Praise for *The Eagle's Throne*

"A literary marriage of two great books from the past, that of Machiavelli's *The Prince* and the eighteenth-century French epistolary novel, *Les Liaisons Dangereuses* . . . a full-blown triumph . . . Fuentes has never written better."
—*San Francisco Chronicle*

"Compelling . . . Fuentes injects the book with uproariously lethal intrigue. . . . [The] reader [is] privy to secret schemes and passions. . . . What makes this satire astute is how Fuentes forces his politicians to face the consequences of their actions."
—*The Denver Post*

"Dazzling, razor-sharp . . . provides a feast of political insight, aphorisms and maxims, in the spirit of Machiavelli and Sun Tzu's *The Art of War*."
—*The Washington Post Book World*

"A nerve-grating cautionary tale, and one of [Fuentes's] best books."
—*Kirkus Reviews* (starred review)

"Daring and original . . . dark, well thought-out . . . The plot is intricate with many unexpected twists. . . . A critical, caustic, analytical, judicious call to arms . . . provocative."
—*San Antonio Express-News*

"[The] characters spring to life as true individuals, fully developed in Fuentes's beguilingly unorthodox fashion. A novel that is truly a tour de force."
—*Booklist* (starred review)

"A political thriller . . . to end all political thrillers. The futuristic tale [is] an old-fashioned epistolary novel in which the characters conspire, deceive, seduce, plea and attack one another entirely through letters. The device is perfect for intrigue. . . . *The Eagle's Throne* is an exhilarating romp through the cruelty of Mexican politics, but it is also a cautionary tale about the price of ambition."
—*The Columbus Dispatch*

BY CARLOS FUENTES

Adam in Eden
Aura
The Buried Mirror
Burnt Water
The Campaign
A Change of Skin
Christopher Unborn
Constancia and Other Stories for Virgins
The Crystal Frontier
The Death of Artemio Cruz
Destiny and Desire
Diana: The Goddess Who Hunts Alone
Distant Relations
The Eagle's Throne
The Good Conscience
Happy Families
The Hydra Head
Inez
Myself with Others
A New Time for Mexico
The Old Gringo
The Orange Tree
Terra Nostra
This I Believe: An A to Z of a Life
Vlad
Where the Air Is Clear
The Years with Laura Díaz

THE EAGLE'S THRONE

THE
EAGLE'S
THRONE

A NOVEL

CARLOS FUENTES

TRANSLATED BY
KRISTINA CORDERO

RANDOM HOUSE TRADE PAPERBACKS

NEW YORK

2007 Random House Trade Paperback Edition

Copyright © 2006 by Carlos Fuentes

Published in the United States by Random House Trade Paperbacks, an imprint of The Random House Publishing Group, a division of Random House, Inc., New York.

RANDOM HOUSE TRADE PAPERBACKS and colophon are trademarks of Random House, Inc.

Published in the United Kingdom by Bloomsbury Publishing. Originally published in Spanish in 2002 as *La silla del águila* by Alfaguara, Mexico, copyright © 2002 by Carlos Fuentes.

Originally published in hardcover in the United States by Random House, an imprint of The Random House Publishing Group, a division of Random House, Inc., in 2006.

ISBN 978-0-8129-7255-9

Library of Congress Cataloging-in-Publication Data

Fuentes, Carlos.
[Silla del águila. English]
The eagle's throne : a novel / Carlos Fuentes ; translated by Kristina Cordero.
p.   cm.
ISBN 978-0-8129-7255-9
I. Cordero, Kristina. II. Title.

PQ7297.F793S5513 2006

863'.64—dc22
2006040806

www.atrandom.com

146122990

To fellow members of the "Half Century" generation,

at the Law School of the

Universidad Nacional Autónoma de México:

the hope of a better Mexico . . .

L'águila siendo animal

se retrató en el dinero.

Para subir al nopal

pidió permiso primero.

[The eagle, being an animal,

had its picture drawn on coins.

Before climbing up the nopal

it asked for permission first.]

MANUEL ESPERÓN AND ERNESTO CORTÁZAR,

"Me he de comer esa tuna"

[I have to eat that prickly pear]

CONTENTS

1

MARÍA DEL ROSARIO GALVÁN
TO NICOLÁS VALDIVIA

You are going to think badly of me. You are going to say I'm a capricious woman. And you'll be right. But who would have guessed that things could change so radically overnight? Yesterday, when I first met you, I told you, When it comes to politics, never put anything in writing. Today, I have no other way of communicating with you. That should give you an idea of how dire the situation has become. . . .

You will say that your interest in me—the interest you showed the minute we laid eyes on each other in the vestibule outside the interior secretary's office—is not political. It's romantic interest, perhaps physical attraction, or maybe even just simple human affection. You must know at once, Nicolás Valdivia, that with me everything is political, even sex. You may be shocked by this kind of professional voracity. But there's no changing it. I'm forty-five now, and ever since the age of twenty-two I've arranged my life around a single purpose: to be, to shape, to eat, to dream, to savor, and to suffer politics. That is my nature. My vocation. Don't think this means I've had to put aside what I like as a woman, my sexual pleasure, my desire to make love to a young, handsome man—like you. . . .

Simply put, I consider politics to be the public expression of private passions. Including, perhaps most of all, romantic passion. But passions are very arbitrary forms of conduct, and politics is a discipline. We act with the greatest measure of freedom granted us by a universe that is at once multitudinous, uncertain, random, and necessary, fighting for power, competing for a tiny sphere of authority.

Do you think it's the same with love? You're wrong. Love has a power that knows no limits, a power that's called imagination. Even if you were to be locked up in the castle at San Juan de Ulúa, you would still have the freedom of desire, for a man is always the master of his own erotic imagination. In politics, on the other hand, what good is wishing and imagining if you don't have the power?

I repeat, power is my nature. Power is my vocation. That's the first thing I want to warn you about. You are a thirty-four-year-old boy. I was drawn to your physical beauty right away. But I can also tell you, lest it go to your head, that attractive men are few and far between in the vestibule to the office of the interior secretary, Bernal Herrera. Beautiful women are also conspicuously absent. My friend the secretary relies on his ascetic reputation. Butterflies don't go near his garden. Instead, the scorpions of deceit nest under his rug and the bees of ambition buzz around his honeycomb.

Does Bernal Herrera deserve the reputation he has? You'll find out. All I know is that, one icy afternoon in early January, in the antechamber to the secretary's office in the old Cobián Palace, a woman pushing fifty but nonetheless still very attractive—your face said it all, darling—exchanged glances with a beautiful young man, every bit as desirable as she, though scarcely over thirty. The spark has been ignited, dear Nicolás. . . .

And the pleasure is to be deferred. *To be deferred*, my young friend.

I admit everything. You're just the right height for me. As you could see, I myself am quite tall and don't care for looking up or down. I prefer to look directly into the eyes of my men. Yours are level with mine, and as light—green, gray, ever-changing—as mine are immutably black, although my skin is whiter than yours. But don't think, in a country as mixed and racist as Mexico, a country so plagued by the issue of skin color (though nobody would ever admit it), that it's an advantage. Quite the opposite: I attract resentment, that national vice of ours, that miserly king lording it over a court of envious dwarfs. And yet my physical appearance does grant me a kind of unspoken superiority, the tacit tribute we all offer the race of the conqueror.

You, my love, enjoy the fruits of true mestizo beauty. That golden, cinnamon-colored skin that goes so well with the fine features of the Mexican man: linear profile, thin lips, long, flowing hair. I saw how the light played on your head, giving life to a masculine beauty that can often conceal a vast mental void. It took only a few minutes of conversation to realize that you're as intelligent on the inside as you are beautiful on the outside. And you even have a dimpled chin, to boot.

I must be honest with you: You're also very wet behind the ears, very naïve. Quite a little green plum, as they say where I come from. Just look at yourself. You know all the catchwords. Democracy, patriotism, rule of law, separation of powers, civil society, moral renewal. The danger is that you believe them. The trouble is that you say them with conviction. My innocent, adorable Nicolás Valdivia. You've entered the jungle and want to kill lions before loading your gun.

Secretary Herrera said as much to me after meeting you: "This boy is extremely intelligent," he said, "but he thinks out loud. He still hasn't learned to rehearse first what he'll say later. They say he writes well. I have read his columns in the newspapers. He doesn't know yet that the only possible dialogue between the journalist and the public servant is the dialogue that falls on deaf ears. Not that I, as secretary of the interior, don't read what the journalist writes and don't feel flattered, indifferent, or offended by the things he or she might say about me—what I mean is that for a Mexican politician, the golden rule is never to put anything in writing and especially never to comment on the many opinions that will inevitably rain down upon him."

Forgive me, I have to laugh at that one!

Today we have no choice but to write letters. All other forms of communication have been cut. We can still, of course, speak to each other in private, but for that, we have to waste precious time making appointments and going from one place to the other, fearful that the one thing still working is the hidden microphone tucked away where we least expect it. In any event, the former tends to encourage a perhaps undesirable intimacy. The latter, on the other hand, may expose one to the most ghastly traffic accidents. And there is no sadder way of being defined than as the casualty of an ordinary traffic accident.

Darling Nicolás, I defy the world. I will write letters. I will expose myself to the greatest danger of politics: I'll leave a written record. Am I mad? No. Very simply, I'm such a firm believer in my ability to lead that I shall now use it to set an example. When this country's political class sees that María del Rosario Galván communicates through handwritten letters, everyone will follow suit. Nobody will want to seem inferior to me. Look at how brave María del Rosario is! I can't let her show me up, can I? That's what they'll all say.

I'm laughing, my beautiful young friend. Just you wait and see how many people follow my example as my audacity sets legal precedent. Amusing, isn't it? To think that only yesterday, on the Paseo de Bucareli, I said to you, Never put anything down in writing, Nicolás. A politician should never allow people to find out about his indiscretions, which erode his credibility, nor his talents, which inspire envy.

Today, however, after this morning's catastrophe I must eat my words, betray my lifelong philosophy, and implore you, Nicolás, write to me . . . you're in the presence of a gambling woman. I wasn't born in Aguascalientes during the San Marcos Festival for nothing, after all. My first breath mixed with horses whinnying, roosters crowing, the sound of knives flying in the cock pits, cards being dealt, tunes played on the bass guitar, the falsetto of the *cantadoras*, mariachi trumpets, and the cries of "Close the doors!"

No more bets. *Les jeux sont faits.* You see, yesterday I placed my bet on silence. I was too busy thinking about how all the things we write in secret could turn against us in public. I was thinking about Richard

Nixon's psychotic fascination with recording his infamy on tape, in the most vulgar language imaginable for a Quaker. I'm telling you straight: To be a politician you must be a hypocrite. To get ahead, anything goes. But, not only do you have to be false, you also have to be cunning. Every politician rises up in the ranks with a bagful of skeletons trailing behind him, like cans of Coca-Cola dragging from the tail of a rebellious but frightened cat. The great politician is the one who reaches the top having purged all his bitterness, his grudges, and his rough moments. A puritan like Nixon is the most dangerous sort of politician, both for his people and for himself. He thinks that everyone has to tolerate him because he rose up from the dregs. His downtrodden humility only feeds his contemptuous arrogance. And that's what brought Nixon down in the end: a longing for the muck, that desperate need to return to the cesspools of nothingness and purge himself of evil, not realizing that he would only sink back into the slime from which he came, having recovered, I grant you, the ambition to crawl out of his hole and rise again.

La nostalgie de la boue is what the French call it (and that, by the way, is another thing I adore about you, that you speak French, that you studied at l'École Nationale d'Administration in Paris, that you agree with those of us who gave up English ever since it became a lingua franca, restoring to French the prestige of a secret, almost elitist, form of communication among enlightened politicians).

Nixon in the United States, Díaz Ordaz in Mexico, Berlusconi in Italy, perhaps Hitler in Germany, Stalin in Russia, although the latter two turned evil into grandeur while the others only turned it into misery . . . Study these cases, dear Nicolás. Learn about the extremes if you want to find the golden mean, my love.

Yes, I remember Nixon and his mad obsession with recording all his plots and schemes on tape, spitting out all that foul language, sounding at times like a little boy lashing out at the world, and at others like a hardened criminal. And what can we say about our tropical local bosses, who record their vilest deeds on tape and take sick pleasure in contemplating their despicable murders, which they know will go unpunished? Can you imagine the almost erotic frisson they must feel when they see a group of helpless peasants fall to the ground bleeding, shot down by the troops of his excellency the governor?

Mexico is stained by blood-soaked rivers, ripped open with mass graves, strewn with unburied corpses. Now as you prepare to make your political debut, my beautiful, desirable friend, remember never to lose sight of the desolate landscape of injustice that is the holy scripture of our Latin American countries. Secrets are paramount, yes, but all it takes is one little revelation to turn the complacent impunity of a governor or president into a collective shame that even the cynicism of the powerful cannot subdue.

Nothing could have prepared me for such a radical turn of events as the one that has ushered in the new year. If indeed all our communications systems have failed, if we have neither telephones, nor faxes, nor e-mails, nor even the humble telegraph machines of the past, nor even carrier pigeons (all poisoned as if by a stroke of witchcraft), and all that remains are the smoke signals of the Tarahumara Indians, waving their colored blankets, and if this communications breakdown is not the result of some millennium bug like the one that was going to make computers programmed in the 1900s collapse as they entered the year 2000, but of the oddly pseudo-palindromic number of the present year, then I can freely confess to you that my life will change more than I can bear, and I will be plunged into a state of dumbfounded shock from which, as always, I will somehow emerge and find the strength to remind myself:

María del Rosario, pay attention to your friend Xavier "Seneca" Zaragoza, trusted adviser to President Lorenzo Terán, who says that when the glitter and tinsel of this deceitful world disappear, the ace in the pack, the card hidden up your sleeve, may very well be the one thing everyone scoffs at as ineffective, unrealistic folly: the noble figure whose dignity can redeem the rest of us from our despicable infamy, the virtuous man who may be able to save our system.

Are you that man, Nicolás Valdivia, or has my judgment failed me?

Has my legendary intuition faltered? Have politics eaten through my brain so severely that one whole side—the moral side—has stopped functioning altogether? Might you, my ravishing friend, be the person who can revive it miraculously?

Well, if the rule of discretion becomes impossible, perhaps the rules governing corruption, hypocrisy, and lies will go, too. If so, necessity will become my virtue and I will surrender to indiscretion with utter recklessness.

This letter I write to you now, Nicolás Valdivia, is evidence of that. There are no other forms of communication beyond the verbal, the immediate presence, which I feel is too dangerous, or the "mediate," which is less risky and, in the end, our only practical choice. The question, then, my very desired young man, is knowing which of the two methods—the oral or the written—will hasten the thing we both want, though our timings may differ. The path to my bed is not free of obstacles, dear Nicolás. You'll have to open a thousand doors before you reach it. It's almost like one of those Oriental tales, you know the kind I mean. I will put you to the test every single day. The reward will depend on you. I know that my carnal delights would be enough to satisfy you. And I admit that I desire your body, but I desire your success even more. Sex can be immediate, only to end up being a brief, unsatisfying quickie.

Political fortune, on the other hand, is one very long orgasm, my darling. Success must be gradual and slow in coming if it is to endure. A prolonged orgasm, my sweet.

Start opening those doors, my child, one by one. Beyond the last threshold is my bedroom. The last key unlocks my body.

Nicolás Valdivia: I will be yours when you are the president of Mexico.

And I assure you: I will make you the president of Mexico. I swear it to you by the sign of the cross. In the name of the Holy Virgin of Guadalupe, I promise you this, my love.

XAVIER "SENECA" ZARAGOZA TO
MARÍA DEL ROSARIO GALVÁN

I don't expect them to pay any attention to me. A trusted adviser like me fulfills his duty by *advising* with goodwill—which is never enough—and good information, which is never forthcoming. If I manage to survive this catastrophe it will only be because this time the president actually, and unfortunately, listened to me.

As I always do, my cherished friend, I invoked principles—after all, principles are the reason the president listens to me at all. I'm the cricket in the ear of his conscience. I rummage through my files of ethical concerns. Perhaps my secret hope, María del Rosario, is that my conscience may remain clear even if realpolitik slides toward pragmatism. As you know, realpolitik is the asshole through which we expel what we've eaten—whether it's caviar or cactus, duck à l'orange or a *taco de nenepil*. Principles, on the other hand, are the head without the anus. Principles don't go to the bathroom. Realpolitik is what clogs the toilet bowls of the world, and in this world of power you have no other choice but to pay tribute to Mother Nature.

Today, for once, principles won out. Perhaps as a gift to an anxious populace in this new year of 2020, the president decided to offer moral satisfaction, not just good news. In his message to Congress, he called for the withdrawal of the United States' occupation forces in Colombia and on top of it all a ban on the export of Mexican oil to the United States, unless Washington agreed to pay the prices established by OPEC. To make matters worse, we announced these decisions at a meeting of the United Nations Security Council. The response, as you can see, was not long in coming. We woke up on January 2 with our oil, our gas, and our principles intact, but with our communications systems cut off from the rest of the world. The United States, alleging a glitch in the satellite communications system that they so kindly allow us to use, has left us with no faxes, no e-mail, no grid, and no telephone service. We have but two forms of communication available to us now, oral and epistolary—as is exemplified by this letter I write to you now, though I fight to suppress the urge to eat it and swallow it whole. Why the hell did the president pay attention to me and put his principles ahead of damn reality this time? Oh, if you could only see me now—I'm banging my head against the wall, I can't stop asking myself, over and over again:

"Seneca, who ever told you to be a man of principle?"

"Seneca, what is so terrible about being a little more pragmatic?"

"Seneca, why do you have to go against the majority of the presidential cabinet?"

Here you have me, my dear María del Rosario, here you have pig-headed old Seneca banging his head against the walls of the republic—Mexico's eternal wailing wall.

At least, my dear friend, the wall isn't made of stone. It's padded, just like in a mental hospital, which is where your good friend Xavier Zaragoza—known as "Seneca" for reasons both marvelous and miserable—should be committed. Born in Córdoba, Seneca was the Stoic philosopher (pay attention if you don't know this, and bear with me if you do and if you still love me nevertheless) who committed suicide at Nero's court. His principles were irreconcilable with those of the empire. And yet to this day, in his native land of Andalucía, the word "Seneca" is synonymous with "sage," or "philosopher."

What shall be my destiny at the presidential court of Mexico, my dear María del Rosario? An enchanted life or death by disenchantment? At the dawn of the year 2020, we certainly have reasons for disenchantment. A communications system that's completely cut off from the rest of the world, riots breaking out here and there, signs of social and geographical fragmentation . . . and a president who is good, well-intentioned, weak, and passive.

Don't blame me, María del Rosario. You know that my advice is sincere and, at times, even brutal. Nobody speaks to the president as honestly as I do, you know that. And I fervently believe that this country needs at least one disinterested voice whispering into the ear of President Lorenzo Terán. Such is our agreement, my dear friend, yours and mine. I'm there to say, "Mr. President, you know I'm your totally impartial friend."

Which is not entirely true. I'm primarily interested in getting the president to shake off that reputation for inaction he's earned during his time in office—almost three years guided by the mistaken conviction that all our problems will just sort themselves out, that an intrusive government creates more problems than it solves, and that civil society should always be the first to act. In his view, the government should always be the last resort. For once, we must admit he's right. What on earth got into him, starting off the new year by invoking principles of sovereignty and nonintervention, instead of just letting the apples fall from the tree, since they were already rotten? What do we care about Colombia? And why not just let Venezuela and the Arabs deal with the dirty business of the oil markets instead of taking sides with a gang of corrupt sheikhs? We've always been good at making the most of others' conflicts without having to take sides. But when you go around giving advice, you never quite know what the outcome will be, and this time, I admit, the whole thing backfired.

"Put some ideas forward, Mr. President, before the people impose them on you. In the long run, if you don't come up with some ideas of your own, you'll be crushed by everyone else's."

"Like yours, for example?" he asked with an innocent's face.

"No," I had the nerve to say. "No. I was thinking of that creep Tácito de la Canal."

I wounded his pride, I realize that now, and he ended up doing exactly the opposite of what his favorite, his chief of staff Tácito de la Canal—who is more than a simple lackey, this guy wrote the book on servility—advised him to do.

One day, my dear friend, you'll have to sit down and explain to me why a man as intelligent, dignified, and kind as our head of state keeps a fawning sycophant like Tácito de la Canal beside the Eagle's Throne. Simply watch how he rubs his hands together and humbly raises them to his lips, his head bowed forward, and you will see that he's nothing more than a depraved man whose hypocrisy is comparable only to the boundless ambition he so poorly conceals behind his false sincerity!

Behold the paradox, my (favorite) friend: My good advice brings about dismal results, while Tácito's terrible advice could have averted this whole calamity. But I had gotten complacent, María del Rosario, I had gotten used to giving all that good advice under the assumption that it would be ignored once again. I know that my words stroke the moral ego of our head of state, who just by listening to me feels "ethical" and considers his duty to principles done, which allows him to follow the advice of Tácito de la Canal, the opposite of mine, with a clear conscience.

Tell me if that isn't enough to make you despair and want to give up altogether. What's stopping me? you might ask. A vague, philosophical hope. I may have my shortcomings, but if I'm not there, someone worse—much worse—will take my place. I am the Shimon Peres of the presidential mansion. As bitter as my defeats may be, at least I can sleep at night: I offer my advice honestly. It's not my fault if they don't take it. There are far too many voices claiming our leader's attention. Some sediment of my truth must have gotten into President Lorenzo Terán's spirit. But on occasions like this, my dear friend, the president would have been better off listening to my enemies, instead of me.

3

MARÍA DEL ROSARIO GALVÁN
TO NICOLÁS VALDIVIA

You're so insistent, my beloved and handsome Nicolás. I see that my letter failed to convince you. My lack of persuasiveness troubles me more than your lack of intelligence. That's why I don't blame you. I must be thick, clumsy, inarticulate. I tell you my reasons directly, and still you, such a clever boy, fail to understand me. The blame, I repeat, must lie with me. Nevertheless, I must admit that I'm not indifferent to your passion, which almost makes me want to go back on my word. Now, don't think that with your fervent prose you've knocked down the walls of my sexual fortress—as you put it. No, the drawbridge is still up and the chains on the gate are padlocked. But there's a window, my lovely young Nicolás, one that lights up every night at eleven o'clock.

There, a woman you desire slowly undresses as if being observed by a witness more human and warm than the cold surface of her mirror. That woman is seen by nobody and yet she undresses with a sensual slowness as if she were being watched. That creature is delectable, Nicolás. And she finds it delectable to undress before a mirror with the slow deliberate movements of an artist of the stage or the court (a fanciful image, I know), pretending that eyes more avid than those of the mirror are looking at her with desire—the burning desire you convey, you wicked boy, you mischievous young thing, desirable object of my desire *only because you can be deferred*. For the price of consummated desire—don't you know yet?—is subsequent virtue or, even worse, indifference.

You'll say that a woman of almost fifty is entitled to fend off the youthful and ardent but perhaps frivolous and transient passions of a *garçon* barely over the age of thirty. Believe that if you wish. But don't detest me. I'm perfectly willing to delay your hatred and encourage your hope, my almost but no longer quite so naïve little friend. Tonight, at eleven o'clock, I will proceed with my *déshabiller*. I will leave my bedroom curtains wide open. The lights will be on so I might be wise, modest, and titillating in equal measure.

We have a date, my dear. For the moment, I can't offer you more.

4

ANDINO ALMAZÁN TO
PRESIDENT LORENZO TERÁN

Mr. President, if anyone is suffering from the recent restrictions on communication it is I, your trusted servant. You know that my time-honored habit is to put all my advice to you in writing. "Opinions" are what some members of your cabinet, my colleagues, like to call those recommendations, as if the science of economics were a question of mere opinion. "Dogma" is what my enemies within the cabinet call them, proof of the insufferable, pontifical certainty of the treasury secretary, Andino Almazán, your loyal servant, Mr. President. But are laws the same thing as dogmas? Was the apple that fell onto Newton's head and revealed the law of gravity dogmatic? And was it merely Einstein's opinion that energy is equal to mass multiplied by the speed of light squared?

Likewise, it is not my idea, Mr. President, that prices determine the volume of resources employed, or that profits depend on monetary flow, or that the productivity of an employee will determine his demand in the labor market. But you already know what my enemies—I mean colleagues—call my "old song and dance." And yet, Mr. President, today more than ever, given the situation that we are now up against, a situation you have wisely chosen to confront with populist measures (which your critics, I should warn you, will call useless posturing and your friends, like me, will call tactical concessions), today more than ever, I must reiterate my gospel for the economic health of this country.

First, avoid inflation. Don't allow anyone to turn on those little bank-note machines under the pretext of a "national emergency." Second, raise taxes to defray the costs of the emergency without sacrificing services. Third, keep salaries low in the name of the emergency itself: More work for less money is, if you know how to present it, the patriotic formula. And finally, fix prices. Do not tolerate—rather, severely punish—anyone who dares to raise prices in the middle of this national emergency.

You once said to me that economics has never stopped history, and maybe you're right. But it's equally true that economics can certainly *make* history (even though it may not *be* history). You've decided to adopt two policies that will ensure you popular support (though nobody knows for how long) and international conflict (with the greatest superpower in the world). As for popular support, I ask you once again: How long can it last? As for the international tension, just so you see that I'm not as dogmatic as my enemies claim, I won't tell you that it will outlast the short-lived patriotic support that we earn when we stand up to the gringos without assessing the consequences. Instead, I'll now turn the other cheek and tell you, Mr. President—and call me cynical if you must—that Mexico and Latin America will advance only if they concentrate on creating problems.

Mexico and Latin America are important precisely because we don't know how to manage our finances. We are important because we create problems for everyone else.

I anxiously await your address to Congress tomorrow, and remain, as always, at your service.

5

NICOLÁS VALDIVIA TO
MARÍA DEL ROSARIO GALVÁN

I don't know what to admire more, my dear lady, your beauty or your cruelty. Beauty has but one name, no synonym can do it justice. To what can I compare the incomparable? Please don't think me innocent, or blind. I've seen many (perhaps too many?) women in the nude. Yet I'd never truly seen a woman stripped of all her clothes until I saw you.

I'm not referring to your beauty, my dear lady—I'll discuss that in due course—but to the obscene totality of your nudity. Nor do I wish to play word games here (you think my knowledge precocious, but in reality I possess only the most meager collection of erudite references), but when I say that, I am saying that your nudity is *ob-scene*, off-scene, incomparable and invisible, and unfathomable if it did not materialize *beyond the stage* of your—and my—ordinary existence, your—our—everyday life, beyond the realm in which you dress and carry yourself in the normal world. . . . When you're nude, *off-scene*, *ob-scene*, and menacing, you are another woman and yet you are the same, do you understand me? You're the same and yet you are transfigured, as if by taking off your clothes, my dear lady, you hinted at a final beauty, the beauty of a death that lives on eternally. A charming paradox. The way I saw you, that is how you will always be, until your death.

No, let me amend that. I should have said "Even in death" or "Only in death." Since the day I met you, I sensed you'd give me extraordinary pleasure, the greatest sensuality I'd ever known, not comparable to anything I'd experienced or imagined before. What an undeserved reward to spy on you from the woods while in front of the one lit window in the house you removed your black cocktail dress, and then, arms stretched behind your back, unhooked your black bra in an equally dark and audacious movement, revealing those two cups filled to overflowing, and you lifted up the front part of the bra and freed your breasts with a double caress, and there you were in nothing but your black panties, which you removed as you sat on the edge of a bed that seemed—forgive me for saying so—too cold and lonely, absurdly so, and instantly you rose, my lady, in all the splendor of your sexual maturity, white all over, twice pink, once black, facing me before turning your back to me so that I could admire that ass, the ass of Venus Callipyge, adored until she sank into the earth with trembling buttocks, so I could have what you spoke of the other day, the vision of a pleasure I must conquer at a price— I laugh at myself, madam—that is very possibly beyond my reach.

Yes, that glimpse of you is all I would have needed. And I would have treasured the trifle you deigned to present to me and only me, María del Rosario, because I thought: This is for me, only for me. This midnight spectacle, unfolding before my eyes from the only lit room in a house tucked away in the middle of a pine forest, she offers it all up to me. . . .

Why did you do it, dear lady, what infinite cruelty, what evil compulsion drove you to make me share the vision that I believed was incomparably mine with another peeping tom, another voyeur like myself, standing a few meters in front of me, whose presence was revealed by the rustling of branches, normally an imperceptible noise but thunderous to my sensitive, lovesick ears? Why? Why that intruder into a vision that I thought belonged to me, or us, you and me alone?

Who was the other voyeur? Was he a random intruder? Does he

know your habits, my dear mistress? Did he, as I did, keep a date that you had made with him, a rendezvous befitting—forgive me if I offend you—a professional courtesan, a high-class whore? Can you tell me the truth? Can you at the very least save me from being a vile, pathetic peeping tom, a madman, a deceived lover?

6

BERNAL HERRERA TO
PRESIDENT LORENZO TERÁN

I write to you now, President Terán, to wish you the best of luck in your annual address to Congress, now rescheduled for early January in light of the current national emergency, so that you, with a courage I admire, will be speaking before the president of the United States delivers her State of the Union address. The White House's reaction to decisions you made over Christmas and the San Silvestre holiday—to keep the price of oil high and to call for an end to the U.S. occupation of Colombia—can only be described as punishment. I don't, however, recommend that you use those terms when you make your address: Instead, stick to the pretext of an international communications collapse. Well, don't say "the system collapsed," first of all, because that kind of wording will bring back unhappy memories of the old-fashioned frauds committed under the PRI's "perfect dictatorship," which we have finally put behind us. And secondly, because "collapse" is the kind of verb that has an unpleasant way of turning into a self-fulfilling prophecy, to use an expression coined by our cousins to the north. Instead I recommend that you avoid any criticism of the U.S. government, and that you present this as a temporary technical mishap in the global satellite-communications network, caused by an unforeseen reaction to the duplication of digits at the start of the present year, 2020. A sort of delayed but likely follow-up to that Y2K phenomenon that had everyone in a panic before the year 2000, when all the computers in the world—personal, governmental, at banks and airports, public, private—were supposedly going to go haywire when their systems went from "19" to "20." It doesn't matter if they don't believe you tomorrow, as long as they buy the story today. Use it. You have nothing to lose. Just don't mention the U.S. government, Mr. President. Talk about a simple technical malfunction. Forgive me for being so repetitive. More than a reminder to you, these things I write are like little memos to myself—you know how I am. In your great wisdom and trust, I ask you to understand and forgive your old friend. Next: Make sure to touch only very lightly on the topics of Colombia and the oil prices, and focus instead on our domestic problems. I know that some members of the cabinet—mainly those so-called technocrats—will blame things on me as interior secretary. They'll say I'm out to profit from the situation. That I'm positioning myself—forgive me for being so blunt, but you and I are more than just superior and underling, president and trusted employee; we're old friends, and I always think of us like that—for the presidential succession that will happen in less than three years, etc. You know me, and you know that I've always advised you with two things in mind. One, I am your loyal colleague, and two, I put the interests of Mexico above all else. I wouldn't be interior secretary if I weren't able to equate those two things. Loyalty to Mexico and loyalty to the president. Having established that, allow me to reiterate with the greatest conviction that the major problems we need to address swiftly and wisely are the three strikes going on as we speak.

First, the students who are refusing to pay registration fees or take admission exams, and who are presently occupying various buildings on the university campus.

Second, the striking workers at the factory in San Luis Potosí that is majority-owned by a Japanese corporation.

And third, the protest march led by peasants at La Laguna who are

calling for restitution of the lands promised to them by President Cárdenas's agrarian reform, lands which have been wrested from them little by little by the corrupt local bosses in the north.

My recommendations, Mr. President, are as follows:

Ignore the students. They can keep on occupying the dean's office
and every other university building until hell freezes over, for all we
care. With the students, anything but repression. Never forget the 1968
massacre in the Plaza de las Tres Culturas, and how, believing it had
achieved some kind of triumph, the system in fact committed suicide
that day by sparking public outrage, collective anguish, and, in the end,
the demise of authoritarianism and the single-party system, in addition
to eternally disgracing the president at the time and forcing his successors to distance themselves from him, the "butcher of Tlatelolco," even
when it meant defying economic logic. Result: We floundered from crisis to crisis, all because we killed some students. Just let the situation sit
and rot. All those students brimming over with solidarity today will
come to their senses and think of their careers tomorrow.

Let us remain calm, Mr. President. More imperturbable than Benito
Juárez.

Now, with regard to the striking workers at the car factory who are
demanding outrageous wage increases and dare to compare their
salaries to those of their counterparts in Japan, break the strike by force
and announce to the world that Mexico welcomes foreign investment
with open arms. We have a massive supply of cheap labor, we'll all end
up winning. As for the disgruntled workers, they'll be happy if you give
them a free movie theater and a decent hospital.

You might argue that police intervention in San Luis Potosí would
work in favor of the inveterate local boss Rodolfo Roque Maldonado,
but I would argue that the mere deployment of forces on our part would
intimidate Maldonado and get those clever Japanese on our side. It's a
risk, no doubt. Consider it, Mr. President. After all, we don't want to
play around when it comes to our bread and butter. Remember the old
Pedro Infante song? The wife's given two pesos for rent, phone, and

electricity. Ah, the nostalgia for those pre-inflation days. Anyway, a little money is better than none, and the families of the San Luis workers won't put up with their men not bringing money home. Foreign corporations will see that the authorities here are willing and able to defend foreign investment. How else did the Asian tigers make all their money? Just ask the ghost of Lee Kwan Yu. Singapore is a safe place because they cut off your hands if they catch you stealing. In addition, my dear president, a show of force in the region of San Luis Potosí will also serve to subdue the local bosses who take advantage of the vacuums in the regional power structure created by our drawn-out transition to democracy. I know I'm repeating something I've just mentioned. Forgive me for belaboring the point. But we have often granted democracy only to lose authority, creating pockets of anarchy filled by an endless string of local bosses and the forces they command: Maldonado in San Luis, Félix Elías Cabezas in Sonora, "Chicho" Delgado in Baja California, José de la Paz Quintero in Tamaulipas.

And finally, Mr. President, pay attention to the peasants in La Laguna. Use the situation to revive some of those agrarian causes that our pragmatism has forced us to drop. Give your government the support of the rural masses that our enemies—the aforementioned local bosses, for starters—have always manipulated through isolation and ignorance, counting on the fact that our hands would be tied by our proximity with the U.S., as if democracy and authority were incompatible. You know my watchword: authority yes, authoritarianism no. Take advantage of the situation to stick it to the local bosses. The domestic business sector in the north will thank you for it, because they know better than anyone that poverty is the worst investment of all and that a starving peasant can't buy food in the supermarket or clothes at the local Benetton.

As for the one topic that secretly concerns us the most, the murder of Tomás Moctezuma Moro, my advice is to leave it as it is, as a secret that is convenient for us all.

Mr. President, I sincerely hope you'll consider my advice in the spirit of patriotism and support with which I offer it. "This," said a German philosopher, "this," the word "this," is the hardest one to say. Very well, Mr. President, that's what I urge you to do: Do THIS. Say, dare to say, THIS.

Postscript: I enclose the memorandum that I asked Xavier Zaragoza to write, explaining the communications breakdown.

MEMORANDUM

Our modern communications system has suffered a grave paradox. On the one hand, we have striven to become part of the largest global communications network in existence. On the other, we have wanted to monopolize access to information for our government's benefit. To attain the first goal, we handed over the management of television, radio, telephony, as well as wireless communications, the Internet, etc., to the Florida Satellite Center and the so-called capital of Latin America, Miami. Our hope was that this decision would ensure our global access to communications. We turned our worldwide operations over to private companies such as B4M and X9N, in search of maximum efficiency and maximum range. What we did not know, however, was that these private companies upon whom we depended were, in turn, dependent upon an infrastructure controlled by the U.S. Defense Department. Nor did we know that the Florida Satellite Center was under the auspices of the Pentagon, which controlled the system's effectiveness or lack thereof, as well as its real, potential, and planned crises, through exclusive access to the synchronized orbits of a number of fixed satellites located 40,000 kilometers above sea level. The precursor to this was the Y2K crisis of the 1999–2000 new year, the so-called "millennium bug" that was thought capable of causing a breakdown in the global communications system, when the com-

puters programmed according to the digits "19" jumped to "20."
The panic, as we now know, was nothing more than the Pentagon's way of reminding everyone of its ability to decentralize
information in the event of an attack on the infrastructure, or to
voluntarily destabilize the system, while claiming to be under
(nonexistent) attack. The Mexican national mistake, then, was to
take the plunge with our eyes closed and with the hope of rapidly
globalizing our communications by latching on to an operation
we didn't control ourselves, while politicizing communications
internally to thwart the democratic, pluralistic use of these
media. The restored PRI government of 2006 opted for external
modernity through Florida and internal anachronism through
an official monopoly of the grid. Governments are organized
vertically. The grid, on the other hand, works horizontally.
President César León decided to verticalize all internal communications, which meant that unions, local bosses, universities,
local governments, and civil society in general were all deprived
of access, while the government's most favored businesses and,
fatally, the entertainment industry were granted horizontal communications access. A lot of Big Brother. No Big Strikes (actually, we haven't avoided them, we simply declare them null and
void; the main thing is to make sure that no one strike senses any
kind of emulation or support from another strike). The point is
that, while the world's systems started out small, grew rapidly,
and delivered value, the Mexican government started out big,
grew slowly, and delivered garbage. Domestically, we restricted
ourselves to a narrow portal. Internationally, we exposed ourselves to a massive portal. Thus we became doubly vulnerable.
The United States has now cut off our big portal, affecting every
aspect of our communications, not just external but internal as
well, given that the latter, negligible as they were, also depended
on the Florida Satellite Center. The hypothetical Y2K bug was
simply replaced by a so-called Y2020 bug exclusively affecting

Mexico, as a way of punishing the country for opposing the U.S. military occupation of Colombia and for supporting the rise in oil prices determined by OPEC. It is known as "Operation Cucaracha." And as you know, Mr. President, according to the ditty, the cockroach can only walk if it's got something to smoke—marijuana, weed, Fu Manchu chocolate. . . . "20/20" is the term gringos use to describe normal clarity of vision at twenty feet. But the thing that really separates our two countries is a border 1,200 miles long. Draw your own conclusions, Mr. President. And think about how long we'll be able to pacify the Japanese investors at Coahuila—although, of course, it's been said they have their own secret methods of making themselves understood.

7

MARÍA DEL ROSARIO GALVÁN
TO NICOLÁS VALDIVIA

Did our date the night before last upset you? Did you feel humiliated
by the way I turned you into a voyeur? Don't lose your patience or
your temper. Show a bit more tenderness, my darling, more fairness,
more sympathy for your poor friend. I did have a life before we met,
you know. And you, my good Nicolás, would like to think, as in that
old song, "that the past doesn't exist and that we were born the instant
we met." That's not how it is, I'm afraid. I'm older than you. And if
you're going to reproach me for the life I lived before we met, you expose yourself to a number of things. First, various surprises. Some
very unpleasant. Some a bit more palatable. Second, you're going to
burn with jealousy of all the men who were once my lovers. And third,
you're going to grow impatient with the time frame I have in mind for
you and me.

"Why them and not me?"

Of the three possibilities, only the second one appeals to me.
Women—and I'm no exception—adore being the object of jealousy. It
fans the flames of passion. Fires up the long cold wait. And ensures the
most glorious erotic culmination. But let me get to the point. You'll see.
Now I'll be a voyeur with you. We're going to sit down together here in

my living room, side by side, and we are going to examine and discuss my version of last night's presidential address. I got someone to film the event, with an emphasis not so much on the president and what he said but rather on the faces of the people in the audience, so that you can get to know the politicians that govern us.

First let me quickly dispose of the president of Congress, who responded to the address. His name is Onésimo Canabal and he is minor in every way: past, present, future, physical size, political stature, and moral fiber. He's one among thousands, but today he feels himself unique. How will he ever learn the truth? Nobody will ever tell him. He'd have to hit himself over the head to find out how stupid he is. But then, most idiots go to their graves without ever knowing what imbeciles they are.

Let's move on to the cabinet, sitting in the front row of the congressional chamber.

The interior secretary, Bernal Herrera, is my friend and confidant. He has experience and solid common sense. He's aware that order has its limits, but that disorder is boundless. His political balancing act consists of avoiding endemic disorder and the extreme evils that feed it: hunger, demoralization, public mistrust. Herrera knows that chaos provokes irrational actions and facilitates political adventures, which eventually prove to be misadventures. Bitterness opens many wounds, and gives them little time to heal. Herrera, then, is a man who promotes three kinds of laws: laws that can be enforced, laws that will never be enforced, and laws that give people hope, whether they are enforceable or not, whether they are more for the future than for today. He is our best government minister and politician.

The foreign affairs secretary, Patricio Palafox, sitting next to Herrera, is another experienced man, idealistic but pragmatic. He understands that we happen to live next door to the single great superpower in the world, and that we may be able to choose our friends but we can't choose our neighbors (just as we can't choose our relatives, as inconvenient as they often are). Palafox is good at working closely with the gringos, but he's especially good at making them see that Mexico is also a democracy and must pay attention to its own public opinion. Sometimes, he tells them, we can't go against public opinion, just as the U.S. can't, either. Unfortunately, however, they tend to stick to that principle at all costs. The U.S. always operates according to polls, congressional opposition, or opinions in the national press, and the executive branch only gets its own way insofar as its ideas jibe with all these factors.

We, on the other hand, pay a high price for our independent decisions—this has been proved in the case of Colombia. We found ourselves forced to support the new president, Juan Manuel Santos, and call for the withdrawal of the gringos from the country. It wasn't enough that we caved in on trade agreements, antiterrorism measures, votes of support in a number of international organizations, and the protection of Mexicans unjustly imprisoned and even sentenced to death in the U.S. All it took were two panic buttons—Colombia and oil—to elicit this cruel, draconian response from Washington: cutting us off from all communications, leaving us in the globalized world's equivalent of a desert.

Nevertheless, you won't see the slightest concern on Secretary Palafox's face. He comes from a very old family that has lived through three centuries of turbulent Mexican history. Nothing ruffles him. He has nerves of steel. He is every bit a professional, even though there are always a few spiteful people around who say things like, "Secretary Palafox's unassailable serenity is not the result of his blue blood, but of his hard-earned reputation as a poker player."

It seems that Palafox's training grounds were not the halls of Versailles but rather the gambling halls, those rooms full of cigarette smoke, dim lights, and card tables. The kingdom of chance, so to speak. And tell me, my lovely protégé, how does one reconcile necessity with chance? That's the great unanswered question of all time, says my dear friend Xavier Zaragoza, misleadingly nicknamed Seneca—I, for one, have learned more from him than I ever learned from studying political science. If you want to know more, have a look at yesterday's paper:

There is a marvelous article by don Federico Reyes Heroles, his reflections on turning sixty-five.

From now on things start to go downhill, my darling disciple Nicolás Valdivia. Now, the comptroller general, don Domingo de la Rosa, is known to many as "the Flamingo" because he never knows which leg to stand on, the left or the right. Since our current president's government is one of so-called national unity, sometimes it has to appease the conservatives, sometimes the liberals. The trouble is that both sides are honest only when they're the opposition. The minute they take over the government, they soon learn the saying coined by that very colorful character from our country's extravagant past, César Garizurieta, aka "the Possum": "He who does not live off the public purse lives in error."

But I can tell you now that the man who, like him, tries to be everyone's friend by granting concessions left, right, and center will never have enough money. And if the comptroller doesn't have enough money, how can the republic?

You're right, my darling Nicolás. Education Secretary Ulises Barragán is a perfect disaster. They say he lies more than a dentist and that his perpetual and endless monologue has but one virtue: It has the power to turn practically any audience catatonic, which is useful when it comes to dealing with the Educational Workers' Union and its two million frightful members when they all gather in the Elba Esther Gordillo Auditorium. The bad thing about Secretary Barragán is that his speeches are so boring that he doesn't just put his audiences to sleep, he puts himself to sleep, too! At one particular event, for example, a prolonged silence aroused the suspicion of the porter at the Colegio Nacional, who found everyone in the lecture hall asleep: the sixty-six people in the audience plus the lecturer, Secretary Barragán himself.

The health secretary, Abundio Colmenares, performs his job with a certain aplomb, panache even. He's an incorrigible lech who uses his political position to get his jollies, all under the pretext of healing. Quite a piece of work, but he can be awfully nice when he wants to. They say he's both tough and passionate: Neither the men he hates nor the women he desires stand a chance when they're in his clutches.

The environment secretary, Madame Guillermina Guillén, sparkles with good intentions. She's so full of fantasy that all she has to do is the opposite of what she thinks in order to be realistic. She protects bird sanctuaries by fumigating them to the point of killing off anything and everything that flies. She hands out logging licenses, turning a blind eye to the fact that soon there'll be no more forests to protect. Problem solved. She recently divorced her husband because she discovered that the good man only put on his false teeth when he visited his lover.

The labor secretary, Basilio Taracena, is exactly the opposite of what he appears to be. Just look at his eyes, the eyes of a *criollo* straight out of Guadalajara—light, but not serene. Hooded, clouded over, misty, and if there's anything that gives him cause for labor, it's his own body. Notice the copious collection of nervous tics, the way he constantly scratches himself, his neck, his armpits, his inner thigh, as if he were plagued by lice. . . .

The agriculture secretary, don Epifanio Alatorre, has been a fixture in national politics ever since the days of López Mateos and is famous for his predictions regarding crops and weather: "Depending on the rains, crops this year might be good, they might be bad, or they might be the very opposite."

Since he's been in politics for over half a century many people have asked him how he's survived so much change, from López Mateos to Fox to Terán. And don Epifanio just licks his index finger and raises it in the air as if to say he always knows which way the wind blows. Don't ever get into a debate with him. It's like arguing with a mariachi band.

You should also be careful not to trust the communications secretary, Felipe Aguirre. You'll notice that his face is the same color as his socks, a sure sign of a vile nature. Or at least a lack of imagination. His famous adage about marriage just about sums it up: "Want to become an old man? Then spend your whole life with the same old woman."

While the advice may be amoral, his conduct is not. He's grown old with the same old woman, a voluminous matron who inspires terror in all who cross her path because she walks with her eyes closed, like a fat vampire blinded by the sun. Proof that our head of communications communicates best via silence and darkness, and by awarding contracts that provide him with some very lucrative commissions. Now, why does the president tolerate him if he knows that the secretary sees nothing and steals everything? A singular and ancient theory, my dear Nicolás: No government functions without the grease of corruption.

Corruption lubricates, but look at the pained face of our national oil company's chairman, don Olegario Santana. He welcomes U.S. capital without denationalizing the industry, but when we defend the price of oil, the U.S. government penalizes us, thus penalizing its own investors. That's Washington's eternal contradiction, caught between the sweeping international claims and the small local interests: The textile factory in North Carolina will always win out over the Brazilian factory and the World Trade Organization, since the latter two don't vote in U.S. elections. As you'll see, the chairman has got the expression of someone who goes around raping ten-year-old girls. How can he allow himself to appear in public with such a guilty look on his face? He is a man to be pitied.

Now turn your attention to the two military officers sitting together. The one who looks like a Prussian *Junker* is, as you know, the defense secretary, Mondragón von Bertrab. Educated at the Hochschule der Bundeswehr, the German military academy, he has an excellent relationship with the Pentagon and has read and memorized all there is to know about the campaigns of Caesar in Gaul and Bonaparte in Italy, he can recite Clausewitz by heart, and there isn't a single page in Tacitus' *Germania* or Livy's *History* that he hasn't studied closely. He's the finest example of the kind of educated, responsible, serious, and loyal officer that the heroic military academy has been turning out for generations. But don't rush to stick your neck out for him, my dear Nicolás Valdivia. Precisely because of his education and professional competence, von Bertrab is a disciplined automaton who fulfills his obligations down to the letter: loyalty to the president, as long as the president remains loyal to the institutions of the republic, but he's more loyal to the spirit of the nation—whatever that means—than to the president himself if he thinks the president hasn't fulfilled his mandate to the nation. And we know exactly what that means! Nevertheless, our admirable local *Junker* never soils his hands, Nicolás, he leaves that to the vicious individual seated at his side, Cícero Arruza, chief of the federal police.

Be very careful with this one, I mean it. Von Bertrab is the friendly face of force. Arruza is the despicable one. His motto is "Blood, death, and fire." He's a wolf in wolf's clothing. His only obstacle is von Bertrab, who said of Cícero, "Giving Arruza any power is like putting a pyromaniac in charge of a fire department."

And yet nobody—and I mean *nobody*—has any doubt that Arruza can be utterly indispensable at the right moment. He knows it, and he anticipates that moment with the stealth of a panther in the jungle. They say that General Cícero Arruza could have forced Benito Juárez to confess that he was working as a double agent for the French. I'm not saying that Arruza isn't constructive, it's just that for him being constructive means turning intimidation into a public service.

I believe I can dispose of the housing secretary, Efrén Iturbide, in a few short sentences. They say he's the best-dressed idiot in the world. He boasts about being the descendant of that preposterous emperor we had at the beginning of the nineteenth century, Agustín I. This is not true. Our dear Efrén uses his looks to falsify his pedigree. Naturally, one can't have such translucent skin without belonging to the "decent people." Decent, my friend? This is what public opinion has to say about him and his position: "Efrén Iturbide is the secretary of state for the housing of Efrén Iturbide."

That's precisely it. He's built but one house: his own.

That man with the dumbfounded look on his face is Juan de Dios Molinar, secretary for information and media, who, thanks to the work of our powerful neighbors, has been effectively stripped of his informative capacity, apart from being able to write letters, as I have decided to

do (and may they all follow my example). Look at him, how badly de-
signed he is, poor thing: saturnine air, timid smile, the eyes of a tiger,
the hands of a carpenter, and the torso of an Italian tenor. Mother Nature can be such a bitch sometimes! And to top it all off, mouth shut like
a padlock. He's the living image of moronic stupor and I feel sorry for
him. My friend Herrera says it's better this way. Since the secretary for
information doesn't inform, the interior secretary can manipulate the
news as he sees fit.

In contrast, look at the smiling attorney general, Paladio Villa-
señor, who goes around saying "That's great, that's great" to everyone.
It's no wonder he's nicknamed "Mr. That's Great," but I think he's a
lot sharper than he seems and that his reputation as a fool saves him
from making crucial decisions or publicly offending the people he
screws under the table. As you can see, that has its virtues and its draw-
backs. Not for nothing, depending on the circumstances, can he be an
eel or a clam.

And now, my darling Nicolás, come the serious players. The treasury secretary, Andino Almazán, is a steely technocrat who refuses to
budge an inch from his convictions about the economy. He's a theolo-
gian of Economics with a gothic and capital "E." For Andino, devaluing our currency would be like having a prostitute for a daughter. What
the poor man doesn't know is that his wife, whom everyone calls "La
Pepa," is a slut who cheats on him day and night. But more about that
later, darling.

I am anxious to get to the worst, to end this presentation with naked
horror itself, the most inexplicable voice in this republican choir: President Lorenzo Terán's chief of staff, the fawning, despicable, grotesque
Tácito de la Canal. Look closely: He shouldn't be seen in daylight. His
head is like one big scar, from chin to occiput, both areas covered with
prickly stubble that does little to hide his egg of a bald skull. Look at
how he rubs his hands together in an effort to appear humble. He culti-
vates the look of the perpetually destitute, as if always on the point of
begging. He's the doormat, the *paillason*, the president's rug in every

sense. He controls access to the executive office and volunteers to clean the president's soles before the chief executive sets foot in the Office of Offices. Tácito de la Canal is the kind of man who looks as though he's never breathed fresh air in his life. That's what they say about him. But I know better. Tácito de la Canal is the man who watches me from a certain spot in the woods every night as I take off my clothes. He's the voyeur who beat you to my window, the repulsive peeping tom you saw the other night. . . .

That is the cast of characters in this little show. I'll wait for a better time to give you the lowdown on another singular group of characters: the third-rate legislators, the congressmen and senators who, pulverized into tiny minority factions, leave the management of Congress in the hands of the inept president of Congress, Onésimo Canabal, while preventing the passing of essential laws, which forces the president and Secretary Herrera to act with a pragmatism that is occasionally legal, occasionally not, but occasionally, like now (Colombia, the oil issue), one that must invoke principle as a way of making up for the pragmatism forced upon them by Congress's fragmentation, which they have had to accept as part and parcel of the system.

And now the good news, my beautiful prince of the night. My very close friend, Interior Secretary Bernal Herrera, has asked the president for a personal favor: to appoint you adviser to the presidential office at Los Pinos, where you'll be working for none other than Tácito de la Canal.

Am I giving you a poisoned chalice? No. I'm giving you the opportunity, my love, to bring me a golden apple from the very heart of a subverted Eden. Make the most of it, Valdivia. Any questions?

8

XAVIER "SENECA" ZARAGOZA TO
PRESIDENT LORENZO TERÁN

Oh, Mr. President! How could I ever forget what you said to me twenty-four hours after entering office?

"They swear you in as president, Seneca, they place the tricolor sash over your chest, you take your seat on the Eagle's Throne and—you're off! It's like being on a roller coaster, they send you down, you grab hold of the chair as best you can and a shocked expression etches itself onto your face, a tight grimace that quickly turns into a mask that you can't remove. The expression on your face that day will stay there for six years, no matter how many different ways you may try to smile or look serious, pensive, angry—you'll always be stuck with the look that was on your face that terrifying moment when you realized, my friend, that the presidential seat, the Eagle's Throne, is nothing more and nothing less than a seat on the roller coaster that we call the Republic of Mexico."

From the moment you said those words to me, Mr. President, both of us understood that you had called me to your side because you wanted someone who would be honest with you, who would offer you objective advice, and who would help you hide the bewildered look on your face that comes from the feeling of being thrown into the void from the steep slope of that fairground ride known as the presidency of the republic.

"They elect you, Seneca. From that moment on, you lose all real contact with people. Not even your best friends are willing to criticize you anymore."

Very well, I've tried to prove myself worthy of your trust and, though my advice may not always be the best, you always have the right to consider opposing points of view—and there is no dearth of them in the editorial pages and the political cartoons. My duty (at least as I understand it) is to tell you what I think with total candor. Now, a few days after you have completed your third year in office, Mr. President, my sincere criticism is that you're perceived as a little ineffectual. People don't see you as a man who *makes* things happen. They see you as a man who *lets* things happen to him. I know what your philosophy is: We're past the age of authoritarianism, when the president's will was the only thing that mattered, from Sonora to the Yucatán, like the hats by Tardán that are back in fashion now. How things come and go!

Now we know that the PRI's soft dictatorship was tempered by a certain degree of tolerance for the Mexican elite and their generally ill-informed opinions, criticism, and scorn. Poets, novelists, the occasional journalist, circus clowns, cartoonists, our ineffable muralists—all of them were allowed to say, write, and draw more or less what they wanted. It was a case of the intellectual elite criticizing the governmental elite, a very necessary escape valve that even extended to comedians—from Soto to Beristaín to Cantinflas and Palillo, they were all granted this very gracious concession. Filmmakers, however, were not, nor were most journalists, to say nothing of the independent trade unions. But then what about governors, small-time mayors, provincial military authorities, the police force in general, even lowly customs officers? A multitude of local powers, Mr. President, acting with corrupt, willful impunity. Only those who were corrupt were free. We created a culture of illegality, even when the president himself worked within the boundaries of the law or launched moral crusades.

For God's sake, Mr. President! Even in colonial times people in Madrid talked about the *unto mexicano,* the Mexican unguent, and about *mordida*—corruption, payoffs and bribes that were used and continue to be used to "influence" people. You know what they say: "He who doesn't deceive, doesn't achieve."

What, then, has happened to you, a pure man who came from the opposition to clean the stables of Augeas? You've turned out to be a democratic Hercules who trusts society's power to do a cleanup job that the mythical Hercules performed with brute force, just as that other divine Hercules—Jesus Christ—drove the merchants out of the temple with lashes.

Morally speaking, Mr. President, you're to be admired. Let society clean itself up. Let the impure among us be purged by the pure—or let them purge themselves. Once again, forgive me for being blunt, Mr. President, and allow me to qualify my criticisms. You yourself are aware that certain areas of Mexican reality are so dark that only people with dirty hands can effectively control them. At the same time, you've gone to great pains to promote honest government officials who can give your regime a pretty public face. Take your defense secretary, a military officer of proven integrity, General Mondragón von Bertrab. Or the interior secretary, Bernal Herrera, an honorable professional who obeys the law but also understands the Latin maxim *dura lex sed lex.* The law is tough, but it's the law. But then, on the other hand, both you and von Bertrab know perfectly well that the chief of police, Cícero Arruza, is a violent thug who won't hold back when it comes to exercising repression with or without justification.

A necessary evil? Perhaps. But there's another case, Mr. President, that you refuse to consider, and I'm referring to your cabinet chief, Tácito de la Canal. Now I know that by saying this I'm going out on a limb: I accuse and yet I have no proof. Very well. I'll limit myself, then, to a simple moral observation. Can someone as ingratiating as Tácito de la Canal possibly be an honest man? Don't you suspect that a deep well of hypocrisy lies beneath his servile fawning? Don't you think that

Tácito de la Canal merits a bit more caution on your part? Or shall I assume that you're playing dumb on purpose and allowing Tácito to be your disagreeable, sycophantic guard just so that you can live in peace, flattered by your slave and defended by your dog? Believe me when I say that I fully understand the need for a shifty-looking dwarf at the door to the castle to keep the bothersome, the undesirable, and the ambitious at bay. But you might want to consider that the guard dog you put out for show might also be driving away the honest counselor, the loyal friend, the useful technocrat, the concerned intellectual, simply because he rightly believes that they, even more than all the other shameless attention seekers, are his greatest rivals in the battle for the president's attention.

I repeat, Mr. President, please pardon the occasionally brutal honesty with which I advise you, but that's why you took me on: to tell you the truth. I warned you of this from the very first day. A politician can pay an intellectual, but he can never trust him. The intellectual will eventually, inevitably, disagree with the politician, and for the politician this will always be construed as a betrayal. Malicious or ingenuous, Machiavellian or utopian, the powerful man always thinks he's right, and the person who opposes him is either a traitor, or at least dispensable.

9

MARÍA DEL ROSARIO GALVÁN
TO BERNAL HERRERA

I realize, Bernal, that you must carry out a full security check before allowing a complete unknown like Nicolás Valdivia into the inner sanctum of the presidency. I've read with great care the dossier you sent me. Born December 12, 1986, in Ciudad Juárez, Chihuahua. Mexican father, American mother. Both worked in El Paso, Texas, but were Mexican residents. Nicolás's birth certificate can be found in the public records office of Ciudad Juárez. Parents killed in a car accident when Valdivia was fifteen.

Then there's a very large gap until Valdivia reappears in Paris, a student at the same college you and I attended. I tested him out. He's very familiar with the subjects and the teachers there. At the Mexican embassy in France he met General Mondragón von Bertrab, at the time the military attaché to the mission. Von Bertrab used the young ENA student for writing up reports, collecting information, etc. It was the general who brought him back to Mexico, where Valdivia spent five years studying on his own in his native state of Chihuahua.

What happened to him between the age of fifteen and twenty-two? I've asked our current defense secretary, von Bertrab, for information. He simply smiled. What can one really know about the life of a teenage orphan forced to earn a living all on his own?

Von Bertrab assuaged my fears. If you need confirmation, just ask him. Nicolás was a bit of a vagabond: working on Mexican tankers and Dutch freighters that often dropped anchor at Tampico, reading a lot, studying when he could find the time, finishing off the subjects he needed for his degree. And then finally, he got himself accepted at the ENA thanks to the intervention of the general, who backed the application with all the necessary documents attesting to Valdivia's unusual and difficult education, his hard work, his tremendous efforts. You know—a youth straight out of a story by Jack London or Ernest Hemingway. . . .

Can you ask for a better recommendation, Bernal? Perhaps he has some mistakes buried in his past, but I must ask you once again to trust my feminine intuition. Nicolás Valdivia looks at me with the face of an angel. He tells me he loves me. And I let him love me. But I've also seen that other look, surreptitious, the one he has when he thinks I'm not looking. That "lean and hungry" look that Shakespeare portrayed in *Julius Caesar*. The look of ambition. A little devil with the face of an angel? What else could we possibly ask for if not this, dear friend, to defeat Tácito de la Canal? Let Valdivia owe us everything, and give us everything, too. My intuition tells me that he's our ideal agent. You yourself have always told me that in politics new blood is necessary, even if it's dangerous.

Darling, let me be the one to take the risk and pay the price for the damage, if any. You and I are playing a game of political realism. Idealistic at times, like our president was, so disastrously on January 1. But in the end, we must be realists, because we must deal with de facto responses to our de jure behavior. The good thing about realpolitik is that you can do an about-face and still keep your basic principles intact. Nicolás Valdivia is an accident of realpolitik, yours and mine. We can get rid of him as easily as we've furthered his career.

Believe it or not, I've gone so far as to tell him that when he makes it to the presidency I'll be his, sexually. And I think he believed me! Or at least my proposal sparked his imagination and his desire.

Be that as it may, we needed to get one of our own into the tarantula's cave. If our little ant Valdivia gets stung and dies, *tant pis pour lui.* We'll just replace him with someone else. For the moment, he's our man in Los Pinos. Leave it to me, I'll take care of duping and manipulating him as I see fit. And rest assured, if he's smart, he'll be a faithful servant.

When I said to him, "You'll be the president of Mexico," young Valdivia didn't even flinch. He showed no astonishment. Perhaps he thought just what you're thinking now: What if he betrays us, what if his indiscretion or ambition gets the better of him and he reveals our plan?

I think this boy is very intelligent. He knows how to read people's eyes. He read mine: If you betray me, nobody will believe you. They'll just think you're an ambitious little operator and perhaps a very big fool. I don't need you as a victim. I need you as an ally. A little Lucifer like you is exactly what I need.

He's as vain as he is astute. He believes me. We will, however, run into problems when he's stripped of his illusions. He may react vindictively. We must make very sure that our victims have no weapons for revenge.

"LA PEPA" ALMAZÁN TO
TÁCITO DE LA CANAL

My love, my precious baldy, how could I possibly mind writing letters to you since writing letters is, in fact, all I've done since the day we became lovers, and I've been careful enough, now more than ever, my dearest love, not to mention your sacred name in writing? You know how I feel: I'd love it if one day, after many years have passed, someone were to open the old trunk that once belonged to my grandmother from the Yucatán and chance upon my bundle of love letters, which by then will no longer be the letters of an unfaithful wife but of a romantic, passionate lover, which is what I am to you, my chubby little baldy, my "better-than-nothing" as the nasty gossipmongers call you simply because they've never been lucky enough to know your scrumptious, delectable tongue, long and soft when you kiss me all over my body, my body as perfect as that of an alabaster Venus, as you like to say. . . . But enough of these pleasures, my anonymous lover, let's get to the point, which is the ever-increasing chumminess between that scheming MR and your rival, Secretary BH. You're too good sometimes, my saintly little sweetheart: Your loyalty to the P blinds you to the people who want to bring you down, calling you an unscrupulous ass-kisser. That's exactly what that diabolical little duo is up to: They want to make you look like another amoral ass-kisser who uses his proximity to the P to rise in the ranks hoping to become P himself at the next election. Let's not play dumb, my darling T, we're past the third year of the "period" (and I'm not referring to my heavenly hormones), and the only thing that matters now is the succession of the P.

This is how I see things. MR has allied herself with BH, whose strength is his alleged serenity and equanimity, his reputation as an honest man in a nation of thieves. He leaves all the dirty work to MR, who commands the P's attention, since the P, as you already know, is a grateful man, and when they were nobodies MR was his sweetheart and taught him all the tricks of the political trade. The good and bad thing about the P is that he's a grateful man. So find a way, my handsome, of making him more grateful to you than to anyone else. Things are getting hairy (sorry, sweetheart, that wasn't a dig at you, my beautiful baldy), and if we really want to get what we're after, you and I will have to find that diabolical little couple's weak spot. We have an advantage that also happens to be a disadvantage. My admirable husband is like the Rock of Gibraltar. Nothing makes him budge; he's boring but safe. Now, were he to hear about some shady move on the part of our little couple, he'd go straight to the P with the information, as sure as Moses appeared on the Mount armed with the Ten Commandments.

My husband is a genius when it comes to making people feel guilty. We all know that the P can't bear to feel guilty. The only thing my husband needs to do, then, to make the P doubt, is reveal one of BH's slipups. Believe me, my adorable tortilla, the best way to get the P on our side is by planting the seed of doubt in his mind. You know he's a man who needs security, security, always more security. Let's not fool ourselves. He's even willing to tolerate corruption as long as it's safe— that is, predictable and reliable. Take the case of our communications secretary, Felipe Aguirre. We all know, as does the P, that for every contract he authorizes he takes a cut tastier than a rumba dancer's ass. The P knows it and doesn't care, he's got that theory of his about corruption as a lubricant, which to me sounds like getting done up the ass (I suppose!). The communications secretary is a swine. It's well-known, accepted, understood, however you want to put it.

But BH! Moral rectitude, honesty, and all those other things that don't feed a man are what people (especially our ineffable Mr. P) expect from him. As such, my sexy baldy, all we need to do is catch BH or that shiftless MR in some kind of sleazy deal to thwart the latter's ambition for power. The P already trusts you like no one else, for his own reasons. He's always saying so: "I don't make a move without T." "T's always more than enough for my needs."

Even here in Mérida everyone knows what they say at the P's office. "T is my most loyal servant, I could never make a move without T, I trust T more than I trust myself, T is the son I never had. . . ."

And so on and so forth.

My adorable little tortilla, we must be even more astute than the eagle that climbed the thorny nopal without asking permission first. The eagle that graces the presidential chair!

What advantages do we have? Our discretion, for starters. There's no better training for politics than adultery. Little secrets, little secrets. Big surprises, big surprises. Nobody suspects us, nor would they ever think of connecting us in any way. I live here in the land of the pheasant and the deer, and there isn't a soul who could possibly suspect a thing about our little romantic escapades in Cancún. Good Lord! In that hippie wig, nobody on earth would ever recognize you at the hotel, and please forgive me for saying so, my sweet handsome thing, but the last time we went to the beach a couple of young gringos invited me to go dancing with them at a disco. "Leave your father at home," they said, "he spends the whole day napping anyway."

Forgive me, forgive me, forgive me, my darling, but I'm telling you this to make you realize that you and I have been discreet, extremely discreet, and on that account we can't be faulted. You, for your part, have always been a teacher of civil law at the National University, a respected congressman for the now defunct PRI, first a loyal campaigner and then a headhunter for the erstwhile candidate, now for the presidency. Unsullied by chicanery. They could accuse you—and with good reason—of being a horny lech, my darling, although that's no sin, not even a venial one. But a thief, never. You don't have to say anything about this, not to me, darling. I know how you live, in that tiny one-bedroom apartment in Colonia Cuauhtémoc. That sickening smell of cooking, garbage, and piss that wafts up the shaft in the stairway. Not even an elevator! And your three Sears suits, your six pairs of shoes, so ancient they're actually from that ancient old shop El Borceguí, your two Basque berets for protecting your bald pate in January. My God! You're an ascetic, my tortilla! What they don't know, of course, is that baldness is a sign—secondary, they say, but a sign nonetheless—of virility, and even if you're modest in every other aspect, your masculine gifts, my irrepressible man, are still peerless. Why, it's as if God the Father gave you almost everything in small sizes with one exception, that Tarzan trouser snake, that Popeye prick, that chimpanzee chili that's very much your own, my bashful one, but it also belongs to me, the woman who so adores you, and asks you to think hard because we've only got two more years to achieve our goal.

I adore you, my dear T. Please tell me when I can see you again, and I repeat: Keep your hands clean and your spine straight, but above all watch it, my love, keep your eyes open, and be prepared to be a bit of a bastard. . . .

11

NICOLÁS VALDIVIA TO
MARÍA DEL ROSARIO GALVÁN

Thank you for allowing me to address you in the familiar, María del Rosario. It's a gift, especially because it makes up for the position you've put me in. I know it's the president's decision. I know that I can thank him through you for the fact that I'm now sitting at a desk in the hallowed halls of the executive branch. But what a price you've made me pay! To have to deal with Tácito de la Canal all day! Everything you told me about him pales in comparison to the dismal truth. If I'm able to bear him at all it's only because I love you and am grateful for all the help you've given me. Besides, I respect your reasons. My first post in the Terán administration is quite close to the president, in the office that's the heart of the country's highest authority, at the service of the president's chief of staff, Tácito de la Canal.

I must be disciplined about this and simply accept the daily company of this repugnant man. Obey him. Respect him. If this is not the best and most genuine proof of my love for you, María del Rosario, I don't know what is, other than romantic suicide in the manner of young Werther. You tell me that I have to start somewhere, and I do hope that my tenure in this office is brief and instructive. I really am repelled by the sickening obsequiousness of Mr. de la Canal: the way he bows before the president, the way he always stands at the president's side like a cardinal next to a king, and that servile way in which he hurries to arrange the president's chair each time Terán stands up and sits down. Must Tácito always unfold and place the president's napkin on his lap at mealtimes? Meanwhile, our casual, unpretentious Lorenzo Terán eats in shirtsleeves and tosses bits of meat to his dog, El Faraón. I can't decide whether the chief of staff would rather feed the dog himself, or if he'd actually prefer to *be* the dog and receive those presidential scraps on all fours.

María del Rosario, if you wished to offer me a crash course in the iniquities brought about by political servility, you couldn't have chosen a better place or a more consummate subject. I can offer you a basic analysis already, and I've only been in this office a week. Tácito de la Canal is a master of deceit, daring in the shadows, humble in the light of day, generous when it suits him, but a miser by nature. Just look at how he treats his subordinates. He evinces fear and resentment because he knows that he is not a subordinate but might go back to being one.

There's a secretary at the office who stands out because of the strange outfits she wears to work. She's about forty years old—and looks it—but dresses like a little girl. Not a teenager, María del Rosario, but strictly, literally, like a little girl. Curly ringlets crowned by a baby blue bow. Blue and pink taffeta dresses, white ankle socks with embroidered angels at the edges, and patent leather Mary Janes. Her only concessions to adulthood are the abundant layers of powder she piles on her face to hide her wrinkles, the bold vermilion-colored lipstick she wears, the waxed eyebrows and mascara-caked eyelashes.

The minute I laid eyes on her I knew this woman had a secret, and the right thing, the human thing, was to respect that.

Imagine my revulsion, my horror, when yesterday I found a Barbie doll sitting on the swivel chair of this child-secretary, who grew very flustered when she saw it and read the card stuck to the Barbie doll's blond mane with a hairpin.

I don't know what the card said, but she read it, burst out crying, and tossed the doll into the trash. I wanted to know what this was all about, and Penélope, an older, stocky, and very forthright secretary, told me that Mr. de la Canal gets his kicks humiliating Doris (that's the woman-child's name). He sends her gifts meant for a ten-year-old girl and taunts her constantly by saying things like: "What would your mommy say? That you aren't a very hardworking little girl. That the teacher should punish you."

Then Doris went into Tácito's office and came out half an hour later, crying but trying to hide her sobs, completely disheveled, carrying the baby blue bow in her hand, adjusting her bra. . . .

Penélope says that de la Canal simply can't live without a female employee to abuse, and in Doris he's found the ideal victim. Now, I always call first or knock on the door before entering Tácito's office, but yesterday I couldn't stand it any longer and I walked straight in when Doris was alone with de la Canal. There he was, clutching that overgrown child, his right hand caressing her breast, his left hand digging into her frilly panties, while he said into her ear, "Don't tell your mommy or else she'll punish you very badly. If you're good to me, I'll buy you more dolls. Respect your mother, fear her, and obey her in everything— except when it comes to the things you and I do together, little slut."

I swear to you, María del Rosario, Tácito de la Canal's cruelty is even more abhorrent than his perversion. He does such infinitesimally hateful things—for example, each week he goes through all the supply closets in the office, counting out all the pencils, the sheets of letterhead, paper clips, erasers, scissors, folders, pens, et cetera. Yesterday, Penélope beat him to it and replaced all the office supplies that had gone missing.

"I keep an exact count, sir," she said. "If you like, we can go through it together and you'll see nothing is missing."

"Did you just put them all back in time, Penélope?" the arrogant de la Canal asked.

"I never took them, sir."

"Have you been snooping through my desk, Penélope?"

"My job is to see that nothing is missing, don Tácito."

Do you know what I did, María del Rosario? I took Doris by the arm, dragged her to Fratina, and dressed her in black from head to toe, black tailored suit, black stockings, black stiletto heels, Chanel handbag, the works, and then I took her to her mother's house in Colonia Satélite. The poor girl was frightened to death, and once we walked through the door I introduced her anew to her mother, a dried-up old hag who was staring aimlessly at a ball of yarn in her hands, sitting in a wheelchair with a jug of lemonade and an arsenal of pills at her side. Oh, yes, and an ugly cat on her lap.

All I said was, "From now on, this is what Doris will wear to work."

"And who the hell are you?"

"I'm her employer, madam, and if you want your daughter to bring a salary home and look after you, Doris better turn up to work looking like this, because if not, I might just kidnap her and take her to come and live with me. . . ."

The old lady began to scream and suddenly I had one of those revelations, like a little thunderbolt flashing through the brain. "And I'd be very careful about saying anything about this to that lowlife Tácito de la Canal. The game is over, madam. If you continue pimping your daughter I'll put you in jail."

The old lady started to shriek in earnest now, and the cat jumped up, meowing with a vengeance, as if defending its mistress. I kicked the bloody cat in the ass and when Doris saw that her mother was defeated she smiled for the first time. Ever since then, she's come to the office dressed like a woman her own age.

Penélope winks at me and gives me the thumbs-up for that one.

But Tácito looks at me with true hatred. He knows I've *read* him like a book, from top to bottom. Servile with the powerful. Contemptuous with the weak. In what intermediate position have I placed myself? I look him straight in the eye. He has no choice but to stare right back at me. But I smile. He does not. And when he calls Doris into his office, I say, "Sorry, sir. Doris is working on a very urgent matter for me."

If the bastard had any hair, it would stand on end.

12

BERNAL HERRERA TO
MARÍA DEL ROSARIO GALVÁN

Are you certain that your strategy is the right one? If your protégé Nicolás Valdivia is working with Tácito de la Canal, it isn't just to gain experience. Not even to gain firsthand knowledge of our adversary. He's there to uncover Tácito de la Canal's weak spot, the truth that will undo him, the act that will condemn him. We already know that Tácito's a lowlife. But how many other lowlifes have you met in politics who still enjoy their ill-gotten wealth with impunity? What we must do is catch Tácito red-handed. What has Valdivia discovered? Not much. Things we already knew. That Tácito is servile. That he's cruel. That in dealing with people he kisses up and kicks down. That he lets the president treat him like a used napkin. That perhaps the president needs a servant to fawn over him. That perhaps the president needs a guard dog with a spiked collar to defend him from inopportune visitors.

Nothing new. Our most exalted leader needs the security of a yes-man, someone who will agree with everything he says. As you can see, our president is following the age-old custom, observed by the likes of Frederick of Prussia and Catherine the Great, of bringing the French Enlightenment to his court. In our case, the roles of Voltaire and Diderot are played by our good friend Xavier Zaragoza, our very own

Seneca. Even so, Frederick still had his valet Fredersdorf to lick his boots, and Catherine still had Potemkin to lick something else entirely. And Lorenzo Terán has Tácito de la Canal.

I'm not satisfied, my friend. Time is ticking away, and in politics timing is at least half the battle. If we can't eliminate Tácito within six months, he'll use his position as a springboard for a presidential bid. And you know what? The idea of running against Tácito de la Canal not only disgusts me. It humiliates me. If I win the 2024 elections against a worm like Tácito, my victory will be as grand as that of a man who has squashed a cockroach underfoot. It will be a hollow victory. And if he were to beat me thanks to his influence with the president, it would mean the end of my political career.

María del Rosario, you know that I'm not a coward and that I assume my own responsibility in this. But life has made us more than just friends: You and I are allies. Our destinies are inextricable. I need you because you're a woman—but not just because of your female instincts. I need you because in addition to instinct you have exceptional political skill. You know how to see what's invisible. You know how to read between the lines. You notice things that escape me. I know I'm not telling you anything you don't already know (or that I haven't already told you). Without you I can never get ahead. You're the person who helps me endure the unpalatable aggression of politics. You've taught me something indispensable in politics: the ability to manage groups of insecure men. You know how to do it, and I've seen it for myself. Somehow you're able to make the most inept cabinet member (and there are several) feel like Aristotle and Bonaparte wrapped up in one. And with the confidence you instill in them, you let them know that you represent me, that you follow my instructions. You are a magnificently talented woman, but you're not a free agent. You are forever tied to Bernal Herrera.

What I mean is that everyone knows you give them all that support and advice because I've asked you to. The agriculture secretary, Epifanio Alatorre, came in to thank me personally for informing him about the imminent decline in sugar prices that he, stupidly stockpiling sugar as if it were gold, never would have predicted. Secretary Alatorre doesn't realize that the United States' and the European Union's agricultural policies will ultimately shut out agricultural exports from the poorer countries: We sell little and cheaply, and we don't gain anything by hoarding our stash in the hopes that prices will eventually go up. There will never be a dearth of anything in the developed world. There will only be munificence toward the beggars, that's all. Handouts. The secretary for public works, Antonio Bejarano, owes me his life because you told him about the contractor Bruno Levi and his ties with the company that was Bejarano's competition during his days as a private businessman—which, by the way, are not quite over yet since he still owns shares through a bunch of false proxies. How I wish we could discover that Tácito is involved in a sleazy deal like that. But Bejarano is irrelevant, politically speaking. He can be as corrupt as he wants. And yet we're the ones who'll exert power over him when the opportunity arises. Without me—without you, that is—his downfall is only a matter of time.

I could go on and on, my dearest lady. But the biggest fish of all, my only visible rival in the 2024 elections, doesn't owe either of us a thing. That's our huge weakness. I don't believe in Tácito's great intelligence, but I know that when it comes to politics he's a sly dog, a Mexican Machiavelli whose capacity for manipulation and cunning is as inexhaustible, my dear friend, as our own capacity for mutual gratitude and affection. We should assume that every secretary of state owes Tácito as many favors as they owe us. Not for nothing is he the holder of the keys to the Holiest of Holies, the president's inner sanctum, our very square "Oval Office."

In any case, we ought to think of it as a fight among equals. Now, will your protégé Valdivia, embedded as he is in Tácito's bureaucracy, be able to come up with the one secret that can ruin him, something more damaging than Tácito's habit of seducing secretaries?

Poor results, María del Rosario, very poor. If we don't produce solid evidence soon to bring Tácito de la Canal down, he and I will start the fight with equal strength. *I cannot tolerate that.* I want to have an indisputable advantage. What will it be? I can only count on your well-deserved reputation as a woman who is intelligent, intuitive . . . and seductive.

13

NICOLÁS VALDIVIA TO
MARÍA DEL ROSARIO GALVÁN

So, my beloved and admired lady, I've yet again followed your instructions (which you euphemistically call suggestions) and traveled to the port of Veracruz in the interest of "earning points" and "polishing my political education," as you put it. I arrived with the letter of introduction you gave me for the Old Man.

There he was, just as you said he'd be, sitting at a table under the great colonnade of the Café de la Parroquia, cane in hand and with a steaming cup of coffee in front of him. He still looks exactly as you and I and the rest of the country remember him. The noble head atop the fragile body. Broad forehead, receding hairline as wide as a boulevard, perfectly clipped and well-combed salt-and-pepper hair. (I don't know why but he gave me the impression of having been combed from head to toe.) And of course, the most arresting thing about him, his gaze: as absentminded as a sparrow and as keen as a hawk! He really is an eagle, though, in every sense of the word, no matter how intense or distracted his perfectly calculated gaze may be. No other president of the republic has embodied such a perfect symbiosis of the person and the symbol. When he sat on the Eagle's Throne, the Old Man was the original eagle.

Now he's known to all as "the Old Man Under the Arches." Although he may change his name and lie about his age, the deep, dark rings that make his eyelids look like two great black curtains remain, softened only by his wide eyebrows. They say that some mountains are covered by "perpetual snow." The Old Man Under the Arches has "perpetual darkness" in those eyebrows that would almost seem diabolical if they didn't contrast so starkly with the petrified smile across his thick lips, rosy for someone so advanced in years, framed and accentuated by deep lines on either side. And in between mouth and eyes, his straight but flat nose, discreet but for the broad, flared nostrils like a bloodhound's.

I'm describing someone you're more than familiar with in order to confirm my own impression of the Old Man. Because that's how he's known around here: the Old Man under the Arches, sitting all day long at one of the Café de la Parroquia's outdoor tables, sipping the aromatic coffee from Coatepec in between sips of mineral water, a copy of *La Opinión* spread out on his lap. Dressed to the nines, as always, in his dark gray pinstriped suit, white shirt, the inevitable polka-dotted bow tie, his cuff links bearing the image of the eagle and the serpent, his flecked socks, and his well-polished black shoes.

I introduced myself, gave him your letter and, just as you warned me, the Old Man Under the Arches launched into a litany of political definitions and recommendations like a priest reciting the Creed. The Old Man doesn't lack a sense of humor. He knows full well that he is an old, old man and that the younger generation condemned him a long time ago to death by oblivion.

"Some people think it would be humane to hasten my journey to the grave," he said, laughing without laughing—a habit of his, it seems. "I won't give them that pleasure. I'll continue to be what some people call 'a political nuisance.' "

Then, without missing a beat (just as you said he would and just as he knew you would tell me he would), he began spewing out his famous sayings, now so old and universally known that they're part of our political folklore. But as I said before, the Old Man doesn't lack a sense of humor, nor is he incapable of deadpan self-criticism.

"Let's get through all those sayings attributed to me, so we don't have to go over them again. . . ."

"I'm one of the young people who wouldn't mind that, Mr. President. Everything about you is new to me."

"What do you mean, 'about me'? And don't call me 'Mr. President.' Remember, I'm not president anymore."

"It's my French education, Mr. President. In France, nobody is ex-anything. That would be considered rude."

"Another Frenchman in Veracruz!" he exclaimed without smiling. "Those damn Frogs again!"

"What I was going to say is that I studied at l'École Nationale d'Administration in Paris. . . ."

"French battleships disembarked here, you know, during the Pastry War."

"The what . . . ?" I asked, revealing my scant knowledge of Mexican history.

"Yes," he said, sipping his coffee. "A French pastry chef by the name of Remortel in Mexico City complained that during a riot the rabble had destroyed his éclairs and croissants, and so in 1838 the French deployed a fleet to bomb Veracruz and demand payment for the ruined pastries. How about that, then? Haven't you ever seen the movie with Mapy Cortés?"

"Mapy . . ."

"A Puerto Rican beauty, oh, yes. A knockout. Thighs so perfect you could cry. She danced a conga called the *pim-pam-pum*," he said, and took another sip.

"Of course," I replied in an attempt to recover a bit of my bruised credibility, realizing now that Mapy Cortés and her *pim-pam-pum* were more important than l'École Nationale d'Administration. "Of course—the whole world has come to Mexico via Veracruz, ever since Hernán Cortés arrived on these shores in 1519. . . ."

"And the French came back in 1862 to help defend the empire of

Maximilian and Carlota." Nostalgia brought a momentary sparkle to his hooded eyes. "Just picture the troop of Belgians, Austrians, Hungarians, Germans, men from Prague, Trieste, Marseilles, the Zouaves, Bohemians, Flemish, who landed here with their flags held high, my little friend, and every last flag had an eagle, two-headed eagles, crowned eagles, heraldic eagles, and here we were with one poor little eagle of our own—but what an eagle, my little friend Valdivia, a bloody fine eagle, incomparable, its talons perched atop a nopal and devouring a serpent. Those Europeans weren't expecting that, now, were they?"

"I suppose not, sir."

"Oh, and the trail of dark-skinned blue-eyed children those imperial troops left behind in Veracruz. Did you ever see the film *Imperial Cavalry*?"

"No, but I read a marvelous novel, *News from the Empire*, by Fernando del Paso."

"Thank goodness," he said, with a note of pity in his voice. "At least you know something."

He looked into the distance toward the sea and the San Juan de Ulúa fortress, an imposing, uninviting gray mass on a forbidding island. The Old Man saw me watching and seemed to know what I was thinking.

I spoke as if he'd asked me something.

"Forgive me, Mr. President. . . . It's just that when I was a child there was a breakwater that connected the castle to the mainland."

"I had the breakwater removed. It was a blight on the landscape," he said, as the waiter, arm raised high above his head, poured steaming coffee with perfect aim straight into our glass coffee cups.

The Old Man kept talking.

"That's why I sit here, looking out at the port of Veracruz, so that I can give warning should any foreign enemy dare to profane our land with his soles, as our national anthem puts it."

I began to think that the Old Man Under the Arches was nothing but a raving monomaniac going on and on with his litany of wrongs suffered by Mexico over the centuries.

"And the gringos, son, the gringos who've sucked the brains out of

Mexico's youth. They dress like gringos, dance like gringos, think like gringos—they wish they could *be* gringos."

He then made an obscene gesture with his left hand as he raised his cane with his right.

"By Santa Anna's lost leg, those gringos can come and kiss my ass! Here they landed in 1847, then again in 1914 . . . When will they be back?"

He readjusted his dentures, which had slipped out of place from all the excitement, and returned to the topic at hand.

"Listen, son, just so you don't leave here disappointed, let me give you some of my legendary maxims. . . ."

And he recited them. Seriously, almost as a meditation, all the while stirring the sugar in his coffee cup.

"Politics is the art of swallowing frogs without flinching."

He didn't laugh. All he did was bite down hard on his dentures to fix them squarely in his gums.

"In Mexican politics, even cripples can pull off a high-wire act."

He took advantage of my feigned laughter to ask the waiter for a *mollete.*

"Refried beans and melted cheese in a hot bread roll. Good for the digestion," he said. "Look, the simple truth is that the presidency is a roller coaster. The expression on your face when they send you off is the expression that stays with you forever."

He took a big bite of his *mollete.*

"That's why you always see me with the same look on my face, exactly the same as my very first day in office."

He continued, María del Rosario, with a slightly macabre smile.

"What nobody knows is that my arsenal of unpublished sayings knows no end."

I gave him a courteously quizzical look.

And then, with a sound like a death knell from the back of his throat, he said, "Make no mistake. I'm immune to bullets and to colds."

I fell silent after that resounding maxim, waiting for him to say something else, wondering what I was really doing there, my lovely lady, aside from simply following your instructions: "Talk to the Old Man Under the Arches. Be patient and learn from him."

"You know what, son? Before becoming president, a man has to suffer and learn. If not, he'll suffer and learn during his presidency, at the country's expense."

Could this mean that María del Rosario Galván—yes, you, my dear lady—had informed the old ex-president of her daring promise to deliver me to the Eagle's Throne, and explained that I was in Veracruz to learn from him? If the thought crossed my mind, I didn't say it out loud, of course.

I merely dared to point out: "Cárdenas became president at the age of thirty-six, Alemán at thirty-nine, Obregón at forty-four, Salinas at forty. . . ."

"I'm not talking about age, Mr. Valdivia. I haven't said a word about age, which is a taboo subject for this old man. I was referring to suffering and learning. I was referring to experience. All the men you mention were young, but they were experienced. Are you?"

I shook my head. "Mr. President, I admit I'm a novice. But one morning with you is enough to teach me everything I didn't learn at the ENA in Paris."

He shook his head very slightly, as if he were afraid that all the parts inside it might become unhinged, that the screws would come loose.

"Right," he said, sipping his coffee. "You do know that every president finishes where the next one should start. That is, where he himself should have started. Am I being clear? The outgoing president speaks to his successor without having to use a single word. That's the experience I'm talking about."

"Except that the successor tends to be deaf to his predecessor."

I thought he would warm to my graceful wit. Instead, his dark-ringed gaze grew even darker.

"Gratitude, Mr. Valdivia, gratitude and ingratitude. The former is a very rare form of political currency. The latter, everyday trash."

Very discreetly he removed a speck from the corner of his eye.

"Just think for a moment of how many PRI presidents were loyal to their predecessors. After all, under the old PRI's rule the man who came to occupy the Eagle's Throne had been placed there by the throne's previous occupant. 'The concealed one' became 'the anointed one.' A perverse consequence of the system: The new all-powerful leader had to prove, as quickly as possible, that he was not dependent on the man who appointed him. How paradoxical, Mr. Valdivia, or should I say how parafucksical. A single-party system in which the opposition always wins, because the new president has to screw his predecessor."

"There were exceptions, though," I said in a Cartesian spirit.

The Old Man picked out three rolls from the bread basket and left the other eight there. He didn't have to say anything else, although with the finger of God he did invisibly trace the numbers "1940–1994" on the tablecloth.

"Now, of course, we live in a democracy," I said with forced optimism.

"And the incumbent still has his favorites to succeed him, he's already mulling over who will best serve the country, who will be most loyal to him, who will respect his people, and who will not. . . ."

"But nowadays the president's own candidate will not necessarily be the successor, as he was in your day. . . ."

"No, but regardless of who wins the elections the ex-president will always be, lethally, the ex-president. And every ex-president, it turns out, has skeletons in his closet. Crooked brothers, insatiable lovers, incorrigible sisters, deviant children, false proxies for his business interests, lifelong friends that cannot be condemned to death, who knows what else . . . What other choice does he have but to make amends for the extravagance of those closest to him by living with monastic austerity? See what they say about me? I go to bed early so as not to waste the candles."

"You know everything."

I flashed him my best smile. He didn't reciprocate.

THE EAGLE'S THRONE 61

"Suffer and learn," he sighed, and once again looked out dreamily toward the misty bulk of the San Juan de Ulúa castle, the fortress guarding the entrance to the port.

I realized that, focused as I was on the Old Man's words and gestures, I hadn't looked very closely at Ulúa's grayish mass, which seemed an architecture apart, embedded in the past, weighed down by a history that couldn't be undone.

"See that castle that used to be a prison? Can you begin to imagine the number of politicians who should be there now, purging their wrongs?"

"If you say so, sir . . ."

He shrugged his shoulders, creaking slightly.

"We have two golden rules in Mexican politics. One is benign: no reelection. The other is more unforgiving: exile. The reason, however, is the same: All delinquents are recidivists, my young friend."

He peered at me from the depths of the lines under his eyes.

"You know, it is a mistake to think that a president controls only the weak. The most urgent but most difficult task is that of controlling the powerful. I'm going to give you a rule for you to share with all the people you know who aspire to public office. Anyone who wants to be part of the cabinet should first take in a liter of vinegar through his nose. That's the best training there is for getting close to the presidency, I promise you. . . ."

The waiter approached us with the massive, steaming coffeepot. The Old Man declined. He had not offered me a third coffee, but he pushed my coffee glass toward me.

It was then that, rather inopportunely, I asked the former head of state, "And you, Mr. President, is there anyone you favor to be Lorenzo Terán's successor?"

The Old Man fell silent for a moment as he gazed out at the crows settling down for the night in the Indian laurels that lined the plaza: flocks of birds making such a racket as they searched for nighttime shelter that luckily they drowned out my voice, even though I know the Old

Man heard me. I've never known a man with as keen an ear as the ex-president, my dear lady, even though all the people who used to ask him for favors would very stupidly steer him over to the most isolated corner of his office and say to him, "Since everyone says that deep down you're a good man . . ."

I don't know if the Old Man Under the Arches is a good man or a bad man. All I know is that he's a sly old dog, that he knows everything, and reveals nothing. Did he hear me? Did he not? Did he not want the waiter to hear? Whatever the case, my admirable though cruel friend, the Old Man used those minutes of silence, interrupted only by the raucous (or was it mournful?) cawing of those birds in the twilight, to give me a political lesson in how to say everything without saying anything.

I urge you to repeat, in front of a mirror, each and every one of the gestures the old ex-president demonstrated for me.

First, he raised one finger to his earlobe and rubbed it. One must know how to listen.

Then he covered his eyes with both hands. If I saw you, I don't remember.

After that, he took his index finger and tugged at one of his eyelids. Keep your eyes open. Careful. Always be on your guard.

After that, he raised one eyebrow as if to suggest skepticism. Don't let this man pull the wool over your eyes.

And at the same time, he tilted his hand left and right as if to say, Be careful with this other one. He's more slippery than an eel. He knows how to sustain a ruse.

For his finale, he placed his index finger on one of his nostrils. Don't let them fool you. Sniff them out.

I enumerate, my dear friend, the quick succession of signals that followed the nasal symbolism. Hand on heart. Both hands flapping to indicate the separation of incompatible issues. Hand on crotch to indicate balls. Thumb pointed upward, like Caesar granting life in the Circus Maximus, and then turned down as if condemning someone to death. Index finger cutting the throat like a razor blade. Index finger and thumb held together in a perfect "O" to indicate success. Lips pursed in a grimace to inject a measure of doubt into the moment of triumph. Squinting eyes to suggest doubt and the question, Who do you think you are? Shoulders raised in resignation, as if to say, What can we do about it? Hands held open, as if to say, Such is life. And then his famous index finger raised in ominous warning. And finally, the same finger passing over the lips like an invisible zipper. Not a word. Shh! Silence is golden.

After this masterful display of body language, my admirable and desired lady, all that was left for me was to thank the Old Man Under the Arches for his advice, his time, his attention. He looked at me from behind his mask of impartiality. He wanted me to look at him as a character playing a role. The benign country patriarch. The wise Mexican Cincinnatus. He was educating me: Son, play stupid. A man has to know how to act the fool. Be the village idiot. Pure gesticulation. Not a word. The master of circumlocution. The juggler of all things unspoken because they are understood by all. The king of the euphemism.

I left, thanking the Old Man, who bowed his head toward me as a parrot settled on his shoulder and the waiter offered him a box of dominoes.

The sun was setting quite spectacularly, hidden crows cawed, and the castle-prison of San Juan de Ulúa, so sinister during the day, looked legendary as night fell.

P.S. You have rescinded my right to speak to you in the familiar until I can prove myself worthy of these circumstances. You have sent me like a little schoolboy to be taught by the Old Man Under the Arches as if the latest version of Plato's Academy were now located in this derelict old port's main plaza. But don't think I'm offended, it only entices me. *NV.*

14

DULCE DE LA GARZA TO
MARÍA DEL ROSARIO GALVÁN

Madam: If I dare to write to you, it is only because I have no other way of contacting you. And you are who you are. The whole country knows that. There isn't a single woman with more influence (I don't know if I've said it properly—perhaps I should say there isn't a single more influential woman?) than you. All doors open for you. The powerful listen to you. But your doors are closed to the powerless. And I am an insignificant woman. Once, I could have been as powerful as you are now. But my name says it all—at one time I could have been, but I wasn't. So I write to you now, madam, I freely admit it, because you are powerful and I am not. But I also write to ask you woman to woman: What has become of my beloved? Can't you tell me anything? Who is buried in my lover's grave in Veracruz? Why are there two graves, one beneath the other? One with a wax model inside melting from the heat, and the other empty? Madam, if you have ever felt love for a man—and I don't doubt that you have—please take pity on me. In the name of the man you have loved most dearly in your own life, think of me, have mercy on me, my loneliness and my pain, and please tell me: Where is the body of my beloved? Where can I go to bring him flowers, kneel down, pray for him, think of him, and tell him how terribly and desperately I miss him and need him? Can't you help me? Is this a lot to ask? Is it too much? Am I asking for the impossible?

15

EX-PRESIDENT CÉSAR LEÓN TO
PRESIDENT LORENZO TERÁN

I wish to thank you, Mr. President, for the friendship and even the trust you have shown toward me by rescinding the unwritten ban that has kept me out of the country during the years of my "ex-presidency." Your generosity toward me is proof of your self-confidence. I haven't come to take anything away from you, Mr. President. If only your predecessors had said the same. As golden as it may be, exile is always bitter. A man carries his country in his heart, his blood, his head. But also in his feet. To be able to set foot on Mexican soil again, Mr. President, is the marvelous gift you have given me, and I intend to repay it with gratitude and loyalty.

On that matter, I had come to believe that the proof of my loyalty to you was my silence. Now you, showing a magnanimity that befits you, and in the spirit of mutual loyalty, have asked for my advice.

Imagine what that means to a man like me, showered with adulation one day only to wake up the next melancholy day and find himself out of office, asking the painful question, "Where did all my friends go?"

It was as though I was Gracchus, the noble Roman who ran to the beach thinking that the approaching soldiers had come to free him, only to discover that they were there to kill him. Loyalties can be changed as quickly as coats. The man who was once my friend suddenly became my enemy in the space of half an hour. . . .

Very well, Mr. President, since you've asked me to speak frankly, this is my message to you.

Though you won the election, never forget that in the end you'll lose your power.

I know what I'm talking about.

Be prepared.

The victory of becoming president eventually and inevitably gives way to the defeat of becoming the ex-president.

Be prepared.

It takes much more imagination to be ex-president than to be president. This is because you will inevitably leave a problem behind you, and that problem has a name: yours.

Mexico's problems go back for centuries. Nobody has ever been able to solve them. But people always blame the country's ills on whoever holds—and above all whoever has just given up—power.

That was my downfall. Perhaps it's not the person but the job that's to blame. How easy it would be to delegate from the first day. But it doesn't work like that. It can't. From the very moment he takes his seat on the Eagle's Throne, the president must prove that there's only one voice in Mexico—his own. That was the meaning of the Aztec emperor's name, Tlatoani, god of the Great Voice. That is what our position as occupiers of the Eagle's Throne demands of us: to claim the Great Voice. The *only voice*.

Naturally we have the power to sack an incompetent (or disloyal) minister. But in the end, all responsibility ultimately falls upon the shoulders of the president. Sometimes we're offered champagne. But more often we're forced to drink something bitter. We all hope to be judged not for the errors committed during our last few days in power, but for the virtues of the previous six years, and there are always a few. Rarely, however, does it work out like that, I warn you with all due respect.

Besides, intentions count for nothing; only results matter. And since you've granted me permission to bring up the subject of the presidential succession that already looms large given the accelerated nature of our new democratic system (those of us from the old PRI always managed to keep our horses locked up in their stables until the last minute before the race, but that was another racetrack, and the jockeys were all too fat), the one thing I'll say is that in the old days, once the candidate had been selected—as late as possible, I insist—the incumbent virtually became an ex-president.

One thing that hasn't changed, however, is that the succession process still takes place primarily in the mind of the man who occupies the Eagle's Throne. There, inside his head, he ponders who among all the possible heirs to the PRI's hereditary republic has the strongest grassroots support, the greatest loyalty among labor and peasant collectives, and the most favorable position in the polls.

Oh, Mr. President, shall I tell you the truth, the nitty-gritty? Public opinion isn't worth shit. The notion that X is a viable successor because he's tremendously popular only works against the incumbent. It's conceivable that, once in office, without debts to anyone but the voters, the popular president will cut off all his obligations to the outgoing president. What you want and hope for is Y, because he has your support and no one else's, because he's trailing in all the polls, because when he succeeds you he'll be indebted to you. Because, as a result, he'll be the most loyal of the lot.

Oh, Mr. President. A big mistake. If you select the man who owes you the most, you can be certain that he'll betray you in order to prove that he doesn't depend on you. In other words: He who owes you the most will feel under the strongest obligation to exercise his independence or, to put it bluntly, his disloyalty. Political cannibalism occurs everywhere, but only in Mexico is the public corpse seasoned with two hundred different kinds of chili pepper—from the tiniest *piquín* to the big and delicious stuffed *poblano,* to say nothing of the *jalapeño,* the *chipotle,* and the *morrón.* The great ritual act of a new president is the killing of his predecessor. Prepare yourself, Mr. President. Watch your back. Very few will stand by you in defeat as they stood by you in victory. There and only there will loyalties be tested and proven. The only opportunity or virtue left to us is the very difficult one of trying to be the best ex-president we can, repressing the desire to complain, overlooking all the damage done to our allies, forgetting about the insults, and above all showing our loyalty to the new head of state. I warn you in advance: This is the most difficult part. We're inclined to feel rage, hatred, resentment, to hatch plots and vendettas. We feel the inevitable temptation to play the Count of Monte Cristo. A big mistake. If the pain of exile (voluntary in theory but compulsory in practice) is compounded by the desire for revenge, we'll ultimately lose all sense of reality and begin to invent an imaginary country where everything continues exactly as we left it when we descended from the Eagle's Throne.

Mr. President, the most serious advice I can give you is that even if you feel persecuted, simply pretend nothing is wrong. Allow your very visible loyalty to be the most subtle and elegant vendetta of all. I assure you that I did everything I could to put it all behind me and I very nearly succeeded. I lived out my exile in Switzerland reading volume after volume of ancient history because the most enduring lessons regarding the exercise of power are those offered by Plutarch, Suetonius, and Tacitus. Chief among the stories they tell, Mr. President, is that of the nobleman Sabinus, murdered for his alleged disloyalty to Caesar. Sabinus' dog, the story goes, refused to move away from his master's body, and even put food into his mouth. Finally Sabinus' body was thrown into the Tiber, but the dog jumped in after it and kept it afloat.

"Kill the dog!" the guard ordered.

Such are the extremes of loyalty, Mr. President. Count on mine.

16

NICOLÁS VALDIVIA TO
MARÍA DEL ROSARIO GALVÁN

If Tácito de la Canal is as slippery a snake as you suspect, my dear lady, then unfortunately I haven't been able to provide any more evidence to support that claim beyond his obsequiousness with superiors and his cruelty with inferiors. The president's chief of staff has been very careful to maintain a facade of exemplary humility. He lives in Colonia Cuauhtémoc in a tiny two-room apartment with a kitchen, a stairway landing that smells like cat piss, furniture from Lerdo Chiquito, and piles of old magazines. A monk, if you will, with no other luxury than that of power for power's sake.

Well, then. Finally I've come up with a bit of evidence that is inconclusive in and of itself but which could open the door to greater mysteries.

You know, my mistress María del Rosario, it's like one of those books our grandmothers used to give us. On a page with a picture of the inside of a home there's a little window that allows us to see the garden on the next page, which in turn has a gate that opens onto a third page, and then that third page opens onto a forest that leads the eye all the way down to the water's edge, where a boat waits to deliver us to an enchanted island. And so on. It's like the never-ending story, isn't it?

Well, having been transformed into a Versace model and duly instructed by yours truly, our little Doris led Tácito to believe that now
that she was such an elegant, modern woman, she would not object to,
let's say, a more intimate sort of relationship with him. As surely as
Tácito is a satyr, so was the god Pan's machinery set in motion, and little by little—duly instructed, once again, by me—Doris, who needed
only to break away from her sinister mother to blossom, began to toy
with Tácito, putting him off, making him take her out to restaurants at
first, and then to bars, to the Gran León dance hall so she could show
off her *tabaré* dancing, but never to any motel, much less a hotel room.

Tácito's ardor only grew. The whole office could tell. Finally she
agreed to go to his apartment on Calle Río Guadiana. As she walked in,
she held her nose and repeated a Bette Davis quote I taught her.

"What a dump! What a squalid hellhole! Vile shack! Shithole!"

Nearly dying of laughter, Doris told me that Tácito was so humiliated by this that he took her by the hand, pulled out a set of keys, went
over to the tiny kitchen, and unlocked a door, revealing a luxurious
panorama within, as if turning a page in one of those picture books. A
sumptuous penthouse appeared before Doris's eyes—a terrace with
large flowerpots brimming with flowers, an oblong swimming pool,
and chaise longues for sunbathing. And behind the terrace, a vast living
room, luxury furniture, expensive collectors' paintings—lots of fake
Rubens, I gather from Doris's description—Persian rugs, fluffy sofas,
cheap glassware, and a door, left ajar, leading into the bedroom.

Doris, following her instructions precisely, exhibited shock and delight, while Tácito registered insouciance and pride. And when our despicable cabinet chief made a more, shall we say, wanton overture,
Doris very coquettishly excused herself and went to the bathroom, as if
getting ready for this late-afternoon tryst, and there she took a handkerchief from her bag and let it flutter down from the window into the
street. I saw the sign, and within five minutes, feigning the rage of a
cuckolded lover, I burst into our incomparable Tácito's bedroom, and
found him stark naked, exposing all that Mother Nature had so cruelly

bequeathed him: the bald head, the dense thicket of hair on his chest and legs, not to mention a number of other shaggy areas that I would rather not describe. He ran after the well-trained Doris who, fully dressed, screamed at the top of her voice, "I can't! What would my mother say!"

I yanked her away from the birthday-suited chief of staff and held her tight. I showered him with insults, saying Doris was my lover and I was her Pygmalion (the latter being true, the former false, of course), and at that the two of us left, barely able to hold in our laughter, while Tácito stood there naked.

Our little farce turned out to be quite amusing. But it doesn't really prove anything, my dear friend, aside from the fact that Tácito's a ridiculous little satyr and that hair loss is a sign—secondary, perhaps, but a sign nonetheless—of virility. In any event, at least you now have proof of how false his alleged austerity is. Let's hope I have even better luck next time around!

17

GENERAL CÍCERO ARRUZA TO
GENERAL MONDRAGÓN VON BERTRAB

General, my friend and my superior (although never superior to the president himself, whose office makes him the commander in chief of the armed forces), hear me out because I smell a rat. Something fishy is going on.

You and I both know that there are times when the deployment of armed forces is our only option. The army intervention in San Luis Potosí against strikers who are causing trouble for the Japanese and acting like real-life samurai made it very clear that around here foreign investment is respected—why, if it weren't for the cheap labor they wouldn't have come here in the first place, and where would that have left us? Twiddling our thumbs. I commend you for executing such a clean, swift operation, General. Anyway, I'm glad that these shows of force are your responsibility. As the saying goes, in Mexico we like our deals crystal clear and our hot chocolate thick, but all too often we end up with watery chocolate and shady deals. What I mean is that, historically speaking, they've always slipped a little goat's meat into our tamales, if you know what I mean. You know well enough, General, that there's always been a big difference between officers trained at military academies, like you, and those of us who've risen up through the ranks.

I'm not saying that one is better than the other. You yourself know that our great general Felipe Ángeles came out of the Saint-Cyr Academy in France and went on to win the battle against his former fellow soldiers in the Federal Army in 1914. But our general Pancho Villa was a fugitive rancher, a man who had killed his sister's rapist, an out-and-out bandit, a rustler, a cattle thief, and so on, and one fine day he found his calling and put together a rural army of eighty thousand men, almost all of them peasants, joined later by ranchers from the north, merchants, and even writers and professionals. And Villa accomplished everything that Ángeles accomplished, but he hadn't attended any fancy foreign academy—he didn't even know how to read and write! Even so, he beat the Federal Army. What I'm trying to say, General, is that I'm not checking up on you, nor should you underestimate me. Deal? We are— oh, what's the word—complementary, like salt and lime to a good tequila, wouldn't you say? You win the big national battles, and I take care of the little local skirmishes. You finish off the car workers striking in San Luis Potosí. But I'm not allowed to beat the shit out of those snot-nosed sons of bitches at the university. They claim it's because the university's autonomy can't be violated. But didn't those little savages already violate it themselves by destroying the science labs and pissing on the dean's chair? You'll tell me, General, that I already have my hands full in a city plagued by fear, express kidnappings, extortion, robbery, murder. . . . You know the problem well enough. Say I decide to clean up the police force. So I get rid of one or two thousand crooked policemen. What do I accomplish? I end up swelling the ranks of the criminal rings by a thousand, two thousand. Ex-cops go straight into kidnapping, drug dealing, or robbery. Nice one. So I find another two thousand boys, young kids, clean, idealistic. Can't be accused of not trying, and you know it. But I'm so unlucky. When will I get a break? Within a year all my men are corrupt, because how can my five-thousand-peso salary compete with the five-million-peso sweetener that my crooked policeman gets for doing a single job for some well-known drug dealer? I'm not lacking in goodwill, General. I'm one of those men who'd gladly kill a thousand innocent people to keep one guilty man from going free. And speaking of policemen, don't forget that I wasn't trained like our dear Cantinflas in that movie, walking the beat and seducing maids to get a free plate of beans (but allow me to share a little joke with you: When it comes to maids, first you wash them, then you screw them, and then, as a reward, you send them to the brothel). What I'm really trying to say here is that I got my education fighting guerrillas, rebels, and insurrectionist groups that have existed in Mexico for as long as I can remember—one day in Morelos, another day in Chiapas, another day in Guerrero. . . . And what did I learn from all that, General? One glaring truth: The night is worth a million recruits. That's why I hate mysteries—they're like the night. It's in the darkness that all those invisible armies are born and, one fine day, without even having to show their faces, they've got us fucked. But in the fight against the guerrillas, General, we have the advantage of being able to break all the rules, because that's exactly what the enemy does. General, the best way to get your troops to love you is to let them pillage what they want and then blame it on the enemy. To go out to kill for food—tell me, can there be anything more appealing to a poor Mexican soldier, one of those crew-cut recruits who are the usual cannon fodder since we don't have blacks like they do in the U.S.? Tell me, you who went to a German academy. Oh, how good it is to give orders like you do, my general, from afar, like in a computer game, knowing that your enemies are a fortress that must be attacked with military might, by discovering their weak side, breaking through their lines, scaring civilians, since all successful rebellions have plenty of civilian support, don't they? Do you think I don't feel some longing, even nostalgia, for the days when I was a line commander, face-to-face with demanding, tough, challenging enemies? Well, just look at me now, using kindergarten stunts to keep things in order—break up the protest, General Arruza, they tell me, let rats out into the auditorium, drop plastic bags full of piss from the upstairs balconies. . . . Every night I still dream of our beautiful countryside, of the dogs barking at the stars, of dead bodies hanging from posts, the wind whistling in their wide-open mouths. And now, General, all of a sudden I spot an opportunity and I very loyally communicate it to you, because its execution will be your responsibility, although the information may come to me first. And if so, we'll have no choice but to join forces, my good general. Some things we feel with our skin, others we see with our eyes, and still others just beat away in our hearts. To cut a long story short, there's a secret, General. A very well-kept secret at the San Juan de Ulúa fortress. Yes, right at the entrance to the port of Veracruz. How do I know this? Because a spy told me. Or, if you will, a little bird. An affectionate little lady bird who is not only mine . . . or in other words she's the very lovely cage where my own little birdie sings. Ulúa, cage, castle, and prison. You may be wondering how this could possibly be connected with all the other issues we face now—whether the president will rise to the occasion, the matter of the gringos who've threatened and isolated us, the question of who will become the next president, the matter of the students, the peasants, the factory workers. . . .

There are a thousand threads in this fabric, General, and yet my old soldier's intuition keeps on asking: Ulúa, Ulúa, what's going on in Ulúa?

18

BERNAL HERRERA TO
MARÍA DEL ROSARIO GALVÁN

Ex-President César León came to visit me. At first I didn't even recognize him. That young man with wavy black hair is now a mature man with wavy white hair. Those matinee idol's wavy locks are what define him for me, politically and morally as well as physically. They remind me of that old song, "The Waves of the Lagoon": "Some waves come, while others go, some to Sayula, some to Zapotlán. . . ." The question is: Where is Sayula in the mind of César León, and where is Zapotlán?

What follows is a summary of the brief conversation we had, along with my conclusions, since León was (and perhaps still is?) your friend. You gave him the advice that ensured his popularity early on. Free the political prisoners, president. Flatter the intellectuals. Attend all the civic and cultural ceremonies. Assume Benito Juárez's republican mantle. Replace the trade unions' leadership. New faces. Change is accepted as a sign of moral renewal. (We all know that the opposite is true: A new bureaucrat has all the ambitions that the old one has already fulfilled. Thus the new one will be more voracious than the old one.) Cooperate with the gringos on everything, except Cuba. Cuba has provided and continues to provide the opportunity to pay lip service to our independence. Thanks to Cuba we're no longer the main target of the campaigns, plots, and occasional violence that the United States has un-leashed on Latin America. The United States is a kind of Captain Ahab on the quest for a Moby Dick that may yet satisfy the American obses-sion with viewing the world in black and white. Gringos go mad if they can't tell who's the good guy and who's the bad guy—and Mexico was the bad guy for a century and a half until, thank God, Fidel Castro turned up and became our lightning conductor. César León made the gringos understand that the problem was a bit more complex than the plot of an old Western. Mexico would be the United States' most loyal Latin American ally, but this would only be plausible if Mexico main-tained a healthy relationship with Castro in the interest of keeping the lines of communication open (issue number one) and playing a role in Cuba's transition after Castro's death (issue number two). It was the latter promise that failed us all. The old comandante is still there, ninety-three years old, and I read in the paper that he's just opened a Sierra Maestra theme park.

Now, I'm not saying that you yourself invented Mexico's policies toward Cuba and the United States, my dear friend, because that would be like saying you discovered lukewarm water. With the seductive wiles for which you are famous, you simply planted these policies in the mind of the young president César León, who was practically a gringo then—trained at Princeton and MIT before he had to take on Mexico's defen-sive foreign policy, a bit like the tortoise sleeping alongside the elephant.

You also reminded him that a newly elected president in the newly restored PRI system (this was fourteen years ago) would do well to be a thorn in the side of relatives and friends of the outgoing head of state, because that was the way to satisfy public opinion and give people the illusion of a fresh start.

César León. We haven't even mentioned his name since he won the 2006 elections. We decided, simply, that he was a nonperson.

But the fact is that he's come back. And President Terán has wel-comed him with open arms.

I said to him, "Be careful, Mr. President. César León is like the scorpion that says to the frog, 'Carry me on your back across the river. I promise not to sting you.' And nevertheless, the scorpion stings the frog. . . ."

"I know the fable," the president said to me, smiling. " 'It's in my nature,' the scorpion says. In this case, though, León is the frog and I'm the scorpion."

"What do you want, then? To sting him or to make it to the other side?"

"That's something I'll decide in good time. Patience."

I'm giving you this background information, my dear friend, so that you can understand my chat with César León last night.

He began with his little "humility" recital.

"I've learned so many things in exile. I want to be a factor for unity. Soon, someone will have to take President Terán's place and we'll be holding elections in the middle of some very serious difficulties."

He enumerated the latter, which you and I know very well: the students, the workers, the peasants, the gringos. . . . He practically volunteered to act as intermediary in every case. He talked about the support he has in the old PRI, splintered apart primarily because of his intolerant, authoritarian, and arrogant attitude toward the end of his term. He even threw in a Latin quotation (he seems to have spent his time in Europe reading the classics): "*Divide et impera.* . . ."

I played dumb, asked him to translate for me.

" 'Divide and rule,' " he said smugly.

So that's it, I said to myself, you're here to triumph by dividing, bastard. I kept the comment to myself. I wanted to hear him say it—it would be like hearing a song that was a hit twenty years ago played on an old scratched record. He repeated the bit about wanting to be the best ex-president ever, a Mexican Jimmy Carter, never complaining, behaving as if nobody had ever done him any wrong. In other words: He's come back, thirsting for power, just like the shipwreck survivor floating adrift on the raft of the *Medusa* for years and years, surrounded by water and yet unable to drink a drop.

He said that he wanted to be a factor for unity and cooperation in what remained of the old, fractured PRI. In other words: He wants to take over the party and rebuild it by making promises to all the old corporate bases, weakened at present but not without latent power, and then bring together all the disparate interest groups, the local power bases and strongmen—unfortunately spawned by our fledgling democracy and our president's laissez-faire attitude—in a unified opposition party that can kick us out of power.

And he very cynically suggested that he could act as a go-between, connecting the presidency and our unmanageable Congress, given that there's no majority at San Lázaro and all bills proposed by the executive branch are either stalled or shelved entirely.

In a word, he was offering me his help to head off these obstacles and to clear the path to the presidential elections.

I sat there looking at him, totally speechless. I don't have to tell you that this didn't make him uncomfortable at all. His scheming little eyes sparkled and he said very slowly, "Herrera . . . Whatever happened . . . didn't happen."

I stared at him intensely.

"Mr. President," I said, with due courtesy, "when you were incomparable, you didn't hate anyone. Now that you're among equals, who is it that you hate?"

His answer was cunning and self-satisfied.

"The question, Mr. Secretary, is to *whom* are you equal?"

I had to laugh at his undeniably sharp wit, but the laugh froze on my lips when his eyes suddenly stopped sparkling and he said something to me in that powerful, menacing voice he always used to use to intimidate his allies as well as his enemies.

"If you want my advice, stay out of the Moro case."

I can only assume that he'd already anticipated my reaction, unless he'd become incredibly stupid or incredibly naïve, which in the end are one and the same thing. My reaction, you understand, was essential in the presence of such a wily, dangerous man.

"Apparently, Mr. President, you don't seem to realize that your days are over. . . ."

"And everything that happened then . . . never happened? Let's see, how can that be possible?"

"Quite simply, the laws you once abided by have nothing to do with the laws we live by today. . . . The problems have changed, the solutions have changed and, I must reiterate, times themselves have changed."

"Ah, but you and I, despite our different problems and times, will always, ultimately, commit evil acts if committing evil acts is necessary, won't we?"

He then raised his leonine head and looked at me with arrogance and scorn.

"Don't touch the Moro case, Mr. Secretary. As long as you don't touch it we'll get along famously."

"Oh, shut up!" I said, losing my patience. "I know what really happened in the Moro case, but I'm not interested in doing the police's work."

"Well, let's see. The police might do their job so thoroughly that you'll be the one who ends up in prison."

At that, I jumped up and snapped, "You're nothing but a lost dream."

"No." He smiled as he walked to the door before turning to face me one last time. "Quite the opposite. I'm a living nightmare."

I slammed my fist into my forehead after César León closed the door behind him. I should never have lost control in the presence of that viper.

In what direction, my dear friend, do the waves in the lagoon go now?

19

NICOLÁS VALDIVIA TO
MARÍA DEL ROSARIO GALVÁN

You have every right to reproach me for being so slow, my dear lady. Allow me to quote that well-known Italian adage, since Italy is the source of all wisdom but also of all political malice: *Chi va piano va lontano.* I only hope that one day you'll grant me the distinction enjoyed by another Italian (one who is less anonymous than the author of this proverb, to be sure), and that you'll recognize me, my dear lady, for what I am: a young boy who was graced with good fortune but who nevertheless lives according to the words of his namesake Machiavelli, who always warned against excessive reliance on Fortune, who, after all, is (and who does this bring to mind?) fickle, inconstant—shameless.

In any case, do you think it insignificant that I was able to undermine the arrogance of Tácito de la Canal and turn the adorable Dorita, so long subjugated by her boss and her mother, into a real woman?

I've continued to employ this tactic, my dear María del Rosario. Yesterday was February 14, St. Valentine's Day, the day of lovers (who knows why), and so I organized a party in the office. I chose to hold it in the Emiliano Zapata room—because Mexico is a country that murders its heroes and then erects statues to honor them. It seemed the appropriate place for the staff of the presidential mansion. You know—all those people nobody ever sees precisely because nobody is ever supposed to see them. I've already mentioned the secretaries, so hard up these days without telephones, computers, and fax machines, forced to haul out the old Remingtons that were gathering dust in the archives.

The archives! Who's ever seen those old people (why doesn't anyone young work there? Have you ever noticed?) who look after the presidential records with the sort of devotion that deserves a medal? They're the invisible among the invisible, living in paper caves, custodians of all that must be hidden and forgotten. The archivists.

I invited the gardeners, doormen, drivers, cooks, waitresses, cleaning ladies, and laundresses to the party. I put the faithful Penélope in charge—never has a woman been so aptly named—of all the necessary arrangements: hanging the lanterns, decorating everything with hearts, hanging up streamers, ordering the buffet, everything.

You can't imagine what a delightful time everyone had—that is, until the illustrious Tácito de la Canal made his triumphant entrance and a funereal silence descended on the party. The chief of staff was pleased by this. He had dressed up for the event, which in his case meant taking off his tie and undoing the top three buttons of his shirt, not to look casual, but because he wanted to show off his chest! Bald as a melon, he wanted us all to see that thicket, the evidence of his strapping masculinity. I must say it was extraordinary: Tarzan himself could have easily swung from one nipple to the other. Very well. But you can't begin to imagine what he had hanging from his neck, all tangled up in the hair. A cameo. And can you guess who was smiling out from it?

None other than you, my dear lady María del Rosario Galván. Wasn't it the Virgin of Guadalupe, you ask? No, my dear lady, it was you, an icon between Tácito de la Canal's hairy nipples. What happened next, you might ask? Well, Tácito boasted to one and all that he was something more than the intimate friend of the president's intimate friend, and that you, my distinguished lady, enjoyed the privilege of Mr. de la Canal's hirsute favors.

Make of it what you will. I'm simply here to provide information, carrying out the brief dictated by my fair damsel (reporting straight from the heart of darkness that beats just beneath Tácito's hairy carapace), reporting on the audacity of the voyeur who spied on your most distinguished and delectable state of undress, madam, and who has now turned out to be the exhibitor of a love that—I hope!—is unrequited.

He left without a word, apart from congratulating me for my "jocular" initiative, and unwittingly unleashed a wave of unrestricted joy, a reaction to his highly depressing presence. Some people just have that effect. I called for drinks to be served and very soon the revelry began to get dangerously out of hand, as if the crowd were about to storm the Bastille. I worked the room, stopping to chat, livening things up, lightening the atmosphere, until I found myself standing before what one might call the "Senate of the Archivists."

How far back did the oldest of them go? Back to the days of López Mateos. And the youngest? Since López Portillo? Did they like their work? Certainly, they had to be highly organized to file documents by topic, date, and name. Did they read all the things they filed away? Blank stares. No. Never. They received the documents, rubber-stamped them with the office seal and the date, made a note of the topic in the upper right-hand corner, and placed them in the appropriate file. Were there any that got marked "Confidential," "Secret," "Personal," or something like that? Of course. Did any of them remember a specific topic filed under such a classification? No, no, all they did was file the documents.

Their eyes revealed one of two things: Either they were bored, or they didn't understand. And anyway, the sheer volume of paper that they received every day was so overwhelming that they could barely keep up with it. And that was that.

Could I visit these archives?

I didn't venture actually to ask the question, dear friend, because I sensed a fraternal spirit among these archivists, a guild of sorts based on old paper, dark basements, long hours of monotony and tedium, short and poorly paid vacations, half-remembered families, and pale faces.

I picked one of them out from the rest. The one who said he'd been there since López Portillo. The one who hadn't taken off that old office-worker's uniform, not even for a party: greenish eyeshade tightly hugging a wrinkled cranium and protecting a gaze that was neither curious nor suspicious. Plastic collar attached to the shirt by a white plastic button. Unbuttoned vest, and arm garters to hide the disparity between the length of the sleeve and the length of the arm, or perhaps to prevent the cuffs from fraying.

"My family is from Jalisco," I lied, though my comment didn't elicit the least bit of a reaction.

"We're related to the Gálvez y Gallo family," I added.

His face lit up.

"The chief of staff I most admire!" he said with joy.

"The very one."

"What a gentleman! Married to a real lady. Would you believe, Mr. Valdivia, that they never forgot a single one of our birthdays? They always had a gift, a smile for you . . . oh, what a difference!"

"You mean between them and Tácito de la Canal?"

"Oh, I didn't mean . . ." The old man raised a hand to his mouth. "I . . . I didn't . . ."

I hugged him warmly.

"Don't give it a second thought, Mr. . . . ."

"Cástulo Magón, at your service. I've been working in the archives since 1982. Different times, Mr. Valdivia!"

"I know, I know. To remember is to live. I'm very interested in our archives, you know."

"Really?"

"Yes, really, don Cástulo."

"Well, at your service. Whenever you please, come downstairs. It would be a pleasure. But I should warn you—there's a lot of paper, a lot of history. Even we lose our way in that maze."

What I didn't tell him was this: I know what I am looking for. Don't you worry.

20

XAVIER "SENECA" ZARAGOZA
TO PRESIDENT LORENZO TERÁN

Time passes, Mr. President, and in your third year in office, you still don't deign to ask me, "What shall I do, Seneca?" This makes me think, of all things, of *The Thousand and One Nights*, Mr. President, and I'd like to remind you of the case of King Harun al-Rashid, who as the sun went down left his palace dressed in beggar's clothes in order to mingle with the people and hear what they really said about him, as opposed to the polite version he heard from his courtiers. Let me tell you, Mr. President, that Mexico is shaped by the dynamics of fate. You have far too much faith in civil society, in giving the people their freedom. My advice, which I have pondered quite carefully, is this: Set some limits. If you let our people move around with no guidance at all, freedom will degenerate into chaos, and that freedom won't be driven by the power of will but by the forces of fate.

This is a country that has buried far too much dissatisfaction over the years, over long centuries of poverty, injustice, and unfulfilled dreams.

If the proper political channels aren't built, if all we have is unrestricted liberty, the subterranean waters will bubble up to the surface and turn into rushing rapids that will demolish everything in their path.

I know that you have faith in two things. First, that the people will value
the liberties you grant them. And second, that public force in Mexico is
exercised by a professional army on the one hand (von Bertrab) and a
vicious police force on the other (Arruza). They'll control the small
local bosses who, instead of disappearing, have in fact proliferated
under the democratic system. That's not enough, Mr. President. Something's missing. Do you know what it is? *You are missing.* People need
to see you. Like so many of your predecessors, you're turning into the
great man all alone in the palace, the ghost that sits on the Eagle's
Throne. React, I beg you. There's still time. Don't let people think
you're a plaything at the mercy of uncontrollable forces. Stop looking
out at the horizon like a mystic when you appear in public on Independence Day, at the New Year, on Cinco de Mayo. Look people in the eye,
let them see you, but make sure it's you they see, Mr. President, and not
your lackeys. Let your voice fill the plazas and find its way into every
corner of this country. Politics can only live and breathe in the places
where the president's voice is heard. Have you tested the limits of your
voice? Have you measured the boundaries between action and passivity? A president must exist for his citizens. If he doesn't, they will with-
draw the veneration he expects from them. The man who is praised as
God one day can be scorned as the devil the next.

Go out to the streets, Mr. President. Throw out some ideas before
they're thrown at you. Because if you don't have any ideas of your own,
you'll never be anything but the mouthpiece of everyone else. Be careful, Mr. President. I see only drones, leeches, and sycophants in your office. Do you really have any use for them, or is it perhaps the other way
around? You're now entering the second half of your term, and you can
safely look back and congratulate yourself for the fact that we're now a
freer, more democratic country than before. How marvelous. But now
you must look forward and proceed with caution because soon we'll be
facing our ides of March: the drama of the presidential succession that
we face every six years. Unlike other presidents, you won't name your
successor. "The anointed one" no longer exists. But there will always be

favorites and presidential darlings in every administration. And the president's support will count for a lot. Within the parties. Within the administration. Even within yourself. Not to mention public opinion.

But be very careful, Mr. President. Having dared to point out that the public perceives you as passive, I encourage you to develop a clear, serene, visible public presence. I must warn you, however, against an overly aggressive leadership, the kind that smothers rather than supports democratic freedoms. Heidegger succumbed to the Nazi belief system in Germany by declaring that land and blood were more important than freedom of expression. He gave academic respectability to the unholy marriage of death and violence; to the kind of leader who channels our energies and forces us to accept—and I quote the philosopher from memory—"the voluptuous passivity of total obedience." How do we know that the Mexican people, tired of a democracy that has become confused with passivity, won't opt for an authoritarian leadership that at least gives them the illusion of security and a sense of purpose?

That is the other extreme. Don't fall prey to it. Examine and assess your public presence. But, and I return to the other extreme, don't let them say about Lorenzo Terán what Georges Bernanos said about France after its defeat by Adolf Hitler: "Our nation has been raped by vagabonds while it slept."

Oh, my dear, esteemed friend, you honor me with your trust, but please, no matter what you do, always remember that the presidency of the republic is a goldfish bowl. Whatever you decide to do, just do it well. Because if you fail, you won't just be the worst democratic leader this country has had. You'll be the last.

21

EX-PRESIDENT CÉSAR LEÓN
TO TÁCITO DE LA CANAL

What a messy little predicament, my old and distinguished friend! "A Mexican politician never puts anything in writing." That was the dogma before. Well, look at us now, you idiot, just look where our notorious, sovereign arrogance—or is it arrogant sovereignty?—has gotten us. Let's not mince words, shall we? I think we both know each other too well for that. Call me Augustus and I'll call you Caligula, even though Caligula was the emperor who decided his horse would succeed him, and in your case the horse will be you if in fact you get where you want to go.

Let me laugh, you Caligulan shit, you revolting traitor. It's funny, isn't it? I'm the one person who can put you on the Eagle's Throne, but I'll humiliate you every step of the way, because you won't just owe me a favor—you'll owe me your life. Remember what I said to you one day, when you were working for me, you ass-licking bastard? Don't start obsessing about conspiracies, because even if there aren't any, you'll end up creating one.

Believe me, I've thought of you many, many times during these years in exile, Caligula. Your Caesar Augustus has never forgotten you—so much so, in fact, that I'm now taking the risk of writing to you.

So we have no telephones, no faxes, no e-mail, no computers, no Internet, no satellites? Well, I can tell you something we do have. We have the unexpected. The unknown. The subtle. General Mondragón von Bertrab and General Cícero Arruza, so diametrically opposed in every sense, have actually managed to agree on a method for keeping tabs on all of us. Don't ask me how they invented it or how they pulled it off. They say that Mondragón has been keeping a million-dollar brain trust on the government payroll—just picture it, moron, the best brains from MIT, Silicon Valley, and the CNRS in Paris.

Well then, can you guess what they've come up with to replace everything that's been lost?

A pin, my slobbering sycophant, a tiny little pin that records our voices and transmits them directly to the intelligence command center at Mondragón's office. Sly devil that he is, von Bertrab conveniently filters out what he doesn't want Arruza to hear. The fact is that all our conversations are being recorded by a pin-sized microphone that's been implanted somewhere on our bodies, though nobody knows where. Not in our clothes, because I know that when I go into the bathroom the sound of the shower doesn't drown out the sound of my singing.

I hope they don't think the boleros I sing as I soap my body are coded political messages: "Stop asking me questions, let me imagine. . . ." Or, "Veracruz, little corner where the waves build their nest . . ."

Every bolero can be interpreted politically. But that's beside the point. The fact is that none of us knows where, when, and on which of our body parts (or worse, inside which body part)—an eyebrow, a knee, an ear, a molar, or perhaps up our ass—Mondragón von Bertrab, aided by meticulous German science, has implanted those almost invisible pins that transmit our conversations.

This means we're reduced to writing letters now. We have no other choice. What can we hope for? That once the recipients read them, they destroy them. What would be the most cunning thing to do, then? To write the opposite of what we think and do. But then again, no matter how simpleminded you might be, Caligula, even you can appreciate the fact that false instructions can also be read and taken literally. Our brilliant and very Teutonic defense secretary has rigged things so that we have no other choice but to write letters and tell the truth.

At the very least we can disguise our names just as Xavier Zaragoza, known to all as "Seneca," has always done. Very well, whether the shoe fits or not, I shall be Augustus and you, Caligula. But let me warn you, you rotten scumbag, don't ever think of yourself as Caesar, because you're nothing but a horse. My point is this: You rose to power with me, in my shadow, and then you stabbed me in the back and gave that terrible order, "Don't even give him the satisfaction of insulting him. Just don't ever speak his name again."

"Silence in the night, the muscle sleeps," as the old tango goes. But ambition never rests, does it, moron? Do you know what a mole is? It's a word with multiple definitions in English. A mole is a hairy blemish. It is an insect-eating mammal with tiny eyes and ears and paws like shovels for digging its subterranean home. It's a breakwater for fending off the forces of the sea's tide. It's an anchor in a safe port. It's a bloody mass of tissue in the uterus. And finally, it's also a term that's used to describe the kind of spy who infiltrates an enemy organization and pretends to be a faithful and patient worker for a very long time until, inevitably, at the behest of his real employer he betrays the people who unwittingly hired him. (Oh, and of course it's also a delicious Mexican dish, *mole*, and a term used to describe the act of beating an adversary to a bloody pulp: *Sacarle el mole*.)

Very well, then. I appoint you my spy, my mole in you-know-where. Damn it if I'm not generous to you, you cockroach. If I win, you win with me. If I lose, you win with my enemies. I can't think of anyone who's ever been offered a better political deal, not since Rudolf Hess was condemned to life imprisonment instead of death by hanging. Be grateful. Did you know that a man grows a completely new set of skin every seven years? We're snakes, and we know it. Of course when it comes to Mexican politics, we shed our skin every six years.

Think about it, Caligula, shed your skin before they skin you. If skinning and flaying turn you on, just think about that Aztec deity, Xipe Totec, sitting in our Museum of Anthropology. Every six years a man needs to change loyalties, wives (in your case, lovers), and convictions. Prepare yourself, my loyal friend. Prepare yourself. And keep on hoping: Tonight I'll sleep in the bed of the vanquished.

The bad part is, if you make it to that bed you'll have to sleep under the mattress. Because I'll be on top. Don't doubt it for a second.

Augustus.

P.S. Oh, how I despise this six-year cycle. It reminds me of a cake divided into slices—just when you're really beginning to enjoy it, you're not allowed to finish it. And I'm warning you now—don't even think of turning me over to your boss. Not only have I dug my trenches with him—I share them with him. He's a good man. Gullible, to be sure. So don't go around telling him nasty stories about me. He'll take you for a gossip, a meddler. And you and your aspirations will then go straight to fucking hell. So be it.

22

ANDINO ALMAZÁN TO
"LA PEPA" ALMAZÁN

Beloved Pepona, this bizarre situation keeps us even farther apart than usual, but it brings us together spiritually more than ever. Distance has always brought me closer to you, my darling, because our separations only heighten the desire we feel for one another. Don't you feel the same, my love? You in Mérida, I in the capital. You in a beautiful, placid, tranquil city. I in this asphyxiated, chaotic, vulgar, noxious metropolis. You, surrounded by gentle people, cordial and unaffected. I, suffocating inside the car that takes me from the apartment to the office, then back to the apartment late at night, with no other reward than that of hearing your voice on the telephone at midnight—at least, until a few days ago. Now we don't even have that. Your sweet voice eludes me, I can only imagine it. I must make do with these letters to you. So here I am, surrounded all day long by enemies, the object of attacks, the butt of endless jokes and caricatures in the newspapers ("Andino, abandon ship," "Andino, head for the Andes") to say nothing of all the plots hatched and traps laid in the corridors of bureaucracy.

How different from my true nature is the mask of the cold, efficient technocrat I must don every morning! There was a time when I needed a mirror to rehearse the facial expression of the implacable bureaucrat.

But I don't need it anymore now, my Pepona. The mask has become a real face, a face with harsh features, furrowed brow, pursed lips, and shit-smelling nose. Eyebrows permanently circumflexed by doubt. Ears pricked up, ready for lies. And eyes, eyes, my love, not showing hatred, but certainly filled with disdain, scorn, lack of interest . . . Did you know I've learned to speak like an Anglo-Saxon, without articles or context?

"Exactly."

"Done."

"Nothing."

"Careful."

"Perfect."

"Warned."

"Face consequences."

I say these things, nothing else. My eyes avert all attempts at conversation—whether they are friendly, unfriendly, unpleasant, sincere, ambiguous, or impertinent conversations. For me, anything and everything people say represents a potential danger. The danger of contradiction in the best of cases. The danger of persuasion in the worst.

I give what's expected of me. My technical expertise. My knowledge of international markets. My macroeconomic parameters. My careful attention to our currency's parity with the dollar, our foreign cash reserves, the payment of our foreign debt, the amount of our national debt, the trade deficit, European and North American aid, the forced fraternity with the directors of the central banks in Washington, Berlin, London, Madrid . . .

And yet I don't give what I'd most like to give: my humanity. You may laugh at me, Josefina, with those noisy cackles that jealous people call "vulgar," as if your vitality—the vitality I'm so attracted to—could ever be considered vulgar. Who could ever describe your capacity for joy, fun, and humor as vulgar? Who could ever dare criticize your delightful wordplay and double entendres? Oh, my darling, if those things make you "vulgar," then vulgarity is what I need—oh, how I come alive whenever I hear your crude jokes, your brazen suggestions, all those things that inspire my fidelity because you make me feel (and this I whisper in your ear, my darling) that I have my whore at home. I don't need to go out looking for women like my boring cabinet colleagues, I already have my woman at home—foulmouthed, horny, and ready for every position and every pleasure under the sun, I have her in my own house. . . .

Oh, how I miss you, Pepona! Hot and sweet, faithful wife and loving mother. How safe I feel knowing that my "three Ts," Tere, Talita, and Tutú, are with you, my darling triplets who came into the world in perfect order, lending a virginal glory to your three successive but actually simultaneous births—for does anyone even remember which of them came first? To me it always felt as if my three angels came down together from the heavens to bless our union, my Josefina, a singularly joyous marriage that goes beyond physical separation, gossip, and beatitudes. A marriage made, just like our three girls, in paradise.

Do you remember our wedding?

Do you remember the Hacienda de los Lagartos, all decked out just for our nuptials? Do you remember the garden, filled with dozens of pink flamingos? And the massive banquet of *papadzules* and *motuleño* eggs, pickled chicken, and stuffed cheese? Do you remember the heat of our passion that night, our loving surrender to each other? Do you remember how nervous your mother was in the bedroom next door to ours at the Hotel del Garrafón, listening for you either to call her for help if it hurt—ow, ow, ow!—or sing the Marseillaise if you liked it— ah, ah, ah, *allons, enfants de la patrie*! How wonderful, my Pepona, that you let me storm the Bastille of your tightly locked jail, how marvelous that you loved Andino's guillotine!

As you can see, you're the only person with whom I can truly express my feelings and rediscover the Andino Almazán you fell for twelve years ago, married eleven years ago, and had triplets with ten years ago. But then, in what feels like a split second, I have no choice but to assume once again my other persona, that of the treasury secretary, completely consumed by the world of economics, hiding behind a mask of statistics, creating an exterior character to disguise my interior obsession, which of course is you, my voluptuous one.

When I wake in the morning, Josefina, I won't be the person you know.

I know what they say about me:

"When Andino enters a room the temperature drops."

"The secretary has arrived. All rise."

"Watch out. For Secretary Almazán only two possible opinions exist: his opinion and the wrong opinion."

My soul is dying, my darling Pepa. But I've assumed certain responsibilities and I must fulfill them for the president, for the country, and for myself. If the treasury didn't have me, the ship would drift out into uncharted waters. I'm the indispensable helmsmann. I'm the one repeating the same old mantra: discipline, discipline, discipline. Avoid inflation. Raise taxes. Lower salaries. Fix prices. I'm the iceman. I may be a native of the tropical Yucatán, but I'm thought of as a miser from Monterrey. Miserly when it comes to the budget and miserly in conversation.

You see, I've already decided simply to say nothing, my Pepa. Every time I open my mouth to chastise Congress, all I do is scare off investors. I'm better off keeping my mouth shut. I can pass as the perfect dumb witness. I say nothing because I have nothing to say, and that, somehow, has earned me a reputation for being wise. I look upon everything with glacial objectivity, but I understand nothing. That's fine. Someone has to play this thankless role. I've already had to fire three deputy secretaries who talked too much. The one who said "Poverty in Mexico is a myth." The one who said "If Congress doesn't approve the new tax bill we're going to go under just like Argentina." And the one who said "The poor possess the virtue of being discreet."

They hired me to disinfect the system. I'm the government's DDT. I hunt down insects.

And my life, darling, is drying up—or at least it would dry up if I didn't have you and my three Ts, Tere, Talita and Tutú. Send me a recent photo of the four of you, will you? You keep forgetting to do that. I, my dear, don't forget you for a minute. Your *A*.

P.S. In the interest of safety, I'm sending this to you via my good friend and colleague Tácito de la Canal. They say that if you want to survive in the cabinet you have to behave as though you're dead. Tácito is the exception to this rule. Thanks to him I'm able to walk in and out of the president's office without any problem. He's an agile man, a man with a future—flexible when necessary, tough when the situation requires grit. Trust him. Farewell. *A.A.*

23

GENERAL CÍCERO ARRUZA TO
GENERAL MONDRAGÓN VON BERTRAB

General, you and I are in constant and amicable communication. You know that I've always acknowledged your superiority and, above all else, above you and me, the superiority of the president of the republic, commander in chief of the armed forces. Well, General, with my usual frankness I must warn you that this goddamn country is getting out of control. Sure, we're all so damn proud of the fact that in Mexico there are seventy million people under the age of twenty. A country full of kids. Have you ever heard them? Have you ever put your ear to the ground? How do you think those kids see the old mummies that govern them?

How old are you? Fifty? Fifty-two? And me, sixty-four, sixty-five? The record books are a little sketchy in the tiny village where I was born, in the state of Hidalgo—that is, if you can say that Hidalgo exists and wasn't just an invention to separate Mexico City from dangerous rival states like Michoacán and Jalisco. Hidalgo is the Uruguay of Mexico, but poor and without any records. Anyhow, General, my point is that you and I are in our prime, as my granny would have said. But to youngsters we're old. They want a young leader. Young like Madero, Calles, Obregón, Villa, and Zapata were when they threw themselves into the Revolution—all of them under thirty.

Keep your eyes peeled, Mr. Secretary. Where's our fresh-faced leader? How old is that ass-kisser Tácito de la Canal? Fifty-two like you? And his opponent, Bernal Herrera, isn't he in his early fifties, or maybe late forties? Do you think today's kids trust them at all? Do you think those millions of kids who cruise on their motorcycles as if their Harley-Davidsons were Pancho Villa's horse, old Siete Leguas himself, and those half-naked party animals who spend all night clubbing, and those DJs who fly from Los Angeles to Mexico City to Honolulu for twenty-five thousand dollars a pop to play CDs, and the children of serial millionaires who've been inheriting fortunes passed down since 1941, will trust any of us?

That's what the elite are saying in the newspapers, General. But what about the middle-class kid who has had to watch how every six years his parents lose their car, their house, and their washing machine because they can't keep up with the monthly payments? Or students who can't even study because public universities are constantly paralyzed by strikes and private universities cost a fortune?

Look at them, General—they wanted to be engineers, lawyers, big shots, but look at them now—they're driving taxis, delivering pizzas, working as ushers in movie theaters, browbeaten into making a living parking other people's cars. They're broken people who should have become something better, and now all they get are kicks in the ass. And all the sweet young things who only dreamed of becoming decent, middle-class housewives? They're out there working as typists, sales girls, and waitresses—if they're lucky. Otherwise it's lap dancing and the brothel. And don't even get me started on the stories of the little farm girls who find work in factories and dream that some gringo will one day want to marry them, the stupid idiots, and then the factory goes under or moves to China, where the workers make 10 percent of what Mexican workers earn, and they're back out on the street again begging, or back in their villages eating *nopalitos*, with their babies bundled up in their shawls, wanting to cross the border and become gringos like so many young men and women trying to find work on the other side of the fence—even if it means drowning in a river or suffocating in some trafficker's truck or dying of thirst in the desert or getting shot full of holes, like a sieve, by the gringo border patrol's bullets. Tell me, General, what can those seventy million kids look forward to? Who will they look to? Think about it while there's still time, General.

And remember, in these matters you have to act quickly.

24

NICOLÁS VALDIVIA TO
MARÍA DEL ROSARIO GALVÁN

So, my lovely and demanding lady, you warned me from the start that everything is politics with you, but I had my doubts the day you told me to come to the woods outside your house at night and watch you undress. As if that weren't enough, I was beaten to it (surely through my beautiful lady's doing) by Tácito de la Canal. Is that politics, too, or is it just sex? Oh, my good lady María del Rosario, how many other secrets do you keep that have nothing to do with politics and everything to do with that region of "the heart that has its reasons" that reason (or politics) doesn't understand?

Well, I've learned another lesson, though perhaps more of a human one than a political one. After all, in our country, can politics exist without that thing we call *endurance*? As I mentioned to you the other day, I've become quite friendly with one of the archivists in the presidential office, an old man I described to you a while back. He was kind enough to invite me to his house. Well, it isn't exactly a house, it's an apartment, a third-floor flat with a little terrace roof, in the Vallejo area, near the Monumento a la Raza.

You enter the place through a little shop between the front door and the stairway. I couldn't describe the building to you even if I tried. It's a place, my dear lady, that slips from the memory the minute one lays eyes on it. Some events, some people, some places are like that—as much as you try to remember them, they simply refuse to appear in the mind's eye. And it's sad not to remember them, until you realize that the memory has no room for the unremarkable. There are some people, though, that we can never forget, my dear lady, because the only possessions they have are the impressions they leave in other people's minds, and their eyes are none other than those of the people who see them.

Do you understand what I mean? For me it was something of a revelation precisely because they asked nothing of me and yet I found myself fascinated, drawn to the pleas of these people who wanted nothing. What pleas am I talking about? you may ask. The archivist is a man named Cástulo Magón, who told me, when I noted the connection between their last names, that he is indeed distantly related to the revolutionaries Ricardo and Jesús Flores Magón, the anarchist brothers who languished away during Porfirio Díaz's dictatorship inside the San Juan de Ulúa fortress at Veracruz, which I saw the other day when you sent me to visit the Old Man Under the Arches. Well, don Cástulo is almost sixty and has been an archivist for nearly forty years, since the time of the López Portillo government. He married late because it took him a while to put the money together for a wedding and to find a woman who suited him and who was willing to work to make ends meet every month.

Don Cástulo has that tired, dreary look of the classic archivist and, as I said before, he even wears the ubiquitous green eyeshade and arm garters that make him look like the typical minor bureaucrat, straight out of a soap opera. Archives are dark places—perhaps out of fear that the papers might grow faded and illegible if exposed to sunlight, or perhaps simply to allow the documents to fall into oblivion as they lie in their yellow folders in gunmetal gray tombs. Perhaps, my scornful mistress, so that they may be exorcised of all, shall we say, luminous content. Yes, don Cástulo is the phantom of the archives. Just like the character dreamed up by Gaston Leroux who lived in the subterranean bowels of the Paris Opera, Cástulo Magón lives beneath the offices of the president of the republic.

His face is gray and his eyes, while not tired, convey a sense of resignation. But his fingers, María del Rosario, are astonishingly nimble—you should see the speed and precision with which he flips through the different files! At that moment his age, his tired, careworn appearance, and his exhausted body are transfigured and Cástulo becomes something like the alchemist of the public records office. He knows where everything is but even more importantly he also knows where to find everything that *shouldn't be there*, those things he was told to destroy. Cástulo, not out of disobedience, but simply because he'd never really thought about it, you see, archived the unarchivable according to an eccentrically Mexican filing system: He didn't file by name (Galván, María del Rosario, or Herrera, Bernal), nor by section (Ministry of the Interior, Congress) but by *reference*.

Arcane references. Where would you think I, for example, might be found in the archives at Los Pinos? Under my name, "Valdivia, Nicolás"? Under my position, "Chief of Cabinet, Assistant to"? "Presidency of the Republic, Office of"? No, my dear María del Rosario. As it turns out, I appear in a file entitled "ENA." Now, what is ENA? you might ask. École Nationale d'Administration, Paris. In other words, the college I went to. Take note, madam! If you're looking for a labyrinth of solitude, this takes the cake. And our friend the archivist Cástulo Magón can find his way around the files using those hands of his, like the hands of a blind pianist, more blind than Hipólito in *Santa*. The fact that his economic status in no way reflects his professional abilities is almost tautological. Cástulo receives a meager salary, some 500 dollars a month, which, given the cost of living these days, is barely enough to spruce up the white locks framing his temples and whip them up into a slick bridge from left to right across his head to hide the balding pate. (For what? From whom? Tell me—after all, you're a woman who knows so much about human vanity, especially that of the dispossessed and humiliated like myself, your hapless *soupirant*.) Don Cástulo, believe it or not, still uses homemade hair pomade, even though it went out of fashion about a hundred years ago. I believe it to be the only evidence of his vanity in the tiny bathroom largely taken over by his family: his wife, Serafina, his daughter, Araceli, and his son, Jesús Ricardo, named after the aforementioned heroes of Ulúa, the Flores Magón brothers.

Don Cástulo, to judge by his bone structure, should be skinny, but he possesses the inevitable pot belly of someone who's eaten bean *tortas* and peppers and fried pork all his life, washed down with the occasional beer. Doña Serafina works miracles, María del Rosario. She contributes to the household economy by baking cakes and pastries. The kitchen is hers. No one else enters it, and it happens to be the largest room in the apartment.

"That was why we picked it," she says.

The kitchen has everything, including a long table coated with flour and even a baker's oven. This is where the good woman prepares her meringues, wedding towers, and all kinds of fanciful concoctions for parties, first communions, and dances, and thanks to this little business, she manages to bring home 1,000 dollars a month—which would be 2,000 if she didn't have to spend half her earnings on "raw materials," as she calls them with pride, efficiently wiping her hands on her apron. Picture Andrea Palma at sixty. Picture that slender, languid beauty from the film *Woman of the Port*, who sold her love "to the men who come back from the sea," only now with a body that's less than slender and a bearing that's anything but languid except in the very deepest recesses of her eyes. And if her husband's eyes are as opaque as a visor, Serafina's are as melancholy as a sudden twilight in the middle of the day.

"Businesslike," the gringos say, don't they? Well, that's what Serafina is, my friend—not a minute of rest and not a single complaint, except in those eyes that yearn for something that never was. I repeat. I emphasize. *Something that never was.* The expression that speaks of a

promise unfulfilled gives both the lady of the house and the house itself
their melancholy. Nostalgia, lost dreams, *what could have been* . . .

Imagine that expression, my powerful patroness, because I've never
seen it in your eyes. It's as if you already had it all—all but the realms
unconquered by your ambition. Doña Serafina has eyes that no longer
aspire to anything. As I watch her working in her kitchen, I see no ambition, just the pure and simple will to survive. And there's Cástulo,
reading the newspaper in the cramped living room. The television, he
tells me, has been pawned, and that's despite the fact that in Mexico
even people from the most squalid slums, the lost cities, have televisions. But he says that he grew up reading newspapers and he isn't
about to give up his slow archivist's habits for those little pills of information they serve up on TV. Of course now without satellite signals for
TV antennae, he couldn't watch anything even if he wanted to. . . .

All in the name of God. Or rather in the name of their irrepressible
twenty-year-old daughter, Araceli, who spends all day lying on her bed
reading *¡Hola!* magazine and dreaming, I suppose, of being Charlotte
of Monaco or someone like her, and then spends hours beautifying herself for a boyfriend who picks her up in a convertible at nine o'clock to
take her out to dinner and then dancing. She's not out of control, her
mother claims. She's just young, she has a right to have fun, and anyway, she always comes back with a plastic doggie bag filled with leftovers from the restaurants she dines at thanks to Hugo Patrón, her
boyfriend from the Yucatán, who runs a travel agency that has been
idling lately since the computers aren't working and the gringos have
their doubts about traveling to Mexico these days. Still, the walls of
Araceli's bedroom are covered with the posters Hugo gives her—of
the Caribbean, the Mediterranean, Paris, and Venice. He's a well-
intentioned boy, doña Serafina says, even if he is a bit old-fashioned.
You see, he refuses to let Araceli work at all; he wants to save up enough
money for an apartment and a honeymoon, and he doesn't ever want his
girlfriend—and future wife—to work. My conclusion is that he associates leisure with virginity.

Serafina occasionally pulls herself together and summons the spoiled young lady from her room to deliver cakes when clients don't send their chauffeurs to pick them up. You should see the scowl that comes over that little girl's face. She was born to be a princess, with that head full of silly dreams, and quite frankly she even flirts with me when I visit. Yes, I'm a better catch than Hugo Patrón, but the minute I start talking she becomes very shy, and as I play the role of the erudite professional educated in Paris, sprinkling my conversation with French, I can see a mixture of ennui, respect, and detachment come over her pretty, moon-colored face, as if I were the "black cloud of destiny," a wondrous soul descended from his pedestal to visit the humble of this world—like her, a girl who has no visible prospects in life other than a marriage to the travel agent Hugo Patrón and a honeymoon in Miami.

The apartment has two bedrooms. One for the parents and the other for Araceli. On the roof, in a wooden hut next to a makeshift pigeon loft, lives the son, Ricardo, who very tenderly looks after those birds, reminding me of Marlon Brando and Eva Marie Saint on the rickety rooftops by New York's waterfront. He's an extraordinary young man, María del Rosario, and I'm telling you straight because I know that you fancy yourself a kind of headhunter extraordinaire (please forgive these occasional ironies of mine, I have no other way to tone down the resentment you inspire in me).

Ricardo is exceptional first of all in the physical sense. A son who was very much planned and hoped for by his parents, he must be about twenty-six, very slim without being skinny, with severe but very delicate musculature. He's taller than me—about five foot eleven—and has the kind of head you only see in Italian museums: every detail finely chiseled, thin lips, sharp nose, high cheekbones, large, almost Asian eyes, broad forehead, and a mane of black hair that reaches his shoulders.

Am I describing an object of desire? In all sincerity, I believe so. You, my beautiful and elusive lady, a woman who has indulged and continues to indulge in so many wonderful delights, surely understand what I mean. This boy is so beautiful that nobody—neither woman nor man—could possibly help desiring him. Tight jeans, short T-shirt, bare feet when he comes out, surprised, to see who's there, and when I tell him who I am he turns to scatter corn for the pigeons. He knows that I've helped his father and he's grateful to me for that.

He looks me straight in the eye, a bit mocking, a bit skeptical, and says, "I don't go to the university because it's been closed down for two years."

He throws some birdseed to the pigeons.

"Would you pay for me to go to a private university?"

His dark eyes are so intelligent that I don't even have to ask the next question.

"It would be a waste of time for me to get one of those rotten jobs that drive you out of your mind with boredom. . . ."

"And end up stifling your ambition and talent forever," I say, finishing his sentence as he looks me over with scornful admiration.

Then he points to the inside of his little "cabin in the clouds," where I see a folding canvas bed, a wobbly table, a stool ("so that I don't fall asleep while reading") and, most importantly, a crudely fashioned bookshelf filled with books, old books, the kind they sell on the Calle de Donceles for two pesos each, with the bindings falling off, from musty old publishing houses, as extinct as animals from some long-gone era: Espasa Calpe, Botas, Herrero, Santiago Rueda, Emecé . . . like a harvest of dry wheat from Argentina, Spain, and Mexico. . . . I have an urge to poke through those shelves, I who have had the privilege of reading in the French National Library, but he stops me, pointing at the three volumes on his desk, Machiavelli, Hobbes, Montesquieu.

He doesn't have to say a word. The look on his face says it all.

"I am a young man who keeps his eyes open, Mr. Valdivia."

Ah, my dangerous lady and mistress, if one day you tire of me (and that day will come), I have a new candidate for you here, a masculine Galatea to satisfy your Pygmalion vocation, my fair lady.

His name is Jesús Ricardo Magón.

He is twenty-six years old.

He lives in a squalid little hut on the roof of a building on Calzada Cuitláhuac.

Hurry up, María del Rosario, or I'll get to him first.

And what, I ask him, does he talk about with his harebrained little sister?

"I tell her all about the lives of the European princesses she reads about in *¡Hola!* magazine and I help her finish the crosswords. She's going to have a very boring life."

25

ANDINO ALMAZÁN TO
PRESIDENT LORENZO TERÁN

Mr. President, you and I can't fool ourselves about the problems our country now faces. Some of these problems are technical: how to control inflation, attract foreign investment, raise the employment level without increasing pay. Others are international and, inevitably and monomaniacally, inextricably linked to our proximity to the United States. Others are domestic: the students, the peasants, the factory workers. Lastly, there are the political problems: the presidential succession in less than three years' time.

With the honesty that you ask of me, I shall put my cards on the table. You have earned a reputation for solving problems by avoiding them. As I see it, this has happened because of your great confidence in civil society, the judicial system and its decisions, and the rule of law. You've relinquished the traditional arrogance of the executive office.

I, on the other hand, have a doubly bad reputation. They say I am "the Job of the cabinet." That I have infinite patience, but that my virtue is also my greatest weakness. According to my detractors, my passivity is such that the only action I should take is that of resigning. I shrug my shoulders, though, and tell you, Mr. President, that I'm the only member of your cabinet who has turned all four cheeks to your enemies. I'm your lightning rod. Now, my strategy may seem paradoxical at first. You'll note that I'm the person who invents the problems that you're supposed to solve. And one of your problems is that you have to turn the opposition into your greatest ally. The more problems I create, the more they shout at me. True enough. But more problems also mean more money that we can squeeze out of the budget for our purposes. It's an infallible parliamentary game, especially when, in cases like yours, the president doesn't enjoy majority support in Congress.

Everyone opposes your tax bills, which I faithfully send to Congress knowing they'll be rejected, while up my sleeve I keep the reforms that I know Congress will approve simply because they don't want to seem like deadbeats, idiots, or enemies of fiscal responsibility. There you have it. We still haven't received approval for a VAT on medicine and food—something we proposed—but Congress is favoring progressive and redistributive taxation, something we didn't propose so as not to alienate the wealthy, even though we obviously want it passed in order to bolster the country's finances.

I tell you all this, Mr. President, to remind you of what we already know. You and I make a good team. The opposition is our best friend. The more they shout at us for reason A, the more budget they give us for reason B. In our case, the opposite is always true: We don't want the things we propose, and we desperately desire the things we ostensibly don't care about.

We live in the most ravaged and, financially speaking, idiotic part of the world: Latin America. Latin America is important because it lacks sound finances. We are important because we create problems for everyone else. I've said this to you time and again. We are not, contrary to the vulgar, populist conventional wisdom, victims of the International Monetary Fund, nor are we slaves of the First World. Quite the opposite. They are our victims. Thanks to all our calculated mistakes and shortcomings, Latin America derives from them its one source of strength: deferral.

One deferral after another. Debt. Devaluation. Floating the currency. Public services. Education. Health. Empowerment of human capital. We defer everything because as long as we continue producing "crises" that other people can save us from over and over again, we can keep on putting off our problems and solutions until hell freezes over.

What do you want me to tell you, Mr. President? The strategy works for us. It keeps us afloat, keeps our head just above water. And that's what worries me. Add up all our problems and think calmly: Is it in our interest to mess with the status quo? Not really, right? That's what worries me, and that's what prompts me to write these words.

Mr. President: The head of the federal police, General Cícero Arruza, is growing dangerously impatient. Luckily, despite his persistence and reiterated arguments he hasn't yet been able to pass his jitters on to the defense secretary (with whom I have a good working relationship, and who apprised me of all this). You do the math: students, factory workers, and peasants demonstrating; foreign aggression; endemic poverty—these are things we all know. But now there's a new factor at play. *Power vacuums.* Power vacuums, I emphasize, Mr. President. The total absence of authority here, there, and everywhere. Mexican workers who can't gain entry into the United States camping out in the northern states or going home, restless and discouraged, to Guanajuato, Puebla, and Oaxaca. Guatemalan workers sneaking in through our unprotected southern border and demanding nonexistent jobs or else robbing Mexicans of the ones that do exist. And then there are the drug traffickers crisscrossing the country from south to north and east to west, from the borders and the coastlines, with no barriers whatsoever and moreover bolstered by a tremendous power base: that of the resurrected local bosses, some of whom are allied with the drug cartels (Narciso "Chicho" Delgado in Baja California and José de la Paz Quintero in Tamaulipas), others who are more independent and as such more dangerous (Félix Elías Cabezas in Sonora), and still others who are more closely linked to the movements driven by unemployment, poverty, and general unrest (Rodolfo Roque Maldonado in San Luis Potosí and "Dark Hand" Vidales in Tabasco, who brags that if he gets killed his "Nine Evil Sons" will succeed him). And then, lording it over the land and sea borders, the King of the Cartels, Silvestre Pardo.

Movements arising from unemployment, poverty, and unrest . . . and generational ambition. What is the average age in your cabinet, President Terán? Fifty, sixty? We are relics, mummies, prehistoric mammoths in a country with seventy million men and women under the age of twenty. These are the armies that the local bosses want to mobilize and Cícero Arruza knows it. He knows it and he wants to control it so that he can create pandemonium and seize power before the electoral campaigns begin, and he has a year to do it.

What do you and I want, then? We want the status quo with all its defects, but without chaos or bloodshed. What do the local kingpins want? They want to fish in turbulent waters. They want a country with no other law but their own, balkanized like Argentina, once a united republic and now an appalling assortment of petty "independent" republics, Córdoba, San Luis, La Rioja, Catamarca, Jujuy, Santiago del Estero, each one with its own local Facundo, its own autocratic local boss, and its own worthless paper currency. Argentina: miserable Cockaigne, ravaged Eden, barbaric Pampa once again . . . Seneca says that culture is what always saves that country. César Aira is, after all, the first Argentinian to receive the Nobel Prize.

Is that what we want to happen to Mexico? Don't close your eyes to Cícero's strategy. First, destroy the established order. Second, balkanization. Third, reestablish unity with military force. And when that happens, the very professional and loyal general Mondragón von Bertrab will join the military regime in the name of patriotism.

How do I know all this? Is it simple conjecture on my part, telepathy? No, Mr. President. Forgive me for being so blunt, but my loyalty is to you, first and foremost. I know all this because it came straight from the mouth of the defense secretary, Mondragón von Bertrab himself. Why did he tell me? So that I would tell you. Did he ask me point-blank to tell you? No, but he must have assumed I would. Why didn't he just tell you himself?

"With the president, I don't assume. I state facts."

So why did he tell me? To warn you about what's going on. With this strategy von Bertrab will remain in good standing with you—but also with the recalcitrants, if they succeed. It's the classic game of two-timing that you find in politics everywhere. But that doesn't make the situation any less dangerous or real, Mr. President. We're walking through this like a bumbling blind man wandering across a busy street while everyone standing on the sidewalk yells at him to get out of the way of the oncoming cars racing toward him from every direction. Is it possible that the blind man is deaf, too?

26

"LA PEPA" ALMAZÁN TO
TÁCITO DE LA CANAL

My love, don't err on the side of discretion, not now. Wake up. The clock is about to strike midnight and our enemies aren't sleeping. Time is slipping out of our hands. As my adorable old grandmother, may she rest in everlasting peace, used to say, "You have to be Beelzebub if you want to beat Satan."

You and I have to be more diabolical than the devil himself. Set your sights skyward. If you want to conquer the heavens you have to look up to God. And bear in mind that you're surrounded on all sides by the crooked and the perverse. Your P only pretends to be an idiot and hopes people will believe it. BH has allied himself with that Lucrezia Borgia of posh Las Lomas, that whore MR. Darling, open your eyes. The couple have planted that rookie NV in your office, but I never trust the so-called innocent. They're cynics who just pretend to be saints so that they can deceive the Lord and get into heaven. You and I will just have to apply that reliable old "Herod's Law": Either get screwed or get fucked.

The return of our ex-leader complicates things somewhat because he plays his own game and neither you nor I have the marbles to compete with him, my sweet. Down there in Veracruz the Old Man plays mysterious with his dominoes and there's no telling when he's going to come around and block our double six. In other words, we're surrounded by enemy forces. On the bright side, you don't have to do all that much to get some good slander going. That old bag from Las Lomas says that you'd kill your own mother if it would help you seize power. Oh, my saint, I know you'd never do such a thing. *Better to kill your enemy's mother.*

Just look at the mess our "regime" is in. The P first, of course. Who doesn't wonder what's going on in the P's head? What's his strategy? What does he know? What doesn't he know? What is he plotting? What is he anticipating? Who does he favor? Who does he despise? There isn't a single soul, inside or outside the government, who isn't asking himself this all day long, and that's why I'm not asking you what you think of the P. Don't answer that. Just remember that there's no mystery there. A P has nowhere to hide.

Don't answer me, I repeat. You're better off asking yourself the question in private. And be careful. You're closer to him than anyone else in the C, and we know that a presidential C is a fruit salad. Who are you going to trust, my love, the cherry or the grape? That's the bad thing about sharing secrets and that's where we must proceed with the most caution. Well, at least nobody can ever make heads or tails of the system for filing documents at Los Pinos, and that old archivist— Magoo, Magón, whatever he's called—doesn't even know his own name, much less where documents are filed, and which ones have been destroyed as per your orders. Your grand idea—or *our* grand idea, if you want to be generous with your little darling—was to make all those compromising documents disappear without destroying them, in case they ever came in handy. If our partners started talking we just might or might not happen to have documents to shut them up. . . .

But the danger's there, my dear, so don't ever let your guard down. You know how a P's mind starts to work when he feels that one of his ministers is no longer useful to him. He doesn't say, "This man is useless." Oh no. He says, "This man betrayed me."

Now, let's go over the usual suspects. Who's your main rival? We know that—Secretary BH. Why is he feared? As far as I can tell he's a man with no sex appeal who, as such, doesn't have the slightest chance of becoming a charismatic candidate. Could he nevertheless ascend to the throne? He's quite an eagle, that one. Everyone considers him a kind of pre-candidate even though his face always seems to say, "Me? I can't imagine why!"

For goodness' sake, of course you and I know why: because he thinks he's utterly beyond reproach, an idea that he's been fed over and over again by that political vixen MR. But me, I've got another idea bouncing around inside my little head. How can we convince him the old bag's fooling him by making him believe he's the P's favorite successor? Nobody will ever say that to him. He'd have to hit himself on the head with a brick to work it out. But those of us from the Yucatán, my darling, we're veritable artists of invention, you know that. And that's where you and I come in to make sure that all this funny business reflects badly on BH and his people. We want everyone to say, "The P made him candidate to get rid of an undesirable politician."

Luckily, there are so many power factors, so much wild ambition, my beautiful one, that you and I can indeed do a fair amount of fishing in those turbulent waters. Turbulent due to all the contradictory fishermen out there—that self-serving ex, for one, then that ex-ex-ex in Veracruz, and then that idiot that presides over Congress (let him hear!), the rookie NV, and even MR herself, who's gotten so out of hand with all that sage advice that one day someone's going to throw it back at her, using the very same words she uses to warn people with that Cruella De Vil face of hers: "You're no longer convincing, dear. No matter what you do, they'll criticize you for it. You're boring everyone with so much advice."

Be careful. Don't let her know that you despise her and much less that you pity her because she isn't as beautiful as me, or because you prefer me to her. You have to realize, my darling, that she already despises and pities you and would be all too thrilled to find out you feel the same way.

But back to our subject, my beloved T. Never forget, not for a second, that all human beings have both defects and virtues, and that our enemies can take advantage of both. Look at me, my lovely. Haven't you ever noticed that I never look at my hands? Can you guess why? Because when I was a young girl I learned that if I looked down at one of my fingers men would think I was asking for a ring. Or worse—that I'd lost a ring because I was too stupid to hang on to it. And if I could lose a ring, I could lose anything—a fortune, a husband, my virginity, the lottery even!

That's why you always see me wearing gloves, even in the sweltering heat of Mérida. But I also wear them so that the tips of my fingers touch no skin but yours, my beautiful bonbon. From time to time you ask, my jealous darling, if there are other men in my life. My love, you don't need to. I'm an object of desire, that's all.

27

GENERAL CÍCERO ARRUZA TO
GENERAL MONDRAGÓN VON BERTRAB

My good general, things have reached the boiling point and very soon we'll have to take action. But please, let it be a joint action, taken by two brothers bound by service like you and me, General. Look at what's happening. Our president's celebrated democratic politics are sinking faster than a rowboat caught in the middle of the gulf during a hurricane. Trust the people, he says, civil society will come together on its own to resolve internal strife. Give the people their freedom, he says, and they'll form unions, cooperatives, neighborhood associations. Like fuck they will! General, loosen up on authority and you create a goddamn void. This country's never been able to govern itself. It doesn't have the experience. It doesn't know how. It has always needed a strong hand, a central authority that prevents chaos and eliminates power vacuums. Just look around you: All over the country those power vacuums have been filled by sneaky local bosses who are always waiting to pounce, like tigers.

I could be talking about a town like Sahuaripa, lost in the desert, where a big shot like Félix Elías Cabezas gains real power in Sonora and exercises it, protected by distance and ignorance, monopolizing the mines, exploiting the export of copper.

I could be talking about a whole state like San Luis Potosí, where a local boss like Rodolfo Roque Maldonado promises Japanese investors order and security so that they can then use San Luis as a launching pad for flooding the United States with technology exports via the Free Trade Agreement. You'll say that Herrera created the situation in San Lázaro, but the one who took all the credit (and the yens, or whatever those yellow kamikazes used for bribes) was Maldonado, boss and governor of the state. In other words, he lets people think that it was the interior secretary who established order there, but those Japs with their Fu Manchu eyes know better and say nothing. Don Roque Maldonado protects their interests.

And as for the Tampico–Matamoros axis, General, where the drug traffic comes in like Adelita in that old song—if by sea on a warship, if by land on a military train—who runs things there? The president? You? Secretary Herrera? No, the guy in charge is the drug-traffickers' top dog, don Silvestre Pardo, along with the local boss working for him, José de la Paz Quintero. On the Tijuana–Mexicali strip, the whole prostitution racket is controlled by Narciso "Chicho" Delgado, the big boss who poses as a whale lover but makes a living trading in monkey flesh, if you know what I mean, General.

Shall I go on? Am I telling you anything you don't already know? Must I tell you that we've lost control of both borders, the one in the north to drug cartels, prostitution, and human traffickers; the one in the south to the European revolutionary-tourist trade that inherited those ski mask things from the late (disappeared) Subcomandante Marcos in order to found the Chiapas Socialist Collective, selling junk— balaclavas, *huipiles*, wooden rifles, manuscripts written by Marcos, condoms with the registered trademark "The Uprising," Zapatista hats, and miniatures of the Virgin of Guadalupe—to tourists looking for a thrill, and devoting themselves to opening "humanitarian" doors to the Guatemalan Indians fleeing the torture, death, and arson meted out by Guatemala's elite. Why don't those white Guatemalans take a lesson from us and promote some interracial mixing so that there isn't a single pure Indian left? Aside from all that there's the whole of the southeast, dominated by the sinister "Dark Hand" Vidales from Tabasco.

For fuck's sake, General! For fuck's sake! Are we going to let things go on festering like this? Or are we finally going to take action, you and I, to save the nation through the purifying work of the armed forces, the last stronghold of Mexican patriotism? Are we going to sit through that endless electoral process that will drag on for almost three years? Are we going to let a couple of damn lapdogs like de la Canal or Bernal Herrera get into Los Pinos so that they can string us along even more? Or are we going to find the way, General, to replace President Lorenzo Terán, who has been badmouthed by the press and the general public as an ineffectual bureaucrat with a cushion stuck to his ass? Are we going to find the way, General, to get ourselves a president with a strong hand and a tough character, who can get this damned country in order?

I know you don't write letters, not even condolence cards, or Christmas cards, but give me a sign, General, my good friend, one little sign—I'm real good at reading them. . . .

28

DULCE DE LA GARZA TO
TOMÁS MOCTEZUMA MORO

Oh, Tomás, I wish I could cry over your grave. But I know the grave is empty. The headstone is there. Your name is there. The dates of birth and death are there:

TOMÁS MOCTEZUMA MORO

1973–2012

But you're not there. There were two coffins, one on top of the other. A box with a false bottom, with a wax model of you melting away in the top part, and nothing below. Nothing, my love, except for the little pin with the eagle and the serpent that you always wore on your lapel, which ended up in the corner of that false coffin—either because the people who buried you were careless, or because you yourself left it there as a sign of your presence, a way of saying to me, "Dulce, I was here, look for me. . . ."

What little I have to give me hope! A forgotten pin! An empty coffin! And your wax figure melting away into a puddle of make-believe.

"Make-believe life." I learned that from you. That's what you always said about politics. And yet my pain and loneliness today are so real, Tomás.

Nobody has helped me. I exist for no one. I existed only for you because that was what you wanted, and I accepted it gratefully.

I bribed the cemetery guard to let me open the grave. You yourself were the one who said to me, "Everything in Mexico can be bought. How can we put an end to that curse?"

After they killed you, nobody ever saw your remains. They said that you had been completely disfigured by the bullet that entered your brain. Respect for the dead! But then why is it that your wax figure in the first coffin didn't have a single wound? Why did your head remain intact, even when it melted? Respect for the dead!

I had no idea who you were. And you had no idea who I was. We loved each other without knowing, without asking questions. It wasn't a pact. We didn't talk about it. The way we met was too mysterious. Mystery is what brought us together and mystery was to keep us together.

I didn't know what my body was until you taught me to love it and discover it because you loved it and discovered it, over and over again, revealing it to me. . . .

"Your eyes change color in the daylight, and at night they become the only light. . . . Your earlobe doesn't need an earring, just as your sweet, clean hands need no jewels. . . . Your mouth is always as fresh as a fountain . . . and your vagina is the wound that doesn't scar so that I can hurt it as much as I want. . . . If you had no hair there, I would paint it on, Dulce María. . . . I travel up your body, touching your belly as if it were the naked field where I want to be buried. . . . Your breasts are restless, they bounce up and cry out for attention. . . . Deeper, deeper, deeper as I caress your ass, strong, hard, and generous, as if to compensate for your waist, slender as a birch tree, and I bury my face forever in your long black hair, and make you swear to me that you'll never cut off that hair, my darling, the black cascade that brings me closer to nature, the true essence of nature that I find in the landscape of your body, the nature I can't live without . . . and if I die, I want them to wrap my head in your hair so that I can breathe in your scent until the end of the world, my love, my woman, my bride. . . ."

I can't remember a time when you didn't make me feel that I was revealing something that I'd never known I had. The right to my body.

"Oh, the majesty of your body, Dulce."

That wasn't your real body in the grave. I didn't know who to go to. And that's because I'm nobody, my love. The secret lover of Tomás Moctezuma Moro. Nobody. Secret. Like at the beginning. The same. My darling, imagine my shock, my desolation, when I didn't find you in your own grave and I became mysteriously, once again, the stranger who saw you for the first time nine years ago, and whom you looked at, too, like the stranger you were to me.

That feeling stays in my soul, my darling. We saw each other without knowing who we were. You were my nameless love, and I your anonymous bride. . . . Because we were already lovers, if not before we met, then from the moment we laid eyes on each other, at that José Luis Cuevas retrospective at the Modern Art Museum in Monterrey, both of us lost in that world of vanished figures and almost invisible colors, as if instead of painting, Cuevas "filled the air," as you said when you walked over. How could I ever forget your first words: "Cuevas fills the air. . . ."

I didn't fully understand what you meant, but I knew, I knew, yes, I realized that only you appreciated what mattered: You had an eye for art and an eye for women.

I said to myself, "I am woman," and I smiled.

I wasted little time in correcting myself.

"I am *a* woman," I said, and stopped smiling.

Then I felt happy again.

"I am *the* woman."

You stared at me boldly, with impudence, desire, tenderness, who knows what else. . . . I looked into your eyes, as black and deep as two pebbles stuck forever at the bottom of the sea, which you offered me as if I were a little girl playing on the beach.

"I am *your* woman."

And then you laughed so I'd feel close to you.

In your arms I became a woman. When I saw you that night at the museum, you had no name. I didn't know what to call you.

"Call me 'Island.' "

I laughed.

"That's not a name," I said. "That's a place."

"No," you said, shaking your head of curls, so caressable. "It's utopia."

I stopped laughing.

"It's the place that doesn't exist."

Your face grew serious.

"It's the place that should exist."

You almost frightened me, you were so serious, almost angry, your teeth clenched.

"I will turn the place that doesn't exist into the place that *should* exist."

Utopia. I had never heard that word. But what's so surprising about that? They were all firsts with you—words, things, ideas, sex, love. . . . Of all the people at the Modern Art Museum why did you pick out a completely inexperienced nineteen-year-old girl from a humble family, without work, anxious to learn, not very ugly but not very pretty either? What did you see in me? The perfect companion to go with you to that happy island in your imagination? Was I like an island for you? Something to discover, something to transform, something to believe in?

Into my hands you put a Mexican novel from the twentieth century by Armando Ayala Anguiano and you said to me, "This is the best title for you, for me, and for everyone, Dulce."

"*The Desire to Believe*," I said out loud, reading the book cover.

The desire to believe. That was your invitation to me, my love, to have faith, and one day you said the same thing to the whole country from a platform raised so high that my hand was no longer able to reach yours.

"We must have faith. We must give Mexico back its hope."

That was when I saw you in all the papers, in all the news reports on TV. In those days you were what they called the *tapado,* "the concealed one." You lived in the shadows, waiting for the sun to come out and blind you. That was when, in the most awful way, both hurt and saved by the truth, I knew that you were mine more than ever because you would never be totally mine, because I saw you in a photograph with your wife and three children, and I accepted the silence, the secret, of being nothing to you in your public life and everything to you in private.

Tomás, my love, you know that I never complained, I understood how things had to be, I never asked anything of you, and I was more than happy; I cherished our love, more secret than ever, far from the stages, the photographs, the speeches. I cherished your confidences because I knew that you shared them with me and only me, and perhaps I never quite understood all the things you set out to achieve—I don't know anything about politics—but you were the candidate, you wanted to make the country a little bit better, give people back their faith, their hope, their trust. Those were the words you used over and over again.

Secret lovers. What joy. I wouldn't change it for anything. I never calculated, I never said to myself, "I'm going to make him choose between me and his family."

It never occurred to me, Tomás, because I knew that being secret lovers was the best thing in the world, I knew that even if it hadn't been for your family and politics, I would have loved you just the same—or rather, I knew that despite your family and political life, I would love you just the same. Your position and your responsibilities only made me love you more, and feel even more pleasure in knowing that you were mine, that you were the master of my body and I was the mistress of yours. I knew that just as surely as I believe in God—you and I, naked and united with no need for explanations, all as inexplicable and joyful as the feeling of your body inside mine. . . .

And now what was once my pleasure is my pain, my agony, Tomás. I have no one to turn to. That woman María del Rosario, who was so close to you during the campaign, that woman whom you did so much for, helping her onto what you called your "bandwagon," doesn't answer my letters. I can see why. She has no idea who I am. I could be a liar, a cheat, a publicity seeker. . . . And when I want to go and talk to someone else, your shadow stops me and begs me to be discreet, cautious, just as if you were protecting me, Tomás, just as if you were saying, from wherever you are, "Dulce, let it be. Don't rock the boat. I'm telling you this for your own good. I don't want you to get hurt because of me."

Do I even have a right, my love, to write to you, to leave a letter of love and desperation on your false grave? May I ask God to intercede, to tell me the truth, since no human being is willing to tell me anything? Wherever you are, think of how many times God hears us. Count for yourself, and you'll see what the answer is. Never.

This makes me think of a heresy, Tomás, and I'll tell it to you here, at your grave.

"How many times can we be expected to rescue God?"

I've reached the limits of my endurance. I will not resign myself, my love. I will not tell myself, "Tomás is dead. Accept it."

No. Instead I spend my nights wide awake, saying to myself, "If no one but God can hear my questions, and even God says nothing, then what can I do to make Him answer me?"

Tomás, my love. Give me back my life. You made me who I am. I was someone else before you. Perhaps I was nothing before you. In your arms I became a woman. And now that I no longer have you with me, I have to hold back my tears because, if I cry, I know that something even worse will happen to me. Tears will release the sadness, the grief that I haven't been able to express.

Will there be no resting place?

I love you, I love you, I think of you all the time.

I hear boleros on the café jukebox (radio and television aren't working; newspapers are selling very well now), and I remember our love.

No me preguntes más
déjame imaginar

que no existe el pasado
y que nacimos
el mismo instante
en que nos conocimos. . . .*

But the music fades away when I walk through the cemetery gate and read the inscription at the entrance:

STOP: THE PROVINCE OF ETERNITY BEGINS HERE,
WHERE EARTHLY GRANDEUR TURNS TO DUST.

**Stop asking me questions/let me imagine/that the past does not exist/and that we were born/the very instant/we first met. . . .*

29

TÁCITO DE LA CANAL TO
PRESIDENT LORENZO TERÁN

Mr. President, I thank God for the crisis we now find ourselves in, caused by the knee-jerk reaction of our neighbors to the north, since it gives me a chance to leave a written record of my loyalty to you. I applaud your decision to place lasting principles above and beyond any and all other transient considerations. I know all too well that for you our ultimate purposes must always be ethical. There can be no other way. All I need is to look at your hands, Mr. President, to know that they're capable of making miracles happen. You have a kind of sixth sense that other humans lack. And that intuition will have told you that I'm here to protect you and to prevent certain people from getting near you, people who might inconvenience you. Or, dare I add, people who aren't humbled by your presence. You know, sir, that I obey your orders before you even utter them. And to this virtue I add another. Keeping things in strict confidence is a habit I've cultivated all my life. What I'm trying to say is that you can place your utmost trust in me. I know that I owe everything to you, and that by doing anything to hurt you I would only be hurting myself. I reiterate my position so that in the upcoming presidential succession of 2024, you remember that you will face opponents who wish to remain in opposition indefinitely because

they are so scared of actually exercising power. But you will also encounter people like me who are already close to the nucleus of power
but have never felt any ambition to wield power themselves. That's
why, Mr. President, I feel I can speak to you with truly impartial conviction.

Bear in mind, Mr. President, that you should possess the imperial
gift of inflexibility. Let other people be the good guys. You don't have
the right to be a good guy. The people of this country will get down on
their knees in respectful tribute to power, but they will not accept bon-
homie and much less artlessness in a presidential figure. We respect the
emperor, we respect Montezuma, we respect the Spanish viceroy, and
we respect the dignified dictator honored by the rest of the world, like
Porfirio Díaz was. And also, of course, we respect the rightful, legitimate man, defender of the nation and distinguished citizen of the Americas, don Benito Juárez. Can you think of anyone more solemn than he?
Have you ever heard a single joke about Juárez? Didn't he go down in
history as Juárez the Impassive? Didn't Juárez come up with that saying: "For one's friends, justice and grace. For one's enemies, the law"?

By this I don't mean to imply that solemnity is synonymous with
imperial arrogance—it's synonymous with republican sobriety, but il-
luminated with the glowing halo of monarchy. Yes, let's always be a
hereditary republic, a monarchy with a six-year cycle, and in the interest of that tradition we must make sure we maintain the dignity of the
presidential throne and restrict access to it as much as possible. For this
reason, I venture to offer you a bit of advice regarding certain members
of the cabinet who like to brag about their "access" to your office and
who are perhaps a bit too chummy with you. Mr. President, don't en-
gage with inferiors. Always show them their place. Don't listen to their
biased advice—because there's no such thing as unbiased advice when
the person being advised is the president of the nation.

Mr. President, I work for you. I'm no different from the majority of
our compatriots. Every good Mexican works for you. Because if things
go well for the president, things go well for Mexico. Allow me to tell

you, then, that at this particular political hour here in this country, there are eight small parties. And then there is you.

The gloppy guacamole that results from this abundance of small parties can only be eaten with the spoon of a strong president who knows how to take advantage of it. Put this idea to the test, Mr. President, now that the elections are looming. Mexicans don't know how to govern themselves. History has proven this. Just watch them welcome the message of your renewed authority with gratitude and relief. I tell you this in the spirit of democracy. There's no such thing as a soft-core dictatorship that doesn't eventually degenerate into hard-core tyranny. You're better off the other way around: starting hard and degenerating into something softer.

Please forgive my bluntness. I'm a guard dog, I know. I accept my role with humility. You, on the other hand, may act according to the free will your position grants you. But what would you think of a cabinet chief—a position I'm honored to have been conferred—who didn't speak to you honestly? On a more humorous note, let me tell you that I'm not like the secretary who was asked the following question by the general, president, and head of state Plutarco Elías Calles: "What time is it?" To which the secretary responded, "Whatever time you say it is, Mr. President."

I am a man who is accustomed to doing things he dislikes.

Use me as you wish.

30

NICOLÁS VALDIVIA TO
MARÍA DEL ROSARIO GALVÁN

My fair lady, there is someone I believe I've mentioned before: Penélope, the secretary who works in Tácito de la Canal's office. Her full
name is Penélope Casas and she's a female freighter. She moves
through the office like a transatlantic ship on the high seas, supervising
the administrative tasks and cheering the girls on (for the lack of cheer
in that office is as deadly as Tácito's bad breath), acting sometimes as
their confidante and counselor, and at other times as a shoulder for
them to cry on. You see, Penélope has a heart as big as her bosom, and
her bosom is covered by a shawl the size of a flag. Her dark-skinned
face is dotted with pockmarks, the vestiges of childhood smallpox,
which she halfheartedly conceals with a layer of matte powder. Her lips
are heavily painted, as if to distract the eye, and presided over by two
dense eyebrows joined in the middle like the celebrated eyebrows of
Frida Kahlo. And as for her hair, María del Rosario, I think our lofty
Aztec goddess must get up at four in the morning to create those rib-
boned braids, those tottering towers that crown her head, and that tor-
rent of bangs that hides her narrow, low forehead.

I'm telling you all this only to emphasize the very powerful figure
cut by our bureaucratic goddess Coatlicue, so that you can imagine how

shocked I was to find her yesterday absolutely motionless, wracked with sobs, the tears soaking the tissue under her forlorn face.

"Doña Penélope, what's the matter?"

She couldn't stop crying. She raised her fist, which was clutching some papers, and only after a moment or two was she able to say, "Totally worthless, Mr. Valdivia, like the Argentinian *patacón*, toilet paper, that's what those shares are worth—nothing at all! Less than a pack of Kleenex!"

She passed me the handful of papers. They were shares of Mexicana de Energía, the utility company that declared bankruptcy yesterday and put thousands of small-time shareholders in the poorhouse—all the humble shareholders who put their faith in the privatization of the national energy company during the presidency of César León, who followed the example of Fidel Castro when he allowed foreign companies to invest in energy, a smoke screen that effectively shushed the noisy Mexican nationalists.

As it happens, MEXEN declared bankruptcy yesterday, putting shareholders like Penélope out on the street. MEXEN's investors, of course, had already earned themselves millions by keeping their mouths shut about the imminent bankruptcy and selling their own shares when they were still worth something.

I'm telling you things you already know, my dear lady, so that I can get to the part you don't know.

Let me take it step by step.

When MEXEN was structured as a private company during the days of César León, the directors put a number of shares up for sale—in the usual fashion, the kind of shares Penélope bought. But at the same time, in order to lure some very robust companies (insurers, banks, industry) to invest in MEXEN, the board gave these companies the assurance of confidential information that would allow them—at the very least—to double their initial investment in a matter of months. To this end, MEXEN was created as a double company. One was the public company open to small-time shareholders. The other was the secret company reserved for the investors with the deepest pockets.

Small shareholders like Penélope did not have access to the more privileged company. In fact, they didn't even know it existed.

How did I learn all this? Through our archivist don Cástulo Magón.

Borne by the sea of Penélope's tears, I said to Cástulo, "Get me the MEXEN file."

The old man replied, "Which one?"

I was taken aback by his response.

"How many are there?" I asked.

"Well, there are three. There are the official files, the confidential files, and the 'shredded wheat.' "

"The 'shredded wheat'?"

"Yes. The files they told me to destroy. Shredded, you know."

"And why didn't you do it?"

"Oh, sir, I respect these documents."

Impassive, I let him go on.

"Did you know that don Benito Juárez, fleeing the French occupation forces, went from the capital to the northern border with three stagecoaches packed solid with the official papers of the republic?"

"Yes, Cástulo, I did know that. But what does that have to do with anything?"

The old man was flushed with pride.

"A paper that finds its way to my hands is a paper that never disappears, sir." And puffing out his chest, he added, "In my hands, a document is sacred. It will never be lost, I assure you."

"Do the people upstairs know about this loyalty of yours?"

"It isn't loyalty to anyone, don Nicolás. It is my duty to the nation and to history."

And how were the famous documents classified? Well, those that were available for consultation were filed under "Mexicana de Energía (MEXEN)." The secret documents, under "Privatization Models." And the ones don Cástulo had hung on to had no title at all, except for the aforementioned breakfast cereal, "shredded wheat."

I've had a feverish night, María del Rosario, reconstructing the shady deals of the MEXEN board. I summarize them herewith. The executives reserve their confidential information for the big investors, keeping the small-time shareholders in the dark. For example: The big investors were once informed that the company owned about a hundred companies that were not going to go public so that they could keep the dividends under wraps, and thereby avoid distributing the profits. MEXEN is a cover, a smoke screen for interconnected investments yielding exponential earnings.

These operations don't appear on the company's quarterly balance sheets. MEXEN discloses its profits to its small, highly privileged group of investors, not to the masses of poorly informed shareholders. In short, the company's main profits favor one group over the other.

The name of the game is confidentiality. But the managers are playing a triple game, because they're cheating both shareholders and investors for their own personal gain. A matter of hiding certain conflicts of interest. If you invest legitimately in MEXEN, your money may go to a company that doesn't allow public investment, or one that is the government's exclusive domain. Neither the small shareholders nor the big investors know this. The former are kept happy with minor earnings and the latter with major earnings. Nobody asks any questions. But the MEXEN managers can be company employees and principal partners at the same time. They distribute 10 percent of the earnings for their shareholders, and keep 90 percent for themselves.

How? By multiplying dual companies. For example, MEXEN Subsidiary A is really a part of Subsidiary B but the directors tell everyone that they're two different companies. When Subsidiary A takes a dip in profits, alleging failed agreements with Subsidiary B (which is nevertheless a simple mask for Company A), the directors of A keep the real profits and make the shareholders absorb B's imaginary losses as if they were A's losses. Meaning: A is not the partner that has been hurt by B. It is exactly the same as B, but makes B take the hit for its losses. The directors and big investors keep the profits. And the losses are passed on to shareholders like Penélope.

But these con men have gone even further, María del Rosario. They created a Company C in order to attract investment and make loans to Company A. Company A promises to issue more shares in the event that C's investments fall, to keep C solvent. Company B invests millions in Company C, and Company C in turn invests in Company A.

But this is where the mistakes and the catastrophes start piling up. Company A forces Company B to buy stocks at fixed prices in six months to protect itself from an eventual drop in the market. B gets ahead and buys when the price is low, earning millions. Company A protects itself by selling shares to C. But when the value of the shares in fact drops, Company A gives shares to C in order to keep the entire operation solvent. And then Company A begins to issue more and more shares, devaluing those held by people like Penélope.

At this point the big guys have already made their killing, having taken in millions at the shareholders' expense. This means they're now free to declare bankruptcy because they've already made their astronomical profits. And anyway, at that point, the best thing for everyone is to wrap up the little game and start a new one before they fall into one of their own traps.

It's like the story of the fox that knows all the traps the hunters have laid out for him, but doesn't know that the trap he himself laid down to trick the hunters will be precisely the thing that nails him in the end.

María del Rosario, one of the advantages of a bureaucracy like ours is that the archivists never change because nobody ever thinks of them. They're forgotten pawns or, depending on the circumstance, people who are easily sacrificed on the great chessboard. And the swift bishops of the game know that the pawns are unaware of their own value. What I mean is, they don't know what they have in their own archives. María del Rosario, the humble archivist don Cástulo Magón has just determined the outcome of the presidential succession in Mexico.

"Where did these documents come from, don Cástulo?"

"Don Tácito de la Canal handed them to me personally."

"Did he tell you to keep them a secret?"

"No, not at all. He knows he can trust me with anything. Only once did he ever say to me: 'Destroy these papers. They're of no consequence. We are going to drown in all these ridiculous papers.' "

Don Cástulo ran his hand across the little hair-bridge he combs over his balding head.

I almost said to him, "He could have destroyed them himself."

Again I thought of Nixon. Of how every last testimony had to be saved, even the criminal kind, even if only for two reasons. Politicians think all their actions have tremendous historical importance. And they are arrogant enough to think they're above the law. And perhaps, as well, they mysteriously fear they will be discovered as the bureaucrat who destroyed documents. Here, of course, the guilty party would be poor old Cástulo.

But when don Cástulo handed me the pile of incriminating papers, there was yet another surprise. The documents had the name "Tácito de la Canal" written on them, in his own handwriting. And that, my dear lady, was when I had to ask myself, "Why would a criminal ever sign papers that would single him out as perpetrator of a colossal fraud?"

31

MARÍA DEL ROSARIO GALVÁN
TO NICOLÁS VALDIVIA

Your information, my cherished friend, is priceless. It makes me want to go running out to the palace balcony, ring the Independence Bell, and proclaim the truth for all the world to hear. In politics, however, timing is everything. In fact, politics is all about knowing how to gauge the moment. Easier said than done. It's hard to reconcile intelligence and passion in the interest of fulfilling one's obligations.

You and I have agreed that our task is to prevent Tácito de la Canal from becoming president. And finally, thanks to you, we have the cards we need to play. We can forget about insulting Tácito. People forget insults. Hatred simmers. Irritation boils over. Frustration is unacceptable and unwittingly gives way to chaos, which then causes people to behave irrationally, and that encourages the most dangerous and counter-productive political adventures. In other words, let us proceed according to some kind of method. Our poor country has suffered too long from endemic dysfunction. It has endured almost constant starvation and demoralization. Oh, Mexico: so many wounds, and so little time for them to heal.

I quote our friend Bernal Herrera: "All these evils can be avoided if we create a country with laws that we are prepared to enforce and obey."

This is the point. Tácito de la Canal has flagrantly violated the law. You know him. You've worked with him. You know he's a cruel, miserable man. Perhaps you haven't yet learned that the most cruel people are also the most insecure. They are cruel because they're afraid of being nothing. Cruelty gives them an identity. It's the easiest path for them. To love, to offer your hand to your fellow man, to attend to his needs—that, my friend, requires time and passion. Few people possess those virtues. I must confess that occasionally even I feel I lack them, and must remind myself: "Patience, woman. Stay calm."

But don't trust chance if you want to destroy Tácito. Chance takes care of itself, so what you and Bernal and I must do is use our will to overcome chance, and govern with well-calculated actions. Never forget that passions are arbitrary forms of conduct. Let Tácito be the one to trust chance and act arbitrarily. The good politician knows how to turn everything into an advantage. Add up the elements yourself: one, your accidental encounter with that archivist, whatever his name is; two, the existence of those documents that were never destroyed; three, Tácito's signature (I am astonished by that, I admit, and I'm still thinking about it); and four, our friendship, my close relationship with Bernal Herrera, and the political ides that are fast approaching, whether we like it or not.

Add everything up, Nicolás Valdivia, and gauge your time. You are the master of a secret that you've shared with me, further confirming the trust I've placed in you, which you occasionally seem to doubt or perhaps not reciprocate. It doesn't matter. Secrets, you know, are our worst political enemies. Look at Mexico, look at Colombia, look at Europe or the United States. Murders, shady business deals, drug trafficking, insider information. Our enemies are united by all these things. And now, the three of us have the good fortune of sharing a secret. You can't imagine, Nicolás, the number of times when, in my younger years, I trusted friends I believed to be discreet, only to wake up from my innocent illusions to the reality of betrayal and recklessness. You give me back my confidence; you give me friendship.

You, me, and Bernal, united by a secret.

And standing before us, like the cast of a play, are all the others. The man who deceives and hides his true passions: Tácito de la Canal. The man who never lives up to his boastful claims: Andino Almazán. The man who performs his job professionally: Patricio Palafox. The man who only cares about getting rich: Felipe Aguirre. The man who reveals all his vices and hides none of his ambitions: Cícero Arruza. The inscrutable professional soldier who might be playing on more than one side: Mondragón von Bertrab. And then, the most dangerous player of all, the man who collects victims like other people collect stamps: our ex-president César León.

And you and me and Bernal Herrera.

And a president who only wants to make his mark on history.

Let's help him.

Oh yes, of course, the medium is petty, even despicable. But since we have no other reality but this, the medium is also powerful. And, getting back to my original point, if we want to move around in this medium, this world, we must remember that secrecy is paramount. Sometimes, the information you give and receive can be more useful to your enemy than to your ally. And only when that information comes out do you realize that you should never have disclosed it. Sometimes, you know, I think you're a bit too naïve. Your heart turns to mush when you deal with humble people—the humiliated secretary, the office worker cheated of her money, the archivist with no hope. . . . Remember, we weren't born to live with the poor or to live like the poor. The poor are to be respected . . . but from a distance.

I'm serious about this. Never be sincere with a poor person. In exchange you'll only be treated with egalitarian scorn and that's something a politician can't tolerate. Don't let them, out of the weakness of your sympathetic heart, treat you like an equal. You are not equal to inferior people. You are not. Calculate. Manipulate. If you don't act astutely, if you betray or disregard our agreement, we'll be lost and you'll be lost. That will be the end of your career. And that would frustrate me.

Remember what I promised you. Wait. Calculate.

32

MARÍA DEL ROSARIO GALVÁN
TO BERNAL HERRERA

Darling, my protégé Nicolás Valdivia has served us well. The wolf has fallen into the trap and doesn't know it yet. Tácito is ours. But he might slip away if we act too hastily. Observe the political panorama that's taking shape. The evil César León is attempting to convince the president of Congress, Onésimo Canabal, that there's still time to change the constitution and reform the laws regarding succession in the event of the president's incapacitation or death.

His idea is that instead of being replaced by an interim president during the first two years in office (which President Terán has already completed) or by an acting president during the last four years in office (the president's current situation), both of which cases are presently subjected to a vote in both houses of Congress, it should be the president of Congress (in our case, Onésimo Canabal) who automatically assumes the executive's duties.

What does our ex-president César León want? He doesn't hold a publicly elected position—and according to his enemies, he never did. He detests Tácito de la Canal. He fears and despises you. But Onésimo is an ass who will let himself be manipulated in a transitional situation. A transition to what? you might ask. I think César León knows something you and I don't. He has a secret. He's a born politician, don't doubt it. The bad thing about him is that he's like soft wax. He can mold himself into any shape, he can adapt to any new situation or requirement that presents itself. You have to realize, Bernal, that this is a war of secrets. You and I (and, necessarily, Valdivia) have a secret that can bring Tácito down and you to victory. But if we reveal it too soon, Tácito will be able to put together his defense with plenty of time to spare. I think he'd be capable of having you killed. And what do you gain, Bernal, what do you lose, if you talk or if you don't? It's a matter of timing. You win if you talk in time. You lose if you talk at the wrong time. I think I have the solution. In a couple of days I'll fill you in.

P.S. It's inappropriate for the institution to send bills and notifications to you. In this matter, I should be the only one to appear on the correspondence. No suspicion must fall on you.

33

NICOLÁS VALDIVIA TO
MARÍA DEL ROSARIO GALVÁN

I thank you for your letter, madam. And I wonder if the hour of my reward has arrived. I've made my love for you clear. You've asked me to
be worthy, if not of your love, then of your mystery. Does one thing
lead to the other? Sometimes you make me wonder if separation unites
lovers more than presence. I console myself thinking that love takes on
as many different forms, and presents as many different challenges, as
any other real feeling. I accept everything from you but indifference. And
I wonder if I deserve my prize now: speaking to you in the familiar.

34

MARÍA DEL ROSARIO GALVÁN
TO NICOLÁS VALDIVIA

Do you want a reward, my impatient sweetheart? Well, here it is. Bernal Herrera is very impressed with your great exploits. He believes, in addition, that it's not only useless but dangerous for you to continue working in the office of Tácito de la Canal. He spoke to the president. You've been named undersecretary of the interior, second in command to Bernal Herrera.

I repeat. Wait. Calculate. And be grateful.

35

NICOLÁS VALDIVIA TO
JESÚS RICARDO MAGÓN

....

I want you to know that the time when I steal away from the office to talk to you is the best part of my day. Luckily for me, Mexican public administration comes to a complete halt from three to six in the afternoon, when no self-respecting government bureaucrat would be seen anywhere but in a luxurious restaurant, in a private room, if possible. Always with a cell phone in hand to answer calls with a frown. It's amazing people don't break their necks with so much nodding! Now, of course, bereft of all telecommunications, this isn't possible. Now we're constantly being pestered by hangers-on who turn up and say things like, "Sir, you have an important message at the door."

Of course there are no such messages. At the most, the distinguished gentleman will exchange a few words with one of the ubiquitous lottery-ticket sellers stationed at the entrances to all the most fashionable lunch spots. "Like a queen of hearts, my country, on a metal floor, you live for the day, by chance, like the lottery." Learn López Velarde's poem by heart, Jesús Ricardo: We Mexicans don't have a more "impeccable and glittering" guide.

I say there are no messages today, but there weren't really any before, either. Cell phone calls were an act staged to show off one's power.

And I tell you all this very honestly because I, like you, harbor no illusions about our political class. *Plus ça change, oui* . . . just like you, I'm sick and tired of the fact that even the street cleaners call me counselor. I'm sick to death of all these Mexican counselors running around everywhere. Would you believe that there are people who come to our office and address Penélope, the secretary there, as counselor out of that false respect, that fawning, exaggerated courtesy? Like you, I wish they would all just vanish and become like the counselor Vidriera in the story by Cervantes, not so that I could see through them, but so that I could do to them what the illustrious character who thought he was made of glass feared being done to him: smash them into a thousand pieces.

And so, knowing you, knowing your ideals and sharing so many of them with you, why am I now inviting you to work with me in the president's office, in the very heart of the artichoke?

I don't dare tell you this again in person because when I first mentioned it a few weeks ago, you attacked me so savagely, you pounced on me, put me in a headlock, and I felt your young brute strength, and smelled your male sweat, and I was afraid of you, Jesús Ricardo. I don't know if telling you this flatters you or alarms you. It doesn't matter. I smelled your youthful sweat. I was blinded by your long rebellious, adolescent mane of hair.

I said to you, "How long do you think your youth will last? Don't you know that an old man with long hair only inspires laughter or pity? Haven't you ever seen those ancient hippies dragging their scraggly defiance through the middle-class neighborhoods they've ended up in, looking for a 1960s San Francisco that doesn't exist, tangled up in their multicolored bead necklaces and shuffling in their old sandals over to the supermarket?"

In Ecclesiastes, the Bible should have added that not only is there a time to live and a time to die, but also there is a time to be a rebel and a time to be a conservative. . . . Have you ever read *My Last Sigh*, Luis Buñuel's autobiography? I highly recommend it. In that book, the magnificent artist of film—among the world's greats—recognizes his anarchist tendencies just as you do, only he regards them as marvelous ideas that are impossible in the practical sense. Blow up the Louvre! In theory, splendid. In practice, stupid.

You still believe rebellious ideas and practice are inseparable. That ideas are meaningless unless we turn them into reality. Let's be realists, let's ask the impossible, the rebels said in Paris in May 1968 before they all became businessmen, professionals, and government ministers. . . .

You frighten me, Jesús Ricardo. The truly consistent anarchist invariably and inevitably becomes a terrorist. I suggest that you go back and reread all those theories you've thrown at me during our "Socratic" afternoons up on that rooftop of yours that looks out over the ugliest city in the world, the city of sand, the dusty capital of Mexico, the biggest garbage dump in the world, that desolate gray panorama: gray air, gray concrete, gray people. . . . The kingdom of the scavenger. The capital of underdevelopment.

Your ideals are noble. Your hero is Bakunin, a Russian aristocrat, after all, who expected, every time he entered his house, to be surprised. . . . From your rooftop, surrounded by pigeons, you firmly believe that the perfect society is one with no government, no laws, no punishment.

"What will it have, then?" I ask you, with genuine concern and interest.

"Managers, obligations, and corrections," you respond cleverly.

"And how will that society, without any visible power structure, place limits on itself? How will that society manage itself, fulfill its obligations, correct itself?" I ask you in a tone of voice that you can't mistake for anything other than affectionate.

"By abolishing property," you spit out at me, like a newspaper editorial, a slogan, a banner, a slap in the face.

"All that is superfluous belongs by right to the people who have nothing," I say, and I'm not trying to show off—perhaps you like this about me, that I'm direct, that all I want is to be honest with you. . . .

"Exactly, Nicolás. If you distribute wealth equitably and give each person his due, then we'll have equality and peace."

I look into your intense, provocative eyes. I doubt that peace is what you're after. Maybe equality. But not peace.

"Who would do the managing?" I repeat.

"Everyone. Each person would govern himself. An unalienated collective."

"Is that possible in a society born out of violence and crime?" challenges Nicolás Valdivia, your devil's advocate.

"It isn't a crime if it leads to the creation of a society without crime, a republic of equals."

How could I pass up the opportunity to dazzle you with a great quote?

" 'Ruthlessly slash the throats of tyrants, patricians, millionaires, all the amoral people who could oppose our common happiness.' "

"You're a walking quotation book, Nicolás!" you exclaim with remarkably good humor.

"It's just part of my rooftop Socratic method, my young friend."

How nice of you to offer me a smile.

"OK, thank you for citing my hero, Gracchus Babeuf. You saved me the trouble."

I swear to you that you smiled, you who are always so solemn, my darling Jesús Ricardo Magón.

"Get me up to speed, Magón. Anarchism was born in the nineteenth century to fight the industrial machine. What are you going to fight? Computers? Didn't Marcos already stage a little mini-revolution on the Internet?"

This time you definitely let out a cackle.

"You can borrow my pigeons, Nicolás. I know you have no other form of messenger."

"True enough. I will have to be my own messenger. I will have to deliver my letters in person, but I can never receive one from you—it's just as if you were a politician from the PRI days: Nothing in writing."

I interrogated with my eyes before saying, "And do you know the message I plan to send with your little pigeons?" I answered my own question emphatically as soon as I'd asked it: "That there is no such thing as an anarchist who doesn't end up a terrorist. That the rejection of authority, and millenarianism, are very beautiful ideas until you start acting on them."

Your face lit up, millenarian that you are.

"You can't deny the beauty of revolt," you said, serious once more.

"Even if the results are horrifying?" I replied with that verbal foil you force me to brandish every time we spar.

"Do you find equality horrifying?" you asked humorlessly.

"No. I can only repeat that the great problem of equality is not overcoming the pride of the rich, but rather overcoming the egotism of the poor."

"Do you know what I like about you? You get angry without swearing. You nurse your rage inside. That's why I find you more dangerous than someone who explodes with violence, verbal or physical."

You look at me and you know I know. I understand you. And if I'm repeating our conversation back to you it's only because, despite our political differences, you and I have a common faith in the word.

Wherein lies the greatness, I ask you, of Plato's dialogues, which serve as the basis for all human discourse in a Western world freed from Oriental despotism? In the fact that they set the stage for you and me talking on a rooftop in Mexico City in the year 2020. The Socrates–Plato duo transforms two random interlocutors into companions in a place and at a time that otherwise—i.e., without the word—would never exist. If we didn't have this time and place to share, we'd know nothing about each other. In fact, we wouldn't even know the other existed. We would be alien to each other, like ships crossing in the night, strangers walking past each other on the great boulevard of the silent.

What is it that unites this time and place we share, Jesús Ricardo?

The word, the word brings us together one minute and then tears us apart the next, the word that, whether friend or enemy, in the end acquires an independent meaning. And it's that transience that drives us, my young and beloved friend, in this hopelessly polluted stoa covered in pigeon shit, to utter the next word, knowing that it too will slip from our grasp and enter into the great realm of reason that engulfs us.

"Don't ever stop talking. Don't ever say the last word."

Plato said that writing was parricide because it continues to signify in the absence of the interlocutor. As long as I write to you, then, it will be fratricide. And only on the day—distant if not altogether impossible—that you write to me, can we begin to speak of parricide. Parricide: Scarcely nine years separate us. And I'm already playing the role of a perverse Mephistopheles, offering the young Faust his chance to be old. To grow up.

Have you read Gombrowicz's marvelous *Ferdydurke*, the great twentieth-century Polish novel? For him, growing up is tantamount to growing corrupt. We kill the advantages of adolescence by becoming adults. We kill the inconsolable youth by corrupting him with maturity. But since we are, inevitably, not alone in our youth, we end up creating one another, running the risk of creating ourselves from the outside, deformed and inauthentic. "To be a man means never to be oneself." If that's how you want to view our relationship, so be it. Let yourself get a bit corrupted.

"Being partly corrupt is like being partly a virgin," you say.

And I tell you the same thing over and over again.

You can't reject what you don't know. Put your ideas to the test. That's the only measure of the intellectual integrity you preach. You don't have to commit to anything. Come and work with me in the president's office—that's where you'll see "the belly of the beast," as José Martí said when living in the United States. You don't have to sacrifice your ideas. In fact, you'll see how resilient they are. All you have to sacrifice is your appearance. You can't work in Los Pinos with that Tarzan hair of yours. You'll have to cut it. And you can't go to work in blue jeans. But you don't need to go overboard, either. Don't dress in that vulgar middle-class office-worker style like Hugo Patrón, your sister's little boyfriend. Let Armani be your best friend. I'll see to that. Make up your mind, you heir to utopia. Stick with me. Let me save you from your impotent language that can only lead to criminal action when desperation sets in.

I ask this of you as a double test.

First of all, a test of your ideas. You're an ideological coward if you don't put your ideas to the challenge.

Second, a test of my friendship, which deepens with each passing day. I love and desire you for who you are—you know that. But also because I see myself in you. Not a duplicate of myself but a similar, separate being. I admit that to love you is to love myself. To love myself as I would like to be. I like women. I love them as intensely as I love you. In women I'm always shocked to see the person that I'm not. I see the other and it dazzles me. That's why I adore women and fall, time and time again, into the abyss of passion for women. The passion for all that's different. With you, Jesús Ricardo, I feel that I can love myself as I would like to be loved by me.

Consider my offer. This gate, unlike the one in the Bible, is not a narrow one.

36

MARÍA DEL ROSARIO GALVÁN
TO PRESIDENT LORENZO TERÁN

My very old and dear friend, the time has come to unleash the hounds
of war. We can no longer put off the selection of the person who will
succeed you as president of the republic. The return of our ex-president
César León is a part in the well-oiled machine of our electoral democracy. And it's not the only one. León is plotting with the president of
Congress to declare you incapacitated so that Onésimo Canabal himself
can take your place and push through the constitutional reform that will
permit the re-election of, guess who, César León. On the other hand, a
constitutional amendment requires time: It will take at least a year to get
a majority vote either way from all the states in the federation. And that
can only happen after the amendment has been passed by two thirds of
Congress.

So César León must have another ace up his sleeve. What it is, we
don't know. And that, my friend, is our weakness. The constitutional
reform has the whiff of a smoke screen to me. The real blow is going to
come at us from another direction. Make no mistake about that. And be
prepared.

Too much time, Mr. President, too much waste. You can be sure that
as long as the pawn in this game, Onésimo Canabal, follows César
León's advice, León is going to give us a scare and end up with all the

chips in his pocket. Which ones? I don't know, I don't know, Mr. President. The only advice I can give you, from my head and from my heart, is that you have to act. Now. Get ahead of the game. Set up separate meetings with your two aspiring successors, Tácito de la Canal and Bernal Herrera. Order them to tender their resignations, announce their candidacies, and launch their campaigns.

They won't have any choice but to do what you say. And if they hesitate, just fire them. You'll see how they listen to you, Mr. President. My feminine intuition tells me that this is all you have to do if you want to win this round against our very astute ex-president.

What have I always told you, Mr. President? Not making decisions is worse than making mistakes. Make a decision. Remember, there are no beginnings in politics. Only moments. And the ability to seize them before they're gone. To be cunning, in other words. Cunning in what sense? you may ask. Well, your interior secretary has shown it in each one of the cases currently at hand. Either you deal with a problem or bury it. What you can't do is leave a request to languish without rejecting or accepting it. You might say, rightly, that the lack of decisiveness in the case of the university strikes means that the problem is unsolvable. But that lack of decisiveness, you see, is precisely the solution: Let there be no solution, until all the parties are tired out. On the other hand, you've kept your investors happy with your policies, and the workers' unrest has subsided because of need—their need to eat. Meanwhile, allowing the peasants a meaningless victory would be a defeat for the local bosses who've always counted on that eternal cannon fodder, the indentured agricultural slave. Very well. But what we're facing now, Mr. President, is a strictly political test.

Who will succeed you in the 2024 election?

What forces can he rely on?

Who will challenge him?

And don't ever let yourself wonder, Who will be most loyal to me?

Everyone, Mr. President, will betray you. Even—and I'm telling you this so that you see the extent of my frankness and my friendship— the man who's my favorite for the succession. . . .

37

BERNAL HERRERA TO
PRESIDENT LORENZO TERÁN

Mr. President, dear friend, I'm writing to you under these new and un-expected circumstances, which must feel somewhat natural to you given that you never respond to messages, only receive them. I suppose that you don't allow anyone else to read them, so I'm going to be completely honest with you. None of your aides can say anything about the letters written to you because it would reveal their indiscretion and prove them unworthy of your trust.

I'm telling you this so that you're not surprised by my honesty and sincerity. Let me be your mirror, my dear president. You already know what people say about you. Power makes even the ugliest person look attractive. But we all have an inner mirror of power and in it we can see ourselves fearful, tired, uncertain. When this internal mirror reverts back to the external, we run the risk of people thinking, Apathy, fatigue, uncertainty, fear—and even worse, This is what the president wants, this is his formula for holding on to the Eagle's Throne. He's an inert president who governs through inertia.

I've always told you that one has to avoid making one's internal doubts visible. You'll say that I'm blowing my own horn and painting a picture of the virtues that would allow me to succeed you as occupant of the Eagle's Throne.

That may be so, Lorenzo. You may be right.

Nevertheless, I'm telling you a useful truth, not only regarding the imminent succession and the campaigns, but with respect to the three years you still have in office. You are no exception to the truth that every head of state must choose from many possible paths, that he's always at a crossroads, pushed this way and that way by a number of different forces.

"Go this way."

"No, better go that way."

There's no force more powerful than the interior force of the president himself. And yet this force is not so easy to identify, define, and act upon because the most insufferable thing about being president is the fact that everyone looks at you as if they could see their own destiny in your face. Especially cabinet members! Unfortunately, most of them believe that the president rewards loyalty more than ability.

I repeat: I have no desire to blow my own horn. I do not speak *pro domo sua*. I'm expressing myself hypothetically. Mexicans have a tendency to blame everything on "the system," no matter what that "system" is. They never blame themselves, not as people and not as citizens. No, it's always the fault of "the system," and the head of that system is the president. One of the unwritten rules of our blessed system—since time immemorial, since the colonies—is that the accumulation of wealth while in power is permissible for one reason and under two conditions.

The reason—and it's an unspoken one—is that everyone knows corruption "greases" or, if you prefer, "lubricates" the system. Corruption makes the system fluid and effective, unbothered by utopian hopes regarding justice or its lack thereof. In any case, Mexico has never had a monopoly on corruption. Remember, if you will, Operation "Clean Hands" in Italy, the Banesto and Matesa scandals in Spain, the alleged corruption of Chancellor Helmut Kohl in Germany, or the virginal Margaret Thatcher's cronies in England, to say nothing of corporate corruption in the United States—the Enron affair, followed by WorldCom, and then Halliburton, etc., all of which may not have exposed President Bush (Junior, a totally clueless man, a ventriloquist's dummy), but certainly exposed his inner circle and its links to the world of high finance and oil. . . .

Need I go on? The difference with Mexico is that, while in Europe or in the United States these things are punished, in Latin America they're either rewarded or ignored. Let me give you another classic example, my dear friend and president. Let's suppose that Mr. X is corrupt and he's caught in the act. Is it wise to punish him for it? What should come first, justice or convenience?

A political system, whatever it is, must create its own taboos to protect the privileged and, more importantly, to protect society itself. Just as there's no such thing as politics without villains, there's no such thing as a society without demons. Sometimes the sins of the state must be either tolerated or disguised, not so much in order to protect the state as to protect society from its own diabolical powers.

They say you're too isolated, and that your isolation has led you to imagine the very best and the very worst of others. The net political result, as you know, is that each of your subordinates interprets the president's imperviousness in his own way, so that they fight among themselves. While you enjoy what in hushed tones you refer to as "my much-needed solitude to think clearly and act properly," those closest to you are all squabbling with one another. Can't you see what a great opportunity will present itself when it's time for the presidential succession? All the contention and rivalry among your subordinates, encouraged by your supposed passivity, will allow you to become the referee.

Don't fool yourself, Mr. President: The country sees your passivity as a flaw. Let's be frank, you've lost your authority. But now, if you set your mind to it, you can win back some power. Win the inexorable battle of the presidential succession. The one thing that everyone considers your greatest flaw can become your greatest asset: Storm the castle without waking up the dogs.

Pardon me for saying so, but don't pay attention to Seneca when he advises you to walk among the people like a king dressed as a beggar.

Remember that if you open the palace windows you'll be letting in both a brilliant sun and a fierce wind. The people will be dazzled, but the government will only catch a cold. Keep your aspirin and your sinus medicine handy.

Add an enema—not for you, but for your disloyal aides. And if you don't know who they are yet, you will soon enough.

38

TÁCITO DE LA CANAL TO
MARÍA DEL ROSARIO GALVÁN

A very brief missive, my dear lady. Everything that is said, written, plotted, or murmured in this country passes through my office. I am the one who, like a sieve, knows what to let through and what to prevent from reaching the president's desk. I know what you, your old lover Bernal, and your young lover Valdivia have recently discovered. Too many secrets, too many love affairs, all that complicated tiptoeing. Be careful. I'm not going to let you get away with what you've been plotting, thanks to the delirious ravings of some decrepit archivist in the basement of Los Pinos. Down with the masks, madam. Or as you, educated by the Frogs, would say: *C'est la guerre*. Don't forget your little weakness. You're more than just a political woman. You're a mother. Would you like that to get out? Or worse, would you like the boy to suffer? Think about it. I'm always willing to cut a deal.

39

MARÍA DEL ROSARIO GALVÁN
TO TÁCITO DE LA CANAL

You're right, Tácito. Down with the masks and up with the curtain. You and Bernal are political rivals and can speak freely to each other. I, however, am not going to lose my temper as you have. Instead I'll take advantage of this moment, almost as a necessary catharsis, to tell you a few truths. . . .

You've always believed in getting to the top at any cost, but you've failed to calculate the price of combat when combat is pointless. For now we've run out of ammunition, and your last round was the president.

You were counting on your obsequiousness to buy you a free ticket to the Eagle's Throne. The whole country has watched you treating the president as if he were an untouchable Japanese mikado. What kind of image could you possibly present to the electorate, my unpresentable friend? Who doesn't know that you push in the president's chair every time he sits down to eat, and that then you lick the leftovers off his plate? Who hasn't seen you standing behind the president as if your sole duty were that of guarding the emperor, making sure nobody touches or listens to him? "Let the president's hair and nails grow, and I'll clip them in private, unbeknownst to him, while he sleeps, and then I'll keep them in a little box. . . ."

Yes, Tácito, just like everything you keep. Like stolen goods. Tácito, you specialize in revealing people's unpleasant pasts. I know perfectly well that you made me the victim of your slander once before, and now you're threatening to do it again. But now it's your own past that's going to haunt you in the middle of the night and rob you of your sleep. You've dug up every last secret except for one: your own. Now, your guilty secret is going to be unearthed, and I swear to you, Tácito, it will terrify you, and with luck dispose of you for once and for all.

I won't be deterred. Mark my words. What you're trying to do to Bernal and me will rebound on you. I know what you're up to, and if you touch a single hair on my head the entire world will hear about it. And even if you were to cut off my head, the evidence against you would come to light, with another charge—murder.

There are petty and evil people who know too much, Tácito. But there are also great and good people who know enough to silence that insufferable high-pitched voice of yours that makes you sound like a newly ordained priest. Do you know who you remind me of with that voice and physique? Franco, my dear Tácito, Generalísimo Francisco Franco. But this isn't Spain, nor is it 1936. You've fallen for the ploy that Lorenzo Terán uses to manage his cabinet. He's made everyone think: "You are my chosen one. You are my natural successor."

Have you ever gotten inside the president's head? Been able to imagine what he imagines?

Poor Tácito. You've read all the letters the president received from his cabinet ministers and you've insinuated that each and every one was proof of their disloyalty to him—until the president himself began to wonder if it was really possible that everyone close to him was disloyal except Tácito de la Canal.

Poor Tácito. You never realized that the more you fawned over the president, the more the public despised you—and the less the president himself trusted you, knowing well enough that in this country the horse you name emperor will kick you to death.

Poor Tácito. Deep down, I don't harbor you any ill will. I just don't like you. More precisely, I'd like to see you humiliated. Rich, in exile, but humiliated.

I'm going to hurt you, Tácito, I swear, and I won't feel the slightest twinge of guilt because I despise you. Then again, perhaps I shouldn't be so free with my contempt. There are too many who deserve it. *Adieu.*

P.S. Next time you go around stealing, be a little smarter about it.

40

EX-PRESIDENT CÉSAR LEÓN TO
ONÉSIMO CANABAL, PRESIDENT OF CONGRESS

I'm back on the offensive, my distinguished though indistinguishable friend, and am here to remind you of the days when you—figuratively speaking, of course—were in the political bathroom with a towel over your arm and your hand outstretched, hoping for tips. Who dragged you out of there and made you an usher at the party assemblies and then "the man with the microphone" at the conventions, the one who called for order, attention . . . ?

"It is my great privilege to present the honorable *licenciado* César León, candidate for the presidency. . . ."

From there you rose to the executive committee of the party, and then the golden exile of an ambassadorship in Luxembourg, where we have so many various and pressing interests (don't laugh—nobody laughs at those bank accounts in Luxembourg) and you fulfilled your obligations as the trusty little guardian-gnome that you are. And now, congressman for the third consecutive time and president of Congress. Goodness, don Onésimo, how far we have come from those toilet bowl days. One should be grateful, don't you think? And you've proved yourself more than worthy of your hometown of Campeche—why, you're what they call a real *campechano*, nice, everyone likes you, sure.

But you've still got to deal with your mortal enemy Humberto Vidales, the so-called Dark Hand of the state of Tabasco. Of course, it might be more accurate to call him the "Hydra Head"—chop one off and a hundred more grow in its place. In his case, however, those hundred heads are what he very proudly calls "My Nine Evil Sons." In other words, an evil dynasty. Tabasco is better at that than any other state, and Dark Hand has his conspiracies and plots planned up to the year 3000.

You also bear the burden, Onésimo, of sharing your last name with another Tabasco strongman, the implacable anticlerical governor Tomás Garrido Canabal. You may remember what Gonzalo N. Santos, yet another name in our long list of strongmen, had to say about him: "He's got the balls of a bull."

And balls were exactly what he needed when he drove every last priest out of Tabasco, shut down all the churches, and even banned crosses in cemeteries. Don Tomás was such a priest-hater that he even prohibited the people of Tabasco from saying *Adiós* and made them say *Hasta luego* instead.

Your secret's safe with me, Onésimo. I know you moved from Tabasco to Campeche to escape Dark Hand and his Nine Evil Sons, so that you could create your own power base, because nobody can compete with Dark Hand. You went to Campeche to make hell for your rival Vidales, and to escape the specter of Garrido Canabal.

Yes, my dear Onésimo, you did your best to get away. Unfortunately, a man can't hide from his destiny, because it resides in his soul— it's not a matter of geography. And your destiny, Onésimo, is that of serving the man who protected you and who continues to protect you from the vengeful hatred of Dark Hand Vidales. The person who protected you in the past, and can protect you in the future, your friend César León.

Let's see just how well I know you. You're politically neutral. You prefer obedience to debate. You would always rather subject yourself to real power than to the grass roots. And you have a tremendous virtue, Onésimo. You're a prehistoric politician, and for you public life has become a succession of ghosts that once were important but now are mere shadows in the platonic Cacahuamilpa grotto that is your memory. They're all "exes," aren't they? And you seem to think that they've been vaporized, that only you remain because nobody watches you as you watch all the presidential contenders turn into ghosts. Let's see, who were Martínez Manatou, Corona del Rosal, García Paniagua, Flores Muñoz, Sánchez Tapia, Rojo Gómez? Ghosts, my dear Onésimo, specters of the misty world of Mexican politics. Light one day, dark the next—and burned-out forever.

Now look me in the eye, Onésimo. I refuse to become a ghost. I've settled my debt with the past, if that's how you want to view things. Exiled, battered, mocked, vilified—but not defeated.

Don't be scared. Your ghost has returned and is going to make you pay your debts. I've been watching you, Onésimo—you feel perfectly secure because you go on playing the same old role and repeating the same old lines without realizing that the stage is different now, as is the playwright. We're in a new theater, and I want to be the star of the show again. You, my favorite friend, will be the man who puts my name back in the limelight.

Re-election? The unmentionable word of our political theater. Although perhaps it's not quite so unmentionable after all, what with the amendment of Article 59 of the constitution and the resurgence of the spirit of the 1917 constitutional congress: The possibility of reelecting senators and congressmen is what has allowed you, my Solon of Solons, to remain in Congress for ten years. Very well, now we must take this further: Allow for the president to be reelected. Reform that damn Article 83 and pave the way for my return.

Reforming the constitution takes time, you say? I know that. That's why we have to start now, nearly three years before the next election. Start raising the issue discreetly with the grass roots, the strongmen, governors, local legislators, businessmen, labor and agricultural leaders, intellectuals. We have to modernize the presidential succession just as we modernized the status of the legislators. Long live re-election.

Don't think I've been wasting my time doing crossword puzzles. I've already spoken to your nemesis, Dark Hand Vidales (though not his Nine Evil Sons), and he seems quite sympathetic to my ideas. He takes the long view, because he's the patriarch of a dynasty. But I must admit, Vidales is his own man. He doesn't like being in debt to anyone and I'm afraid—alas!—that he wants to use me, and knows how to use me, more than I know how to use him.

You, on the other hand, are my beloved Play-Doh. You can and will do what I want because you owe me everything. You have one political virtue that will give you staying power, Onésimo. You're ugly but not outrageously so. You're ugly, fat, dark, and short in the most typical sense. You're not even pockmarked or scarred. You could pass for a truck driver, or a rest room attendant, which is what you were when I met you. But since you're invisible you're not dangerous, and since you're not dangerous, you know how to placate and handle large groups of insecure men. And who could be more insecure than our vociferous legislators?

Oh, Onésimo. Let's work together. Remember, you can keep on pretending to serve the current president as you start to lay down the rules that will pave the way for me—and you, of course. The real problem of the presidential succession is not who, but how. You just keep on assuring the outgoing head of state, Lorenzo Terán, that you're going to protect his property, his privileges, his family. That's more than enough. Security is gold. In fact, it's priceless. We all dream of it. Let the incumbent and his people dream of it, too.

Do you realize what a massive banquet of vengeance is going to take place in three years? Who is exempt? Our shameless Tácito, with his closet full of skeletons? The irreproachable Andino, with a wife who cheats on him all day long with every pair of trousers that comes her way? The untouchable María del Rosario, cold as an iceberg but who, like any iceberg worth its name, keeps three-quarters of herself submerged, revealing only the tip of her true self and none of her secrets? The upstanding, energetic Bernal, whose love affair with the aforementioned is a mere screen behind which lies an even bigger secret that will soon come to light? My old predecessor under the arches in Veracruz, keeper of another secret that he holds on to like a domino player hanging on to that double-white? And then we have the mysterious wild card in this great game, the callow Nicolás Valdivia, hoisted up to the position of undersecretary of the interior, thanks to the efforts and good graces of María del Rosario, and who, consequently, has set his sights on becoming secretary so that when Terán leaves office he can become a presidential candidate. There isn't a single one of them, Onésimo, not one, I'm telling you, who isn't expendable. But let me give you three rules of good political conduct.

First, kill your political enemy and mourn him for a month.

Second, if you're going to be the executioner, make sure you're invisible.

And third, be afraid of the ghost of the political enemy you've killed.

In other words, my near-illiterate Onésimo, you'd do well to read a little play called *Macbeth*, and wait for the day when the woods of your crimes begin to move toward the castle of your power.

And don't rule out pure dumb luck. Like the kind that came my way the day three separate strikes broke out simultaneously on my watch and I crushed them, causing the death of thirteen strikers, but nobody realized because that was the day Axayácatl Pérez—the so-called Sultan of the Cha-cha-cha, and the most popular musician at the time— died. Everyone went to pay their respects to the great idol at the Gran León dance hall and then followed the coffin to the cemetery, and everyone forgot all about the nameless dead. The ones I was responsible for.

I write to you openly, Onésimo. I know that you're the very soul of discretion, simply because nobody believes in your disclosures and you're able to hide conveniently behind a veil of silence. Keep on doing that and keep me informed.

P.S. Don't worry about keeping this letter. As soon as you've finished reading, it will self-incinerate chemically. You can't copy it or show it to anyone, you bastard. Didn't you ever see *Mission Impossible?* The past is full of lessons for our present situation. Just ask yourself, in these dark days of our republic, how many letters, how many tapes, how many cassettes are being destroyed by their terrified recipients as soon as they read or listen to them? Just imagine. And don't burn your sweet little fingers with my message.

41

TÁCITO DE LA CANAL TO
MARÍA DEL ROSARIO GALVÁN

Most dignified lady, is it possible to blackmail the blackmailed? I wouldn't want to debase myself in your eyes, since I'm already so far down that you don't even deign to look at me. I, on the other hand, look up: up, up, and away. Farther up and farther away, I dare say, than the two of you—and by "the two of you" I'm referring to Bernal Herrera, interior secretary, and you, María del Rosario Galván, his lover and the mother of his child. Yes, you.

Allow me to quote from a classic: "In the midst of the broad expanses surrounding Berchtesgaden, isolated from the quotidian world, my creative genius produces ideas that shake the world. At these moments, I no longer feel my mortality, my ideas transcend the mind and are transformed into facts of enormous dimension."

Don't think me presumptuous for invoking the words of Adolf Hitler. Whatever you think about the German *Führer,* he got as high and went as far as he wanted. His fall was terrible, true enough, but to fall from such heights is, in and of itself, a victory.

In other words, if I don't know the limits of my own ambition, how will others know them? The question is one of proper timing, just as you yourself say in your letters to Bernal Herrera, which I take delight in reading before I go to sleep, as if they were a romantic advice column in a newspaper. Believe me, my dear lady, I know how to time things. Don't forget—I have power because I, more than anyone else, have *access*. Need I say more? Other people have access, too. But I have it before anyone else. And don't think I'm fooling myself. You and Herrera tell each other: "Tácito has access, but he's totally unpopular."

You, you diabolical little duo, lay traps for me. Very amusing ones, by the way. I know that you two are behind all those tributes in my honor carried out by powerful interest groups—unions and business associations where someone paid off by you praises me to the skies before some other crony of yours rips me apart. Nobody gets up to defend me. You think, don't you, that you've both flattered my vanity and mocked my pride. That you've undermined me.

Wrong. You've only strengthened me. Every humiliating act, every cheap shot you fire my way strengthens me, stokes my courage, steels my spirit. Would you like to know how good I am at resisting offense? The other day I received a visit from César León, the ex-president for whom I worked as a young aide, some ten years ago. He complained about the way people have treated him since leaving the Eagle's Throne, and accused me of mounting a smear campaign against him.

"I make you uncomfortable only because that's what the president wants," I replied.

"They aren't making me uncomfortable—they're hunting me down," said the ex, in a voice that was commanding, not plaintive.

"I simply work for the president."

"Were those his orders?"

"No, but I can predict what the president is thinking."

Madam, I want you and Herrera to see the risks I'm willing to take, so that you understand that I'm not easily offended. I'm hardly a sensitive, romantic fifteen-year-old girl.

So that you see the extremes of my endurance, my serenity, and my determination, I'm going to tell you a little story.

President Terán made it clear that he hadn't authorized what he considered to be my tactless treatment of ex-President León.

"But, Mr. President, I did it for you."

"I never asked you to do that, Tácito."

"Well, I thought it was obvious. . . ."

"Ah! So you think you can read my mind, is that it? And did you read my mind when I thought to myself, If Tácito does this again, he's sacked?"

I didn't have to read anyone's mind, my dear friend. I *knew* that the president would have to reprimand me pro forma, but that deep down he was glad that I'd done something he could never have done himself, or ordered me to do in any explicit way. I'm not called Tácito for nothing, you know. . . .

My distinguished friend: I know how to take risks. I know how to suffer humiliation without flinching. That is my strength. Do you think I don't know what you tell the president?

"Tácito is a sign of your weakness, Lorenzo. You don't need him. Only the weakest leaders need a favorite."

Oh, the court favorite! An adviser who exercises real power on behalf of a weak or harebrained monarch. Nicholas Perrenot de Granvelle for Charles V; Antonio Pérez for Philip II; the Duke of Lerma for Philip III, Philip IV, and the Count-Duke of Olivares. Some are more fortunate than others, some return from previous obsolescence, others betray and flee to enemy ranks disguised as women (Pérez, who only had to slap on an eye patch to imitate his one-eyed lover, the Princess of Eboli), while others drown in their own incompetence, even worse than that of the real monarch (Lerma), and still others are lionized for their success in running the empire.

Historical models, madam. Which of them will I resemble in the end? Oh, a favorite is as good as his protector—but also as good as his enemies. And to tell the truth, you and Bernal are completely useless to me.

"You are nothing but a flimsy reed disguised as a sword," our beloved interior secretary once said to me.

"And you are a sardine who thinks himself a shark," I replied.

"And me?" you dared to ask, petulantly.

"A noodle, nothing but a noodle."

You say that I'm a masochist who derives pleasure from recounting the humiliation I'm forced to endure in my service to the president. The simple truth is that I walk through the corridors of the presidential house thinking about these things, and I chastise myself for the vileness of my acts, but I congratulate myself because my despicable nature not only keeps me alive, it keeps me on top. Your friend, the so-called Seneca, has this to say about me: "Tácito could corrupt the devil."

And as I walk by, he murmurs, "There goes His Excellency the Evil One."

(He borrowed that one from Talleyrand, as you probably know since you were educated by the Frogs.)

But me? I put lead in my shoes so that no sudden gust of wind can carry me off into thin air. I endure everything, madam, because the man with the greatest endurance is the man who laughs last. And as you so carelessly say in your letter, I too could fall at any moment. But I warn both of you that I'll drag you down with me into the abyss.

You once said to me, "You're a bat, Tácito. Don't show your face by day."

I didn't dare confess that I admire you by night, madam, as you strip off your clothes with the light on. I was a gentleman.

"Certainly not, I'm nothing but a harmless little dove."

"That would make you the first hawk ever to turn into a dove."

"Nonsense. You and I are birds of the same feather."

Your comparisons are not very accurate, María del Rosario. You'd be a lot better off thinking of me as "the man in the mist." You'll see that I'm not so easy to catch, and that I can get in under unguarded doors. Like yours, and your lover Bernal Herrera's. Not to mention that of the wretched bastard born from your love affair and abandoned in an asylum for idiots.

42

BERNAL HERRERA TO
MARÍA DEL ROSARIO GALVÁN

Marucha, my Marucha, what's happened to you? I hardly recognize you, I hardly recognize myself. Why have you let a vengeful impulse get the better of you? Why haven't you controlled your passion? Why have you let your hormones hasten the plan that you and I agreed to, the two of us together, as ever, always so synchronized? You and I have never confused our loyalties. . . . Our political bond grew out of a carnal bond, and only now am I struck by how very different we were when we met and fell in love, before we paid the inevitable price of all romantic beginnings. It was in our nature, psychological and political, to doubt everything. We met. We were drawn to each other. But you doubted me, just as I doubted you. Until the night we shared a bottle of Petrus and realized that we loved each other even though we couldn't trust each other. We laughed (was it the wine, was it the lust, or was it the risk, without which no erotic encounter is possible?) and said to each other, "If we doubt everything, we'll understand each other perfectly."

I told you that a public figure should never stop doubting, even though that means living in perpetual anguish and insecurity without ever revealing it to anyone. That's the other rule, my Marucha. Doubt

and anguish leaven our public clarity and serenity. We've become professional politicians because we don't suppress our insecurity—that is,
our capacity for suspicion. Profession: politician. Party: suspicionist. In
other words, we make the most of our anguish so that our serene facade
is fed by human matter. We had a son, María del Rosario. A mongoloid
child or, to speak scientifically, a child with Down syndrome. We had to
make a choice. We could have lived together, looked after our child, and
sacrificed our political ambitions. Or you could have kept the child and
set me free, free and doubly condemned for having frustrated your ambitions and abandoned our child. Or we could have done what we did:
Put him in an institution, visit him now and then—increasingly less
often, let's be honest, increasingly less connected to that fateless fate,
increasingly worried that that defenseless creature with a face tender
and happy yet distant and indifferent, that child whose future holds
nothing but premature death, will wrench our lives away from us in exchange for nothing.

These were our reasons and we've kept the secret for fourteen years.
I warned you, María del Rosario, that I was never to receive the bills
from the institution at my office. I'm so scrutinized and besieged, I'm so
surrounded by spies working for my enemies (who are also your enemies, don't forget) that the least little oversight can and will be used
against me—and you.

So it has happened. Guess who saw the bill from the institution and
sniffed out the truth. Do you think I don't know? My friends claim to
despise Tácito—but I can only suspect they say the same thing to
him: "We are your friends. We despise Herrera. We're with you all the
way."

The schemes you and I have to use to test the people around us are
occasionally useful, usually useless, and always detrimental to one's
peace of mind. Eventually you decide that friends and enemies can con-
ceivably be friends among themselves, and, whether you want to or not,
you end up repeating that sentence by Stendhal you taught me, "How
difficult it is to bear this continued hypocrisy!"

How many times have you and I pondered together one of the central issues of political life: How should one treat the enemy?

Appease him?

Attack him outright?

Use violence, sever his head?

Defeat him first, only to honor him immediately afterward?

Betray him, without letting the ignominy of your victory come crashing down on your own head?

Chop off his head first, never forgetting, "That could have been my own head"?

Turn your defeated enemy into your protector and friend, erecting statues and plaques in his honor—as long as he's dead?

I'm very worried, María del Rosario. Your rash behavior violates the law of political justice. The political executioner should be invisible. By responding to your purely feminine, maternal emotions you've violated your own laws.

Tácito has forced our hand. He's forcing us to reveal our game, to publicly condemn his shady dealings with MEXEN. Now, more than ever, we have to be extremely careful as we consider our opportunities for attack. Tácito knows we know because you, my impatient friend, told him so without considering the consequences. You tasted the sweet nectar of victory before it was yours. Mistake number one. And Tácito, in his response, has very skillfully proven himself worthy of our own rule: In politics, never make your intentions clear. Act.

You know, Marucha, I'm a man who always has a court in session inside his head. The judge is a "we" and sometimes a plural "you." Today, the judge sitting in on our case is an "I-you" and he's telling me, "You trusted this woman with a secret that is the key to my success and my rival's defeat. But if this woman—my ally—reveals the secret, my rival will destroy both of us."

That's exactly what he's done by going to the press and telling them about our retarded son. Face it, understand it: I, the pre-candidate for the presidency and you, the most renowned female politician in the country, have been reduced to a pair of heartless parents, despicable and callous ogres, two cruel monsters. . . .

You can breathe easily, María del Rosario.

The president has personally contacted the heads of the five or six major media organizations to tell them:

"Make no mistake. The child is mine. The result of a very old love affair with María del Rosario Galván. Look in the mirror, each one of you, and tell me you don't have a secret love affair in your past. Kill the piece. I've never asked any of you for personal favors in the past. But I'm doing it now because it involves a lady. And, of course, as you well know, the office of the president."

"But, Mr. President, the person who leaked the news was Mr. De la Canal, your chief of staff. . . ."

"Ex-chief of staff. Mr. De la Canal handed in his resignation this afternoon."

"Mr. President, your interior secretary, Bernal Herrera, has just announced his resignation as well."

"That's right, gentlemen. Tácito de la Canal and Bernal Herrera have resigned from their governmental positions so they can devote themselves fully to their respective presidential campaigns. And I'd like to thank both of them for their tremendous service to their country and to me. I think this news is a bit more important than prying into my personal life."

"You're absolutely right, Mr. President."

"Let me reiterate my respect for the integrity and hard work of these two close aides who are leaving us now. They were trusted advisers who were loyal and steadfast to the end. That is the real news of the day."

"We'll treat this with the utmost discretion. Say no more."

"Thank you, gentlemen."

So proceed with a cold heart, María del Rosario. Remember who we have for a president, and let Tácito start his campaign before exposing the MEXEN scandal. Compose yourself for a few minutes, please, and remember what you said to me the day we decided to keep the boy a secret: "No. If I confess my disgrace, I'll lose all respect. And even love."

And I replied, "Never punish yourself for being happy. Don't forget, we got where we are because we never let feelings drag us down."

P.S. This tape will be delivered to you personally by Jesús Ricardo Magón, the young man who recently started working alongside your little protégé, the undersecretary of the interior, Nicolás Valdivia, who trusts him implicitly. Once you've listened to the cassette, destroy it, just as, as I know, you've destroyed all the other recorded messages I've sent you. And, María del Rosario, please don't make me doubt you as I did when I first met you. . . .

P.P.S. I've just had lunch in my office with the editor in chief of the newspaper *En Contra*, Reynaldo Rangel. I thought that the president had summoned the newspapers and (though televisions are now useless) TV magnates to his office to speak to them personally. But the meeting Rangel described to me sounded very bizarre. Host and guests were separated by a big curtain in the middle of the room. The president didn't allow his visitors to see him. He carried out the conversation from the other side of the curtain, but since they all know Lorenzo Terán's voice, and the conversation flowed normally, it didn't occur to anyone to doubt that it was him. In any event, even if they did have their doubts, it was in their interest to grant the president his request. . . . But there's definitely a mystery here. Destroy this tape, please. And I repeat, remember who you are, who we are, don't let your hormones get the better of you, and don't break your own rules. Let a cool head rule over fury.

43

CONGRESSMAN ONÉSIMO CANABAL TO CONGRESSWOMAN PAULINA TARDEGARDA

My distinguished colleague and loyal friend, you know how I go about these things. I believe scientists call it "mimicry," chameleons that change color to blend in with their environment. In other words, if they're sitting on a rock, they blend in with the rock, and if they are perched on a tree trunk they change their color accordingly. Well, my esteemed Paulina, I find myself at a crossroads. A path that is unpaved, muddy, mucky, a valley of slime, some might call it.

I won't bother to tell you what you already know. Or perhaps I'll tell you again so that you get the full picture.

The parties are divided. The president's party, the National Action Party, has splintered into the ultra-reactionary and clerical faction, the center Christian Democrats, and the left-wing faction that associates itself with liberation theology. The PRI, our Institutional Revolutionary Party, has split into eight groups. The far right, which wants order and repression. Dinosaurs who are gathering dust in the Museum of National Political History. Neoliberal technocrats who keep alive the flame of their goddess Macroeconomics. Nationalists who believe that the reassertion of sovereignty is the PRI's raison d'être. Then, the populists who promise everything and deliver nothing. Not to mention the factions of agrarians, unionists, and old bureaucrats dating back to the corporate culture of the Cárdenas era.

Take a look around you. Instead of the great steamroller of the once "invincible" PRI, we're now facing eight mini-parties in search of lost unity.

And then, on the left, we have the Green parties, but they're only as green as the dollar bill; the Social Democrats following the European model; the neo-Cardenistas who want to go back in time to 1938; the Marxists of the Leninist and Trotskyist persuasions, and Marxists who read the young Karl Marx and proclaim that Marxism is a form of humanism.

And don't think I've forgotten about the indigenous factions, or the strung-out extremists—both sides, anarchists and fascists.

My method for controlling this circus in Congress, as you know, is to pretend not to notice anything and wear my dunce cap as much as possible. I make myself invisible. So that nobody pays me the slightest attention.

As for the tactics of our president and his treasury secretary Andino Almazán, I know them like the back of my hand. First they present the measures that they know our "confetti Congress" will reject because they offend popular or nationalist sensibilities and can be denounced as neoliberal, reactionary, or antinationalist laws: taxes on books, drugs, and food, privatization. . . . And then, to avoid being taken for lazy slobs (if you weren't a lady I might use another word), Congress goes ahead and approves bills that the executive would never put forward for fear of offending the wealthy—progressive taxation, higher income and capital gains taxes, etc. You know, the things that really make money for the government, not the tax on aspirins or those Isabel Allende books I know you devour.

That, then, is how you and I manage our unmanageable Congress. That has become our rule, and you are my greatest ally because you're a woman, because you're austere to a fault (forgive me, I know you like dressing like a nun, I'm not criticizing you for that), and because you're from Hidalgo, an improbable state if there ever was one simply because people seem to have forgotten that it exists.

And now, my austere and improbable lady, I need you more than ever to organize the legislative chaos and to face up to the pressures that will soon be upon us.

First of all is the threat of an armed uprising. I have very good reason to believe (as the bolero says, "Stop asking me questions, let me imagine. . . .") that Cícero Arruza is running around spreading panic among officials, local strongmen, as well as the top general himself, Bon Beltrán, or whatever his name is. I can't spell that name unless I have it in front of me—foreign languages have never been my strong suit. Anyway, Paulina, Arruza wants to declare President Lorenzo Terán unfit to govern on the basis of "grave shortcomings," as stipulated in Article 86 of the constitution. And since the majority of Congress considers Terán incompetent, the scheme might just work. The only catch is that Congress would then have to choose the appropriate acting president to complete Terán's six-year term.

I have no idea who Cícero and his allies have in mind for this. But who are his allies? Paulina, you must find out if the strongmen and the defense secretary with the unpronounceable German name are, in fact, joining forces with General Arruza in his attempt to stage a military coup, because that, in the end, is his objective.

The other person breathing down my neck is our ex-president César León, and he's as shady a character as they get. He's also trying to manipulate Congress into declaring the president incompetent, but he refuses to reveal who he wants to replace Terán, finish out the rest of his term, and call for elections—that is, only after amending Article 83 so that former presidents (such as César León) can be reelected by the time those 2024 elections come around.

Be very careful, Paulina, because the ex-president is a sly snake in the grass who knows every trick in the book and is fueled by an ambition that knows no limits. Go to the old ex-president, who sits around all day playing dominoes under the arches in Veracruz—visit him, see if you can get any information from him. Don't even try to seduce César León, because he only lets himself get taken for a ride by centerfolds. Although, who knows, he's so lecherous that even you might strike him as a sort of Venus from Hidalgo. I say that with all due respect, Paulina.

But to go back to the old man in Veracruz, the most I've ever gotten out of him—so far, but you know better than anyone that I'm stubborn as a mule (my enemies call me pigheaded and my allies persistent)—is this:

"Mexico already has a legitimate president," the Old Man says.

"Of course, Lorenzo Terán," I reply.

"No, another one, in case Terán resigns or dies."

"Resignation? Death? What are you talking about, Mr. President?"

"I'm talking about fucking legitimacy."

(Excuse me, Paulinita, all due respect to you.)

"That's all?"

"That's all, Onésimo."

You know that the Old Man is half mummy, half sphinx. And, since I don't get anything but riddles out of him, I put on my little holy innocent face and turn to the cabinet in search of advice. They all tell me the same thing, with their own particular ifs, ands, and buts:

"The constitution's clear on that," says Herrera of the interior office. "If we're left without a president during the last four years of his term (as would be the case now), Congress names an acting president to finish the term and then calls for new elections. That's the law, and it's crystal clear."

"The constitution could be changed, and we could have a vice president," Tácito de la Canal remarks. "But that would require the vote of two thirds of all present congressmen and the approval of the majority of the state legislature. How long do you think that might take?"

He scratches his bald head and answers his own question.

"One, two, three years. It's irrelevant to our situation."

"Why don't you have a vice president like we do?" the U.S. ambassador, Cotton Madison, asks me. "Kennedy gets shot, Johnson takes over. Nixon resigns, Ford takes over. No problem."

I try to explain to him that, during the nineteenth century, when we had vice presidents in Mexico, these fine, upstanding characters spent most of their time undermining and overthrowing the presidents they served, starting with the revolt of Nicolás Bravo against Guadalupe Victoria in 1827. And then Santa Anna, "the immortal leader from Cempoala," according to our national anthem, struck out against his own vice president, Valentín Gómez Farías, even though old "Fifteen Nails" (that's the one-legged Santa Anna, Paulina) actually managed to overthrow his own government in the end, a maneuver that the sinister Hugo Chávez, admirer that he is of Bolívar, imitated to perfection not twenty years ago.

I could give you a laundry list of disloyal vice presidents—Anastasio Bustamante against Vicente Guerrero, for one. And I could also tell you about generals who preferred to strike out against their leaders rather than defend the country from foreign invaders, which is what happened with the traitor Paredes Arrillaga during the war against the Americans. That's a depressing story, no doubt, but it's one worth keeping in mind, my discreet friend, if you want to keep all the cards in your hand and don't want to be surprised in the middle of a siesta, like Santa Anna was by the gringos at the Battle of San Jacinto, which cost us Texas.

As I said before, you're going to want to know the opinions of local bosses like Cabezas in Sonora, Delgado in Baja California, Maldonado in San Luis, and the fearsome Vidales in Tabasco. Without a doubt they'll lie to you.

Sonora: "Our problem is creating assembly plants, not conspiracies," Cabezas will say.

Baja California: "We've got enough problems with the waters of the Colorado and dealing with the drug traffic in Tijuana," Delgado will say.

San Luis Potosí: "The only thing we're concerned with around here is protecting foreign investment," Maldonado will say.

Tabasco: "In this state, the buck stops with me," Vidales will say.

So they say, so they say, so they say. . . . Lies, all of it. But they won't (forgive me) try to seduce you. No. Let us, then, interpret the lies in reverse to find out the truth. The seduction will not take place because, in the first place, let's just say you inspire more respect than that magistrate's wife, doña Josefa Ortiz de Domínguez, heroine of our independence, and secondly (I'll say it again) because you're from Hidalgo, and Hidalgo's a state that doesn't register on Mexico's political radar.

Keep me informed, my dear and respected friend.

44

NICOLÁS VALDIVIA TO
MARÍA DEL ROSARIO GALVÁN

I'm back because you asked me. I'm back in Veracruz, in the port's main plaza under the arches. I'm back in the Café de la Parroquia to meet the Old Man again.

The famous déjà vu. The parrot perched on the Old Man's shoulder. This time the Old Man is not wearing his bow tie. Today he's wearing a *guayabera*. It seems appropriate given the sticky, humid, suffocating heat beneath an umbrella of black clouds heralding a storm that refuses to break and clear the melancholy tropical air. The Old Man's still there, with his coffee in front of him and his dominoes in an asymmetrical ivory pattern on the table.

I think he's taking his afternoon siesta. I'm wrong. The minute I stop in front of him, he opens an eye. One single dark-ringed eye. The other one stays shut. The parrot shouts, or chirps, or does whatever it is parrots do: "NO RE-ELECTION! EVERY VOTE COUNTS!"

The Old Man opens the other eye and gives me a dark look. He doesn't hide it. He doesn't want to hide it. He wants me to know that he knows. He wants me to know that he knows I'm no longer the novice that came to visit him in January. He wants me to know that he knows I'm the former undersecretary now in charge of the office of the interior because Bernal Herrera has resigned as interior secretary to become a pre-candidate for the presidency. He wants me to know that he knows that I'm now the head of domestic affairs in our country.

Nevertheless, I feel like I'm meeting someone who behaves as if nothing at all has happened in Mexico since 1950. He acts and speaks as if we lived in the past. As if the bonfires of the Revolution were still burning. As if Pancho Villa were still on his horse. As if all the country's generals didn't drive around in Cadillacs. As if the Mexican Revolution (as was acknowledged half a century ago) hadn't ended in the suburban Lomas de Chapultepec.

And nevertheless (oh, the endless number of *cependants* I hang from your lovely ears, my wise lady), I can't fail to notice that the Old Man is aware of my political youth—interior secretary at thirty-five—and that he wants to warn me, with his Veracruz wisdom plucked from Lampedusa's *The Leopard*, that *plus ça change, plus c'est la même chose*, that I shouldn't harbor dreams of radical change, miraculous transformation, etc. That there's a permanent substratum, a bedrock, not only of Mexican politics but of politics *tout court*.

Tiens, for some reason (our secret French-speaking alliance? An evocation of the shared world of our studies? A form of code, now that French is out of use?) I use French expressions that couldn't be farther from the world of the Old Man Under the Arches.

"So is this what Mexico's much-vaunted democratic transition has come to?" he asks me without moving a muscle of his famous mummy face.

"What do you mean, Mr. President?"

"Ah," he says, his smile falling apart like a mask made of sand. "I forgot that you studied with the Frogs. Monsiour le Presidan!"

He pauses to sip his coffee.

"You know, sometimes, in an effort to keep up my education (since they say education never ends), I play dominoes here in the plaza with a group of Mexican intellectuals who were educated in Germany. Chema Pérez Gay, for example, meets me here, and I say to him, 'Talk to me in German, even if I don't understand a damn thing you say. I like that guttural noise. It has an authoritarian ring to it. And anyway it makes me feel philosophical.' Well, the last time Pérez Gay was here, he said, 'When the Weimar Constitution opened the door to democracy in Germany for the very first time in 1919, after centuries of authoritarian rule, the Germans stopped wide-eyed at the threshold, like peasants invited into a castle. . . .' "

There was no mimicry in the old man's words. He maintained his somber, penetrating gaze, the circles deep and dark beneath his eyes.

"Well, let me just say that the same thing has happened in Mexico. We've stood here wide-eyed, not knowing what to make of democracy. From the Aztecs to the PRI, we've never played that game here."

"Did they do things better before—I mean, in your day?"

"People were given some measure of security. There were rules, and everybody knew them. Everything was predictable. The public was spared the anguish of making their own uncertain decisions. I invented the institution of 'the sealed envelope.' All it took was a sealed envelope with signed instructions from me. Whenever a governor, a congressman, a local president received the sealed envelope he did exactly as I said."

He stopped, looking like a pirate about to attack a galleon from the Indies filled with Spanish gold.

" 'Propose the candidacy of X.' The rest was easy. The candidate I'd selected, the candidate in the sealed envelope, garnered general and widespread support. Woe to the strongman who dared dissent. Woe to the rebellious governor. Woe to the congressman with the independent spirit."

He licked his crooked teeth.

"They would be eliminated from politics forever. And if any of them dared protest my decision, I'd just remind him, 'You've had your pleasure. Now crawl back to the hole you came from. I'm telling you for the sake of your health.' "

Is it possible that someone could deliver such terrible threats so agreeably? Clearly, steely resolve and serenity went together. Lesson learned, María del Rosario.

The Old Man pressed down on his dentures.

"Envelopes sealed, ballot boxes stuffed in advance, carousel voting, and other methods for sending voters from polling site to polling site, raccoons running all the electoral fraud—we performed whatever alchemy was necessary to win an election in advance with double, even triple votes. And in the end there were more votes for the PRI than there were registered voters, what with all the citizens we dragged out of the cemeteries, all the voting booths we stole, and all the dissenting votes that were destroyed—if and when it was called for, of course. And all this, Mr. Valdivia, was presided over by his sovereign majesty the president who, from the Eagle's Throne, declared to his designated successor, 'You will be president.' "

The parrot said, "I swear to uphold the laws . . ." and then fell silent as if expecting the Old Man to gaze at him with affection, the green, yellow, red, and blue bird perched atop his shoulder, the shoulder of a political pirate.

". . . the laws of the republic," the Old Man solemnly intoned.

"The written laws?"

"The unwritten ones, Mr. Valdivia. Think of how easy it was. The unwritten rules of authoritarianism were clear. Just look at the current uncertainty and the chaos it has caused. How could I not feel nostalgic for the calm old days of our benevolent PRI dictatorship?"

Before I could even respond he interrupted himself, raising a stiff finger in the air to keep me quiet.

"In reality, our vices were virtues. But let's just say that I've resigned myself to change. I always knew that the system would come to an end one day. Still, the question remains: What will we replace it with?"

"Everything was better in the past," I said with melancholy.

"Yes, despite some pretty stupid politicians."

"Who were the wise ones, then?"

"Not who, my friend, but how."

"How, then?"

"Everyone kills fleas in their own way, Valdivia. Excessive ambition either fails, or else it comes at a very high price. Some men have made it to the presidency feeling that Mexico owed it to them and then relinquished their positions feeling that Mexico didn't deserve them, and that's why they feel they deserve to return to power one day."

"Are you thinking of someone in particular?"

"I'm thinking of myself. I did nothing to get to the Eagle's Throne. That was my strong point. I got there with no strings attached, no favors to pay back."

"A process of elimination of sorts?" I dared to ask, with only a hint of impudence. He didn't pick up on it.

"I got there just like Jesus," he said, extraordinarily still, like an icon. "How many prophets and pseudo-messiahs were on the loose in Judea just like the son of Mary?"

Then, out of nowhere, he began to sing a line from an old Spanish *zarzuela:*

"*Ay va, ay va, ay vámonos para Judea. . . .*"

At that, the parrot picked up on the tune in his shrill voice. "*Ay ba, ay ba, ay Babilonia que marea . . .*"

I ignored these eccentricities.

"Yes, but that isn't the rule, Mr. President."

"Shut your mouth! Each president creates his own reality, but since the law against re-election forces him into retirement, this reality fades away and historical legend takes its place."

He looked as if he were swallowing bile. Even the circles under his eyes seemed to be turning green.

"What happens? The ex-president is left with no power, but he's still surrounded by ass-kissers. He doesn't have to fool the people anymore. Now his aides want to fool him. They offer him the temptation of revenge. They intoxicate him with the idea that he's incomparable, a cross between Napoleon and Disraeli."

"*¿Dónde vas con mantón de Manila?*" the parrot began to sing, and the Old Man whacked him so hard that the poor bird nearly went crashing to the floor.

"It's like the old story about the whale and the elephant. The thing is, the poor slob ends up treating his allies like he treated his enemies. It's a waste of time. Destroying them isn't worth the effort. A lot of energy for nothing."

He let out a sigh that the parrot didn't dare respond to.

"Better to be alone and respected, even if they think I'm dead."

There was a pregnant pause, as the Anglo-Saxons would say.

"Look at me here, drinking coffee and playing dominoes. I escaped the sad fate of most ex-presidents. I escaped the vicious cycle. And do you know why, Valdivia? Because I didn't become president believing I'd be getting into bed with my own statue."

He smiled as the parrot, having taken his punishment, sat once more on his shoulder.

"Don't let that one get out. It's the truth."

"Mr. President, you were famous for shielding yourself with silence, for answering without speaking, for elevating the gesture into a sign of political communication, for turning the elliptical response into an art form, and the authority of your gaze into gospel."

I looked him in the eye.

"I don't want to waste time, Mr. President. I've come here for your guidance through the labyrinth of the presidential succession."

Did I glimpse affection in his expression? Was he grateful for my attention, my respect, my interest? The look in his eyes seemed to say, I've known the depths of misery and disaster, and I'm the only one who left the palace without being disillusioned . . . because I didn't have any illusions in the first place.

"I never became disillusioned because I didn't have any illusions in the first place," he said, uncannily echoing my thoughts.

At that moment María del Rosario, your words came into my mind like a flash of lightning: "You will be president, Nicolás Valdivia."

And I felt dizzy, as if I were on the edge of a cliff, seeing myself reflected in the Old Man. Was that how I'd end up as well, in a café in Veracruz, playing dominoes with a busybody parrot perched on my shoulder?

The vision sent me into a cold sweat in the middle of the sticky heat of the Gulf of Mexico.

The Old Man brought me back to reality.

"Do you think I didn't know what kind of people I'd have to deal with as president? Damn it, Valdivia, the only cure for a hunchback is death, and in politics there are legions of them, all crooked, all of them incurable. They never straighten out, not even when they die."

I was uncomfortable now. I scratched my back, I couldn't help it—the Old Man's tone of voice was so solemn, so gloomy, even fatal.

"As far as I'm concerned," he went on, "a politician should be like a Japanese pilot: He should carry pistols but no parachute."

He made an unusual gesture—a cinematic flourish straight out of an old Tyrone Power movie.

"Between the two extremes of Quasimodo and the kamikaze, I chose to be Zorro. The masked man everyone believes to be perfect."

Did he sigh? I placed my two hands on the back of my chair.

The Old Man noticed and in a compassionate voice said, "Don't rush. I haven't breathed my last sigh yet. Oh, if you only knew how many times I've been taken for dead!"

I leaned forward. I took my chance.

"Don't die on me without telling me first, Mr. President."

"Tell you what?" the parrot said, as if he'd been preparing for that question all his life.

I had to laugh.

"The secret that you're keeping."

He didn't move an inch. Unexpected or not, my question did not disturb him.

"Nobody should know everything," he said after a long pause. "It's not good for the health."

"Don't you mean, 'Nobody *can* know everything?' Isn't that more to the point?"

"How straight you are, Mr. Valdivia. Get real. No, it's not a question of *can*. It's a question of *should*."

"But we're running out of time. I'm pleading with you now, like the young man you once were. Don't send me back to Mexico City empty-handed."

"I was never young," he replied with a hint of bitterness. "I had to suffer and learn a lot before I became president. Otherwise I would have suffered and learned during my presidency and that would have been at the country's expense."

He looked at me with unconcealed scorn.

"Who do you think you are?"

He paused.

"You have to have lost a lot in order to be someone before and after you wield power."

"But sometimes it's the country—not the powerful leader—that loses with all that secrecy, intrigue, and personal ambition. And that's what I'd call a catastrophe," I said in the most dignified voice I could muster.

"Catastrophes are good," said the Old Man, licking his lips like the Cheshire cat. "They reinforce the people's stoicism."

"Aren't they stoic enough?" I asked, somewhat exasperated by now.

The Old Man looked at me with a mixture of pity, sympathy, and impatience.

"Look: Everyone thinks they can lock me up in an old age home. They underestimate my craftiness. But my craftiness is what makes me indispensable. The chitchat I leave to the parrot. You're here because I know something everyone wants to know, information that could be critical for the presidential succession."

He narrowed his eyes diabolically, María del Rosario.

"Do you think I'm going to spill the beans and let myself get thrown out in the garbage? Are you an idiot or are you just pretending to be?"

"I respect you, Mr. President."

"What I said stands. I'm keeping my mouth shut."

"Believe me, your honesty in no way diminishes the respect I have for you."

He laughed. He dared to laugh.

"Comrade Valdivia, I believe in the law of political compensation. What I give with one hand, I take away with the other. If I give you what you want, what will I take away in exchange?"

Disquieted, I said, "Are you asking what you can expect from me?"

His response, lightning fast, was, "Or from the people who sent you here."

"My protection," I murmured, realizing my stupid mistake as soon as the words came out.

The Old Man who never laughed stopped laughing but didn't stop smiling.

"Never believe in the improbable. Only believe in the incredible."

"But you're offering me neither the improbable nor the incredible. You're offering me nothing."

"Oh my goodness. What if I told you Mexico needs hope? Someone to create absolute ideals and relative realities? To fuel the imagination?"

"I'd think you were fooling me."

"See? And yet I'm telling you the truth, the whole truth. And I'm also giving you the key to my secret, just in case you really do want to know what it is."

"You're giving me a pebble, and I want the whole rock, Mr. President."

"A pebble thrown into the water creates a tiny ripple, but the tiny ripple makes waves."

Pause. Sigh. Resignation.

"And in the end, all those waves are the same."

In an instant he recovered the energy that had been sucked out of him, as if the Gulf of Mexico were a giant drain. And that afternoon, perhaps it was. On my first visit, the Old Man had talked of the tide of invaders that had entered Mexico through Veracruz. But tides have to go in, taking some of the land with them, land that's used up, no longer wanted or needed. What would the tides of the gulf carry away with them now? Everything, I thought, if the Old Man let them. Nothing if he was stubborn enough to stop the ebb and flow of the sea.

"The mist of conspiracy hovers over Mexico and no man's head is higher than the air he breathes," he said, and for the first time I detected a dreamy note in his voice—perhaps incongruous and rather unjustified, but dreamy nonetheless. Then he looked away toward the docks, the castle, the water. . . .

"Polluted air, sir."

"I'm going to tell you one thing," said the Old Man, his face and tone of voice back to normal now. "If you want to breathe easy, if you want to cut through some of that fog and put an end to all those conspiracies, you need to give the country back its hope."

"Again?" I asked, resigned.

"I'm talking about a symbol," the ex-president said, his voice growing stronger. "Cheated, lost, corrupted, this country can only be saved if it finds the symbol that can deliver it the promise of new hope."

"But for a long time now we've given the people new hope—every six years, in fact—and then they lose it. Do you have the key to eternal hope?"

He went silent for some time because he was thinking. Out of courtesy I tried not to look at him. That was when I noticed that the vultures were no longer flying over Ulúa, and I wondered if I'd noticed them in January when I made my first visit to the Old Man. The sense that the vultures weren't circling overhead may have been something I'd felt before and that now, as if life were a dream, I was feeling for the first time, having only dreamed it before. Or was it the other way around? Did I feel it first and then dream about it afterward?

"There once was a cat with feet made of rags. . . ." the parrot interrupted, chirping away.

"A symbol that will offer new hope."

"Again?"

Silence.

I dared to speak for him.

"You've just said it. Mexico needs a symbol. Have you got one?"

He nodded his graying head. His receding hairline lent a noble air to his features. He looked up.

"Haven't you wondered why the vultures aren't flying over Ulúa today?"

Now I was the one to respond without words. I shook my head.

"I had a very foolish and tactless government minister working under me. My advice to him was this: 'Be careful. You've been accused.' "

"Of what, Mr. President?"

"Of telling the truth."

He went silent, María del Rosario.

I think I understood, María del Rosario.

"The moment still hasn't arrived?"

"No. Not yet."

"What message shall I take to the capital?"

"When the coyotes howl, howl along with them. You don't want people thinking you're a cat."

"Do you want me to tell you again?" the parrot chanted.

"Thank you, Mr. President. Is that all?"

"No. One more thing. But it's for your ears only, Valdivia."

"I'm listening."

"My only regret is that I know every last story, and yet I'll never know the full story."

He turned to look at San Juan de Ulúa.

"I'll summon you again for a visit, young man. When the moment arrives."

The sun-drenched palm trees were nowhere to be seen in the deep circles around his eyes.

"Meanwhile, I can offer you the title for a novel that has yet to be written."

I waited for him to speak.

"The Man in the Nopal Mask."

45

GENERAL CÍCERO ARRUZA TO
GENERAL MONDRAGÓN VON BERTRAB

General, if anyone respects hierarchy it is I, your loyal servant Cícero Arruza. Forgive me for being insistent. This time I'm sending my faithful assistant Mauser with a tape for you of my voice so that you can hear out loud my sincerity and my anguish. Now is the time, my general. Things are boiling over and this is our opportunity for action, to make the things you and I want happen. The one thing we can't have is a power vacuum, but we're heading straight for that cliff. Ask yourself this: When was the last time the president was seen in public? I can tell you, I've been keeping track. The beginning of January, when he read his address and got us into this mess with the gringos. For three months we haven't seen the so-called head of state's face! If that isn't the famous power vacuum we've all talked about, it's a hell of a hole. Holes, holes, everything in life is holes. Crawl out of a hole, get into a hole, shit down a hole, stick it up someone's or let them stick it up ours . . . I'm going to be frank with you, General. Either we act now or they're going to stick it to us both. You're waffling, I can tell. I can tell you've even distanced yourself a little from your loyal subordinate Cícero Arruza. What's the matter? Isn't it kind of late to suddenly discover the kind of man I am? Forgive the frankness. I'm back where I was, at a bar, General—you know what they say, we only win battles in the bar and in bed. Do you remember that man from Tabasco, González Pedrero, who made our lives hell with "the dart of truth"? Wasn't it González Pedrero who said that the Mexican Revolution may have left a million men dead, but that they'd died in bars during shoot-outs and not on the battlefield? I tell you that just to remind you: You know who I am, you know where I come from, and you know what I'm capable of. And I'm reminding you because I want you to be certain of one thing: Put the violence on my tab. The deaths are on me. . . . I'm not going to hide anything from you, General, I want you to know who you're dealing with so that you won't be cheated on like the husband in the song who asks, "Whose gun is this? Whose watch, whose horse whinnying in the stable?" . . . Sorry about my voice. Whenever I drink I always feel the urge to sing. . . . Remember who's on your side. . . . I once told you, didn't I, how much I miss real violence—not those little exercises where we bust up meetings by letting loose mice or pouring piss down from the balconies. Let me remind you of my credentials, for your peace of mind. As regional commander in various states of our union, General, I finished off the malcontents as well as the rebels in a single stroke of pure genius. I disposed of the opposition leaders in Nayarit by slipping Benzedrine into their rum and Cokes while they were celebrating some supposed electoral victory. They've got nothing to celebrate anymore. The opposition candidate in Guadalajara disappeared quietly at a building site for the metro. Building site, my ass, General. More like a grave site . . . I eliminated those annoying university students ten years ago by locking them up in a laboratory full of infected rabbits. And people don't mess around when it comes to hunger, you know. . . . As for those rebels in Chiapas, I ordered them to be shot in a laundromat in Tuxtla Gutiérrez just because I knew the blood would contrast so well against those white sheets. . . . When the Yucatán tried to secede from the federation again, backed up by official and popular support, I made the whole bureaucracy disappear (don't ask me where they ended up), and then I invited the townspeople to visit the empty government offices. There wasn't a soul there.

"Take your places at the desks," I ordered them. "Sit down and start working. Don't you get it? The people who used to work here aren't coming back."

When the umpteenth Zapatista uprising broke out, this time in Guerrero, I ordered the troops to paint crosses on two out of every three doors in Chilpancingo, with a sign reading, "Here died everyone who opposed General Cícero Arruza and the government."

Did you know all this already, General? Maybe yes, maybe no. It doesn't matter. Now that the alcohol's loosened my tongue, I want to make it real clear who you're dealing with, I want you to know I'm not trying to fool you. You can count on me for laundry operations like the one in Tuxtla Gutiérrez, and you can keep your white gloves on— I won't let anyone get them dirty. *[Long silence, followed by a mariachi yelp.]* Aee-aee-aee, this is Cícero Arruza here, one hell of a general who knows how to give his enemies a nugget of shit and pass it off as a hard candy. Enemies, me? You've got to be fucking kidding. Erase that, Mauser, General Bonbon's a decent man, we don't want to offend him. . . . Mauser, you've got to learn to tell the difference between vulgar louts like you and me, and queers like General Bonbon.

"Forgive your enemies," the Bishop of Huamantla once said to me.

"I can't," I told him, dead serious. "I haven't got any left. I've killed them all."

Have you ever seen my photos of the men I've shot? There's one that I keep above my bed. It's famous. A rebel ringleader just before getting it. He's got his cowboy hat on. Cigarette dangling from his lips. One leg in front of the other. Thumbs tucked into his belt loops. And smiling from ear to ear. Waiting for the grim reaper with the biggest smile you've ever seen. That's how I want to die, General, now that I'm five sheets to the wind I'm telling you because you're like my brother, my soul brother and my comrade-in-arms, that's how Cícero Arruza wants to die, laughing his head off in front of a firing squad of traitors and sons of bitches. *[Another long pause in the recording.]* Oh, General, I've never had a shred of luck in life—when's it going to get better? That depends on you. You give the order and I'll carry it out. Easy as anything. The police take the blame for the crimes—that way we keep the army in the clear. I swear to you, I know how to carry out orders to the limit. Not for nothing people say I've got the face of a man with no friends. I've got no friends! Not even you, General. I obey you. You're my superior. But you're not my friend. That wouldn't be good for you. I assure you. Being my friend would be hazardous to your health. On the other hand, you can count on me for loyalty and solid knowledge of the territory I'm heading to. I know I have the support of people who count. Governors and local strongmen who exercise the power that our democratic president refuses to exercise because he thinks society is capable of governing itself. Yeah, right. Hell will freeze over first. Mexicans only understand brute force. Cabezas in Sonora. Quintero in Tamaulipas. Delgado in Baja California. Maldonado in San Luis. They're all sick of the dumbass democratic government and are ready to join forces with us. . . . I can't speak for the big man in Tabasco because you can never tell how that one's going to react. One day he promises his full support and then the next day he goes back on his word. Just so you can see I'm not hiding things from you, General. And as for all those other candidates jockeying for the succession, they'll be scared shitless when they see that the hard core, guys with the military leading them on, have beaten them at their own game and are ready to take control in the interest of national security. I've already got ex-President César León's public funeral all set up. No, no, I'm not going to kill him; you don't announce crimes, you commit them. For the scheming César León I'm going to organize a funeral procession that will go past his window at noon. To see if he gets the hint, you know. As for Bernal Herrera, we can just let him be. He's like President Terán's double, and nobody wants a second act in this play. As for Tácito de la Canal, we've got no choice but to eliminate him. That bald bastard knows too many secrets that could damage too many people. The new kid at the interior office, Valdivia, is wet behind the ears. I doubt if he's got any underarm hair yet. I'll fix him. Right on, man! And as for that gossip María del Rosario Galván, I've got a little surprise in store for

her. They say she likes a fuck, don't they? Well, she's really going to
have her fun when twenty of my men break into her house, destroy everything, and then fuck her, all of them. Let's see, who've I left out,
General? Ah yes, the treasury secretary. He's going to be our candidate
for interim president, and I really mean interim because he won't last
more than two days on the Eagle's Throne before he turns it all over to
the armed forces—I mean the junta, General, presided over by you,
with my patriotic support to reestablish order, restore people's sense of
security, reinstate the death penalty. And we'll chop off the thief's
hands, the rapist's penis, the attacker's legs, and the kidnapper's eyes if
we have to because that's priority number one in this country—safety
and crime, and that's what drives our patriotism, the safety of our people, not personal ambition, and that's why we'll get unanimous support. The days of impunity are over. No more robberies. No more
kidnappings. No more murder—except for the ones you and I consider
necessary. Order, order, order, order. My wish . . . is for . . . natural
death . . . to no longer exist. *[Fading voice, garbled words.]* General,
only stupid people play it safe . . . ooh, I know I'm a full-blooded Mexican because, I'm telling you, for me every night is Independence Day.
[Loud burp.] And don't think any less of me because I've been straight
with you. And answer me quickly, will you? We have to move *now*.
We've been down a long road together, General. Answer me. You always just sit there listening and you never say a damn thing. I understand your silence to mean alliance and agreement. Shh, no flies are
going to get into my mouth . . . just tequila, pal. . . . Forgive me, General. Don't make me think you're having second thoughts about our
plan. Don't make me feel like a prickly old nopal that's ignored unless
it's got fruit. . . . And you know something? Have you ever killed a
man? After the first one, the rest are easy. . . .

46

NICOLÁS VALDIVIA TO
JESÚS RICARDO MAGÓN

My love, this letter goes out without a signature but you know who it's for and who it comes from . . . what a lovely verb, "to come." It can be conjugated in every imaginable form. . . . I'm leaving Veracruz today and I'll be waiting for you at the Hotel Mocambo. Don't let it faze you. It's a kind of Marienbad-on-the-Gulf. A hotel with a hundred years of solitude behind it, inhabited by the ghosts of its golden days circa 1940. Picture it. Eight decades ago. It's like a white labyrinth, *délabré*. You go in and out without knowing where you're going. Just getting to your bedroom is a delicious adventure—or it will be if you're there waiting for me. I've reserved separate rooms, but I can hardly bear the time and distance that keep me from your cinnamon body, like a living tropical statue, replete with jungles and flowers, blackness and sun, secret places and wide open fields. . . .

I don't think I need to remind you that I love women with equal intensity because in women I see and desire the one thing I'm not. But I also love you, without denying my heterosexual nature, because I see myself in you. In women I see the other and I find that equally alluring. In you I see myself and my passion is enhanced by melancholy. Yes, we're men, we're young, but I'll grow old before you and in that sense,

I know that when I make love to you I'm giving you what's left of my youth. I entrust you with my youth. I love you just as Saint John of the Cross said one should love, unrestrainedly repeating the word "beauty."

> Let us, through this exercise of love I have professed, arrive at seeing one another in your beauty, where, being one and the same in beauty, we see the both of us in your beauty, possessing your singular beauty; such that, looking at one another, each of us may see in the other his own beauty, since one and the other are both your beauty, and I am engulfed by your beauty, and in that way, I will see you in your beauty, and you will see me in your beauty, and then I will appear as you in your beauty, and you will appear as me in your beauty, and my beauty will be your beauty and your beauty will be my beauty; and that way I will be you in your beauty, and you will be me in your beauty; because your beauty will be my beauty, and that is how you and I will see one another in your beauty. . . .

You are not Narcissus' mirror. You are the pool in which the two of us swim naked. You seal my wound. You are my delicate wound. I have loved only one man in my life, and it is You.

P.S. Don't even think of going into the water at Mocambo. There are sharks off the coast and the nets a few meters from the shore often have holes in them. They could give you quite a scare! Remember, the good thing about sharks is that they never stay still. If a shark stops moving, he sinks to the bottom and dies there. Do you think the shark dreams while moving around like that? Ah, what a question, my love. And don't walk along the beach. There isn't any sand. Just mud. Wait for me with clean feet. And throw this letter to the sharks. If they eat it, perhaps they'll learn something. They'll learn to love. Did you know that sharks only fuck once in their sad lives?

47

XAVIER "SENECA" ZARAGOZA
TO PRESIDENT LORENZO TERÁN

It is with great pain, Mr. President, that I review the course of our relationship, for as I do so I realize that all along I've been the gadfly that criticizes your inactivity. A king sitting on a throne, motionless, believing he was ensuring the kingdom's peace. If you moved your head to the left, it meant war and death. If you moved it to the right, it meant freedom and well-being, desired but utopian.

And now, as I've just seen you, as you've allowed me to see you, lying in your bed, emaciated, my friend, now only my friend, good and honest man that you are, a president inspired by his love for his country . . . Now that I see you in the throes of death, now I truly understand that a president is neither born nor bred. He's the product of a national illusion—or perhaps a collective hallucination. Once, I said to you, "Less glory, sir, and more freedom."

How terrible and cruel politics is: Once you disappear, it's only a matter of days before your glory and our freedom are lost forever. Mr. President, you've left the question of your succession unresolved. How can we make sure the next president is someone like you, a politician who is a decent man like Bernal Herrera, and not a snake like Tácito de la Canal?

How empty and melancholy, my beloved president and friend, my earliest advice to you sounds today: "Take advantage of the grace period at the beginning of the presidency. Honeymoons are brief. And democratic bonds get devalued from one day to the next."

"The first rule for the exercise of power, Mr. President, is to disregard the immensity of your position."

"The presidency is like the solar system. You are the sun, and your ministers are the satellites. But you are not God, nor are they angels."

"The art of politics," I told you then, "is not the art of the possible. It is the graffiti of the unpredictable. It is the scribble of chance."

My poor president! Badgered for three years by Herrera's pragmatism, Tácito's fawning, and Seneca's idealism! What would I say to you if this were your first day on the Eagle's Throne? I'd remind you of the best aspects of our traditional benevolent dictatorship, so that you could endorse them or avoid them as you saw fit: "You don't have to fear the president who's passive, rather the president who's unstoppably active."

With you the opposite has always been true. Your passivity sparked more doubts than your action. And now, perhaps, you feel the supreme temptation of power. To be a leader who summons the energy of the nation and subjects us all to the voluptuous passivity of total obedience.

That is the easiest thing.

The most comfortable thing.

But it's also the most dangerous. And you avoided that danger, my beloved, cherished president.

One day you said to me, "They think they're fooling me by giving me those endless reports to read. They think I'm lethargic—as if I've been bitten by a tsetse fly. Wrong. I read at night, and I know everything. I've fooled them. I can sleep well at night."

Yes, but the passive image you projected might be misinterpreted now. People might begin to demand a hyperactive president because authority can change its face from one day to the next (think about the past presidential successions, from Madero to Fox). The public feeds off paradox and adores contrast and contradiction.

Thank you, my dear friend, President Lorenzo Terán, for allowing me into your bedroom, where you're bedridden, surrounded by nurses, doctors, intravenous tubes, sedatives. Thank you for giving me the opportunity to see your life complete.

I don't know if we'll ever see each other again. I know that you haven't allowed anyone other than your faithful mosquito Seneca to enter this room where power is approaching its end.

Goodbye, Mr. President. . . .

48

CONGRESSWOMAN PAULINA TARDEGARDA TO CONGRESSMAN ONÉSIMO CANABAL

This letter will be delivered to you by Jesús Ricardo Magón, a young aide to the new interior secretary, Nicolás Valdivia. I'm laughing. I can see you now, red as a beet at the idea of me divulging secrets to a government employee, no matter how lowly. You and I, Onésimo, with our determination and political wiles, can pull our Congress back into shape and put a few obstacles in the government's way. . . . You and I, Onésimo, have all the gray matter we need to exploit the diffused power of our party-ocracy and make life hell for Lorenzo Terán. . . .

You asked for discretion. I'll give you discretion, Onésimo, together with a present. The medium is the message, they said fifty years ago, and so if Valdivia's little helper Magón is the medium, then he's also the message.

This is it. The coast is clear for us to take action. I'll get straight to the point. Cícero Arruza's reading of the country's domestic situation is all wrong. Arruza is a relic left over from another era, his day is over. He believes brute force is the only answer to problems, and that brute force can only be delivered by the army. This is his rather extravagant fantasy: He wants to unite all the governors and local bosses and then stage a military coup so that he can fill what he calls the "power vacuum" (where would he have learned that?) created by President Lorenzo Terán's passivity.

I've spoken to the leaders of each one of those local power bases, and I tell you, they're delighted by the president's passivity. Delighted because it's in their interests. How could they not be happy about the absence of a central authority? Now they can do exactly what they want. You tell me if Cabezas in Sonora isn't happy to govern his state with no interference whatsoever from the government. Or look at "Chicho" Delgado in Tijuana, making deals with the coyotes who smuggle illegals across the border and the U.S. immigration patrol that won't let them through—until Governor Delgado extorts one and pays off the other. It is shameful, my dear Onésimo, an outrage that the forces of law and order in the United States have become so corrupt. I'm blushing. Haven't I always said that the gringos know how to multiply any Mexican vice by the thousand and hide it by the million?

You will allow me a little joke every now and then, Congressman, won't you? You who treat me like a nun. . . . I'm being serious again now. You tell me if Roque Maldonado in San Luis Potosí is unhappy about the fact that he deals directly with his Japanese investors; closes deals in El Gargaleote, that mysterious Potosí refuge that once belonged to the legendary strongman Gonzalo N. Santos; and possesses a fortune that the hardworking revolutionary Santos could never have dreamed of, since Maldonado takes a hefty commission with no interference from central government.

You tell me if the *capo di tutti capi* Silvestre Pardo wants some meddlesome government making waves in his Narcomex empire. Need I say more? There isn't one governor, local boss, or drug trafficker who wants a military government with Cícero Arruza at the top, making off with the lion's share when it comes to so-called profit distribution. Our general is either blind, crazy, or a complete imbecile. His calculations have failed him miserably. He's going to find himself all alone in this coup.

Now do you see why it's important for the government to know, and why the little heartthrob Jesús Ricardo Magón, with his irresistible angel face, should be the emissary?

I laugh, Onésimo, but look at me. The only one who escapes us is the sly, ambitious strongman of Tabasco, Humberto Vidales, "Dark Hand." He's always had his eye on the Eagle's Throne, but since it's always been just beyond his grasp (to be a soap opera villain, you have to know how to be discreet; you can't go around curling your mouth, raising your eyebrows, and sniffing, wearing Cruz Diablo's cape). He's convinced that sooner or later one of his Nine Evil Sons, as he so lovingly refers to them, will sit on the throne and reclaim his God-given right—or so he thinks—to the presidency.

As for the candidate we're supporting, Onésimo, let's keep telling him to stay calm and that the only thing he needs to worry about (just a bit) is that sinister man from Tabasco. As far as the other local bosses are concerned, if we keep out of their affairs, they'll go along with what *we* want—which is to not rock the boat and to leave their businesses intact.

And who are *we*, my distinguished friend? What do we want? What we want is to be the decisive factor in the presidential succession of 2024. Do a head count, Onésimo. Contrary to what one might believe, Arruza is irrelevant for the reasons I've already explained, the best possible outcome of the mission you saw fit to entrust me with.

César León has no immediate chance of re-election. That would mean changing the constitution and God knows how long that could take. Anyway, you and I can make sure things are prolonged indefinitely.

Listen: Congress has three missions. One, to pass laws. Two, to prevent laws from being passed. But the most important mission is to make sure that issues get delayed indefinitely, that nothing ever gets resolved, that the agenda remains full of unfinished business. . . . If not, my dear friend, what are you and I doing here? What's the point of this operation if we don't use our ability to put everything off for as long as we can?

"Be careful," you said, "you don't want to end up the founding member of the Ides of March Society."

How well-educated you turned out to be, Onésimo. No wonder you were agriculture secretary under César León. You and I should found the Greek Calends Society. . . .

Let me continue. Andino Almazán, very simply, doesn't pass muster with the people. Apart from López Portillo, no treasury secretary has ever become president. He really is the villain in this little soap opera, spending six years saying no to everyone who asks him for money. It seems his profession is to be hated, and what the voters want is to love, even if only for a little while before disillusion sets in.

We are left, then, with two serious candidates. Bernal Herrera and Tácito de la Canal.

Don't be alarmed if I say Tácito must be eliminated.

Nicolás Valdivia sent me, via young Magón, copies of the documents that prove Tácito's criminal conduct in the MEXEN negotiations. How such a crafty operator allowed an archivist to file such incriminating papers, I have no idea. Magón, who is the son of the archivist, says that his father never lets a single paper disappear. That may be true. But still, why did Tácito let the documents get to the archive instead of sending them straight to the paper shredder? The only thing that occurs to me is that perhaps this is part of the muddy terrain of pride associated with power—hubris, Onésimo (a word I've already explained to you twice and which I'm not going to explain again). Hubris was what made President Nixon, for instance, zealously save all the tapes that proved him to be a revolting criminal and that ultimately got him expelled from the White House. . . . At every level you'll find them, Onésimo—governors who save videos of their murders, military commanders who have their shootings filmed, torturers who adore replaying their atrocities on-screen. . . . Is Tácito any different? I don't think so. Nixon, to return to our best example, had an archive labeled "The White House Files," which contained a full record of all his unethical deeds and crimes, but which was ready to be removed from the White House if he lost the election.

There's definitely something fishy going on with Tácito. His signature is on the documents. But signatures are easily forged. What I'm asking myself now is this: Who handed those papers over to Cástulo Magón, the archivist? I don't think it was de la Canal. If we can find out who said to him, "Don Cástulo, don't forget to file this . . ." then our mystery will be solved.

I repeat. Eliminate Tácito. María del Rosario has all the original documents and she's already shared the secret with her darling Nicolás Valdivia, whom she's pulled up to the top, and of course she's also shared it with Bernal Herrera, her ex-lover and the other candidate for the Eagle's Throne.

Nicolás Valdivia, I repeat, sent me (via young Magón) copies of the documents that prove Tácito's criminal conduct in the MEXEN case. Again, how could such a sly dog have overlooked the fact that the archivist was holding on to such incriminating evidence? I can't figure it out. But I now see why President Terán did everything he could to accelerate Tácito's resignation.

And Herrera's, too. Herrera emerges, then, as the favorite. Magón told me the president himself killed the story that Tácito had cooked up against María del Rosario and Herrera, making it very clear, in the process, that Herrera was his chosen one.

This is the best picture we have of things as they stand now. Very well, Onésimo, the real picture encompasses all these possibilities, with one small exception: The invisible issue here will not be the presidential candidate issue, as we've all been led to believe, but the issue of the acting president in the event of the resignation or absence of the president in office.

I can just see your face. Cover up your astonishment. And don't think César León's scheming or Cícero Arruza's threats can prompt the president to resign. There's something bigger going on here. Something very big. Young Magón told me that Valdivia told him that the president's trusted adviser Seneca saw Terán in a state of acute physical debilitation.

How does Valdivia know this? Because Seneca told María del Rosario, whom he's secretly in love with, and our little Eva Perón told her protégé Valdivia. There it is, Onésimo. Everyone's spying on everyone else, stealing documents from one another, and maybe even spying on themselves when nobody's looking. . . .

Which confirms the notion that in politics secrets are open and only the loudest voices tell secrets. Work out the mystery that's there in what you know, Onésimo, and forget the secrets: They're empty vessels. Distractions. Better to think—and think hard—about what you know.

That's where the mystery is.

49

MARÍA DEL ROSARIO GALVÁN
TO BERNAL HERRERA

President Lorenzo Terán has died. It's like losing a good father, Bernal. All my life I've lived with the repugnant image of my own father, who was tyrannical and corrupt. Sometimes he appears in my nightmares. I wake up, shouting at him, "Go away! Disappear! You're worse dead than you were alive!"

When Franco died, Juan Goytisolo, anti-Franco always (he's now eighty-nine and lives somewhere in the medina in Marrakech), couldn't help giving a requiem for the stepfather who subjugated the Spanish for forty years.

Lorenzo Terán, on the other hand, was a good patriarch. Perhaps too good. I call him "father," but really he was our son. Your son and mine, Bernal. We made him. We persuaded him to give up his business in Coahuila and become president in the midst of our multiparty catastrophe, from which not one political group has emerged unscathed, as if they were eight spoiled, measles-ridden children locked up in a room together.

Lorenzo Terán, on the other hand, was clean, unfettered, industrious. And as if that weren't enough, Bernal, he was ours. Nevertheless, you and I made a decision. We were not going to manipulate him. We'd be loyal and we'd respect his position and his autonomy. We'd serve him. We'd advise him. But we wouldn't treat him like a puppet. Were we wrong? Should we have pressured him more? Should we have been more than mere counselors and loyal servants? Did the president realize that he had you to thank for all those shows of power: the strikes, the students, the peasants? You were the one who acted. You always handed the president faits accomplis. Because Lorenzo Terán, so contentious on the campaign trail, decided to be a saint in office. He climbed up to the top of a column so that he could serve God and he chose to let society govern itself.

You and I had to act on his behalf. That was our way of being loyal to him. We didn't manipulate him. We respected his autonomy. But we filled the gaps for him. Since he never called us to task, we did whatever we could. You could do a lot from the interior office but not everything. I think there was a utopian lost somewhere in Lorenzo Terán's heart. The only person he listened to—unfortunately, for us—was Seneca, and that elicited a vicious response from the gringos. It was to be expected.

My own role was limited because I am a woman. For all that we've progressed, an unwritten law still holds sway in this country: A man can be forgiven all his vices. Not a woman.

I can see you smiling, Bernal. You're a good man. You're generous. Only once did you reproach me for being indiscreet, when I got into that argument with Tácito de la Canal. You were right. My hormones did get the better of me. Once again, I ask you to forgive me. Not only did I break our political pact. Discretion, discretion, discretion. The bad thing about power is that it gives one a sense of impunity. The more you get used to it, the more indiscreet you become.

I swear never to make that mistake again. That's why I'm putting everything down in writing, so that we have a record this time of what you proposed to me yesterday at President Terán's funeral, as we knelt side by side in the Metropolitan Cathedral.

You're thinking of your future, as am I. The president's death doesn't only move the political calendar ahead. It changes it. How quickly things change in politics! There are more cracks, winding paths, waterfalls, gulfs, narrow passes, hidden islands, bottlenecks, and gorges than in the whole length of the Amazon! When I said to Nicolás Valdivia, "You will be president of Mexico," I was only stringing him along. I thought it would be one thing or the other. Either he would take it as an erotic dare, a sexual promise I kept putting off, a woman's fancy: "Come to my arms, my sweet young thing. . . . Be the president of my bed. Didn't you understand what I meant? My bed's the real Mexican presidency, silly. . . ."

Or he'd be spurred on by ambition. He was under no illusions. I was working for you. But politics is "what a man does so that he can hide what he is and what he doesn't know." And Nicolás Valdivia was clever, daring, and beautiful enough to understand this proposal. All or nothing.

It turned out to be all. He's going to be acting president. Don't look at me like that, my love. I have to be able to keep a secret or two. No woman can be denied that right. Have you ever noticed how easily we get secrets out of men? From the old "If you don't tell me, I'll get angry" to the "Keep your secrets, I'm leaving." Bernal, you knew about my relationship with Lorenzo Terán. He was the one who protected our poor doomed son. I wanted to thank him. We had only a few weeks of love when I went to the United States. We met in Houston. He showed me the X-rays. Bernal, I always knew the president was going to die. I didn't know when or how, but we had to be prepared. I did it for you, my love. If the president lived through the 2024 election, Valdivia would watch our backs in Los Pinos. But if he died in office, who more malleable than Valdivia, our creation, to be acting president while we prepared for your election? That was my plan. Yes, politics is "what a man does so that he can hide what he is and what he doesn't know." And with Valdivia it was a win-win situation. From the office of the president to being undersecretary of the interior to being in charge today. Forgive me if I made mistakes. Let's share our success. Congress will have to name an acting president. We have our man. Valdivia. We groomed him for this. He'll call for elections in July of 2024 and you will once again be the people's candidate. Who elects the president of Mexico? Seventy percent of the population claim no party affiliation. Who can possibly challenge you? Tácito has been eliminated. Andino isn't man enough for the job. Nobody in that "cabinet of champions," as they called it at the beginning of the century, has got what it takes.

There are temptations: the military. There's the mystery of Ulúa and the Old Man Under the Arches who won't reveal it, even if he's tortured. He'll take that secret to his grave. Torture could kill an old man like him, and anyway, it would be a reprehensible act of cruelty. Then there's the question of the unfortunate Miss de la Garza, who still writes love letters to the dead presidential candidate Tomás Moctezuma Moro.

In short, Bernal, you need to find yourself a rival. López Portillo was the last president who ran uncontested, and remember how that turned out. His vanity and arrogance were all-consuming.

Who will be your opponent in the 2024 elections, Bernal?

That's what should concern us, not your mad serenades of love. You're fifty-two, Bernal, and I'm forty-nine, let's face it.

As the funeral prayers were being said in the cathedral, you whispered to me, "María del Rosario, we've put off our marriage for a quarter of a century. We know why. But now . . . think of how important it is for a presidential candidate to be married."

"President Terán was a bachelor. . . ."

"But he lived like a monk, everyone knew that. He was irreproachable. But two in a row, María del Rosario, two in a row, come on— they're going to think I'm a queer."

I hid my laughter behind my black veil.

"Find another woman, then, Bernal."

"Marucha, you're the only woman I've ever loved."

Forgive me. I didn't mean to break the rosary I had in my hand. The beads scattered noisily all over the place.

"Let's talk about this later."

"No. Now."

"In the communion line, then. We'll have to whisper."

What did I say to you, Bernal, as we waited in the long, slow line for communion? What did I tell you? Let's put it on record:

"All men fear women who are able to think and act for themselves. All men fear women who are strong and able to fend for themselves. I choose to act of my own accord and not inspire fear in a husband. I'm telling you this for your own good. That's why I never married you when we were young. Don't ever pity me. Would you ask a man to give up his friends? His restaurants, his habits? I would never accept it. Why should I force someone else to be what I don't want to be? Let me be my own woman. Don't forget, I'm the daughter of a man who inspired fear, and I feel justified in behaving in the political world just as he did in the business world. I justify myself, Bernal, by saying that he had an evil energy—he didn't just want to *make* money, he wanted to *be* money— whereas I am inspired by the common good, in a devious way, you could say. Laugh if you want, but you'd better do it silently because we're in the middle of the Te Deum. Think about it, though, and re-member, I have one great fault. I don't know how to be a good wife. I don't know how to share, to laugh, to soothe. The only thing I know how to do is scheme, but that—*j'espère*—I do with a certain style well worthy of my allies. I may not know how to love a man. But I do know how to respect a friend, like you. . . ."

On our knees, side by side at the high altar, we received the body of Christ from the hands of the archbishop of Mexico, Pelayo Cardinal Munguía.

As the service came to a close, you offered me a ride in your car. As you drove you told me that I hadn't helped solve your problem. A man needs a first lady by his side at Los Pinos. The president has to be able to say, "I have a private life."

I had to laugh at that.

"We all have the right to a private life. As long as we're able to pay for it. If I were to marry you, no amount of money could compensate for our unhappiness."

"You're the only person I can confide in outside politics, do you realize that?"

"I feel the same about you. Let's just leave things as they are. To be married would be a lie."

"Isn't the political life a lie?"

"Yes, and that's why it's so demanding."

"What do you mean?"

"That lying successfully requires an enormous amount of time and attention. The successful cultivation of lies is a full-time job. Which is precisely what the political life allows for."

"Have you still got the energy?"

"Look at yourself in the rearview mirror, Bernal. Let's both look. Do you think we're the same people we were twenty years ago? What does that little mirror tell you, Bernal?"

Your voice sounded so sad, my love.

"That we can't turn back the clock."

Chapultepec transformed into a shrine to rock music, quavering from all the benefit concerts, so noisy that some people claim to have seen the sleepless ghosts of Maximilian, Carlota, and the boy soldiers who died there rising up from the dead and wandering through the throngs of Mick Jagger fans. Mick Jagger's here to celebrate his seventy-seventh birthday—he's less of a rock star than a constipated old hag, like all aging hippies.

And finally Los Pinos, the presidential residence and office where all the foreign heads of state, ambassadors, and political groups have come to mourn. Who's there to receive them? Naturally, the president of Congress, Onésimo Canabal, the president of the supreme court, Javier Wimer Zambrano, and the interior secretary, Nicolás Valdivia. The election of the acting president will not take place until the memorial ceremonies in honor of President Lorenzo Terán have concluded and the foreign politicians have gone home—although Fidel Castro says that he plans to visit Chiapas "with a very important announcement to make."

You and I find ourselves back in the line. We're no longer part of the government. We can only admire the composure of our Three Powers. And I search in vain for the woman, Bernal.

Because President Lorenzo Terán did have a woman at Los Pinos. An invisible woman, and she's there peeping into the López Mateos room. Crying. With a handkerchief over her mouth. Dark-skinned. Pockmarked. As square as a safe. Loving. Grieving.

That woman is Penélope Casas.

She cries, but through her tears she gazes tenderly at Nicolás Valdivia.

She knows he will be president. And she is grateful, for he is her protector.

I watch the scene with you, Bernal, and I repeat, politics is my passion. How lucky we are, you and I, that we never married. I was able to give the darkest part of myself, the part I inherited from my father, to politics, without hurting you.

"Nicolás Valdivia, I will make you president."

What I didn't tell him was that I knew that President Lorenzo Terán was terminally ill.

50

XAVIER "SENECA" ZARAGOZA TO
MARÍA DEL ROSARIO GALVÁN

Lorenzo Terán has died. The president has died. Are you and I still alive, María del Rosario? No, no, I won't drag you into my own Viking funeral, the burning ship whose fiery sail will not survive the night of death. No. All I'm doing, my friend, is offering an assessment, which is perhaps a funeral prayer as well.

Was Lorenzo Terán a great man? Might he have been and failed? Or was he only what he always was: a decent, well-intentioned man and—*de mortuis nil nisi bonum*—without true intelligence? His presidency will not go down in history. Terán let things happen because that was his democratic credo. But what happened wasn't what he wanted. Consider the situation. Power vacuums, entrenched local fiefdoms, uncontrollable palace intrigues . . . and civil society incapable of governing itself in an atmosphere of tolerance, respect, and moral initiative. You, Bernal, and I know better than anyone that the man who died was honest and decent. But I must ask you this: Can anyone effect change with words? The words that the civilized world loves—Law, Security, Democracy, Progress—seem insipid, a lie, here in Mexico, and everywhere else in Latin America, a land ravaged by pain.

And I, a man everyone calls Seneca—what can I do but propose radical utopias, given that *topos* is, in itself, so absolute in the political realm? Faced with the inherent extremity of realpolitik, I championed the equally extreme notion of idealpolitik in the hope that, somewhere between two extremes, the coin of virtue might land. *In medio stat virtu,* as they say.

With this philosophy in mind, I accepted the position that President Terán offered me, so close to the Eagle's Throne. I knew that life could be wretched even when thoughts sailed high. I accepted my place with serenity in the belief that, even if my advice was not always taken, at least a moral echo, if only a faint one, would always resonate in the president's ears. Yes, I am a utopian. I will die dreaming of a society governed by men of knowledge, integrity, and good taste. But since this is impossible, aren't we better off taking this conviction to the grave, where nothing can thwart or contradict it?

I've sought virtue so that we might better exercise our liberty.

I've believed in a country that belongs to everyone, that embraces everyone, regardless of sex, race, religion, or ideology.

It's been difficult, but I've tried, María del Rosario, to extend my love to the bearers of evil, thinking of them as people who are simply "sick with passion," as the original Seneca, native of Córdoba, called them.

But most of all, I've followed the Stoic advice: When it comes to aggression, never allow yourself to be conquered by anything but your own soul.

María del Rosario, I want you to understand this farewell note from your friend Xavier Zaragoza, the man everyone calls Seneca. I want you to feel that my despair is also my peace. That I still have the desire. What I've lost is the hope. I know, now you're going to tell me that I should have been more aware of the realities the president faced, that I should have regarded my ideals—an enlightened, fair government—as merely corrective, a call to the refuge of the interior life in stormy times. Resigned myself to the crumbs of utopia. Yes, María del Rosario, you yourself believed that my presence was useful, like the condiment that's unnoticed if the stew is tasty, but considered indispensable the moment someone asks, "Where's the salt?"

The salt on tables piled high with well-seasoned dishes—how many times was my counsel heeded? Why did I fool myself into thinking that my advice counted for anything? Didn't I realize that the political weight of an intellectual could only be felt outside the power base, though even in the opposition an intellectual can scarcely exert much more than relative pressure? Within the power base his influence is not even relative. It is nil.

In other words, at one extreme you shit, at the other you eat shit. It's as bleak as that.

As I look back on these three years I've spent in the antechambers of power, all I see is misery and all I feel is disgust. Yes, I've seen the president suffer. There were times I said to him, "Don't think so much. That's what I'm here for."

But whenever I did that, someone else had already saved him from his suffering. Tácito, in the interest of evil. Herrera, in the interest of goodness. And I was always left with, "You're right, Seneca. There was another path. Perhaps I'll take it next time."

And then he'd smile at me.

"You bastard, stop keeping me awake at night, will you?"

It was the inner circle of sycophants, demagogues, and schemers that was keeping him awake.

María del Rosario, this is your friend Xavier "Seneca" Zaragoza, the man the president listens—listened—to with enthusiasm but without conviction.

These imbeciles think success will make them happy. They don't know what's coming to them. I was isolated and discredited. It was only thanks to the president's goodness that I kept my position. I was the gadfly. I was the one who said the things that had to be said, no matter how unpleasant.

"Nothing will ever convince me that wisdom lies in statistics, Andino."

"When I look at you, General Arruza, I am filled with revulsion."

"People can sleep in the same bed and dream very different dreams, Mr. Herrera."

"Crown yourself with laurels, President León, lest a thunderbolt strike you dead."

"Your cowardice is like a stench that you leave behind everywhere you go, Tácito."

And you, María del Rosario, tell me this: "Seneca, don't drink poison to quench your thirst. It's not worth it."

Isn't it, my dear friend? Do you think I want to die because I'm disillusioned with the world? Do you think that the only thing left for me, an idealist without convictions, is death? Do you think I'm betraying the Stoic belief in keeping the soul's passions at bay? Tell me, isn't it possible that death is yet another of the soul's passions? And since it's our inevitable end, why not accelerate it?

No. I've put my convictions to the test and I know that the price of intelligence is disenchantment. Nothing can match our use of reason. I've been too close to the sun for too long, and since I'm nothing but a statue made of snow, I melt when the sun burns out. Oh, if you only knew the things I've felt since the death of my wonderful friend Lorenzo Terán. I'm like a cat: I can't make sense of my reflection in the mirror. I try to remember my name, and I have such a hard time. I shouldn't remember it, for I've lost it forever, I know. And I feel that nothing is worth the effort, nothing satisfies me. Everything has gone sour. Is that proof of moral greatness? Can a dog feel boredom? Only the idiot has no doubts. Only the idiot doesn't suffer.

When the president died, I peered into the mirror of my soul and it trembled. My emotions were in flux. My spirit was wavering between life and death.

It was the immense unfulfillment of my love, a hollow between life and death. My love for you, María del Rosario. It was my desire to possess you, never expressed, forever silenced, a prisoner of my dreams. And I'm sure you never guessed.

In the end, it was the absolute certainty that my interior life was the only reality. The untouchable fortress of my inner self. My freedom to decide whether that should remain in the world or be left behind. It meant—it means, María del Rosario—that rational thought will never take root in Mexico. Time after time we've done it, and we'll go on doing it, killing the hen that lays the golden eggs—after stealing the eggs. It means that, though he said it in 1800, Humboldt was right: "Mexico is a beggar sitting on top of a mountain of gold."

In a detective novel, we don't know who the criminal is until the end. But in Mexico, everyone knows who the criminal is in advance. And the victim is always the country itself. Oh, my dear friend, ignore the demagogues who promise salvation, our Mahatma Propagandis. But be careful of the comedians who are the repressors, our Robespierrots.

Listen to the desperate.

Listen to the rumors in Mexico City, where everyone knows what goes unsaid. Write it all down. Nobody will believe you.

Keep your mouth shut. They'll find out.

Yes, my more than valued friend. If I were a politician I'd betray them all. Just as well I'm only an intellectual and know that the politicians will betray me.

Yes, my beautiful and enlightened lady, nothing has any value outside the inner life, the silent self. Don't talk to anyone about it. They won't understand.

I go in the knowledge that our life is in our dreams. Nothing is more real than our Utopia. There's no other reality, you see. Only a suicidal man would dare say this. They're not my final words. I'm not asking for them to be inscribed on my tombstone.

HERE LIES XAVIER ZARAGOZA

KNOWN TO ALL AS SENECA

1982—2020

IN MEXICO, ALL THOUGHT IS

CONTRABAND

I'll tell you in secret that there's no mystery after death. The dead man doesn't know we're alive. What it amounts to is that before birth and after death we experience our own untouchable worlds.

My farewell sentence, María del Rosario, is much simpler.

"I am leaving before the sky above Mexico City disappears forever."

And I reproach myself for leaving with rage, without serenity. . . .

I go with rage because I allowed myself to be seduced by politics. I discovered that the art of politics is the lowest form of art.

I go with rage because I was unable to convince the president that the head of state can't matter more than the people, or the times.

I go with rage because I was unable to stop the six-year cycle of political madness that appropriates all of Mexican history and reinvents it every six years. What madness.

I go with rage because it's my fault that the president listened to me when I gave him good advice. It's my fault, not his.

I go with rage because my reason and logic were unable to defeat the propaganda, which is the food of fanatics.

I go with rage because I never learned how to grow magueys.

I go with rage because where once I was provocative I'm now an irritation.

I go with rage because I preached morality from the top of a mountain made of sand.

I go with rage because I was never able to say to you, *I love you.*

I go with rage because I envy only the dead.

51

NICOLÁS VALDIVIA TO
JESÚS RICARDO MAGÓN

Darling, it's very hard to trust anyone else. Who knows what the consequences will be of the information you gave to María del Rosario? She used to be my regular correspondent . . . but I'm not sure about her now. Too many crossed wires. Too many interweaving stories. Should I just keep my mouth shut? That would be the safest thing, but I'm terrified of taking the secret with me to my grave. I trust you enough to tell you that. My feelings for you have deepened since I first saw you on the roof and we started working together. At last I've found a kindred spirit, someone who reads the same books and who thinks as I do. I feel you very close to me and I want to keep you there.

My secret is your secret, but then you and I are one and the same.

I'm warning you that knowing what I know is dangerous—for me and for whoever hears me. Destroy the tape after listening to it. It will be delivered to you by your father don Cástulo, the safest messenger I can think of.

I went back to Veracruz to talk to the Old Man because he asked me to. There he was, as always, wearing his double-breasted suit and bow tie, with the little parrot on his shoulder and the dominoes laid out on the table, and the waiter, artful as an acrobat, pouring his steaming coffee.

"Sit down, Valdivia," the Old Man said.

He could tell from my eyes, from the way I moved my head, from my hands open in supplication, that I wanted to meet in private, not in full view in the plaza in Veracruz.

"Sit down, Valdivia. When you do things openly you don't arouse suspicion. It's secrecy that wakes up the wolves. We're not drawing attention to ourselves here under the arches. Look: The vultures are flying over Ulúa Castle again. That's what people are going to notice, not you and me sitting together over a cup of coffee."

I didn't say anything. I didn't ask anything. I knew the Old Man was going to talk. By the look on his face I could tell that everything that was going to happen had already happened. I went cold as I realized this. The Old Man was a sorcerer, I knew it, and he understood, Jesús Ricardo, those subtle but significant changes in time and space that affect us all. That was the wisdom he'd gained from living so long. Space and time. How to read them, endure them, and find ourselves in them. Whether we like it or not, space belongs to the order of things that co-exist, whereas time belongs to the realm of things that happen. What unites the two is their effect on what *already is* and on what is possible, what can happen. In themselves, they're abstract notions. They need the concrete here-and-now to have substance.

Didn't Susan Sontag say that years ago? "Time exists in order that everything doesn't happen all at once. Space exists so that it all doesn't happen to you."

In political life, strictly speaking, can we say that chance, sequence, and recurrence belong to the world of the everyday, just as the intensity, simultaneity, and harmony of personal, internal time, yours and mine, my darling, are properties of the soul?

Now, you know what joy it is for me to have a companion whose mind works like mine. Whom else but you can I talk to about things like this? Who else could possibly understand me when I say that the time we're living in now isn't just an abstract idea but a useful way of understanding life and *that politics is one way of making time a reality*?

I want to believe that the Old Man read my thoughts. Not literally, of course, but through his intuition—though in his case you'd call it something else, malice, even perversity. . . . He's a sly old dog.

Anyway, this is what he said to me: "My only regret is that I know all the stories, but I'll never know the full story."

"Nor will I," I ventured.

"Nobody, for sure," he said, nodding his well-groomed, graying head.

I didn't want to add anything. He was the boss.

"Just as a person measures out the sugar for his coffee," he said, "he should know what to tell, when to tell, and to whom. . . ."

"And when to take a secret with him to the grave?"

I don't know why he found this so funny. He bared his teeth. That was the only time I ever saw him looking hungry.

"Sometimes with a heavy heart, or in the interests of discretion, or out of pride—how many secrets have we never revealed, and only when we're dead do we regret it? If I'd told this at the right time, everything would have been different. Or better."

I wasn't going to rush the Old Man. I'd already decided to keep a very formal, respectful distance that I hoped would intrigue him more than his secret intrigued me. Because there was a secret there, Jesús Ricardo. If you were to add up all my visits to the café in Veracruz, you might think I'd come here because María del Rosario had asked me to, as part of my political education. But little by little I understood that the Old Man was keeping a secret and was waiting for the right moment to reveal it. Maybe at the beginning this was coincidence, whim, or chance. But in the end it was inevitable, necessary.

I was interior secretary at the moment of the president's death. Congress was selecting an acting president to complete Lorenzo Terán's term and call an election. My political education, which was the reason for all my trips to Veracruz (how distant it seems today!), was now my political decision. Who would be the acting president? And who would be the candidates in 2024?

I already knew that for the Old Man declarations of conviction came, like hors d'oeuvres, before the main course.

"You know something, Valdivia? I'm tired of keeping secrets that most people have already forgotten or don't care about. So a president's brother had his wife's lover killed and then was poisoned to death? Mystery! So some stripper rammed a guitar into the face of a jealous ex-president and left him with only one eye? Mystery! So a certain ex-president was ruined by a dozen women who conspired to abandon him under the sun on a deserted beach until he burned to a crisp? Mystery! Anecdotes from our national political comedy. You tell me if anyone cares about these things now."

With his index finger he lifted up the silent parrot and stroked his many-colored feathers.

"There are other secrets, however, that could change the course of history if they ever got out."

He closed his mouth. The parrot returned to its spot on the Old Man's shoulder. I kept my expression blank.

"In politics," he went on, "one mustn't let the train guide the driver. María del Rosario sent you here for your baptism of fire. That was what she said, the old bitch. Really she sent you here to find out my secret. And you found out nothing. You went back each time with a heap of advice. A bag of potatoes."

Then he did something unusual. He tossed his cane aside, and it clattered against the floor. Now, I said to myself, everyone will turn around and look at us. But no. Nobody flinched. The pact between the Old Man and the regulars under the arches was indestructible. He grabbed my fist and with the strength of an athlete tightened his grip until my hand hurt. Strangely, I started to imagine him naked, to wonder what his muscles were like, because at his age flesh usually sags, everything goes soft, but that old man pressed his iron fist around mine with a vigor that seemed to come from his head and his balls.

"Not this time, Valdivia. Not this time."

What did he mean? The parrot stayed mysteriously silent, as if the

Old Man had filled him with Nembutal, or perhaps the parrot knew when to play the fool and distract people, and when to behave with what the Old Man's nemeses, the French, refer to as *sagesse*—a wisdom that is knowledge, experience, restraint, and courtesy.

"You know, the dirty and the sacred have something in common. We don't touch either," he said, gazing at the parrot instead of me.

The rings under his eyes seemed to darken further.

"Do you remember Tomás Moctezuma Moro?"

I was almost offended by the question. Moro was the candidate who had won the 2012 presidential election and then was assassinated before taking office. New elections had been held while the country was still in shock, and in 2013 the colorless president of the Emergency Coalition was sworn into office—a dull, forgettable secondhand president known only for his inefficiency, his obliging transience, his weakness. Congress governed during that period, and governed badly. United at first in elevating a Mr. Nobody to the presidency, they quickly reverted to a gorilla guerrilla war, so to speak. Congress dictated policy to the best of their knowledge and belief, and the president—what was his name, for God's sake?—simply obeyed, his fingers crossed.

That's why Lorenzo Terán sparked so much enthusiasm in 2017, when his strength and personality—so evident, so strong—carried him to the presidency on a wave of triumph and hope. He won 75 percent of the votes, the remaining 25 percent divided among the small parties that had long since been unable to inspire the voters.

Tomás Moctezuma Moro. A forgotten moment. Another political ghost. A presence yesterday, a specter today.

"An honest man," the Old Man said. "I can vouch for that. He thought of himself as the Hercules who was going to clean the stables of Mexican politics. And I warned him, 'It's dangerous to be really honest in this country. Honesty may be admirable but it ends up becoming a vice. You have to be flexible about corruption. I know you're honest, Tomás, but close your eyes—like divine justice—to the corruption around you. Remember, first, that corruption lubricates the system.

Most politicians, government employees, contractors, et al. won't have another opportunity to get rich once the six-year presidential term is over. They'll go back to oblivion. But they want to be forgotten, so that nobody accuses them of anything, and rich, so that nobody bothers them. Then another gang of villains will turn up, but denying them the chance to pocket anything would be a mistake.

" 'What you need,' I told Tomás, 'is to surround yourself with opportunists because you can control the corrupt. It's the pure man who's the problem, he's the one who just gets in your way. In Mexico there should be only one honest man, the president, surrounded by a lot of tolerated and tolerable yes-men who in six years' time will disappear from the political map.

" 'The bad thing about you,' I said to Tomás Moctezuma Moro, 'is that you want the map and the land to match. Look, live at peace in the center of the map and let the corruption brokers cultivate the land.' "

The Old Man sighed and I could almost feel a tremor in the hand that was still pressing down on mine with incredible strength.

"He didn't listen to me, Valdivia. He proclaimed his redemptive intentions right, left, and center. That way, he believed, he'd gain the greatest popular support. And he was acting out of conviction, without a doubt. He was going to put an end to corruption. He said it was the lowest form of stealing from the poor. That's what he said. The thieves were going to go to jail. The poor would have protection against abuse.

" 'Slow down, Tomás,' I told him. 'They're going to crucify you if you go around playing the redeemer. Don't announce what you intend to do. Do those things when you're sitting on the Throne, just like Cárdenas did. Don't destroy the system. You're part of it. Good or bad, it's the only one we've got. What are you going to replace it with? You can't just invent something overnight. Be satisfied with making an example of a few scapegoats at the beginning of your term. Make a moral statement early on and then you can rest.' But he didn't listen to me. He was a messiah. He believed in what he was saying."

I was stunned. He crossed himself.

"Who killed him, Valdivia? The list of potential murderers is as enormous as the cast of *The Ten Commandments*. Do you remember? Drug traffickers. Local bosses. Governors. Local presidents. Corrupt judges. Crooked policemen. Bankers fearful that Moro would take away the public subsidies that financed their private incompetence. Union leaders afraid that Moro would force them to be voted in and approved by their union members. Truck drivers overpricing their merchandise. Millers exploiting the corn-producing local farmers. Loggers turning forests into deserts. New landowners controlling land, seeds, and tractors while impoverished farmers continued to use the ox and the wooden plow."

Did the Old Man sigh, or was it the parrot?

"The list is endless, I tell you. Then add the mystics, all those madmen who want to save the country by killing presidents. And then the international conspiracy theories. The gringos scared that Mexico would get out of hand because they knew they weren't going to have an easy time manipulating Moro. And as always the Cubans—both the ones in Miami afraid that Moro would help Castro, and the ones in Havana afraid that Moro, apostle of human rights that he was, would make problems for Castro. The list of problems went on and on . . ."

Now he looked me in the eye.

"I've never met a politician who made as many enemies as quickly as Moro did. He was a thorn in everyone's side. I told him that he had too many enemies, that he was an obstacle for everyone, that he was in danger. . . ."

He didn't let go of my hand. But his eyes weren't his. They were the eyes of the night, of a bat, of prison.

"I ordered the murder of Tomás Moctezuma Moro."

Need I tell you why you must destroy this tape? And why I had to communicate with you so urgently?

I love you,

N.

52

NICOLÁS VALDIVIA TO
TÁCITO DE LA CANAL

Sir: I'll be brief. This letter will be delivered to you by Jesús Ricardo Magón, whom I trust implicitly. I won't waste time on matters you and I know about already. I simply want to warn you that the incriminating documents are in my possession, and well protected.

Someone as undeniably intelligent as you will understand why I'm not going to make them public. If they were to become public knowledge that would be the end of any higher political aspirations for you. Such a scandal would seriously impede your candidacy. President Téran was aware of this. Your rival the ex-secretary of the interior, Bernal Herrera, whose position I have the honor of filling, knows. María del Rosario Galván, whom you have treated in such an ungentlemanly way, also knows, but given her fine political mind, she understands that it's better to lose you, Mr. De la Canal, and to see you retire from public life. In exchange, those of us who know about your objectionable dealings will maintain a discreet silence.

The papers will remain locked away for one simple reason. They incriminate too many people. Bankers, administrators, and businessmen who are more useful to the country stimulating growth than purging their sins in the Almoloya jail. After all, what did their indiscretions in

the MEXEN deal really amount to? Streams in a mighty river of investments, tributaries of the river of essential capital and savings that the
country needs to move forward.

There are two things you have to weigh here: On one hand, Mexico's progress; on the other hand, your guilt. Which is heavier? You're
going to say you're not the only guilty party. Are you spiteful enough to
drag down your accomplices? As for me, I think we will all be better off
if everyone keeps their composure and remains silent. Also, I think it
would be a good idea for you to take a long vacation. A permanent vacation, I would even suggest. Acapulco is surely more tempting than
Almoloya. And we won't say anything to your mischievous little
friends, neither you nor I. Why don't we just leave them in peace? What
I'll do is promote stricter laws governing the management of publicly
and privately held companies, in the interest of eliminating fraud and
insider trading, ensuring access to corporate accounting data and
severely punishing the PDGs (excuse the French, that means *Présidents
Directeurs Généraux*) who sell shares at high prices weeks before they
plummet, knowing that those who take advantage of inflated prices, like
the despicable Bush Jr. and Cheney, get out in time, leaving the smaller
investors to take the hit. Like that woman Penélope Casas, who worked
in your office. Do you remember her?

I propose to establish a presumption of guilt *jure et de jure* for those
corporate pirates, so that it will be up to them to prove their innocence
in court. I repeat: I'm going to protect the small-time investor who was
cheated for lack of information, confidential information that the company chiefs and their accountants possessed. But I'm going to look to
the future, not the past. Punishing the past only shows an inability to
manage in the present, or plan ahead. I won't make that mistake. But
your file still exists, de la Canal, and it contains the evidence of a crime
that we might be forced to expose, not to condemn the past but for the
sake of the future.

Consider yourself warned. I won't initiate any action against you or
any of your co-conspirators in fraud. However, if you start making

waves, either to save your own skin (which would be very imprudent), to get buried along with your accomplices, or to have the masochistic satisfaction of taking others down with you as you kill yourself . . . in that case, Mr. De la Canal, the full weight of the law will come crashing down on your bald head.

Consider yourself, then, under the sword of Damocles.

I remain your loyal and steadfast servant,
Nicolás Valdivia
UNDERSECRETARY OF THE INTERIOR

53

TÁCITO DE LA CANAL
TO ANDINO ALMAZÁN

Mr. Secretary, my esteemed friend, I turn to you from the bottom of the pit into which my political enemies have thrown me. That is the state of things. Some win, some lose. But in politics there are many twists and turns. Perhaps my present disgrace and the low profile I'm being forced to maintain are in fact the best possible mask for me to use as I prepare my surprise comeback.

They say all is fair in love and war. I'd say the same goes for politics and business. I know that the undersecretary of the interior, a former subordinate of mine, has sent you a series of documents that implicate me in the MEXEN case. He himself has told me that he's not going to pursue me because I would drag too many other powerful people down with me. I claimed that I was only following the orders of the president, César León.

Nicolás Valdivia looked at me coldly.

"The president is untouchable. The secretary is not."

"Principles are good servants of bad masters."

"That's true, Mr. De la Canal. Don't worry, from now on your hands will be clean. Because you won't have any hands. . . ."

I do not surrender, Secretary Almazán. Not even if they were to cut off my hands, because I'd still have feet to kick with. I've spoken to the other people involved mentioned by Valdivia, to remind them that we're in this together. That I only signed those papers under orders from President César León.

They laughed at me. Below I offer a literal transcription of the conversation I had with the banker most deeply involved in the complex MEXEN business scheme.

"I've come to discuss the MEXEN affair," I said to him.

"I don't know what you're talking about."

"The MEXEN shares."

"But you don't know anything about that, do you?"

"Excuse me?" I admit I was shocked, but I knew what he was playing at, and said, "No. That's why I've come here. To find out about it."

"If I were you, I'd stay in the dark. You'll be better off."

"Why?" I persisted.

"Because it's secret," he conceded for a moment, like a fisherman dangling a worm in front of a fish, and then ended by saying, "And it's best to leave it at that."

"Secret?" I said, giving away my shock. "Secret for me, who made it all possible with my signature?"

"You were just a tool," he responded, barely hiding his scorn.

"For what purpose?"

"For keeping the deal secret."

He looked straight through me, as if I were a window.

"Don't lose your grip, Mr. De la Canal."

"But I . . ."

"Thank you. Goodbye."

I haven't given up, Mr. Almazán. I spoke to one of the press barons. He owes me, a man who always found the doors to President Lorenzo Terán's office open, thanks to me.

I'll be brief.

When I asked him to defend me, at least by publishing a favorable profile of me, and maybe launching a personal rehabilitation campaign, he said, "A good journalist should never annoy his readership by eulo-gizing. He should only attack. Praise is boring."

I admit I was furious, Andino.

"You owe me a lot."

"True. The powerful always need charity."

"All it takes is an order to one of your lackeys. . . ."

"Mr. de la Canal! I've never done anything like that! My contribu-tors are independent!"

"Do you want me to prove the opposite?" I shouted, indignant. "Do you want me to bribe one of your journalists?"

I expected a cold stare from the businessman. Instead, he looked at me with the charity he'd just mentioned.

"Mr. de la Canal. My journalists are not dishonest. They're inca-pable of being dishonest."

I know that what I'm transcribing could damage me and tarnish my image. But I haven't got many rounds of ammunition left, Mr. Almazán.

In truth I have only one.

Let me be frank. I've come to respect and admire you—and your family. You're lucky to have a devoted wife, Josefina, and three lovely little girls, Teté, Talita, and Tutú. What you don't have is much of a bank account. You live off your salary and your wife's inheritance—what remains of one of the old agave fortunes of the Yucatán's "Divine Caste." . . .

I have a proposition. The fact that the MEXEN deal failed doesn't rule out the possibility of other profitable ventures. Perhaps my politi-cal fortune is in the doghouse right now, but a good deal is always a good deal. And although I'm no longer in power, you still are—in charge of public finances, no less—which means that you can generate the kind of money required for something one might call an *investment opportunity*.

This is my plan.

Through a publicly held company you and I will offer investors with good credit ratings the chance to acquire mortgages that have been preapproved by the authorities (that is, you, Mr. Secretary) with the promise that, as of a certain date, they may be sold to any bank at a profit of two percent. In other words, guaranteed profits and very little risk. There won't be any shortage of sharks or sardines for this venture because before the first period of investment's up, you and I will recruit new investors, and with the money we get from them, we'll pay the dividends to the first group, who'll be very happy—and taken in.

The first group of investors will be grateful for the profits and will help us recruit new partners. The new partners will inject the necessary money to pay the dividends out to the previous group of investors.

This way, Andino, we'll ensure a financial pyramid in which we attract new investment because of the profits of the existing investors, and quickly build up capital.

Unfortunately, the number of investors isn't limitless, and once people stop investing in the pyramid it'll collapse like a house of cards.

You and I, however, will have made our pile by extracting the profits at each stage of the operation. Then the company will be declared insolvent, we'll be in the hands of the bankruptcy laws, and the company will be given an administration order rather than going into liquidation.

In other words, you and I can't lose. We win every step of the way. Moreover we don't even have to show our faces. Felipe Aguirre, communications secretary, and Antonio Bejarano, public works secretary, will do that for us. They're ready to be our front men. Since Valdivia's going to get rid of them, they're eager for revenge and want our acting president to start off with a scandal. They'll take their share, and if it occurs to Valdivia to accuse them of embezzlement while working for the government, nobody can be judged twice for the same crime. It's a question of weighing the risks, Andino, and being willing to spend a short time in Almoloya prison in exchange for millions waiting for us in bank accounts in the Cayman Islands.

You and I, prudent as we are, will have saved our earnings offshore, so that in Mexico we pass for bankrupt and the minimum is seized from the company.

I do hope you'll consider my proposal. And don't forget to discuss it with your dear wife. We shouldn't do anything, you and I, without involving Josefina. After all, we're talking about your future well-being, and Teté, Talita, and Tutú's. I don't think Valdivia will keep you on in his new cabinet, Mr. Secretary. And it isn't right that you and your family should be watching the public parade of advantage and wealth from behind the window.

And remember: You're an honorable man, and principles must always be good servants to bad masters.

Yours ever, *T*

54

THE OLD MAN UNDER THE ARCHES TO
CONGRESSWOMAN PAULINA TARDEGARDA

My beloved disciple and favorite friend, I turn to you with a sense of ur-
gency, yes, but also with the reflection and deliberation that you know
me for. "Slow and steady wins the race" has been my motto since the fig
tree blossomed and Felipillo was made a saint—a real Mexican saint,
crucified by the brutal Japanese in the sixteenth century, not like that
third-rate Juan Diego de los Nopales.

Well now, just think, the fig tree is about ready to topple over with
ripe fruit and the lonely nopal is flowering at last. Ah, the nopal, my
darling Paulina. The symbol and the strength of our nation, for if in our
emblem it is the eagle who rules and the serpent who suffers in its beak,
the eagle still needs something to stand on so that it doesn't fall into the
waters of the lagoon.

I suppose I'd rather come off as a sly but ignorant old man, because
the well-educated politician doesn't inspire the trust of the common
man. In the United States, Adlai Stevenson wasn't accepted because he
was too educated. "Egghead," they called him. Bill Clinton had to hide
his education from the public while Little Bush, on the other hand, actually showed off his ignorance. You know that sitting here in Veracruz
I like to make the most of my francophobia, but the truth is, like every-

one else, I grew up reading French novels. Dumas, Hugo, Verne—most of all Dumas and two novels, the one about the man in the iron mask, twin brother of the king who sent him to prison to eliminate any doubts as to who was in charge. Thrones have to be for one man only (or woman: sorry, Paulinita) because power depends on legitimacy for its authority. *The Man in the Iron Mask*, of course, and *The Count of Monte Cristo*, yes, unjustly imprisoned for years and years in a castle remarkably similar to our Ulúa, here in Veracruz . . .

Well, there you have it, my dear Paulina. Your old friend, the Old Man Under the Arches, is going to introduce you to the Man in the Nopal Mask.

He is a prisoner.

He lives in the dungeons of the Castle of San Juan de Ulúa.

He wears an iron mask to ensure that he remains unrecognizable to all—even himself, of course; to make it Mexican I had it painted nopal green.

Nobody knows. And I can rely on the absolute silence of the guards because in Veracruz my word is law. One blabbermouth ended up as a snack for the sharks. That's why Dulce de la Garza was allowed into the funeral crypt. Because I gave orders to let her in. All part of the plan.

I have kept this secret for eight years.

I've been patient. I'm more patient than those old ladies shuffling their cards. They say one old woman died while dealing cards. Your servant has survived by dealing his cards the way he likes. Quietly and unobtrusively, I rule this port of Veracruz. In a "balkanized" country, as Héctor Aguilar Camín would put it, divided into more fiefdoms than Argentina, who was going to deny me my little patch? Doesn't Vidales rule in Tabasco, Quintero in Tamaulipas, and Cabezas in Sonora? They've respected my little republic in Veracruz, which doesn't stretch farther than Boca del Río on one side and Hernán Cortés's crumbling old house on the other and the road to Tononocapan just beyond. . . .

Here, I do and undo. And anyone who gets in the way gets thrown into the aquarium to learn how to wrestle with the sharks. . . . Here I am, still, untouchable, smiling. Or rather, untouchable, smiling, and *patient*. You know I've never stopped educating myself, but I don't brag about what I know. You read Machiavelli's *The Prince* out loud to me when you were a young girl. You came to console me after I was widowed. Virtue, necessity, fortune. I've never forgotten that. The qualities of a ruler. In Mexico in the nineteenth century, Juárez depended on virtue, Santa Anna on necessity, and Iturbide on fortune. In the twentieth century, Madero was the virtuous, Calles the necessary, and Obregón the fortunate. You see, only the necessary one wasn't murdered. Virtue, necessity, fortune? I think only my good general Cárdenas combined all three. I, my dear Paulina, took advantage of all three, used all three, but I didn't possess them. How could I be virtuous, necessary, or fortunate if I spent all my time being suspicious?

My vivid political sayings have been repeated ad nauseam. But there are others I keep to myself.

"In the great battles, after the heroes come the villains."

"In politics, the noontime butterfly is the midnight vampire."

"In Mexico, the thief precedes the honest man, who will in turn be the next thief."

"The rear guard of Mexican politics are ass-kissers, thieves, blackmailers, villains, and perfumed groupies."

"Look at the doves flying. The vultures are right behind them."

Paulina, there are periods of national fright and there are periods of national fever. Today a feverish fright threatens. President Terán's death may well open the floodgates. Arruza is betting on a military coup. César León, on re-election. Herrera on becoming the late president's favorite son. As far as I can see it Tácito is out, he's too obviously corrupt, a lackey and an idiot.

I said as much to him once, "You're a rat climbing onto a sinking ship. You're too clever for your own good, but you're still nothing but an idiot."

"I serve the president, Mr. President," he had the nerve to say to me.

"What you do really well, Tácito, is obey the president's orders before he's given them."

"Sir, I'm what they call an independent courtier," the creep said.

"Never was there a better slave for a worse master." I sighed.

An amusing aside, Paulina: Knowing that Tácito's vanity is his greatest weakness, and that he thinks himself so popular, I organized a tribute to him, hosted by the so-called interest groups here in Veracruz. In that very place, when it was time for the toast, I accused him of being ambitious. Nobody stood up to defend him.

Tácito smiled, and extraordinary as it might seem, said, "What the hell do you want from me? I'm nobody. Don't waste your time attacking me."

"I'm not attacking you," I said loudly. "I'm defining you. You are a parasite."

"Since when has it been a crime here to do nothing?" he said with a broad smile.

As everyone present knew he was referring to them, the little gathering broke up with laughter and hugs.

[Brief pause in the tape, chuckles from the Old Man, and then a sigh.]

Andino Almazán is nothing but a puppet of his ambitious wife. The one I fear is Nicolás Valdivia. He's young, he's innocent, he's intelligent, I like him, and I'd put my money on him. The question, Paulina, is this: Is he ours? I don't think so. He's young, he's pure, he's independent. That is to say he's ambitious and is looking out for his interests and his interests alone. María del Rosario supports him. But does he support María del Rosario? That remains to be seen. I know you don't get on with the Dragon Lady of Las Lomas, as you call her. Think about it objectively, weigh it up, gauge your potential for influence. And finally, your president of Congress, Onésimo Canabal, he's pure Play-Doh. Between you and me we can shape him as we want, as long as César León, who has more power over him, doesn't get there first.

[Long pause in the tape.]

Paulina. A ruler can be good or bad, but he must always be legitimate. Or at least he must appear to be legitimate. In a matter of days, perhaps hours, Congress will grant legitimacy to the person it makes acting president. You know how patient I am. I've reached old age because I've always taken the long view. I've never indulged in instant gratification, unlike so many people do today. I know that times change. There is a time to live, and a time to die, a time for war, and a time for peace. . . . You read me that years ago, my darling girl, and it left me more impressed than a condom in the rain.

A time for war, a time for peace. How are we to separate them, to distinguish them? Let me tell you. Eight years ago, Tomás Moctezuma Moro started his candidacy with a platform of combative idealism that stirred up a lot of animosity—and there's plenty of that in this country. His government would have been impossible. They would have attacked him from every side. They would have paralyzed him and plunged the country into a tub of molasses. They would have frozen him as ice freezes, without the slightest breath of wind. Because wind is a hammer, but ice is a tomb. And that is that.

Paulina, you were the person who gave me the idea when you were inspired to say that the cold was the "secret ministry." And Paulina, is there any place colder, darker, more humid, more resistant to wind, but hammer and ice at the same time, than a prison cell in the fortress of San Juan de Ulúa?

The Man in the Nopal Mask. A symbol, Paulina, a symbol in a world that can't live without them. A symbol. The iron mask, but painted nopal green so that the poor prisoner feels comfortable, at home, less displaced. For eight years he's been believed to be dead. A wax figure melting under his tombstone, which reads:

TOMÁS MOCTEZUMA MORO

1973–2012

and a man in a green iron mask languishing in the dungeons of Ulúa for his own good, Paulina, you must understand that, for his own good, to save him from the death to which his impetuous idealism would have condemned him, to save him from the inevitable bullet of the hit man, the local boss, the drug trafficker, to save him from the vultures ready to eat him alive, I killed him, Paulina, I ordered his kidnapping for his own good and I myself, with the authority of an old patriarch from Veracruz, announced his assassination to the shocked country, and ordered the immediate capture and death of the assassin, an Argentinian madman called Martín Caparrós, a militant from the underground party Cattle to the Slaughterhouse: pure fiction, all of it, but the best fiction—that is, impossible to confirm. . . .

I organized the funeral here in Veracruz, since Tomás was originally from Alvarado, where every May the landscape is a forest of crosses asking forgiveness for that obscene language they use. In Alvarado that means a lot of crosses. You'll think I'm digressing, getting carried away about the place I came from. No, Paulina, Tomás Moctezuma Moro was the favorite son of this state; he deserved all the crosses in Alvarado.

I made all the people who participated in the funeral farce disappear (don't ask me how or where). The bogus embalmers, the manufacturers of the wax model, the inevitable witnesses (very few, only two or three) of the invented crime . . . And then one dark night, Tomás Moctezuma Moro entered the Ulúa fortress with no identity beyond that of "The Man in the Nopal Mask." And he's been there for the past eight years, his existence unknown, his mask part of his face, stuck to his skin. . . .

Why, what for, my dear child? To save him from himself, from his fatal idealism, from the inevitable swarm of enemies he'd aroused. Anyone could have murdered him! He was a threat not to too many, but to *all* vested interests. My idealistic, pure, dedicated, passionate disciple, why, he was like my son: Tomás Moctezuma Moro, eight years locked up in the castle fortress, eight years with the nopal mask, eight years waiting to be released and brought back into the light, when his virtues would no longer be a threat but a guarantee of legitimacy, butter instead of mustard for the national sandwich, my dear Paulina.

Let them not look for five legs when the cat's only got four. Let's not deceive ourselves, because Mexico already has a president elected according to the constitution.

His name is Tomás Moctezuma Moro.

He's our cat—but tomorrow he'll be a tiger capable of finishing off all those mediocre pretenders aspiring to succeed Lorenzo Terán.

Paulina. Set the wheels in motion for Congress to reinstate Tomás Moctezuma Moro and inaugurate him as the legitimate president elect—we don't need an interim president, an acting president, or new elections. Stop César León in his tracks. Push that pusillanimous Onésimo Canabal out of the way. We have our president. It's Moro's hour. Eight years ago he was killed. And today his restless idealism is the best medicine we can give this country after Lorenzo Terán's infuriating spinelessness.

Look me in the eye, Paulina. Look at me and see everything that's going to happen. Better still, imagine that everything that's going to happen has already happened.

And when you look at me again, don't be afraid. My blood has to run cold in order to freeze everyone else's.

55

"LA PEPA" ALMAZÁN
TO TÁCITO DE LA CANAL

So, my precious little melon, you were going to become president with my help? So first you had to become the perfect smoke screen that would fool the world, and you and I were going to form an alliance to make my husband Andino Almazán acting president so that he'd haul you up onto the Eagle's Throne? So I was to deceive my husband and lead him to believe I was working on his behalf to make him president? Is it possible I actually trusted you and your cynicism to get me where I wanted to go?

"My morals are inferior to my genius," you whispered to me as you blew your fetid breath into my ear.

Let me laugh out loud at your vanity, you disgusting idiot. You've been the doormat of Mexican politics. They say you chose the wrong vocation. That you should have been a priest, not a politician.

"You're wrong. He's both."

That's what my husband said when he told me that the interior secretary, Valdivia, had you by the balls with that MEXEN scheme, and that he had to appeal to Andino to make sure the treasury kept it under wraps. . . . And now, as if that weren't enough, you're trying to rope my husband into your corruption with a new financial scam.

You're a priest. You're a politician. But you're also an idiot.

In other words you're a piece of shit, and your only consolation is that in this goddamn country shit attracts ass-kissers, who are like flies. How will you go down in history, poor Tácito?

"Tácito de la Canal? He had problems with his digestion. A saintly aunt. A senile father. A bald head. Nails that went farther than his eyes could see. Programmed nightmares."

"Was he a fag?"

"Not that I know of."

"But he was a bachelor."

"That doesn't prove anything."

"Who did he sleep with?"

Oh, you bastard, they can link you with every last secretary and waitress for all I care, but I don't want anyone mentioning my name in connection with you. I'm warning you. I don't want to hear anyone say, "Of course. He was sleeping with Josefina Almazán, 'La Pepa,' you know. . . ."

Did you think I'd go that far to defend you, you loser? What haven't you done in order to get to the top? Do you think I haven't seen you talking on the phone to the late president (when we had telephones, you bastard), standing up as you talked, clicking your heels every time you said "Yes, sir!"? Do you think I haven't seen you saving the stubs of the cigarettes that killed President Terán in the end? Do you think I haven't seen you standing in front of the mirror, saying, "Nothing defines me more than my desires. They are unique. Mine and mine alone!"

Oh, and to think of how I put up with your nonsense, your vain pretensions. I was working on you the way they do in the Yucatán, using you to help my husband—I was always Andino Almazán's loyal wife, even when I let you lick my ass, you worm. Look at yourself in the mirror. Do you really think a woman could fall in love with you, my beautiful darling? Do you think I didn't want to piss myself laughing when after your pitiful orgasms you'd say, "I'm devoured by ambition. I want to leave my mark on the wall of time, and all I have, like a lion, are my claws"?

How dramatic of you, dear! God, what I've had to put up with! And all of it for Andino, to help him on his way to the presidency, to forge an alliance between him and his opposite, General Arruza, and then strike. President Almazán—and not acting president, but president for six years, with the aid of Arruza's coup. That was the real plan, not yours, you miserable shit. I even slept with Arruza and used you as a cover to get you to believe that all the scheming was for your benefit. Oh, how Arruza and I laughed at you! My general—now there's a man who really knows how to fuck. Not like you, you worm . . .

"Careful," the general said to me. "He may be a worm. But remember that when you cut worms down the middle they keep on moving."

You know, the best thing about all this is that nobody will ever believe that a delectable, sexy Yucatecan woman like me could want a slob like you in her bed.

And you know something else? I'm being open with you because I don't give a fuck if you show this letter to everyone in the world. You've got no credibility left. Everything you say or do will be taken for fraud, fraud, fraud. . . . That's what's written across your melon head: LIAR AND THIEF.

"I have the features of an ascetic and the ways of a libertine."

That was the first thing you said to me, you slug. That was your calling card. I had to hold back the laughter. I was ready to play all my cards. With the general, so that he would declare Terán incompetent, push him out of office, and name Andino interim president. Then we'd just leave him there as a puppet while Arruza and I ruled the country together. You were the second option in case you made it to the presidency "on your own merits" (after all, in this life anything is possible) or Congress named you president and Andino only interim. How long would you last? As long as the general and I wanted, no more than that.

Or at worst, you, as the interim president, would have backed Andino for president, with Arruza ruling from behind the throne.

You see, it was a game of chess in which I was the queen, Arruza the king, Andino the bishop, and you the bloody pawn.

Goodbye, my poor Tácito. You crawled out of a hole and now

you're going straight back to where you came from. And tell Nicolás Valdivia that ideals aren't important, that convictions aren't worth a fucking thing. Tell us whose side you're on. That's what matters.

Oh—by the way, Valdivia has banned you from entering any government office. FYI.

56

DULCE DE LA GARZA TO
THE OLD MAN UNDER THE ARCHES

Mr. President, I can no longer bear my joy and my sadness, which is why I'm writing to you. I don't know if I'd dare look you in the eye, you who have caused me so much pain and who now give me back an impossible happiness that I stopped dreaming about long ago. You summoned me to the café by the port. I knew that Tomás respected you immensely. How many times did he tell me that you were more than his mentor, that you were like his father; and like a father you always advised him not to be so good, to be tougher.

"The worst enemy of power is the innocent," you said to Tomás, and those words are engraved on my heart, like everything my love told me. "Up until now you've been a docile pre-candidate, which is as it should be. Now you want to be a reformer. Wait. Don't be too eager. Don't start your day in the middle of the night. Make your reforms when you're sitting on the Eagle's Throne, like I did. Take advantage of my experience."

Yes, I know Tomás was brave, that he never held back, that he threw himself into the ring. Yes, I know that all the powerful people in Mexico saw him as a threat. That's why they killed him.

I've endured eight years—I was twenty-one then, and I'm twenty-nine, nearly thirty now, "in the flower of my youth," isn't that what they say? Eight years of suffering, Mr. President. At least my pain was solid, real. Now, all of a sudden you appear and plunge me into a pit of desperation and misery worse than before.

Yes, Tomás is alive. And you have the nerve to tell me what you told my love when you—and nobody but you is to blame—took him away from me. . . .

"Tomasito, think of yourself as a privileged prisoner. Think of life as ugly and dangerous and cruel. Look, my boy, close the door to the world for a little while, and come back rejuvenated. Wait for your moment: It hasn't arrived yet. It will come. I swear."

You didn't have the courage to go to that cell yesterday. Instead you sent Tomás a written message via me. I have it here:

I wanted to give you power. I wanted to give you the chance to do the things I couldn't do because in my day the system was different. I'm so sorry, truly sorry, Tomasito. You didn't understand. You didn't know how to judge the moment. What I did, I did for you. It was neither the first nor the last time I would offer you my good counsel and try to shield you from your idealistic impulses. Now your time has come. Now the country wants legitimacy, symbols, drama, hope. Not since the Resurrection of Christ has there been a resurrection like yours, my son. I who shun publicity will have an army of photographers and reporters waiting for you when you come out. From Ulúa? God, I'm better than that. Listen to me, Tomás: You were never in Ulúa. You got lost in the jungle, you were kidnapped, disoriented by torture and peyote—you got lost in the goddamn jungle. A witch from Catemaco buried your fingernails and your hair underneath a ceiba tree. You've been under a spell for eight years, Tomás, lost in the natural world, part of the jungle yourself, no different from the vanilla creeper, the pepper plant, the prickly pear, the hawthorn, the *jonote* tree, the sugarcane, the vast, abundant natural world of Veracruz that was there before we were born, Tomás, that enveloped you like a splendid cloak, that swallowed you up and made you part of it. . . . Don't forget, Tomasito, you are under a spell. You sleep sitting down because if you lie down the sea breeze won't blow over you. You sleep with the windows open so that the rain from the Gulf of Mexico soaks your skin. And if you die, they can just say that the "North Wind" was an accomplice in the crime. You thought you were dead, Tomás. And now your girl Dulce has appeared to rescue you, to tell you, "We've found you at last! You got lost in the jungle."

Oh, Mr. President. What were you thinking? Do you really believe what you said to me?

"Everything in Mexico requires symbolism. If they can turn an amnesiac, impressionable, ignorant Indian like Juan Diego into a saint, why not make Moro president at the right moment, which is the year 2020—not 2012! Miracle, miracle! Miracles, faith, trust—what motivates Mexico more? A president-elect lost in the jungle, amnesiac like a saint, who reappears to reclaim nothing less than the Eagle's Throne! A sensation, Miss de la Garza! And what a sensation if you, his saintly girl-friend, are the one who rescues him and delivers him back to his rightful place. A love story! Love and miracles, my dear! Who could be opposed to that? It is my masterpiece. Now I can die in peace, I can leave behind the sealed envelopes, 'the concealed one,' the electoral racket, the carousel voting, the ballot tricks, all those dead people's votes, everything else that went on when I was president. This is the culmination of my political career: I've given Mexico the right president at the right moment, I've resurrected him just like God the Father resurrected his son Jesus Christ. I've brought him steeped in mystery back to the world. All the ingredients are there: cloak-and-dagger adventures, mystical ascensions, inevitable pain, melodrama, lovers reunited . . . Miss Dulce, sweet lady, can't you sense the emotion in my voice, my recovered strength, my masterpiece completed?"

Yes, Mr. President, I feel it and I feel sorry for you, and I feel hatred for you, as well. Shame on you. I think you've gone mad. You're deranged, a senile monster who plays with the lives and emotions of others without any humanity. . . . You were right to send me to Tomás, and I went happily, but I was scared to death, too; my heart was pounding because I didn't know what I'd find.

They led me down those dark tunnels that smelled like the forgotten dead. A filthy rat looked at me as if it wanted to seduce me. Saltwater dripped from the ceiling, and the whole castle creaked as if offended by my footsteps. I'm telling you this so that you can see the eloquence that took hold of my head and my tongue, preparing me for the most intense emotion of my life. . . .

He was wearing his mask when I entered the cell.

"Tomás, my love, it's me. . . ."

Nothing but silence. The longest of my life, long enough for me to remember how Tomás and I first met, at the museum in Monterrey, and then to remember every moment of our love.

"Tomás, my love, it's me. . . ."

He turned his back on me.

Then, he scribbled something on the wall with a piece of chalk, something he'd written a thousand times before, as the cell was covered with those white marks, fading in the humid air:

BREAD. TIME. PATIENCE.

I embraced him. He freed himself from me with a violent shrug of the shoulders. It threw me—it was like being struck by lightning. I sank to my knees and held his legs.

"Tomás, I'm back, it's me. . . ."

I looked at him, imploring him.

He remained silent.

I caressed him, still down on my knees, and then I looked up, imploring him.

"Take off your mask. Let me see you again."

He laughed, Mr. President. Never in my life have I heard laughter like that, and I hope I never hear it again. It was as if he had chains in his throat, iron instead of words. My own voice began to tremble, as if death were my lover, as if I had risen from the grave that I visited for eight years, taking flowers to it, sometimes crying, sometimes refusing to let my tears fall onto that gravestone. My own voice trembled, as if I were a lover who, having resigned herself to disappearing, was now back to court death, because that man you cruelly deceived, imprisoned, and perversely—yes, perversely—manipulated is no longer mine.

He is another man, and I don't know what to call him or how to speak to him.

He didn't respond to my words. I pulled at his mask, I tried to pry it open like a can. He only laughed. Then a voice escaped, stifled, indistinct, a voice that I didn't recognize, asking me who I was, what I was doing there, how I dared enter the place that was his and no one else's.

"Your face . . . let me see your face, Tomás. . . ."

He told me not to be an idiot, that I wouldn't want to see the face beneath the mask because why would he be wearing it, if not to hide something awful, the face of a monster, an eagle's head, snake's eyes, and a dog's mouth? Is that what I wanted to see, idiot that I was, a man with the face of a lunatic, smothered by his beard and unable to speak properly, so that even the guards couldn't bear to look at him when they took off his mask to feed him? They'd put the mask back on and he'd just let them, not even putting up a fight. He'd gotten used to the mask—"bread, time, patience"—and he'd go completely insane in the daylight. Reality wasn't outside, it was here inside, and he'd believe that until he died. He was a prisoner, yes, but free from the shams, the lies, the illusions, and the dreams of the outside world.

"This is my house: truth, peace, time, patience."

What he said hurt me. He spoke without recognizing me, or he pretended not to recognize me, I don't know, but he refused to look me in the face, and his voice was muffled by the huge clump of hair, as thick and dense as that jungle you cruelly invented, the voice shut in behind the mask, and then those bizarre words: "Wake the dead, since the living are asleep. . . ."

He didn't recognize me. But I tell you, and I knew Tomás Moctezuma Moro better than anyone: He's found his home inside those four frozen walls. He can't even see the water or feel the sea spray down in that hole at the bottom of the Gulf of Mexico. San Juan de Ulúa is the only reality he knows, or wants to know. And that, Old Man, is your cruel and evil accomplishment.

How did I know it was him?

That voice was unmistakable, even distorted.

How could I tell he was alive?

From the fear in his eyes, which were visible through the slits in the mask.

From the fear in his eyes, Mr. President. A fear that I can't imagine, not even in my worst nightmares, a fear of everything, do you understand? A fear of remembering, loving, desiring, living, dying . . . The fear that you put there, Mr. President, and may the devil bury you in the deepest pit in hell the day you die. And I'd pray for that day to come soon, but I know that your life is already a living hell.

It was all in vain. You sacrificed the man I love for nothing. Tomás Moctezuma Moro will never leave Ulúa. Neither alive nor dead. That cell is impenetrable. It's his womb. He wouldn't recognize any other home.

Your home is a house of shame. Or perhaps—and this would be even worse from your point of view—the house of lost opportunity. I think this must be the first time things haven't come out the way you hoped. You sicken me. But most of all I pity you.

I have only one thing to ask of you. Keep on bribing the cemetery guards so that I can open Tomás Moctezuma Moro's false grave, as I did before.

57

TÁCITO DE LA CANAL TO
"LA PEPA" ALMAZÁN

Don't worry about me, my love. I've lost everything. Except the most
intimate refuge of my soul, which is my love for you. I don't care if you
mock me, insult me, push me away forever. I don't care. I've come back
to the safest harbor. I want you to know that. It's neither a triumph nor
a defeat. You reproach me for my servility and vanity. You humiliate me
and I deserve it. Everything I thought was fortune has suddenly, instantly, changed.

Yes, I'm the man to whom the president could say, "Tácito. Jump
out the window." And I would reply, "With your permission, sir, I'll
gladly jump from the roof."

I had a premonition, you know, the day a foreign head of state came
to Los Pinos to see the president. I was waiting for him at the door, and
he handed me his raincoat as if I were a servant. That's what he thought
I was. I should have crossed my hands behind my back, like British roy-
alty do, to indicate politely that I was not a palace servant. But since that
was, in fact, exactly what I was, I took the man's raincoat, bowed my
head, and ushered him into the office. He didn't even glance at me. And
there I was, clutching the president of Paraguay's raincoat, as he walked
away from me remarking, "It's so cold here in Mexico!"

I was definitely the servant. And again I asked myself what I'd asked when I started working for President Lorenzo Terán. "What the hell do they want from me? I'm nobody."

You'll say, "Sure, now that you're no one you can play at false humility."

Believe me. Don't believe me. What does it matter? I'm writing to you for the last time, Pepona. I'll never write to you again, I swear. I only want you to know how and where I've ended up, and I want you to know that I accept it with genuine humility.

My father lives in a tiny, isolated house in the Desierto de los Leones. It's a modest, decent little house, very hidden away. The only way to get there is by taking those very steep, winding roads from where you can see Ajusco. My father is very old. I call him my AP, my "Aged Parent," as a tribute to something I read in a novel by Dickens when I was young. Yes, I was young once, my Pepa, hard as it may be for you and the rest of the world to believe. I was young, I studied, I read, I prepared for the future. I was driven by ambition and by something else: my father's destiny. Not to repeat it, to be precise. I couldn't bear to be like him.

For three consecutive six-year cycles, the AP was a significant influence on Mexican politics. He went from one government ministry to the next, always wielding his power from the shadows, always as a political operator working for the big payoff—that is, getting the PRI to put his minister on the presidential ticket, and then push him into office. He never managed to do it, and so he always gained the winner's trust. Nothing gains people's trust quite like losing. Always in the shadows. Always a secret operator. He couldn't hope for anything more than that because he was born in Italy of Italian parents, the Canalis of Naples. That was why people could trust him: His ambitions were thwarted by the law. He himself could never be president. Three six-year periods. But then the day came when he had too many secrets under his hat. That was the problem. So many secrets, in fact, that nobody believed they could possibly all be true because secrets are, by nature, contradictory and ambiguous, and what is inevitable for A is nonsense for B, what is virtue for X is vice for Z, and so on. In other words, everything my father knew, everything he knew too much about, turned against him in the end.

"A" reproached him for keeping a secret when it could have been useful to expose it.

"B" pounced on him because he didn't understand that my father's silence protected him, while what B really wanted was for his secret to get out and become a political threat.

"X" wanted my father sacrificed precisely because of his secrecy: The secrets he kept were crimes of state.

And "Z" reproached him, on the other hand, for a series of supposed indiscretions. . . .

Yes, he was pulling strings on too many puppets and the theater of his life was a house of cards.

My father was clever. *Too* clever. Too clever for his own good. He overdid it. He forgot to purge those who purge. He forgot that the best way to secure your enemy's life is by killing him. He forgot the immortal lessons of the longest dictatorships: Invisible service to the powerful can bring reward but also punishment. After a time my father knew so many secrets that people began to fear him, and he became famous. His silence didn't save him. On the contrary, they decided to bury him before he could open his mouth.

How did they destroy him? With flattery, my Pepa. Heaping praise on him. Dragging him out of the shadows that were his natural habitat. Showing him off and applauding him at the political circus, trotting him around the ring. My poor father suffered—he couldn't decide if he should stay in the shadows or revel in his public adulation. He forgot the cry of one of Stalin's close collaborators: "Please! Don't flatter me! Don't send me to Siberia!"

Yes, my AP had too much applause. Not the public kind, which doesn't matter, but the private: the applause of the president, which inspires people to feel envy and spite for the president's favorite. . . .

In short: He spent too much time being both the light of the house and the darkness of the streets.

They say that public figures are condemned to live in constant anguish but must never show it. And yet sometimes anguish must be translated into action. Stalin was terrified of dentists. He preferred to let his teeth rot rather than risk going to the dentist. In other words, one believes that loyalty, not ability, is what gets rewarded in the end. Laugh at me if you want, remember all my despicable acts, mock me for my vanity. And take pity on my defeat. It is simply act two of my own father's downfall.

It had been years since I'd last seen him. I always sent him money, but I was afraid to go near him. Failure is contagious, and I didn't want to end up like him. I was going to succeed where he failed. I was going to make it to the Eagle's Throne. Bernal Herrera, María del Rosario, my great enemies, you, the woman who betrayed me, the little enemies that one should never underestimate, the little snakes inside my own office: Dorita with her sky-blue ribbons; Penélope with her hulking frame and dark skin; and the true architect of my downfall, Nicolás Valdivia, who is now interior secretary, the man who thought up the scheme that cost me my power, those damned documents kept by that imbecile archivist Cástulo Magón, those documents that I signed only because President César León asked me to, a request that was an order and a consolation:

"Don't worry, Tácito. I have an archive all ready for the moment I leave office. I need it for my memoirs. I'll be selective, I promise. But I can't sacrifice a single document from my administration. You understand. A president of Mexico doesn't govern for just six years. He governs for posterity. Everything must be saved, the good and the bad. Who knows, my good Tácito, time might prove you were right about those necessary legal oversights. What will matter more in the end, the fact that we cheated a group of small shareholders or that we saved the great companies that are the driving force behind an export economy like ours?"

He smiled mischievously.

"And besides, the archivist has orders to put the originals through the shredder. I'll keep certified copies."

There was a blatant threat in his beady fly's eyes. Oh yes, my Pepa, that man is just like a fly, his eyes can look in every direction simultaneously. He has very long antennae on his head. He has two pairs of wings, one for flying and the other for keeping his balance. He always lands on trash dumps. He's an old fly, gray with a yellow belly. That's what gives him away. Be wary of him. He can stick to walls and crawl across ceilings. He uses maggots as bait, and everyone knows maggots feed on dead flesh. You despise me. I don't despise you, and that's why I'm warning you now: Don't rest on your laurels with Arruza. Don't be taken in by the pure brute force of the general. And keep your eye on César León. He always has an ace up his sleeve.

I told Valdivia all this and now I'm telling you, especially now that you're in bed with a wolf. Let Arruza the wolf fear León the fly. Whoever thinks the ex-president is willing to retire is sorely mistaken. He'll keep on being a nuisance until the day he dies.

But I want to get back to my Aged Parent. The world was his downfall, my Pepa, just as it was mine, but it was worse for him because he never aspired to the Eagle's Throne; all he wanted was to keep on operating from the shadows. Yes, and since he was less ambitious, it hurt more to lose. It was like an affront to his moral code of discretion, you see. Thanks to his modesty, a vast horizon stretched before him, as long as his career as a trusted political adviser—like Talleyrand, Fouché, and Father Joseph Le Clerc de Tremblay, the original éminence grise at the side of Richelieu. Look how quickly my memory comes back—I'm the passionate student of history again. Oh, but that only shows how much I've changed, Josefa. I'm someone else—do you see? I feel purified by this moment of emotion. My father's greatest gift, his greatest strength, was that of being invisible. It earned him the trust of powerful men. But it made him expendable when he finally knew everything but was still nobody.

I went into the little house in the Desierto de los Leones.

The girl that looks after the AP was wearing the traditional outfit of the *china poblana.*

"What's your name?" I asked her, because although I pay her salary I'd never seen her.

"Gloria Marín, at your service."

I smiled.

"Oh, just like the actress."

"No, sir. I *am* the actress Gloria Marín."

And it was true, she looked exactly like one of those disturbingly beautiful belles of the Mexican cinema. Gloria Marín: jet-black hair, eyes wistful and suspicious but sensual behind the inevitable defensiveness of the world-weary Mexican woman. Her profile was perfect, her face oval, light brown. And those lips, always on the verge of a bitter smile. In appearance, submissive. In reality, a rebel.

"Where is my father?"

"Where he always is. Watching television. Day and night."

She wrapped her shawl gracefully over her breasts. I didn't bother telling her that the television antennae had been dead since January.

"Oh. Day and night?"

"Yes. He sleeps there, he eats there, he says he can't miss a moment's television. He says those people might come and kill him at any moment, and he has to be ready to defend himself."

"Who wants to kill him?"

"Bad people."

"What are their names?"

"Oh . . . Sute Cúpira. The other one's Cholo Parima. I dream about them, sir. He says they're Venezuelans and they live in a jungle called Canaima."

I stared at her, more and more bewildered by the minute.

"All right. Your name's Gloria Marín. And the man you work for, what's his name?"

"Jorge Negrete."

"No. His name's Enrico Canali. Where did you get the name Jorge Negrete from, bitch? Negrete was a movie star, a matinee idol, the kind of heartbreaker that women like you used to dream about. He died nearly a century ago."

Gloria Marín started crying.

"Oh, sir. Don't tell him that. Don't kill him. He's Jorge Negrete. He really believes that. Don't take that away from him. I swear it will kill him."

She lowered her eyes.

"Call me whatever you want. At your service."

I sighed as I used to sigh when I was a young man. Then I walked into the tiny living room, which opened onto a neglected patio where grass grew between the cracks in the tiles, and a solitary *pirú* tree made its penance. And there, in an easy chair facing the television sat my AP, my Aged Parent, his eyes fixed on the screen. He was talking to himself, in a reverie.

"Now I go into the bar and I give everyone a dirty look. 'Machine gun's here!' I shout, my hair in my face, and the whole place goes quiet, they're scared, and I grab the prettiest girl by the waist—I'm sorry, Gloria, not you, you weren't in this movie—and I sing 'Oh, Jalisco, don't back out . . .'"

He felt my presence, and his cold, freckled hand that felt like marble settled on top of mine and guided it up to his shoulder, as if thanking me for being there without knowing who I was. He changed the picture with the remote control. You see, he was only watching a homemade montage of scenes from a bunch of different old movies. Suddenly, there was Jorge Negrete dancing away on a Veracruz stage to the melody of the Niño Aparecido *son* with the stunning Gloria Marín dressed like an aristocratic lady from the nineteenth century in a mantilla and ankle-length silk skirts, and Negrete dressed up like a *chinaco*. The two of them gaze at each other with a defiant passion until the villain, an apothecary named Vitriolo, mad with jealousy, stabs Gloria with a knife. . . . My AP fast-forwarded the tape, his hand trembling in anticipation of the excitement of watching Jorge give Gloria a long, slow kiss in the film *A Letter of Love*.

My father paused the film as the two characters kissed, and sat there in rapture, savoring the moment.

Then, after a long while, he turned to me.

"Thank you for coming to see me. I've been waiting for my squire."

He looked at me with a blank stare.

"Who are you, young man? Mantequilla or El Chicote?"

"Chicote, Father."

"What?"

"I'm sorry. Chicote. I'm Chicote, your loyal companion."

"That's what I want to hear. Come on, have a tequila and lime over here in the corner, it's on me, we'll drink until we fall over, and we'll dream of all the women who let us down, you and me, soul mates. . . ."

Negrete sang on the screen, my father sang from his chair, and I sang too, holding on to my father's hand, as we watched scenes from the movie *Me he de comer esa tuna.*

> *L'águila siendo animal*
> *se retrató en el dinero.*
> *Para subir al nopal*
> *pidió permiso primero.**

Out on the patio, not paying us any attention, Gloria Marín watered her flowers and sang her own song: "I am a little virgin, I water the flowers. . . ."

She directed her gaze, coy and coquettish, at me.

I looked back at her.

You can say what you're thinking, Josefina: "Of course you'd end up fucking her. . . ."

How sorry I am that your husband, honorable to a fault, had to tell you about my financial recovery plan, calling me a scumbag and a criminal. Let's see how you and he navigate these turbulent political waters. I offered him a transatlantic liner. He's willing to put up with a canoe. It's in God's hands now.

**The eagle, being an animal, / had its picture drawn on coins. / Before climbing up the nopal / it asked for permission first.*

No matter what you read, no matter what they tell you, remember this: I'll always be a politician, and politics is a business with many twists and turns. In politics, you assume your responsibilities and you get what you put into the job. That's the way it has to be, that is the simple truth.

Yours,
T.

58

NICOLÁS VALDIVIA TO
EX-PRESIDENT CÉSAR LEÓN

Distinguished president and esteemed friend: I know that nobody knows the rules of national politics as well as you. Every president leaves behind a rosary of more or less famous sayings that become part of our political folklore.

"In politics, you have to swallow frogs without flinching."

"A politician who is poor is a poor politician."

"He who doesn't deceive, doesn't achieve."

"Onward and upward."

"We are all the solution."

"If things are going well for the president, things are going well for Mexico."

I remember only two of yours.

"In order to preserve customs, we must break laws."

"Becoming president is like reaching Treasure Island. Even if they expel you from the island, you'll never stop yearning for it. You want to return, even though everyone—including yourself—tells you no."

Very well, Mr. President, the moment has arrived. It's time to abandon Treasure Island. I understand your feelings. You would like to be an agent of reconciliation at a difficult time for the republic.

You've stated publicly, "The struggle for power destroys the one thing that gives power any meaning, which is to create wealth for the country within a framework of peace and legality."

I couldn't agree with you more. And I understand your dismay, Mr. President. You're anticipating the struggle ahead. You fear that it will degenerate into riots, civil war, balkanization, dog-eat-dog, and all that. And you see yourself as an agent of unity, experience, authority, and continuity.

Mr. President: I see how you act and I think that the politician who goes around thinking he's more than he is will never know who he is.

This confusion, this lack of self-awareness, might be interesting material for psychoanalysis but it's fatal for the person in question and, above all, the political health of the country.

I know what's going through your mind—some matadors will die and some will shield themselves behind the barriers, but the fierce bull will never abandon his favorite spot in the arena.

Yes, I want to eliminate them all until he and I are the only two left.

So now the question is: Who is "he"? And who am "I"?

Yes, Mr. President, power effects its own fiction, according to the distinguished Chilean philosopher Martín Hopenhayn, in a reference to Kafka. And fifty years ago, Moya Palencia, interior secretary as I am now, said that in Mexico Kafka would be considered a chronicler of local customs.

I find it amusing that Mexicans call "customs" what the rest of the world, the *serious* world, calls realpolitik—which is nothing less than the politics of my friend Machiavelli: "Since all men are wicked and do not keep faith with you, you also do not have to keep it with them." The Prince's skill lies in his ability to use this evil reality in his own interest, while seeming to be acting in the interests of the people.

The crack in Machiavelli's system, Mr. President, is the belief that the Prince's enemies have been blinded by his glow and scared off by his power. The powerful man believes that wrongs can be righted by showering gifts.

"He's deceiving himself," my namesake would say.

The Prince would be better off decapitating all his enemies immediately and in one fell swoop. Doing it little by little, he would run the risk of leaving someone out.

"For injuries must be done all together . . . and benefits should be done little by little, so that they may be tasted better."

That was your mistake, President León. In your eagerness to consolidate the power you achieved through elections (questionable elections, let's face it), you lavished the benefits, adulation, perks, lucrative deals, in one fell swoop. You wanted to gain allies who could give you legitimacy, without realizing that no matter what you give to a bloodhound, it will always want *more*.

And that *more* is power itself.

So you, Mr. President, have no cards left because you've dealt them all. In the process of seducing so many potential enemies you lost your chance to chop off their heads. The result? You're loved by neither your friends, to whom you gave everything, nor your enemies, to whom you gave a little. And you know it.

"A few minutes ago, he was my friend. Half an hour was enough to make him my enemy."

Be honest. Don't lie. How many times have you said these words to yourself?

Believe me. I'm your friend, and I fully understand your complaint:

"Yesterday they were all cheering me! Today they're all silent. If only they'd insult me at least! Yesterday I was indispensable. Today I'm a nuisance. If only they'd kick me out at least!"

I feel exactly the same way. And that is exactly what I am doing now, Mr. President.

My aide, Jesús Ricardo Magón, will be delivering this letter to you personally. He will then accompany you to the door of your house. From there, a military escort befitting your status and rank will escort you to the international airport, where a very comfortable seat awaits you in the first-class cabin of a Qantas Airways plane, which will take you directly to the beautiful land of the kangaroo, Australia. Once there, don't forget to take note, please, of the marsupials who carry their young in pouches, so as to ensure the healthy growth and development of their offspring, and in turn of their descendants.

Extending you the assurance of my distinguished consideration and wishing you a good journey,
Nicolás Valdivia

59

GENERAL MONDRAGÓN VON BERTRAB
TO NICOLÁS VALDIVIA

Mr. Secretary, esteemed friend, in keeping with the principles of the republic and in compliance with Article 89, section VI of the constitution,
I would like to inform you that in the early hours of the morning of
today I saw to the death of General don Cícero Arruza, found guilty
of sedition and of attempting to overthrow the legitimate government
of this country by the ad hoc military tribunal that I assembled to address this urgent situation, in the knowledge that my actions would be
fully supported and sanctioned by you, in the absence of an acting president following the terrible loss of President Lorenzo Terán.

You know as well as I do that there are times when it is incumbent
upon the armed forces to act with speed, as long as these actions are in
the interest of protecting our republican institutions.

General Cícero Arruza's criminal intent is patent in the numerous
letters he has sent me since the onset of the crisis in January, written
with a recklessness that I can only attribute to drunken spirits. Reader
that I am of both Clausewitz and Machiavelli, I cannot help but invert
the German's terms here and remark that politics is a continuation of
war by other means. And as to the Florentine thinker, I would say that
it is better to take preventive measures during times of peace than allow

ourselves to be surprised during times of war. The threat posed by General Arruza's coup attempt has been thoroughly eliminated.

I regret to inform you that General Arruza was discovered in bed, in the throes of an adulterous affair with Josefina Almazán, wife of our honorable treasury secretary, Andino Almazán. The general attempted to reach for a gun from beneath his pillow, and this, as you might imagine, provoked a response from the men sent to apprehend him. Unfortunately, the gunshots did not spare Mrs. Almazán, whose body has since been delivered to her husband, whose resignation, if I am not mistaken, should already be in your possession.

Mr. Secretary, I trust that you will understand and support my decision to remove General Arruza's wounded body from the bed and to transport him in his last hours to the military headquarters of Military Zone XXVIII in Mérida. There, his body was placed standing up against a wall so that he could be put to his death in a manner worthy of his unquestionable military merits. I would like to say that he was afraid. He was not. Not because he was brave. Bravery was not possible for him at that moment: He no longer had a gun to speak his truth.

His last words from the bed were, "Nobody makes a fool of me."

Later, as he took his last gulps of air, his body against the wall, he managed to say, "What's the matter with you? Fire! Or don't you have the balls?"

With respect, and in recognition of my obligation to render a faithful account of the aforementioned events, I remain, as always, under your command today and in any and all future circumstances that I may consider favorable for you and for our nation.

General Mondragón von Bertrab, DEM

P.S. The Yucatán is full of rock pools and underwater caves. Arruza has gone to a watery grave.

60

CONGRESSMAN ONÉSIMO CANABAL
TO NICOLÁS VALDIVIA

To the president: With great satisfaction I hereby fulfill my constitutional obligation and inform you that, in strict adherence to Article 84 of the Political Constitution of the United Mexican States and in the absence of the plenary of the Honorable Congress of the Union that I am proud to preside over, I have convened the permanent commission of the same in the interest of pursuing the proceedings with respect to the appointment of the acting president who shall conclude the presidential term of don Lorenzo Terán, following his unfortunate death last week.

In the presence of all the members of the permanent commission and following the initiative of Paulina Tardegarda, congressional representative of the state of Hidalgo, the members of the commission have unanimously voted in favor of you, Nicolás Valdivia, currently serving as interior secretary, to assume the functions of the chief executive of the country, in the capacity of acting president.

The Congress of the Union, which I have convened in an extraordinary session in its faculty as electoral college, has unanimously ratified the aforementioned decision and, as such, you, don Nicolás Valdivia, are hereby invested as Acting President of the United Mexican States effective as of this date and until the date of the constitutional change of powers on the first day of December of the year 2024.

I would like to extend my congratulations to you, as well as my invitation to assume your position in a solemn ceremony on the fifth day of May of this year at five in the afternoon. I would also like to take the opportunity, Mr. President, to offer the assurance of my highest esteem and my best wishes for the success of the appointment that the nation has bestowed upon you.

Onésimo Canabal
PRESIDENT, HONORABLE CONGRESS OF THE UNION

61

JESÚS RICARDO MAGÓN
TO NICOLÁS VALDIVIA

Mission accomplished, Mr. President. With the authority you lend me, I find all doors wide open. Even the doors of a fortress like the one at San Juan de Ulúa, that castle to which you sent me because you can trust me, because I answer only to you, because I hold your secrets and because if I betray you I betray myself.

"Only you can do me this immense favor," you said to me, Nicolás. "There's no one else I can trust."

With sadness I looked at your sadness. It was almost as if you were saying to me, "This is the last favor I'll ask of you. After this, if that's what you want, we won't see each other again! . . ."

Instead, you said, "You're going to drink from the most bitter chalice of all."

You looked at me with an intolerable air of philosophical complicity. (Oh, how I have begun to identify and despise your tics.)

"Drink it down to the bottom. This act is the culmination of the political education I promised you on your pigeon-infested rooftop. Do you remember? Set off on your own path, if you want. Go back to being a long-haired anarchist, if that's what you want. Your *paideia* is complete."

If only you'd sent me alone, Nicolás. That was my one consolation. I'll do what he asks me, I said to myself. When I accepted the pact with this devil disguised as an angel, which you are, Nicolás Valdivia, I knew in my heart of hearts I couldn't avoid a final test, that "test of God" to which the old Norse heroes were subjected. Afterward I'd leave in a Viking ship. Even if the ship burned like a funeral pyre and I were the sacrificial victim. . . .

I was going to a funeral. But it was my own funeral. You've tested my loyalty to the point of making me a murderer. Your armed thug. And despite everything, look at how things are, look at what twins you and I've become, in the way we speak, walk, dress. . . . You Pygmalionized me completely, Nicolás Valdivia, you turned me into the mirror that you needed in order to feel secure, to feel that you, too, were young, intelligent, beautiful, rebellious. I've been your clone—in the way I talk, the way I walk . . . and now, in the way I kill.

"Is it necessary?" I dared to ask you, recovering some of that old rebelliousness that you crushed with equal measures of passion and tyranny. . . .

"We can't go on living with a ghost."

"No. *You* can't go on living with a ghost, Nicolás. Don't generalize."

"All right. I can't live with a ghost."

You chewed on those words like a bull until you belched in my face, "A restless ghost."

You made me believe that I was going to the Ulúa dungeon alone.

"Nobody will know but the two of us."

You didn't have to say any more. You and I always keep our secrets.

One by one, the prison guards opened the heavy metal doors for me, each one closing behind me like a symphony of iron, like in those old black-and-white James Cagney films that we loved to watch late at night, you and I. A melody of metal that I heard for the first and last time.

But it was just me. Me, with my own name, Jesús Ricardo Magón, son of an archivist and a baker; sole inhabitant of a utopia of pigeons and words; avid reader of Rousseau and Bakunin and Andreyev; the Anarchist of the Clouds; the Tarzan of the Rooftops; long hair and no more clothes than a pair of torn jeans and a Che Guevara T-shirt. Stained.

There I was, the pure young man who was going to depose all the corrupt tyrants, standing in front of the prison cell of Tomás Moctezuma Moro inside the San Juan de Ulúa Castle—the purest hero, the incorruptible politician who was so very irritating to everyone, and intolerable to you. A restless ghost, did you say? So restless that he could turn you into a scheming, weak person—one more over-ambitious, vulgar political *arriviste*. Is that why you feared Moro, because of the brutal contrast between his personality and yours? Was he such a threat to you, even in prison?

Tell me, have you thought about it? Even dead, might he still be a threat to you, *my love?*

And there I was, standing in front of the door to Moro's cell, almost agreeing with what you said: "There's no such thing as an anarchist who doesn't eventually turn into a terrorist. Your language is impotent, so you compensate with criminal action. *Quod erat demonstratum.*"

I accepted it. It's a crime, but a crime of state. Weren't all the anarchists' acts of terror against the kings, presidents, and empresses of the Belle Epoque? Don't smile. Haven't you read Conrad's *Under Western Eyes?*

"Women, children, and revolutionists hate irony."

Anarchists don't have the right to humor. Not even black humor, Mr. President?

I stopped in front of Tomás Moctezuma Moro's cell. I was about to go in, to kill that symbol of legitimacy and purity that so many people find uncomfortable.

That was when, just behind me, I heard faint steps, as light as a butterfly. The cell door opened and I turned away from the infernal stench, as if that subterranean tunnel were the road to hell itself, the meeting place of all demons, this underground tunnel beneath the Castle of San Juan de Ulúa, its ceilings dripping not just with saltwater but liquefied blood, blood so old that it had become part of the universal currents of the oceans, the blood of hungry dogs and drowned sharks and hanged pirates and mermaid whores, and in that tunnel were vast jungles of seaweed and tightly shut oysters with baroque pearls. All this I felt pounding inside my head, Nicolás. The sunken, watery crypt of Ulúa, and I was going to have to walk through it alone, no one else would have this wretched experience but me.

No one but you and I would know what happened on that evening in May in the dungeons under the Ulúa Castle.

"Good evening, young man," the greasy creature said to me. His presence engulfed me, like the smell of rancid pig's fat. He was breathing in and out, in a stinking gasp, his voice both sleepy and threatening, like the voice of a sleepwalker who doesn't know what he's doing. . . .

A fetid odor emanated from his body, even from his sickly eyes— and from his insolent hand brazenly holding a Colt .45 automatic that seemed like a natural extension of his arm.

He wore black gloves.

Even in the darkness of the tunnel his raccoon eyes blazed with insanity.

"Come on, what are you waiting for, you idiot?" he called out, shoving the barrel of the gun into my ribs.

"I . . . I thought I was alone," I stammered.

"Alone? The crabs in Tecolutilla—now, they're alone, and they walk backward. But me and you, my friend, we're going to walk forward now."

"I don't want witnesses," I said, summoning up my courage. "I thought it was just supposed to be me."

"Yeah, so did I," laughed the legendary strongman from Tabasco, Humberto Vidales, also known as "Dark Hand"—as if you, Nicolás, didn't know he was going to be my partner in crime. "But the new president's clever, he wants two witnesses for every crime. Even if both of them are guilty. That way, he says, one cancels out the other. As if murderers were marbles—same color, same size—that you could just swap, one for the other," he said, laughing monstrously and expelling another gust of that sickly breath that could have awakened the dead.

Vidales opened the door to the cell.

Tomás Moctezuma Moro was asleep.

The famous nopal mask covered his face.

"He never takes it off, not even to sleep," the obliging warden had said to me.

He didn't want anyone to be able to tell what he was feeling, to detect tenderness or passion, to see the "still life" of his inner world, Nicolás, the "cold wounds," as we put it one day here in Veracruz—but in very different circumstances.

Vidales sensed what I was feeling.

"Don't be sentimental. I know what you're thinking. It's better like this, while he's sleeping, don't you think? He won't even know. More charitable, wouldn't you say?"

He cackled.

"Only nuns are charitable. That's what my old mentor Tomás Garrido always said, governor like me of Tabasco. He's got his memorial stone in the Arch of the Revolution. You and me, boy, we'll be lucky if we get ourselves a little brick in the Arch of the Transition, in the service of Lady Democracy. . . ."

Again he laughed in his sinister way and nudged the back of the sleeping Tomás Moctezuma Moro with his foot. As quick as lightning, the Man in the Nopal Mask was awake and on his feet, peering out at us through the terrible slit in the mask that was like a metal gash. Moro stood still, like a heroic statue. Serene and unshakable. A statue—it was frightening, as if he were dead before he'd died.

Vidales fired.

Moro didn't speak.

He fell on his face, as it were.

There was no display of emotion.

He didn't cry, "Murderers!"

He didn't beg for mercy.

He didn't say a word.

We heard the dry sound of the iron mask hitting the floor.

That was how Tomás Moctezuma Moro died for the second time.

That, Mr. President, is how the ghost of Banquo was laid. Only it wasn't Macbeth who occupied the empty seat of power. Because although it ended as it did in the Shakespeare play, this drama smacked of Veracruz, Mexico City, and Tabasco, as "Dark Hand" Vidales pointed out.

"Very clever, this new president," he said, smiling and offering me a cigar. "I don't turn you in and you don't turn me in, right?"

He gave me an ugly look.

"Don't forget—if anything happens to me I've got my dynasty of Nine Evil Sons to take revenge. Who've you got, smartass?"

Now he smiled.

"Go on, take it. It's a Cumanguillo. I don't go around offering these cigars to just anybody."

He glanced down at Moro's bleeding body.

"Get out of here. And don't forget: this didn't happen and neither of us was here. I'm in Villahermosa celebrating Son Number Eight's eighteenth birthday. What about you, you little bastard?"

He closed the cell door and we were out in the eternal cold of the Ulúa labyrinth. There was no end to his conversation.

"You know who committed this crime?"

I shook my head, disquieted.

"One-Eyed Filiberto and don Chencho Abascal."

"Who?" I asked idiotically.

Dark Hand laughed.

"One-Eyed Filiberto and don Chencho. They commit all my crimes. They're invisible. No one will find them, because I made them up." He stopped laughing.

"Don't you forget. I'm not just the governor, I'm the boss. And when I die, I told you, I've got Nine Evil Sons to carry on the killing. We're a dynasty, and we have our own motto: 'Stone by stone and hit by hit, the Vidales men win with grit and spit.' "

And he went, leaving behind an aroma of Cumanguillo cigar and narcotic weed.

Don Jesús Reyes Heroles was right when he said that barbaric Mexico dozes but never dies, and wakes up furious at the slightest provocation.

Thank you, dear president, for making me see that with my own eyes.

Thank you for letting me be the person I was before I met you.

Thank you for proving to me that the anarchist always, inevitably, becomes a terrorist in the end.

Thank you for making me see that the doctrinaire rebel will inevitably make his insurrection a reality.

And watch out, Nicolás Valdivia, because now I'm a murderer.

And my next victim will be you.

62

NICOLÁS VALDIVIA TO
MARÍA DEL ROSARIO GALVÁN

My beautiful lady, I don't want to seem insistent, but I do feel it's time for you to honor the promise you made to me when we first met. I am what I am and that was your condition, wasn't it?

"Nicolás Valdivia: I'll be yours when you're president of Mexico."

That's why I'm at your window. I adore your coquettish ways. Before you open the doors of your house to me will we be repeating our initial rite? That's fine. I'll go along with your whims. You have the right to ask what you want of me. Your prophecy came true. I've arrived, as you so boldly foretold in January. Or should I say promised.

I realize that I owe my position not to María del Rosario Galván, but rather to a chain of events that nobody could have predicted at the beginning of this fateful (or very fortunate) year. Once again, need is a matter of chance. Don't think that I'm any less grateful for that. On the contrary. I came to you with no commitments, pure and free. I have you to thank for my political education. I'm the star student who has come to give his teacher her prize. Might I now complete my erotic education in her bed?

I'll follow your instructions. Tonight I'll return to the woods surrounding your house and from there I'll watch you take off your clothes in front of the lit window. Give me a sign. Turn off the other lights, light a candle, as if you were in one of those old mystery films—and I'll come to the "beds of battle, soft field."

Anxiously yours, *N.*

63

MARÍA DEL ROSARIO GALVÁN
TO NICOLÁS VALDIVIA

"In the dark night, a beautiful stranger . . ." as the song goes. You, a stranger? Someone I don't know? You're my creation, my clay, my male Galatea. Yes, you do owe me. A lot. Everything, I'd say. Everything. Except the final prize. The jackpot. You owe that to people less significant. You used the dwarfs to get where you are. Why? Were you afraid of me? Were you afraid that if you owed me everything I'd turn you into nothing?

You've learned a lot, apart from knowing whom to trust. All we can do, Nicolás, is study character as much if not more than actions. What did Gregorio Marañón say about Tiberius? That power corrupted him. No! *He was always evil.* But, you see, the light of power is so *powerful* that it reveals what we've always been but have kept hidden in the shadows.

Your power and my power reveal our true selves. A couple of opportunists. Gangsters. Blackmailers. Predators. Criminals. Surely both of us know that the most ambitious person is always the one who dramatizes himself the least.

Be careful, then, of the least conspicuous. I told you this at the beginning so that you wouldn't be taken in by Tácito de la Canal's pretensions—he was the most transparent politician I've ever known. The only thing you could trust was his untrustworthiness. How could a hypocrite like Tácito have become president, a man who pretended to be on the brink of abject poverty so that one of us would rescue him?

And poor Seneca—he was the anti-Tácito. He wore his intelligence on his sleeve. He was what the fastidious English most deplore. Too clever by half. Too much brilliance blinds those who live in the shadows of mediocrity. Seneca offended people with his intelligence, just as Tácito offended people with his hypocrisy.

Seneca criticized himself: "My principles are solid, but my practice is terrible. All I can do now is grow old and cynical."

No. He committed suicide. Despite not being married, marriage being the surest path to suicide.

César León. There you have him, discreet with the people who were useful to him, but brutally indiscreet with those he despised. Indiscretion won out. In his heart, he was a sentimental person. Outside politics, though, he felt displaced. As if the land he lived in as president was the only land that existed. In a play this would have been his closing speech: "I spoke to Destiny like an equal. I defied Fortune. I said: I dare you, bitch. I'm invulnerable to goodness. And better still, I'm invulnerable to evil."

Did you know he always carries a miniature guillotine in his pocket, and that he plays with it the way other men play with their penises?

President Lorenzo Terán, on the other hand, was *too* discreet. He said very little or nothing at all. Yes, he did have perfect muscular reflexes. That was why he was so good at handling public relations. He knew that in Mexico the forces of nature are on our side. If it isn't an earthquake, it's a flood. Or a drought or a hurricane. In Mexico natural disasters get turned into public profits. All a president has to do is make an appearance at the site of a disaster and disappear again. That's how he avoids having to deal with the deeper issues.

But tell me, has there ever been anyone more inconspicuous than Onésimo Canabal, president of Congress, that fugitive of the public rest rooms? Mediocre, submissive, embarrassed by his ugly physique and humble background. But wasn't Jesus born in a stable? Nobody would ever imagine that the real kingmaker of this succession would be poor old Onésimo Canabal.

Nor did anyone know that he was conspiring with your good friend Paulina Tardegarda, a viper capable of repainting paradise with the colors of hell. And I thought it was I who was the double of Madame de Maintenon, the princes' tutor who ended up marrying the king! Is that what I should do, retire like Louis XIV's other lover, Madame de Montespan, to a convent to train young nuns to be better courtesans than I? Or do you think that with your current power, Nico, you can somehow prevent the succession process, the 2024 elections that I swear will take Bernal Herrera to the presidency? Yes, Bernal Herrera. For the good of the country, Nicolás. Because Bernal is discreet—that is, if the word "discretion" means prudence, caution, tact, good judgment as well as the measured, intelligent use of uncontested force.

We're going to fight, you and I, Nicolás Valdivia, because you can't fool me. You've become merely a substitute president until 2024. Did you think I couldn't sense your ambition? You can't succeed yourself. But you can immortalize yourself. That's what I fear. A colossal scheme of yours to stay in power.

You have an arsenal of pretexts. The economic crisis, internal revolutionary uprisings, foreign invasion, power vacuums. What won't you do to keep yourself in power! Everything short of aspiring to the Nobel Peace Prize. And that ambition will wound you irredeemably, for sure. That aside, I fear you. This is the struggle now. Bernal Herrera and I will do whatever is necessary to make you relinquish the presidency in 2024. Whatever is necessary—even the impossible. Just as you will do all that is necessary and even impossible to stay on the Eagle's Throne forever.

You're not Lorenzo Terán, a good and democratic man who was not in love with power. Ah, we always need a dignified, noble figure who can redeem the wretchedness of the rest of us. Now that man is Bernal

Herrera, as it was Lorenzo Terán before, but he was ill. You think you'll go on forever. You do have one virtue, I admit. You stand for new blood. But you'll be old soon enough—as soon as you begin to spill the blood of others, something you'll do if you want to stay in power. But remember the price of blood. Tlatelolco, October 2, 1968. It lasted one night but cast a long shadow.

Today you're lauded for being young and clean. A reason for hope. Worthy of your position. But power will corrupt you in the end. Take it from me. You don't know how to resist temptation. I know you. You don't know when to stop. And you've proven as much, efficiently and perhaps a bit hastily, ever since you became president. You got rid of Tácito, César León's back in exile, Cícero Arruza has been assassinated, Andino Almazán publicly cuckolded, and Moro put to rest forever with a lying-in-state, his body riddled with bullets from that little episode in Veracruz that robbed the Old Man of his raison d'être because without the Moro secret he's just a pathetic old man playing dominoes. However, you still have to face the cabinet you inherited from Lorenzo Terán. And the local bosses in the rest of the country. Let's see how you do—I'll be watching.

You know, Nicolás, a man can cease to act in politics, but the consequences of his political actions are there to stay. You do know—and that will be your dilemma. You'll cover the holes of your mistakes (and your crimes?) but for every hole you cover up, three more will be exposed. That's what they call "consequences." That explains President Terán's passivity. He didn't want "consequences." He wanted to retire and live in peace. Then he got blood cancer, leukemia combined with pulmonary emphysema. And yet he still always feared that the "consequences" of his actions—or his inaction, which is also a kind of action, perhaps the most dangerous kind of all—would plague him far beyond his days on the Eagle's Throne. Destiny intervened. We'll have to wait and see how he goes down in history.

History. You haven't made much yet, Valdivia. Remember that you'll be governing a destructive country that protects itself and deceives itself with false psychology and a sensitivity, born of suffering, to art and death. You tried to court the middle ground. You had no other choice when you were a nobody. But now you harbor, and I admit I encouraged it, what the Germans call the *dunker-instinkt,* the much-misunderstood but profound desire to have power and exercise it with style.

Style makes the man, they say. Style is everything.

And beauty? Is that part of style? No. Only fools believe that. Beauty, like style, is a question of will. Beauty is also power. Look at me, my conquered one. Do you think I don't look at myself in the mirror every morning? Without makeup? Do you think I deceive myself? I'm a coquette: I do my best to deceive the rest of the world. Did I tell you that I'm forty-five, forty-seven? I can't remember. It's not true. I'm forty-nine. The fact is, I have to recreate my beauty every morning, like someone painting a picture, creating a design, or perhaps more pejoratively, shaping an advertisement. Whether I'm convincing or not, I want to be admired so that I can get what I want. Admired but untouchable. I'd like to be a statue.

Do you know what a lover of mine once said to me? "The trouble with you is that you're so beautiful on the outside, you must be appalling on the inside."

"No," I replied. "The trouble with beauty is that it condemns you to sex, and the trouble with sex is that even though it's a pleasure it can't turn bad news into good news."

"But maybe it saves you, despite the bad things," he said.

"I want to save myself despite all the good things," I told him, confusing him forever and forcing him to run away from everything he didn't understand, which was a lot.

Do you understand me, my poor little Nicolás? Look at me properly. Age is a woman's unpunished murderer. You're younger than I. I bet you thought you could enjoy the benefits of my maturity and perhaps be my last good fuck.

Were you stripped of your illusions yesterday, my stupid little sweetheart?

I saw you the day you were sworn in as president at San Lázaro. And

I saw a dangerous smile I'd never seen before. You frightened me. It was more a smile of deception than power. The smile of a real-life villain. A smile that said, "I've fooled them all." That's when I decided to make you suffer for all that I've suffered, though not because you've done me any harm.

I decided to make you the reason for all the bad things I'd ever experienced—you were to be the bag into which I'd put my suffering, even though you weren't the cause.

As I watched you fasten the sash with the eagle and the serpent, I realized, "Nicolás Valdivia has become great. But his love is small. He's a man who doesn't know how to love."

I read you in an instant, like an open book. There's no love in your life. Father, mother, family. Girlfriends. Lovers. You're like an island in the middle of a huge river. Preoccupied by ambition, never creating a deep connection with anyone. Licked by the waters of the river but unable to bathe in them.

Tell me if you know of an absence of love that can't be healed by the experience of being loved. That was my promise. I showed you the path that led to me. But you went off course. You postponed things. You humiliated me. You separated "achieving power" from "achieving power because she allowed me to." Do you think I can forgive you for that?

I want you to suffer how I've suffered. See how truthful I am? See how I debase myself? See how I let myself get carried away out of passion, against the calm, better judgment of my true soul mate, Bernal Herrera? But understand one thing. I want you to suffer for all that I've suffered since I was born, not because you've done me harm. Nor because I believe for an instant that you ever loved me, or that I ever loved you.

You kept to our arrangement, our rendezvous in front of my window, just as you did in January.

Did it hurt to see me last night in the window?

Did it hurt to see me naked again?

Did it hurt to see me in the arms of another man?

Did you hear, confused with the weeping of the trees, my sighs of orgasm, my moans of pleasure?

You postponed things. Forgive me. You always told me how much you liked him. You shouldn't have. I took him away from you. You played your cards well—all of them except that one.

Should I thank you for having introduced me to the best, most beautiful lover I've ever known, someone who shamelessly licks my ass, my clitoris, puts his fingers inside, and makes me come twice, with his tongue and with his cock, crying out to me, begging me to stroke his anus, which is what all men secretly wish for, to help them come faster and harder—the anus, closest to the prostate, the hole of the most secret, least confessed, least demanded pleasure.

He asks me for it.

"Your finger. Up my ass, María del Rosario. Please, make me come. . . ."

Dark, tall, muscular, tender, rough, passionate, and young . . .

What a marvelous lover you gave me, Nicolás! From the beginning he spoke to me in the familiar!

But be very wary of him.

Jesús Ricardo Magón is convinced that you want to kill him.

This is my final piece of advice. I think you're the one who should make sure that he doesn't kill you.

Crimes committed out of the fear of being killed are far more common than crimes committed from a desire to kill.

Forget about me as your lover. Fear me as your political rival.

And go. You're searching in vain for a crack in my soul. You'll never find it because it doesn't exist. Am I different from everyone else? Who is master of his own soul? The man who believes he is is only deluding himself. We can't be. We are in the process of being. We don't submit ourselves to reality. We create it. Go, little creature, *mon choux*. . . .

64

MARÍA DEL ROSARIO GALVÁN
TO BERNAL HERRERA

I know there's a hint of mockery in your smile, Bernal, but there's affection in your eyes, an affection we've always shared. By "always" I mean since we were young.

Since then we've never hidden anything from each other, you and I. We know each other's personal history and family history, which in the end are one and the same. In fact—you know this better than anyone—the most mysterious thing, and perhaps the most exciting, is that ever since childhood we've learned to create an interior world, and we've developed a kind of double commitment: to our objective environment and to our subjective one. The exterior world changes and so does the interior. On the one hand, there are the things that are outside us and contain us; on the other are the things inside us that we contain. All of life is a struggle between these two forces. Sometimes it's harmonious, as it's been mostly for you. Other times it's an uphill battle, like swimming upstream, difficult as mine's been.

How lucky we were to have met when we were young, and to have known instantly that we each gave what the other lacked. Your steadfast nature comes from your parents. You're the son of humble and honest social activists, Bernal and Candelaria Herrera,* labor organizers at a factory up in the north. You owe them your solidarity with the people who most need to know that they too count and that they have the shelter of a political roof. That is the mission of the eternal left, you say, to tell people, "You're not alone. You have a roof here."

From your parents you also understood that purity of ideals is not enough in itself. That in order to gain half of what we want, sometimes we have to sacrifice the other half. Your parents never accepted that compromise. They were heroes of the labor movement and their sacrifice was surely not in vain. Who deceived them? Who made them cross the Rio Grande by night, making them believe they were saving a group of illegal immigrants, only to fall into the hands of the U.S. immigration service? They were shot in the back as they fled and subjected to the "Fleeing Fugitives Law," Bernal—the unjust and searing lie—you who knew your parents, Bernal and Candelaria, so well. They never ran from anyone. They never turned their backs on anyone.

The "Fleeing Fugitives Law." How can they call such an abominable act a law?

When we met in Paris, you told me all about your life and about how your parents had been sacrificed because of a sinister conspiracy hatched by the drug traffickers in the north, the corrupt politicians on both sides of the border—Chihuahua and Texas—and the corruptible forces of law and order in Mexico and the United States.

You told me, "I'm not going to be a pure idealist like my parents. I'm going to be able to tell the difference between the lesser evil and the greater good. I'll serve the greater good by making concessions to the lesser evil."

I envy you those parents, Bernal. I said it then and I'll say it again now as I look back on the farce and tragedy that was my family life. I wasn't born into poverty like you. I didn't have to escape hardship as you did. On the contrary. I had to overcome wealth. The table was set.

*See "Malintzin of the Maquilas" in Fuentes's *The Crystal Frontier.*

I was born into privilege. My father made me a rebel; I had to oppose him, be different from him, ignore his cynical tirades, his rather admirable lack of hypocrisy as he openly talked of his frauds, his illegal schemes, his business acumen. In politics, one must pretend. In business, one can be openly brutal and cynical.

My father frightened me so much I had to spy on him if I wanted to see him at all. I began listening in on his telephone conversations from a phone in the hall.

"Sell the fleet of old trucks to the Ascent to Heaven Company for the highest price you can. . . ."

"But Ascent to Heaven is our company, sir."

"Exactly. We claim the capital profit as earnings and then sell shares at the highest price possible."

"The Herreras are stirring up trouble in the north, demanding legislation for job security in your factories, sir. . . ."

"Well, let's do the same as we did when they wanted to save that ecological mountain site full of birds and ocelots. No laws protecting the environment, no laws protecting job security, Domínguez. Buy as many legislators as you have to."

"Buy?"

"All right, persuade. Pardon my brutality."

"There is one legislator, pretty stubborn, who wants to pass a law that sanctions lawsuits against fraudulent investments. . . ."

"Look, Ruiz, you just worry about inflating the value of those bull-shit shares so that we can sell them and make a profit. That's our business. Don't confuse the issue."

"The company in Mérida is reporting losses, sir."

"No company of mine reports losses if I don't want it to. With Mérida, hide them by selling the subsidiary at a high price."

"Who is going to want to buy it?"

"We will, stupid, the company in Quintana Roo. . . ."

"How is that going to happen?"

"With a loan from us. That way we keep it in the family, our companies finance one another, we hide the losses and attract more investors. . . ."

"And what happens when we can't do that anymore?"

"Look, Silva, only when we've made ten times our personal holdings, only then will we declare bankruptcy and let the shareholders take the hit. Meanwhile, I need you to make everyone think that we're doing just terrific, take the idea and stretch it like chewing gum, as far as it'll go, so that the shareholders keep on investing, so they don't catch on that we're about to go bankrupt. Understood?"

"You're a genius, sir. . . ."

"No. My mother was the genius—she was the one who came up with the brilliant idea of giving birth to me!"

"What are we going to do with the executive bonuses this year, sir?"

"Maximize them, Rodríguez. Maximize them with share options and hide the expense so the investors don't get wind of it. Never record options as expenses. You hold on to your millions."

"What about the employees?"

"Fuck 'em."

"I should warn you that Quique, your speechwriter, is getting a little out of line, he's been going around and saying that he gives you all your ideas, sir."

"Get rid of that ass-kissing bastard now. Take his things out of the office and put them out on the street."

"He has been a faithful employee for twelve years. . . ."

"There's always work out there for a good ass-kisser. . . ."

"And the investors?"

"They can go to hell."

"And the prosecutors?"

"Don't you go worrying about them. Don't say a word. Nobody's going to send us to jail. There are too many people out there who depend on us."

My mother was better. Just like my father, she always wore black.

"I'm in mourning for Mexico. Eternal mourning," he used to say.

And so she imitated him and went even further with that funereal severity by wearing a long black skirt all the time.

Do you think you can picture me as a little girl, sitting at the dinner table between my father and mother, both wearing black from head to toe, eating their meal without exchanging a word?

He stared at her with his wildcat eyes.

She never looked up from her plate.

The servants had learned not to make a noise.

And yet there was more hatred in my mother's downcast eyes than in my father's fierce scrutiny.

If there was affection it was there in my father's yellow eyes as he looked at me—but it was guilty, cagey. Over and over again, I'd hear him rebuking my mother behind closed doors.

"You couldn't give me an heir. You're completely useless."

"You may be everyone's boss, Barroso Junior, but you can't give orders to God. It was God's will that she should be a girl."

It was as if the Virgin Mary were apologizing to the Holy Spirit for having given birth to a girl.

My father's resentment, though, ended up working in my favor. He had no male heir. The doctors had advised my mother, Casilda Galván, not to risk a second pregnancy. It made them both bitter. My father decided to educate me as if I were a boy, thinking that one day I would inherit his fortune and run his businesses. That was why I was able to study in Paris, meet you, and fall in love with you, Bernal. I was the rich little Mexican girl who went to study at the University of Paris, all expenses paid, so that I could hang on to all those millions my father would eventually leave me. And you were the government's young scholarship student, a protégé that Mexico sent to France almost as a compensation for the death of your parents and the injustices you suffered for having the same name as your father.

"Since my name is Bernal Herrera, just like my father, they arrested and tortured me, thinking I was him. Then, finally, the Juárez police chief came in and told them, 'Don't be idiots. The father's dead, and we even buried him.'"

There was suffering in your expression, but it was combined with serenity, and I envied that; it was a look inherited from pain and courage and faith . . . I don't know.

You, on the other hand, could see the family bitterness in my eyes, and you reproached me for it.

"Sweetheart, resentment, envy, and self-pity are poison. Turn what you feel into the will to love. Into the freedom to act. Don't wear yourself out hating your father. Overcome it. Be more than him. Better than him. But be different from him. That's what will most rankle inside him." You laughed, my love.

You and I in love, Bernal Herrera. It was love at first sight. A love born in lecture rooms and the books we read, in the cafés on the Boul'Mich, on our walks along the Seine, in the old films on the Rue Champollion, during our hurried meals of *croque-monsieur* and *café au lait*, our impassioned readings of the immortal *Nouvel Obs* and Jean Daniel, our study sessions, our book-hunting expeditions along the Rue Soufflot, our passionate nights in your attic flat on the Rue Saint Jacques, the dawn views of the Panthéon, our protection. It was love at first sight.

"We're in Paris. Nothing changes here. The city's always the same. That's why lovers in Paris will always be lovers!"

Tra-la-la.

There were two reasons why I had to rush back to Mexico.

First, because I found out that my father had cheated my mother out of her money. Once they were married, they combined their assets. My mother had inherited a large beer consortium and it was understood that my parents' common assets didn't include my mother's involvement with the company, only her personal estate.

One fine day, the executive board of the company summoned my mother and informed her that my father had not only driven her personal fortune into the ground through a series of fraudulent financial operations but that he had also forged the signature of Casilda Galván de Barroso, taken control of the company stock, and cheated everyone out of their money.

I returned to Mexico in the middle of this melodrama. I only made it worse. That was when I announced to my father that I was in love with you and that I intended to marry you.

"A Communist! And dirt poor, no less! The son of my archenemies, those trade-union ringleaders in the north! You've gone mad!" my father shouted, as he threw his bowl of scalding soup at me, got up from the table, and started hitting me while I cried, "Stop it! Hit me but don't hit my child!"

Bernal, my love. Melodrama is inevitable in private life. There's no family without its soap opera. And what is melodrama, but comedy without the humor?

"I don't want sons-in-law!" my father exploded.

The furies that had always tormented him were unleashed on the accumulated disgrace: the "lost daughter," the wife who had "ruined him." Even though he had, in fact, been the one to ruin everything for us with the rage that was too much even for him. It was a storm, a tempest on open ground, the rustling of dry trees and sterile plains and raging skies, Bernal, a raw fury like a resurrection of all the dead seasons of his life—silent springs, long, hot summers, black autumns, discontented winters. Yes, Bernal, my father's rage was let loose, as if poisoning himself weren't enough—he had to poison the rest of the world as well.

"My daughter! Some communist's whore!" he howled like an animal. "My daughter, the lover of a man who harassed the Barroso family and tried to ruin all of us! My grandson, a child with poisoned blood!

"Whore, swine, you belong in a pigsty," he shouted, and he hit me, tearing the tablecloth off the table, destroying all the glasses and plates, staining the rugs, all of it in front of my mother, motionless, cold, dressed in black, reproaching my father with a deadly look. Then, suddenly she stood up and took a gun from her bag, observing the fleeting shock that crossed his face. At that, my father took out his own gun and they faced each other, like in a Posada etching or a Tarantino film, pointing their guns at each other and me in the middle, battered, terrified, wanting to separate them but defeated by my womb, by the instinct to save my child, our child. . . .

I moved away from the dark, obscene figures of my parents. I backed out of the dining room. I saw them looking at each other with hatred, dollar bills and bile in their eyes. Standing opposite each other, both armed, pointing their guns, waiting. Who would shoot first? The duel was a long time coming.

Outside the dining room, I began to scream, covering my ears so that I wouldn't have to hear the shots, trembling, clutching my belly, not daring to go back into the dining room.

They were dead.

My father was on the table, his face half-buried in a plate of strawberries and cream.

My mother was under the table, her black skirt pushed up high above her sex. For the first time I saw the milky whiteness of her legs. She wore ankle socks, I said to myself.

They were both dead.

I inherited both fortunes. I liquidated all my father's debts. I saved my mother's shares. The beer company was very understanding, even generous with me. But bad luck prevailed. Or rather, bad luck came along with the good luck, as is often the case.

"Oh, how small my fortune is—when will I see it grow?" as the late general Arruza used to say.

You came back to Mexico. You asked me to marry you. Now there was nothing in our way. My father was dead. But the little boy was born.

What is a chromosome? It's the messenger of heredity. It communicates genetic information. Every human somatic cell has a nucleus that contains twenty-three chromosomes, organized in pairs. One half is paternal and the other maternal. Each chromosome can duplicate: It is its own twin. But when an intrusive chromosome—a "third man"— suddenly appears, the total number of chromosomes is raised to forty-seven, and this abnormality results in a strange creature: a flattened face, mongol eyes, deformed ears, flecked irises, broad hands and stumpy fingers, weak muscles, and the forewarning of arrested mental development. Down syndrome.

What were you and I to do?

Keep the child with us, treat him as our son, which is what he was— is? Dedicate ourselves to him? Look after him, me the devoted mother, freeing you to pursue your career?

Kill him, Bernal, relieve ourselves of the unwanted burden?

Love him, Bernal, peer into his odd little eyes and see the spark of divinity, that creature's desire to love and be loved?

Together we decided that fighting for power was less painful than fighting for a child.

How cold, how clever we were, Bernal. What did we want, you and I? The same thing. To be active players in politics. To carry out the things we learned at the university in France. To build a better country on top of the ruins of a Mexico cyclically devastated by a combination of excess and shortage: poverty and corruption equally rooted, evil people who were far too competent and good people who were far too incompetent; affectation and pretension at the top and grim resignation down below; lost opportunities; governments blaming everything on the people and their civic passivity, and the people blaming the government's ineptitude; a general belief in signs, as if instead of federal law, our constitution was the *Popol Vuh* of Mayan antiquity . . .

You and I were going to change all that. We had immense confidence in our talent and our education in a country of amateur politicians. We wanted to act legally, but we were also willing to be flexible.

"Politics is the art of the possible."

"No. Politics is the art of the impossible."

Who said what? You first, then me, or was it the other way around, as our unforgettable agriculture secretary would put it? The fact is, Bernal, we stopped being parents to one little boy because we thought we would become godparents to a whole country.

The boy was deposited in an institution. We visited him from time to time. Less and less, after a while, discouraged by the physical distance, the mental wall.

We didn't listen to the voices that told us, "Get closer to him. These children are more intelligent than they seem. They have a different kind of intelligence."

"And what kind is that, doctor?"

"The intelligence of a world unto itself."

"Impenetrable?"

"Yes, possibly. We still don't know. But real. Whose job is it to try?"

"To try what . . . ?"

"Whose job is it? Yours, as his parents, or his?"

We didn't explore these enigmas. We distanced ourselves from these options. We did what we had to do without the burden of an *idiot,* yes, I don't mind going to the root of the word. *Idio,* what is ours, *idios,* what is loved, *idiosyncratic,* what belongs to one person . . . Do you remember Emilio Lledó's extraordinary lecture at the Collège de France about Plato's *Phaedrus,* about that speech that is the seed of language? The language that when "unjustly condemned needs the help of a father, since it is not able to defend itself." For that reason, Lledó taught us, all language must be interpreted so that it can be "submerged" in "the language of which we are comprised, the language that *we are.*"

We've spent nearly twenty years, you and I, speaking the conventional language of politics. Wouldn't we have been capable of speaking the creative language of a child? Perhaps a poetic language?

What was the price, Bernal? Accept it. Not only did we distance ourselves from the boy that was ours, our own. After a while, deeply involved in our respective political careers, we distanced ourselves from each other. We never stopped loving each other, seeing each other, talking to each other, conspiring together . . . but we were no longer *idiots,* we were no longer *ours,* we no longer lived together—sometimes we'd go out to a bar and sometimes, even, we went to bed together. But it didn't work. There was no passion. We preferred to abstain so as not to sour our great friendship.

You are a good man, and that's why we couldn't live together. Without you, I could freely exercise the dark part of my soul, the part I inherited from my father, without hurting you.

I've always told you about my love affairs before the poisonous gossip reached your ears. I know that in politics skill, not truth, is what wins arguments. I've told you before, "A liar falls sooner than a one-legged man." Being a good liar is a full-time job. You have to devote yourself to it entirely. And that's precisely what politics allows you to do.

Long ago, the liar was often sent to purge his guilt in a monastery. But Mexico is neither a convent nor a monastery. It's a whorehouse. And you've been the austere monk of the whorehouse of Mexican politics. That's always been your strength. Morality. Contrast. You've cultivated them in the name of what used to be called "moral renewal." You've been tough and pragmatic when necessary, fair and legalistic when appropriate.

You never told me anything about your private life and sometimes I think you had no private life at all. Or, as my father, Leonardo Barroso, Jr., once said, very cynically, "We all have the right to a private life. As long as we have the wherewithal to pay for it."

I've worked with you unconditionally. I knew Lorenzo Terán was terminally ill since the day he became president, in fact. He wasn't the first ill man to take office. François Mitterrand became president of France knowing he'd die in the Elysée Palace. Roosevelt knew it, too, when he allowed himself to be elected for the fourth time. Perhaps that knowledge gave them the will to survive with the energy we remember them for. And the will to keep their secrets, just as Terán kept his. He trusted me completely. His illness was the reason I began to prepare an inexperienced young man, someone who'd barely started to shave, someone I could mold. He'd take over the presidency if Terán died—he'd be interim president if Terán died during his first two years in office, and acting president if he died in the last four years. But he was only meant to be passing through; Nicolás Valdivia would only be passing through, until your own presidency, Bernal, once your adversary Tácito was eliminated.

Valdivia complied very conscientiously with all I told him to do. But he always believed that when I said, "You will be president," I meant a full six-year term. He never suspected that I only considered him feasible as acting president because President Terán was ill. A new Emilio Portes Gil. He was obedient and loyal. There were certain things that he—and nobody else—could control. The Old Man Under the Arches. The simpering passion of that soap opera queen Dulce, whatever her name is. The impenetrable mystery of Ulúa. The Moro affair that you and I wanted to make invisible by eliminating it from public discourse, as if it didn't exist at all, a secret sealed up forever at the bottom of the sea . . .

But then again, Valdivia was useful for spoiling the ex-president's little schemes, not to mention the heinous general Arruza's plot—we never imagined Nicolás would overtake us and get in with General von Bertrab to find out what Arruza was up to, to say nothing of what he found out about the idiotic pretensions of Almazán, that Yucatecan whore, and Andino, her bottomless pit of economic science and political mediocrity.

All of it under control and all of it in your favor, Bernal. Fate smiled on you. The coast was clear. Onésimo Canabal, the president of Congress, plays the fool, but he's craftier than a pirate, and he knows which way the wind blows. All of us have our secret vendettas. And Canabal's vendetta was that of avenging the humiliations heaped on him by the terrible ex, César León (no adversary should ever be underestimated). Eliminating César León has been Onésimo Canabal's obsession. Andino made him laugh, but not Pepa, because he knew about the Mexican Madame Pompadour's secret affairs with Tácito and Arruza. Onésimo, sneaky son of a bitch that he is, calculated that these deceitful affairs would end up like the liar and the one-legged man—flat on their faces. Onésimo also knew how to take advantage of our balkanized Congress, so that he could divide and conquer.

What neither you nor I calculated, Bernal Herrera, was that Onésimo, more astute than we gave him credit for, would co-opt a secret agent, an unglamorous old woman, more changeable than a chameleon, a woman who could blend into anything from the Chihuahua desert to the jungles of Tabasco, Paulina Tardegarda, who has the air of a nun, a virgin, a martyr. Not only was she a bottomless pit of information for Onésimo, but she was something far worse, something that, quite frankly, makes me seethe, Bernal.

I promised Nicolás Valdivia: "You will be president of Mexico."

Subtext: "I will *make* you president of Mexico."

It wasn't like that. The person who made Valdivia president was that convent escapee Paulina Tardegarda. Valdivia can thank Paulina and Onésimo, not you and me, for making it to the Eagle's Throne.

I'm seething, Bernal, I admit it, and I'm frightened.

Nicolás Valdivia was going to be the don Tancredo, the sitting duck in our monumental bullfight, the immobile buffoon in charge of diverting the bull as it entered the ring, so that the matador could shine. Well, well. Now it turns out that you and I have been the Tancredos and that Nicolás Valdivia owes his position to Onésimo and Paulina, not you and me.

However, you are who you are, my old sweetheart, and your candidacy has the most promise and the best chance to win the 2024 elections. But "life brings us surprises," as the Panamanian bard Rubén Blades said. Life brings us surprises. Other candidates may appear on the scene. That's to be expected. In fact, I think we should encourage other candidacies. When I survey the political horizon, I don't see a candidate stronger than you. In any case, you can breathe easy. Article 82 of the constitution states that any citizen who has served as president of the republic—whether elected, interim, acting, provisional—may not serve in that position again. Under no circumstances, the law says. That was why César León was trying so hard to intimidate Onésimo Canabal into starting that complicated constitutional reform process—because he wanted to scrap Article 82 and become president again. Blessed reelection, Bernal. Nobody has the right to screw us twice.

Except Nicolás Valdivia perhaps?

My creation.

My anointed one, *à la mode démocratique.*

The docile puppet who was going to deliver us to the presidency without a problem.

Well, look what happened. The maid turned out to have a mind of her own.

No, I don't think that you'll be defeated in free, democratic elections. Your victory is assured. But what I am afraid of, Bernal, is that Valdivia will find some way to stay on the Eagle's Throne. Do you think he's going to be satisfied with a mere three years? Do you think he isn't already plotting with that Paulina to see how he can hang on to the throne?

Maybe not. But better to be safe than sorry. Remember always that under no circumstances should we forgive Nicolás Valdivia for deceiving us. But you leave that to me. If you forgive the person who did you wrong, your enemies will take note and screw you over twice as badly.

I'm telling you this, my good Bernal, because you're the one who always goes around saying, "I can't be unjust with my enemy."

You're wrong. Be unjust. Because your enemy will be unjust with you.

CONGRESSWOMAN PAULINA TARDEGARDA
TO NICOLÁS VALDIVIA

Dear Nicolás, I think you're covered from all sides. You were wise to leave President Terán's cabinet intact with the exception of the secretary for public works, Antonio Bejarano, and the communications secretary, Felipe Aguirre. Their corruption was too well known. By sacrificing them you'll satisfy public opinion and demonstrate your commitment to justice. That's the system's weakness: justice. We don't have a culture of legality, and we resign ourselves to throwing meat to the lions every six years. But the system doesn't change.

It would be a good idea to reform the judiciary right away in all those states where doing so doesn't compromise our political power. The public will be paying so much attention to the acts of justice you carry out in Oaxaca and Guerrero, Nayarit and Jalisco, Hidalgo and Michoacán, that they won't have time to think about Sonora and Baja California, Tamaulipas and San Luis Potosí, where you won't touch any of those old local bosses. I've spoken to all of them. To Cabezas, Maldonado, Quintero, Delgado. They understand your proposal. Low profile. Nothing showy. Invisibility. Local authorities will work with them, do whatever they want, but all with the utmost discretion.

"What do you want, money or fame?" I asked them on your behalf.

"Because you'll have to choose, gentlemen. Fame you've got a lot of, and it's not the good kind. You've got a lot of money, too, and you could have more. And bad money is a contradiction in terms. Doesn't exist. Money or fame. You can't be political bigamists."

Obviously they prefer money. They'll be your silent allies. They pull the strings of repression and persuasion, too. Everything on the sly. They know you can rule with an iron hand. Your decision to extradite the *capo di tutti capi* Silvestre Pardo has terrified them. And they know that if you want to, you can connect any of them to the drug cartels and send them straight to the U.S., where they would await the death penalty. And you, the gratitude of the White House.

Another immediate success for you. The gringos have pardoned us. Your decision to support U.S. military intervention in Colombia has been presented as part of the war on drugs. What would become of the U.S. financial markets without all that money being laundered for the drug empires? And as for oil, you convinced President Condoleezza Rice that you'll let the market determine the price, and we won't need to make any statements of support for the Arabs.

"Necessity knows no law," you told Condoleezza over the phone, something she understands perfectly.

Over the phone, Nicolás! Can you believe it? That was all it took, a few little acts of deference for Washington to lift the sanctions. And as President Terán was discreet enough not to complain, what happened between January and May . . . never happened. That's all.

"There are blank pages in all history books," Condoleezza said to you.

The fact is, starting today all communications will resume and we can finally say goodbye to this tedious task of writing letters.

Why then do I write to you now?

For the record.

You know, I love poking around in the archives. Like you. Thanks to the absentminded Cástulo Magón, Tácito de la Canal is through. When I saw your folder from the ENA in Paris, I started connecting the dots, and like Sherlock Holmes I set out on my investigation. Is that how you spell "Sherlock Holmes"? Because I had a Cuban friend once who used to pronounce it "Chelmojones." He was one of those memorable Cubans who reinvent a whole life on the basis of pronunciation. How do we know who the famous film actor was if they pronounce his name "Cagable"? And how can we recognize "Retamar" if it's pronounced "Letamale"?

Anyway, I started to make my deductions, from the specific to the general, piece by piece.

You came to Mexico straight from the ENA in Paris, and settled into your "native" city of Juarez, crossing the border every day so that you could study at the library of the University of Texas at El Paso, where you devoured everything that had to do with Mexican politics, from Salinas onward. You applied for residence in Juárez and produced a confusing birth certificate—the son of a Mexican father and a North American mother, both accountants by profession, employed by companies that were fronts for a U.S. business empire with double and sometimes even triple accounting, run by the business magnate Leonardo Barroso, Sr. In other words, your family background was shady, and any revelation could compromise a number of companies on both sides of the border. The secrecy was justified. You were born in a clinic in Texas, but granted Mexican citizenship thanks to Article 30, section A.ii, which guaranteed it to all children born out of the country to Mexican parents. You were more fortunate than José Córdoba or Rogerio de la Selva, strongmen in the Carlos Salinas and Miguel Alemán administrations, but constitutionally barred from the Eagle's Throne because of being "foreign." But you know all this, because nobody knows more about Mexican political history than you, since you studied it so intensively and so recently, too. . . . Not like the rest of us, who learned it in elementary school. Or were weaned on it.

Moving on, my good friend Valdivia, your parents died in a car accident in Texas when you were fifteen. Since you had the right to dual citizenship, you buried them in the U.S. That's where the documents are with the name you used on the other side of the border, "Nick Val," so you could get work, you said, and avoid discrimination.

There's a gap between the Nick Val who buried his parents in Texas and the Nicolás Valdivia who studied at the École Nationale d'Administration in Paris and was much engaged with Mexican student groups in France—they vividly remember you talking to them, observing them, finding out about their family backgrounds, trying to score points for being an orphan as well as a foreigner.

You wanted to know everything about the country you missed so much!

You were preparing to serve Mexico by studying in France—just like María del Rosario Galván and Bernal Herrera—as is fashionable now. It distinguishes us from the gringos and gives us cachet.

You're not the only one who knows how to use the archives. Take the file you're familiar with because Cástulo Magón showed it to you when you went to work at Los Pinos.

ENA PARIS

VALDIVIA NICOLÁS

Student. Open courses. École Nationale d'Administration, Paris. Mexican passport. Date of birth: December 12, 1986. Residence: Paris, France. Professional plans: Return to Mexico. Education and discipline: Optimal. Physical description: Darkish skin. Green eyes. Regular features. Black hair. Height: 1.79 meters. Distinguishing marks: Dimpled chin.

That's the file on you from Paris, with photo and everything. But then, my curiosity got the better of me. Where were you before you went to Paris, during that gap between the age of fifteen and twenty-two? Well, since I'm a member of Congress, I had no trouble sending your details to the people at Interpol. They needed only your initials. In that, my dear Nicolás, you weren't very clever, no. All I had to do was go through the lists of Mexican students in Europe between 2010 and 2015. A little exhaustive, but it wasn't that hard, what with modern methods of locating information—methods unknown to men like our good Cástulo Magón.

Nicolás Valdivia in Paris disappeared without trace. A file on someone named Nico Valdés, however, did turn up, and it included a dossier from the Swiss police department and a photograph: yours.

NICO VALDÉS, Student. University of Geneva, Switzerland. Registered for courses in political economy and constitutional theory. Expelled upon discovery of falsified academic record. Address unknown.

What were those false documents? The Swiss hang on to every scrap of paper, as you know well. It turns out that "Nico Valdés" was already registered as a foreigner—same photo as "Nico Lavat"—and the Swiss justice system doesn't like double identities because they can lead to double indemnities.

Who was this Nico Lavat unjustly detained in Switzerland? As you know, photographs can be scanned through electronic imaging processes that can show how a person ages—fascinating, isn't it? The point is, though, among these facial "identities" was one of your twin brother, Nicolás.

NICOLÁS LAVAT. Spanish employee hired as doorman to the building that was the main office of the Le Rhône publishing house, April 25, 2006. Considered an exemplary employee. Dedicated reader when not fulfilling professional obligations. Perfect French. Accused of conspiring with a gang to rob banks and of the theft of 250,000 Swiss francs. Released due to inconclusive evidence. Physical description: Dark skin. Light green eyes. Normal features. Black permed hair. Height 1.79 meters. Distinguishing traits: Dimpled chin.

One thing leads to another. Elementary, my dear Watson. Just use Hercule Poirot's little gray cells—he's another of my favorites when it comes to the art of detection. Consider, for example, this report found in the files of the Barcelona police department.

> NICO LAVAT, b. December 12, 1986, in Marseilles, France, Catalan parents, migrant workers. Associated since adolescence with Marseilles criminal elements. Drugs, male prostitution, "scab" gangs. Active in Le Pen's National Front. Two years in prison for anti-Semitic and anti-Islamic vandalism, 2000–2002. Whereabouts unknown following release from prison. Failed to meet obligations to report to authorities and renew documents. Physical description: Dark skin. Green eyes. Normal features. Shaved head. Height. 1.79 meters.

Good Lord! First a black woman president and now a Catalan president!

I'm sending you copies of these documents, my sweet. I'll keep the originals in my office at Congress, in a sealed envelope that I'll open only in the event of violence against my person. A remote possibility, if I've got someone as affectionate and understanding as you to protect me. No, I don't think I should accept your marriage proposal. If you want me to be your Evita Perón, fine, as long as I don't have to sleep under the same roof as you, hire a food taster like the Borgias did, or go mad, thinking I'm in a Hitchcock film every time I have a shower.

No, we're better off as we are, affectionate friends, secret conspirators, highly discreet lovers.

Let me tell you something, Nicolás. There is nothing I want more than to be the companion of a politician whose personal passions don't concern me. I can save you from the perils of love. With me you don't have to pretend, like you had to with your Mexican Dulcinea, María del Rosario Galván.

It's difficult to assume power knowing that it's impossible to exercise it in a calm and objective fashion. Power is always subject to passion, pleasure, pain, love, fear. You know, I'm enormously impressed by the amount of knowledge and experience you've managed to acquire, coming from where you come from. No wonder you're always quoting those Greek philosophers. "Power is a slave to everything else." (Protagoras? Nice name. If you and I ever had a baby . . .) But I live for my own destiny, and for the years I have left. I have no dynastic pretensions like your friend "Dark Hand" Vidales and his Nine Evil Sons. I can't wait to see how you settle things with him! But as for me . . . I don't have to subject myself to the terrors of marital intimacy. I don't need a man. I'd lose my independence. I'd squash you, don't you see? Protagoras Valdivia Tardegarda? Or just plain old Protagoras Lavat? They could be names from a Joaquín Pardavé film comedy. Now there's a name: Pardavé. No! Nicolás Laxativa!

With me you won't run that risk. I'll protect you from all the snares, Nicolás. I'll protect you from others and I'll protect you from yourself.

I like the cold, efficient, practiced way you make love to me. They say all young women are beautiful. Not me. I think I've learned to make up for my lack of beauty with talent, and to make my personality more attractive than my ugliness. I want them to envy my personality, not my face.

And you, handsome? Who's really handsome when the time comes to uncover his soul and confront his truth, his secret, his transgression?

How fortunate that you and I have no intimacy to remember. We have no shared moments of laughter, confiding, cuddles. None of that nonsense. What we have is politics.

What we have is the determination to keep you in power for longer than the three years granted by law. Three years. That should be enough time, if we play our cards right, to amend the constitution and allow for re-election. Enough time if we keep up the legalistic energy and practical flexibility. If we choose the right sacrificial victims—Galván and Herrera (I don't know if that sounds like a trademark or a comic strip). If we maintain the facade of seriousness and credibility.

Proceed with caution, Nicolás. Remember that folly has destroyed more Latin American governments than ineptitude or crime.

A Mexican witch discovering the bones of a disappeared congressman in her garden, except that they turned out to be the bones of her grandfather, or something like that. (It was a long time ago.)

An Argentinian witch making decisions for a cabaret dancer who rose to the presidency. (That was a thousand years ago.)

Argentinian, Brazilian, Peruvian presidents publicly airing their marital conflicts.

An Ecuadoran president dancing to rock music and hula-hooping in public around the male member of a certain gringo who'd been castrated by the voracious Judith of Quito.

All this against the very real backdrop of widespread corruption, international loans that end up in Swiss bank accounts, intimidation campaigns, torture, all those Vladimiros and their vladi-videos. . . . How is Latin America ever going to be respectable? How can Latin America avoid derision, scandal, condemnation, humiliation?

With discretion, Mr. President. With liberty and democracy. With the horizon open to opportunity. In the great words of the greatest political genius of the modern age, Bonaparte: "Let the path be open to talent."

A person is allowed to have a shady background. If you'd like some consolation after reading this rather unconsoling letter written by a friend who always finds consolation in the truth, here are two more police records for your perusal.

SCHICKELGRUBER, ADOLF, known as Hitler. Born in Braunau, Austria, 1889. Corporal in Great War. Vagrant on streets of Vienna. Taken in by Shelter for the Homeless. Joins extreme right-wing organization. Gains followers with impassioned anti-Jewish and anti-Marxist rhetoric. Participates in beer-hall *putsch*, Munich, 1923. Tried for treason and condemned to two years at Landsberg Prison, where he writes *Mein Kampf.* Obsessed with Aryan racial superiority and elimination of Jewish parasites.

DJUGASHVILI IOSIV VISSIARONOVICH, known as Stalin, Koba, Soso. Born in Gori, Georgia, 1879. Imprisoned Irkutsk, 1903, Volgoda Camp, 1908. Assault on State Bank, Tiflis, 1907. Gives anti-Semitic speeches. Calls Jews "circumcised Judases."

I'll spare you the sordid details of the more advanced careers of these two tyrants. Suffice it to say that their backgrounds were not only humble, but criminal, yet this wasn't an obstacle to their ascent. All they had to do was fabricate new personalities. How was a bum called Schickelgruber going to dominate Germany and the rest of the world? How was a bank robber called Koba going to dominate Russia and the rest of the world? How was a little Catalan thug called Nico Lavat going to become president of Mexico?

Yes, a person is allowed to have a shady background. The presidential sash is like detergent. It cleans and makes everything gleam. The Eagle's Throne elevates, true, but "nobody can sit higher than their own ass," as they say. You're no worse than Menem or Fujimori. You know what depths Hitler and Stalin emerged from, and they had more power than you've ever dreamed of, Mr. President. Much more.

But they were careful to eliminate those who paved their way. Hitler's co-conspirators in the Munich *putsch*. Stalin's communist comrades after the death of Lenin and despite Lenin's warnings ("Comrade Stalin has unlimited power at his disposal and I'm not sure he will exercise it well"). Now do you see why I'll never take a shower in your bathroom?

Very well. Fiddlesticks, as our grandmothers would say. Let's bury the hatchet, Mr. President. The simple truth is that politics is a barbarian feast. Every Aztec sinks a dagger in the chest of his Tlaxcaltecan neighbor and vice versa. And there we are, you and I, sitting high up above the banquet, gazing down as our tribes of aboriginal Attilas beat one another to death. You and I, my dear Nicolás, apostles of restraint and mediation.

Restraint, Nicolás. If you want to gain an enemy, show him that you're sharper than he.

Discretion, Nicolás. Never allow your unavoidable acts of illegal authority to become public.

Modesty, Nicolás. Let us only be satisfied with the best.

Power is a terrible sum of desires and repressions, offenses and defenses, moments lost and won. We bear the secret arithmetic of our accounts. And I must repeat: We cannot allow the things that should remain secret to become public knowledge. Even if the secret is a relative one. It's stupid to think that something that's happening to one person isn't happening to anyone else. Every single thing that happens is happening at the same time to millions of other people. Never forget that. Protect the secret. But remember our strength. We're all humans, and we're all the same. Our presidents and our cabinet secretaries often forget this fact. But we're politicians because we're not the same as everyone else. What wretched consolation, I know! And what an irritating paradox!

Inevitably, you'll arouse envy. Everyone wants to be close to the president because everyone wants to enjoy his privileges. Now we'll have to act alone, my dear. Turn everything to our advantage. But careful when it comes to our weaknesses. I say this as a woman. Women hate one another, you know that, and they're very good at learning to hide their hatred. But men love one another and learn to disguise their affection. Our virtues are our weaknesses, in both cases.

Now, there's a man who loves you so much that he'd kill you. And whom you love so much that you can't bring yourself to kill him. Jesús Ricardo Magón.

Decide, Nicolás. I can't offer you any advice. Politics is the public expression of private passions. Could public politics exist without private passions? At this stage in the game, need I repeat your Florentine namesake's ABC?

It is much safer to be feared than loved. . . . Love is held by a chain of obligation, which, because men are wicked, is broken at every opportunity for their own utility, but fear is held by a dread of punishment that never forsakes you.

The prince should nonetheless make himself feared in such a mode that, if he does not acquire love, he escapes hatred.

Choose your words carefully. Don't let a single word that can't be interpreted as charity, integrity, humanity, rectitude, or pity escape your lips. The people judge more by what they see than what they understand.

Choose your words carefully. Mussolini, early on, spoke badly of the last remaining independent deputy of the Italian left, Matteotti. His aides—his lackeys—heard him and killed Matteotti. The fascist dictatorship was strengthened. Because of a verbal faux pas. How wise Obregón was when he said, "A president speaks badly of no one."

Have your last words ready, Nicolás. "Light, more light," at one extreme. "*Après moi, le deluge*," at the other. The words of a humanist and the words of a monarch. But don't end up like the aforementioned Álvaro Obregón, the best military officer in the history of Mexico (why didn't we have him in 1848 instead of that one-legged traitor Santa Anna!), Obregón, the man who vanquished Pancho Villa, the brilliant strategist and politician, killed at a banquet by a religious fanatic just as he stretched out his hand to say, "More tortilla chips, please. . . ."

More tortilla chips. Don't let these be your last words. Why did they kill Obregón? Because he wanted to be reelected. You need to be able to say, "Light, more light," if you win and "*Après moi, le deluge*," if you lose. But never, and I mean *never* say, "More tortilla chips." It would be such a disappointment to me. I'd hate to see you in the back streets of Marseilles again. I'd say what Bernanos said about Hitler: Mexico has been raped by a criminal while it slept.

Eliminate your tortilla chip, Nicolás. My information is thorough. In 2011, the military attaché of the Mexican embassy in France was General Mondragón von Bertrab. He gave you your official identity papers. He invented your life history. He forged your documents. Everything is in my safe deposit box in Congress.

You have eliminated the little tortilla chips. Tácito de la Canal.

Andino Almazán. Pepa, his wife. General Cícero Arruza. The Old Man. That weeping woman of the cemeteries of Veracruz, little Miss Monterrey, Dulce de la Garza. And the phantom of this opera, Tomás Moctezuma Moro. It's just you and me now, Nicolás. And a shadow over our lives. General Mondragón von Bertrab.

We have to act quickly. Early to bed, early to rise. True enough, if you're a baker. A politician has to wake up as early as the night before sometimes, otherwise he—or she—might be the victim of a very rude awakening.

Rest assured that everything we've discussed is between the two of us. Gypsies don't tell one another's fortunes, as they say. And anyway, I'm unconvinced by all these reports on you. Pure fantasy. I trust you. I give no credence to your enemies. It's all conjecture. And if any of it comes to light, we'll simply accuse María del Rosario Galván and Bernal Herrera of libel and slander. Remember what the ex, César León, said to his enemies: "I'm not going to punish you. I'm going to vilify you."

Count on my loyalty. And don't stop calculating the cost–deceit ratio.

GENERAL MONDRAGÓN VON BERTRAB
TO NICOLÁS VALDIVIA

For the very reason it's no longer necessary, I'm writing you this letter. You may surmise that my desire is not to communicate but to leave documentary evidence. Everyone has told you about my military education at very demanding schools of exceedingly high intellectual caliber. The Hochschule der Bundeswehr in Germany is excellent in that sense. Nobody leaves there without having read Julius Caesar and Clausewitz (obviously), but the students are also made to read Kant so that they learn how to think, and Schopenhauer so that they learn how to doubt. The Honorable Military Academy of Mexico is also an excellent institution. While in Germany one learns to strive for victory, in Mexico one learns to endure defeat.

We shouldn't fool ourselves, however. There are still men like Arruza around. Survivors of Mexico and its barbaric past, harbingers of a barbaric future. They dwell in our country's subterranean depths.

Educated Mexican officers are something else entirely, but every bit as real as the savages. In every human relationship there's a battle between truth and lies. We could never answer the question "What is truth, what are lies?" if we didn't apply both absolute and relative criteria. For example, in military strategy courses the first thing they teach you is to question the information you receive.

Are you familiar with an old *corrido* song from the revolutionary days, "Valentín de la Sierra"?

> *El coronel le pregunta,*
> *cuál es la gente que guías?*
> *Son ochocientos soldados*
> *que trae por la sierra Mariano Mejía.**

True or false? Should the colonel in question accept the confession of the captured officer, or should he question it? How will the truth be known? Truth can be stubborn, cautious, as the *corrido* reveals in the following lines:

> *Valentín, como era hombre*
> *de nada les dio razón.*†

So Valentín gives out no information and the other man claims that there are eight hundred men under Mariano's command. Ah, but Valentín, to make his quatrain rhyme, adds something even more confusing to the mix:

> *Y soy de los meros hombres*
> *que han inventado la Revolución . . .*‡

What does the officer do with all this information? If he really believes the "Mariano" story, he must prove it or expose himself to failure. He can interpret Valentín's silence as proof that "Mariano" is a fabrication. But "Valentín" gives the information an unexpected ideological twist when he says that he is one of the true men who "invented the Revolution."

---

*The colonel asks him,/how many men are with you?/Eight hundred soldiers/led through the mountains by Mariano Mejía.

†*Valentín, being a man,/told them nothing.*

‡*And I am one of the true men/who invented the Revolution . . .*

True or false, the information must mean something. The poor officer asking the questions might assume that the "Mariano" truth is an objective one in the sense of using a singular proposition to speak of the other person, "Mariano Mejía." But Valentín de la Sierra doesn't do that. He speaks of the proposition itself: He is one of the true men who invented the Revolution.

Therein lies the difficulty of making decisions, Nicolás, by adhering to the solid basis of what is true and what is false. Those of us who are military officers, fortunately, are beholden to a code that dictates our conduct. Up to a certain point, of course. Because even when you obey the written code down to the letter, the paradox of the lie is that what we say is only true if it is a lie.

This is what I want you to understand, Nicolás. In this letter I shall confess my lie only to justify my truth.

Perhaps the criteria for speaking the truth should be a question.

"If I tell the truth, will I be a source of pain or relief?"

A lie is true because it has meaning. Things that have no meaning cannot even be false. For that reason, the meaning of the truth is only one part of what the truth conceals beneath its surface. Lies are one half truth. Truth is one half lies. Because all that we say and do, Nicolás, is part of a relationship that cannot exclude its opposite. For example, as an intellectual I can say that everything created is true. Even lies.

But as a military man I cannot grant myself that luxury. I can only conceive of the truth as coherence, as conformity to the rules that govern us. But even when I obey the rules down to the letter—that is, as the rule book establishes—I still have a doubt, a secret, a fissure in my soul. The truth cannot be reduced to the verifiable. Truth is the name we give to what is, ultimately, a *correspondence* between me and another person. That *correspondence* makes my truth relative.

Turn it around and consider these questions from the opposite angle:

When are lies justified?

When, instead of causing harm, do lies bring relief?

Every existence is its own truth, but always in correspondence with the truth of the other. And every lie can be its own truth, if it is protected by the other's supreme truth, which is his life. . . .

When you were born in a clinic in Barcelona (not Marseilles as the unfortunate Paulina Tardegarda believed) on December 12, 1986, I was stationed at the military zone of Ciudad Juárez, far away from your mother. She was already married, but everyone knew that her husband was impotent and her elderly lover was an invalid. Her son therefore must have been fathered by a third man. She was treated according to the customs of upper-class Mexican society—as if she were an unmarried young woman who'd gotten herself pregnant. Before the birth she stayed in a maternity home run by nuns in Sarrià.

I wasn't able to be with her. I was very young. More cowardly than irresponsible. And more in love than irresponsible. I had to comply with military discipline in Chihuahua. That was my excuse. That was my cowardice. I should have been at your mother's side in Barcelona, I should have picked you up, I should have made you mine from the very first day. . . . Judge me, condemn me, but let me make up for the lost time between us, let me wring the neck of destiny and reclaim now all that could have been, but never was.

Your mother's family was extremely dangerous. The Barroso clan controlled the northern border from Mexicali to Matamoros. The Barroso family, Leonardo Barroso and all his descendants, including his granddaughter María del Rosario Barroso Galván. Now she is just Galván, like her mother, because she was so disgusted by the last name of her father and grandfather, old Barroso, who turned your mother Michelina Laborde into more than just a lover. She was his sexual slave. His imprisoned odalisque. He made her marry his own son—a sensitive, shy boy who people said was a bit simple. Bad blood. He never touched Michelina. He lived all alone in the country, on a ranch filled with deer and *pacuaches*, those "erased Indians" from Chihuahua.* Leonardo Barroso the elder kept that stunningly beautiful woman— your mother, Nicolás—all to himself, more beholden than ever to the

*See "A Capital Girl" in *The Crystal Frontier*.

Barroso millions after an attempt was made on the old man's life on the bridge between Juárez and El Paso.

He was given up for dead. He ended up a paraplegic, the bottom half of his body useless. Condemned to vegetate in a wheelchair for the rest of his days, just like his brother, Emiliano Barroso, the communist leader. What poetic justice!* Leonardo an invalid in a wheelchair, with all the perverse energy in his brain focused on humiliating his son, despising his wife, and keeping his mistress locked away. He did have another descendant—Leonardo Jr., a child from his wife's first marriage who became his second son. This adopted child was the father of your friend María del Rosario Galván. And Barroso Sr. was so evil that he urged your mother to become Leonardo Jr.'s mistress as well, so that he could spy on them and enjoy the vicarious thrill. . . .

So doesn't it make sense that thirty-five years ago your mother would seek and find solace and passion in a young, attractive military officer like me?

I want you to understand, I want you to know, I want you to ask yourself, "At what point does absence become more powerful than presence?" What is it about absence that sparks our passions to the point of driving us mad?

On the other hand, at what point do social pressures force us to abandon the light of love and descend into darkness, filth, and vice? And finally, why is it that instead of reaching a golden mean these extremes of passion—the hunger of presence, the vice of abandonment—come to rest at an evil mean in the middle of oblivion? Or worse, indifference?

Michelina Laborde was unable to return to the bosom of the powerful Barroso family, who were all *somebodies,* with the child of a *nobody* like me. And so she went back to the border with her secret protected by family conventions. She had been "on vacation" in Europe. Visiting museums.

I never saw her again. She died shortly afterward. I think she died of

---

*See "The Line of Oblivion" in *The Crystal Frontier.*

sadness, and of that nostalgia for the impossible that you sometimes feel when you know that what you desired could have been possible.

You were handed over to a Catalan family by the name of Lavat. The Barrosos gave them a certain amount of money for your education, though they didn't use it for that but for the pursuit of their mediocre lives, and sent you out onto the streets and into a life of crime, which was your real education, Nicolás. It began when you were a child in Barcelona, and continued in Marseilles, where the Lavats, who were migrant workers, moved when you were ten.

And nevertheless, something in you, perhaps that nostalgia for the impossible, drove you from an early age toward risk, but also to want to sharpen your mind, your wits, your ambition, to be more than you were, as if your blood were crying out for a heritage, inevitable, obscure, at once strangely luminous and scarcely formed in your mind's eye. You educated yourself in squalor, on the streets, in crime, with a discipline that was second only to your need for survival, and with the profound conviction that not only would you one day be someone, but that you already *were* someone, a disinherited son, a child stripped of his legacy. *Algo.* Something. *Hijo de algo.* Son of something. *Hidalgo.* A man of noble birth.

You were no blind criminal. You were a lost child with your eyes wide open to a destiny that was different—not unlucky—a destiny forged by your unknown heritage and the future that you yearned for.

I didn't forget about you, my son. I didn't know who you were. I knew that my lovely Michelina had had a child in Europe. When she went back to Chihuahua, she managed to scribble me a little note:

> We had a child, my love. He was born on December 12, 1986, in Barcelona. I don't know what they named him. He was placed in the hands of workers, I know that. Forgive me. I will always love you—*M.*

Finding you was like finding the proverbial needle in the haystack. My professional ambitions, my career in the armed forces, prevailed. My positions both inside and outside Mexico. And then I was appointed military attaché of the embassy in Paris, which had jurisdiction over Switzerland and the Benelux countries. That was when a certain file found its way to my desk, a file about a young man who claimed he was Mexican and who had been sent to prison in Geneva for supposedly plotting with a gang of bank robbers.

I visited you at that prison in Geneva. You had long hair then. I stopped cold in my tracks. I was seeing your mother with a man's body. Darker than she was, but with the same long, straight black hair. Perfectly symmetrical features. The classic *criollo* face. Skin with a shadow of the Mediterranean, of olives and refined sugar. Large black eyes (in your case green, my contribution). Dark circles under your eyes, high cheekbones, restless nostrils. And one tiny detail that was your mother's signature: the dimpled chin. The deep cleft beneath your bottom lip.

Who else but me would have noticed such details? Who else but your father? Who else but your mother's sleepless lover, trying to make up for lost time by lying awake and remembering her sleeping face?

I interrogated you, trying to maintain my composure. I pieced things together. It was you. Your birthdate, your physical appearance, everything fit. I declared that you were Mexican and I paid your bail. Very solemnly I began to look after you, but I asked you—as payment for my testimony—to agree to a period of study at the University of Geneva. But the Swiss are bloodhounds. They expelled you because your previous documents were found to have been forged.

Once again I intervened, driven by my heart but trying to keep a cool head. You see, I've never wanted to compromise my position. Isn't that important, to be able to exercise some influence? I brought you with me to Paris and registered you as a student at the ENA and I told you to read everything, to learn all you could about Mexico, and we'd sit up for hours together late at night, and you would listen to all my stories about Mexico, our country, our history, our customs, our economic, political, and social realities, who was who, speeches, songs, folklore, everything.

With what you read about and learned from me, you returned to Mexico more Mexican than the Mexicans. That was the danger—that your imitation would be detected. I sent you to the border, to Ciudad Juárez, for five years. With the help of the authorities there, I doctored your papers, changing your birthplace from Catalonia to Chihuahua. It's all there in the public records office of Ciudad Juárez: son of a Mexican father and a North American mother. The documents for your imaginary parents were easy to forge, too. As you know, everyone does it in Mexico. If you don't deceive you don't achieve.

When I became secretary of defense under Lorenzo Terán, I felt more sure of things and so I brought you in, I put you into circulation, sent you to deliver my messages, especially to the interior office. That was where you met María del Rosario Galván. What happened next was inevitable. María del Rosario is a fool for attractive young men. And if she thinks she can groom them politically, an affair is inevitable. She's a natural Pygmalion in a skirt.

She knew the president was suffering from terminal leukemia. And as the head of national security, I knew as well. It was my obligation to know. Both of us played our respective games. She made you think that she was putting her money on you for president. Now you know the truth. President, yes, but only for a brief period after Terán's death, just enough time to prepare Herrera's campaign and election. In order to do that, we had to eliminate a formidable cast of characters. The "usual suspects," as they say in the movies. Tácito de la Canal, César León, Andino Almazán, General Cícero Arruza. We had to outfox that other ex-president in Veracruz and defuse the plot he hatched involving his secret prisoner in the Ulúa Castle. We had to see to the sentimental accidents of the sniveling woman of the port, Dulce de la Garza; but calming women down is so easy, especially when they're simpleminded and smitten like Dulce de la Garza, idiotically scheming and crassly licentious like Josefina Almazán, or intelligent—perhaps too intelligent for their own good—like Paulina Tardegarda, a woman you'll never hear from again, I assure you. One personal, perhaps even romantic detail:

Paulina's only possible companions now, as she's chained by the legs to her safe deposit box, are the sharks at the bottom of the sea.

No, she's not short of water now, your dubious friend Paulina Tardegarda, keeper of too many secrets—which turned you into the perfect blackmail victim. Learn not to trust. Don't even trust me, your own father, Nicolás. And don't cry for Paulina. The sharks in the Gulf of Mexico will eat her, but her heart will survive. The advantage of a poisoned heart is that it's immune to fire and water. If it's any consolation, think of how her heart will survive, like a cocoon of blood at the bottom of the sea.

There are still some loose ends, my son, lest you've forgotten. Your protégé, Jesús Ricardo Magón, is so disillusioned that he has no anarchist or homicidal tendencies left. I had him deported under charges of drug trafficking. He's in prison in France. As he stepped off the plane he was detained by certain members of the Sûreté with whom I am connected. Don't worry. I paid for his ticket, first class. His parents, don Cástulo and doña Serafina, think he's gone to Europe to study. He's so young! They keep thanking me for the "scholarship" that I got for him as per your orders. And Miss Araceli now has a lifetime subscription to *¡Hola!* magazine. She's since married (or rather, I made sure she married) Hugo Patrón, who's thrilled with the disco-bar he now runs in Cancún.

Then there's the question of our two official rivals, María del Rosario Galván and Bernal Herrera.

Their calculations are correct. In the democratic elections to be held in July 2024, Herrera will win. Nobody could possibly challenge him successfully. And you yourself are out of the running because of your present position. There's no way you can succeed yourself.

In the space of fourteen years, from the age of twenty to thirty-four, you acquired an impressive education, what with your natural talent and my guidance and teaching. Now, however, I have to give you a piece of advice. Don't be so precocious. Don't reveal your true colors by shining too brightly now. Remember how the Old Man tried to trick you a couple of times—the Pastry War, Mapy Cortés, the conga, pim-pam-pum? You had no reason to know anything about Mapy Cortés or the conga. But you should have known about the Pastry War. Be careful. Don't overestimate your newfound education. Don't ever give anyone a reason to scratch your gold-plated surface and discover a baser metal beneath. Don't give people cause for jealousy. Keep quiet about your education. Keep the illicit activity in check. It's not always justified. We're doing everything possible to consolidate our power base. But it has to stop there. A few dead people now and then? Only when absolutely necessary. You've already seen what it did to Arruza's reputation. He was so busy showing off about his criminal activity that he never stopped to think that someone else might beat him at his own game, that someone would kill the great Cícero Arruza. And Moro—he had to be killed. But you made a mistake sending "Dark Hand" Vidales—he's vindictive and convinced that his dynastic succession will keep the vendettas alive. You thought you were compromising him with your own guilt when you sent him to Ulúa. Don't believe it. He's the one who could compromise you. He's going to give us a few headaches. What we have to do now is think of how best to neutralize him. Poisonous gifts, that's what we have to give that viper. From now on, we have to seduce him to the point of putting him to sleep. Presidential lethargy has its advantages, you know. Terán just didn't know how to exploit it. You need to figure out how not to be perceived as a violent man—make sure whatever violence you resort to is carried out in the name of "justice." And be careful to keep the moment of truth at bay. But don't think for a minute that the time for violence in Mexico is over.

My son, my beloved son. Surely you can understand the depth of my feelings—the feelings of a father who lost a precious—unequaled—woman, your mother, to the tyranny and brutal prejudice of her family, the Barrosos. She was the fragile altar of my strongest passion. Let the two of us rebuild this temple ruined by the lies, pretension, greed, and arrogance of the unscrupulous ruling class epitomized by the Barroso family, whose only heir is the perverse María del Rosario Galván. Do you think I'll allow her to scheme in peace? Why should we have scruples with people who are unscrupulous with us?

Always remember: María del Rosario is from up there, the same social class as your mother. Think of María del Rosario as your mother, but with a fortune, mistress of a life that was denied Michelina. Avenge your mother's cruel fate on María del Rosario.

I will take care of Bernal Herrera.

You are my creation, Nicolás. My heir. My partner. Together we'll win. It's all that matters: attaining power and keeping it forever.

Nicolás Valdivia, my son, power unites us as a longing for the truth. You and I are going to take possession of that truth.

I want to give you one more piece of advice. From now on, don't let anyone find out what you're thinking—not even me. Especially if you plan to betray me.

I promise you: In politics, any betrayal is possible. Or at least imaginable.

CONGRESSMAN ONÉSIMO CANABAL
TO NICOLÁS VALDIVIA

Mr. President, I write to you in the strictest confidence. And with alarm. The heart and soul of the Congress of the Union have been violated. Well, only one office, but Congress is, after all, an inviolable whole. It is the sanctuary of the law, Mr. President. In any event, today I woke up to an urgent phone call from the building custodian, Serna.

In the middle of the night, someone entered the San Lázaro Legislative Palace. Someone deactivated the alarms, slipped past the guards, perhaps bribed the security people. I don't know. Someone with power, evidently. Mr. President: The office of our friend the congresswoman Paulina Tardegarda, the woman to whom you and I are so indebted, has been ransacked. Her safe deposit box has been wrenched, yes, literally and completely wrenched out of the wall, leaving a gaping hole in its place, which makes the office look awful—we'll have to have the whole wall rebuilt, do you realize how much this will cost? (Speaking of expenses, when are you going to name a new treasury secretary now that Andino Almazán has left us?)

The worst thing isn't that the safe deposit box has been stolen. The honorable congresswoman has disappeared, Mr. President. She isn't at her apartment on Calle Edgar Allan Poe. Her housekeeper says she didn't come home last night. We've already launched an investigation, on the quiet, of course. But she's nowhere to be found. She's vanished without a trace.

What could possibly have become of her? Do you know anything? If it were just that she'd taken a sudden vacation, or was having a good time with someone—well, fine. But the safe deposit box, too, Mr. President? The two things at the same time are what I find most alarming.

I need to know from you. Should we put out a national alert because Paulina Tardegarda has gone missing? Poor thing. She was no saint, but she wasn't a sinner, either. I can't imagine anyone would kidnap her out of passion—she wasn't exactly attractive. She was big enough to kidnap someone herself if she wanted to.

In any case, I need you to authorize the national alert. I can't do it; only you can. Otherwise, her remains will never be found. Or else they'll turn up in a witch's garden, and then turn out not to be hers. Or Paulina will have suddenly undergone plastic surgery like the famous drug trafficker, the "Lord of the Heavens." Forgive me if this is out of line, don Nicolás, but you know, I think she had the hots for you. . . . Oh, sorry, sorry, who knows, maybe she was just trying to make herself a bit prettier. Poor Paulina, she could use it. . . .

Well, anyway, enough of all that. You do agree that this is a most urgent matter, I trust. I await your orders to take action or to let the issue die, whatever the president thinks best.

Your humble and loyal servant,
Onésimo Canabal
PRESIDENT OF THE HONORABLE CONGRESS OF THE UNION

68

BERNAL HERRERA TO
MARÍA DEL ROSARIO GALVÁN

You're right, María del Rosario. They've changed the rules of the game. Valdivia may appear to respect the electoral calendar but I don't believe there's anything in his head or heart that will compel him to hand over the presidency on the first of December, 2024, if in fact I'm elected. We have a problem: There's no viable politician out there to challenge my candidacy. Tácito, at least, would have been from the presidential cabinet like me. The mini-parties have no charismatic candidates to speak of. The local bosses will support whoever offers them the most protection. The danger for me is that I may end up alone out there. I'll stand out, my stature will only make me vulnerable. The bad thing about being tall, said de Gaulle, is that we're people who get noticed. His conclusion? "Tall men have to be more moral than anyone else."

You once said to me, referring to Tácito, that hatred is more intelligent than love. And I'm going to keep on protecting myself from the illustrious Mr. De la Canal. I don't trust his newfound humility. He wears it as if he just found it at a flea market. The filial love he professes is not to be trusted. Only believe in his loyalty to sex. According to my sources, he's already seduced his father's maid, a woman who calls herself "Gloria Marín." Oh, well, as you once said to me, "Fidelity is so sad!"

María del Rosario, you and I are going to continue to act as a team, but this time we'll be at a disadvantage. Don't laugh at me if I warn you against any attempt to rekindle our old flame. It's better to be frank. Falling in love again would only demonstrate that as a political couple we've suffered a setback and are trying to compensate for it. It would be proof of our weakness and disillusion.

I'm telling you this as a preventive measure. You seem to have become more sentimental lately, and perhaps that could help our situation. I have, too, and I'm tempted by the idea that you and I might be able to love each other again, the way we did at the beginning.

But it would be a weakness, and you know that. We'd be together only in order to lick each other's wounds. We'd console each other today. And detest each other tomorrow.

Take a cold look at what our relationship was like at first. I only wanted to give you love. You wanted to want love. I believe the only kind of love that would satisfy you is a love that is pure desire. You couldn't bear a secure, everyday affection. Without risks. You're a woman who adores risks. You take it to extremes that some—people who don't love you as I do—would call immoral. Stealing a man from another woman—or another man—makes you happy. Your erotic passion is so deeply ingrained that it has become completely and totally intransigent. Don't deny it.

I am not obstinate. I am steady. And in my steadiness there's no room for nostalgia for passion. I know: For you, being unfaithful doesn't necessarily mean being disloyal. And for that reason, living with you would force me to do something that I don't ever want to have to do again. I don't want to be constantly examining and reexamining my relationship and my heart. Living with you would expose me to that agony, and it would be a never-ending one. Marucha, have you been faithful or not?

Thank God we never married. We managed to act as one without having to put up with each other. We can't go back to what we were. You couldn't bear it. I'll give you the reason. Be lovers again? You and

I know that the second time wouldn't be just a mistake. It would be lunacy. Wouldn't it? The best you could give me would be the necessary distance to love you so much that I would consider you unworthy of my love.

(You know that I admire you for what others despise in you.)

(Don't torment yourself. Think of all the things we didn't say to each other.)

Let's not be tempted at this difficult moment to rekindle our passion. After all, it's not as though we've broken up. We've just untied things. What do we have in common? We are powerless over *love*, and we are powerless over *power* if we're not together.

I want to reaffirm our pact.

Remember that you and I could destroy each other. Better to stick together. Let there be peace between us. Our pleasure was too tempestuous. Now more than ever, let us proceed calmly.

Never forget that you and I have always been able to reach agreements even when we haven't technically been *in agreement*.

Resign yourself as I have resigned myself. Surrender to my imagination, just as I surrender to yours. There, inside our minds, we can experience our passion forever.

I do have to admit, however, that right now the doors that open on to my mind are like the doors of a saloon: They swing open, they close, they slam shut. . . . But there is one thing I know: We have to find Nicolás Valdivia's weak spot. The wound that makes him bleed. His most shameful, shamefaced secret. That's our only hope of defeat. If we want to prevent Nicolás Valdivia from staying in power, we're going to have to put our heads together.

And in the final analysis, remember—a little bad luck is the best antidote for the bitterness that has yet to come. And the greatest bitterness is that of those who wield absolute power. Nothing satisfies them, they always want more, and that's where they lose. We identify Nicolás Valdivia's weakness and we'll have the key to his downfall.

69

MARÍA DEL ROSARIO GALVÁN
TO BERNAL HERRERA

I've walked a long way this morning, Bernal, in search of a high, open spot from which to look out onto our Valley of Mexico and renew my hope. The seedy, garish city that horrified (and prematurely killed) the great poet Ramón López Velarde. It is the "Valley of Mexico, opaque mouth, lava of spittle, crumbling throne of rage" that Octavio Paz whipped with a fury that saved him. Or perhaps it is the exact, balanced image of José Emilio Pacheco, the poet of intelligent serenity whose eighty-second birthday we've recently celebrated, when he allows himself to be carried along by the facts, and sing in a wounded voice of the "Twilight of Mexico, in the mournful mountains to the west . . ."

> *Allí el ocaso*
> *es tan desolador que se diría:*
> *la noche así engendrada será eterna.* *

Mexico of eternal seasons, "immortal spring" . . .

The rainy season has begun, washing away the eternal night, the

---

**There nightfall/is so bleak that one might say:/night thus begotten will be eternal.*

opaque mouth, the seedy, garish look. . . . Settling the dust. Clearing the air. It's true that on rainy afternoons, between shower and downpour, even from our disastrous highway, the Anillo Periférico, you can make out the sharp, clear outline of the mountains.

I decided to climb up to Chapultepec Castle so that I could look out over the city and the valley from a height that seemed more human, intermediate, where I could see the mountains whose names I know—Ajusco, Popocatépetl, Iztaccíhuatl—in the intimate light that I want to rediscover, Bernal, at the end of this episode in our lives.

Do you realize that we've lived through this story in confinement, as if we've been acting on the stage of a prison? A story completely divested of nature. Pacheco was right: "Are stones the only things that dream? . . . Is the world nothing but these immutable stones?" That's what I'm doing here now, trying to remember the natural world that slipped away from us, lost in a wood of words, buried in a swamp of speeches, cut down by a knife of ambition. . . .

Before I went outside I looked at myself in the mirror without makeup, without illusions. I have managed to keep my figure, but my face has begun to betray me. I now realize that I was a natural beauty when I was young. Today, the beauty I have left is an act of pure will. It's a secret between me and my mirror. I say to the mirror, "The world knows of me. But the world no longer tastes of me."

Why do we waste our youth and beauty? I see how I handed over my youth and my sex to men who turned to dust or statues. I touched my body this morning. Nothing wounds the body quite like desire. And I haven't been able to satisfy mine—I admit that to you, since you are the one, true man of my life. Nothing has ever satisfied me, Bernal. Why? Because I have presided over too many altars where God was absent. My altars are the kind that cause hearts to age prematurely. Fame and power. But I am a woman. I refuse to surrender to the evidence of time. I convince myself that my sexual appeal is unaffected by age. That I don't have to be young to be desirable.

I look back on the people, the places, the situations since the crisis began in January, and I find that there's no sense of taste in my mouth. I wish I could summon sweetness, or bile—or even vomit. But my tongue and palate taste of nothing at all.

I consult my other senses. What do I hear? A cacophony of empty words. What do I smell? The excrement that ambition leaves in its wake. What do I touch? My own skin, every day less elastic, more vulnerable, grown thin. What do I touch with? Ten fingernails like knives that lash out at me. Not only do they fail to caress me. Not only do they scratch me. They sink into me and ask, what will become of my skin, how much longer will it last, what wasted pleasure awaits it? Nothingness.

I have my eyes. This afternoon, I shall become pure vision. Everything else betrays me, turns me into someone I don't know. I retain nothing but my gaze and I discover, with shock, Bernal, that my eyes are filled with love. I don't need a mirror to prove it. I look out from Chapultepec and I feel love, for the city and for the Valley of Mexico.

A loving gaze. That is my gift to my city and to my time. I have nothing else to give Mexico but my loving gaze on this luminous May afternoon after the rain, when the bougainvillea are the patient ornaments of urban beauty, and for one glorious instant the city is crowned by the lavender color of the jacaranda trees. The valley has such powerful light at this time of day, Bernal, that it transports me out of myself and then abandons me on the great terrace of the Alcázar with its black-and-white marble surface, and then transports me as if on a magic carpet around the city, high above the clusters of multicolored balloons sold on the avenues, and allows me to caress the heads of little children in parks, to walk in the muddy waters of the reservoir in Chapultepec Forest, and to continue walking, now in the hyacinth waters of Xochimilco, as if my bare feet were trying hard to become clean, Bernal, in the lost canals of what was once the Venice of the Americas, a city that embraced water and life, a city that slowly grew dry until it died of thirst and suffocation.

But not this afternoon, Bernal—this afternoon on which I've chosen to be reborn is a miracle, for it is a liquid afternoon, it has rained and all the avenues have become canals, all the limestone deserts have become lakes, all the sewer pipes have become cascading waterfalls. . . .

With my newborn eyes, I survey the city that your namesake Bernal Díaz del Castillo surveyed in 1519, resurrected through the force of desire, and I leave behind all the political melodrama you and I have lived through, and I resuscitate the old city, fanning out into boulevards made of gold and silver, rooftops of feathers and walls of precious stones, cloaks made from the skins of jaguars, pumas, otter, and deer. I walk past the Indian pharmacopoeia of remedies made of snakeskin, shark teeth, funeral candles, and the seeds known as "deer's eyes." I walk into the plazas painted with cochineal and I breathe in the aroma of liquidambar and fresh tobacco, coriander and peanut and honey. I stop in front of the stalls selling jicama, cherimoya, mamey, and prickly pears. I rest upon seats made of wooden boards and beneath tiled canopies, listening all the while to the concert of hens, turkeys, ducklings. . . .

How can we not delve back into our Mexican consciousness (unless we lose it) and return to that lakeside city that awakens our great lyrical passions, the city that seems to be the very cradle of our origins? "The flowers come out, they open their petals, and from within emerge the flowers of song." But oh, my most cherished friend, is there a single poem of the indigenous world that does not possess the wisdom of uniting the song of life with the harbinger of death? "Bitterness predicts destiny. . . . With black ink you shall erase what was once brotherhood, community, dignity. . . ."

What, Bernal, warns us of impending disaster? The memory of the beauty and the happiness that was, or was not, I don't know. I do know that beauty and happiness were imagined and that the imagination exacts a price from us that is also a gift: memory. And since I believe this, I pray that nobody and nothing can ever rob us of our memory. That is a gift from above: to remember. Because I can promise you, our bodies will be wounded by desire. Will you and I ever be able to recover all the things we put aside in order to become the people we are now? The moments of love, the duty, the dreams? Even those losses can be redeemed by the memory.

Yes, I've been looking out from Chapultepec at the city that no longer is, Mexico-Tenochtitlan, and suddenly I see wildcats and badgers in its streets, and suddenly, Bernal, I hear a bark and then another and then I can no longer count because hundreds of dogs are now running down the valley, all of them vicious mastiffs, barking—with each bark they drown out the squawking of the hens, the scent of liquidambar, the hammering sounds of the daily grind, until the whole valley is invaded by that massive pack of wild dogs, set free by their evil owners as night falls. . . . A terrifying procession of giant, mangy, slobbering hounds with hungry eyes and spiteful noses, dogs without masters, dogs abandoned because their owners went on vacation or couldn't be bothered to take care of them, or beat them for fun: the entire city, in the clutches of these rabid dogs, Bernal, every one of them glaring at me with eyes of fire, every one of them climbing uphill, toward the balcony where I stand, coming closer and closer, more and more menacing, with their filthy coats and their yellow fangs, led by one sole mastiff with a human-sounding cackle and a collar of deadly spikes around its neck, and it's almost ready to attack me, Bernal. And then I recognize it. It's the dog that belonged to our late president Terán, El Faraón, searching for his master's grave.

Dogs with frightful voices, screaming at me, "Go. Don't hesitate. Don't ever look at him again."

"Who? Who?" I shout. "Who are you talking about? Who should I never look at again?"

The Valley is filled with spikes.

The lake of time, not just the lake in this valley, grows smaller and smaller.

The only thing left for us is the dust of time.

And then, suddenly, the true king makes his appearance. The King of the valley. I don't want to look at him. I tell myself it's a mirage.

I desperately search for a silent space where I can hear and understand.

I feel my forgotten life emerge from the dead lake.

Or the life I never lived.

I wish I could be an arrow and defend myself.

The King of Mexico looks at me, without eyelids, and opens a mouth of mud and silver:

"Storms will come."

He says nothing else, and then disappears together with the dogs that preceded him and the dust that followed him.

Oh, Bernal, how heavy my heart feels, and how impatient my soul.

How the shadow of pain and sin pursues me.

How I ask myself why I didn't kill myself before the pack of hungry dogs could rip me apart.

How I would love to plunge into a bottomless pool of freezing water that might clean me and give me back my spirit.

The noises died down.

The city emptied.

The dogs grew quiet and they fled, returning to their lairs in the vast landfills of the city.

Only El Faraón wanders still, howling for his master.

And I return to my home in Bosques de las Lomas.

Once again I am me.

Never again will I feel tempted by suicide.

Because falling in love with you again would be a form of suicide for the personality I've created—with such effort on the one hand and such weakness on the other.

Don't worry.

You are right.

What kind of marriage can possibly exist between two people who only conspire against each other?

I'll deliver myself back to the slow suicide of politics.

I wanted to empty myself so that I could be born again.

Instead, I surrender to the world.

Bernal Herrera, you will be president of Mexico.

I swear to you.

70

(LORENZO HERRERA GALVÁN)

(i am playing hide-and-seek in the garden i laugh a lot they can't find
me i hide behind the tree and they say there he is we'll get him now run
over there and i hide behind another street and shout there he is but i am
the one who shouts because i am alone playing all by myself and i think
i should shout here i am, right? here i am playing all by myself in the
middle of all the trees in the house where i have always lived was i born
here? the lady doctor says no that they brought me here who brought
me here i ask and she says nothing and i try to remember who brought
me here to my house i hear the house talking but i only say my house because i have never had another house and i know that i will never leave
here but i don't mind i have a fuzzy picture in my head of a man and a
woman who came here when i was little but they came less and less and
the lady doctor told me they love you they love you they are very worried about you they are people who are good and i don't know what that
means good people but i know i love them too i love everything that
comes near me and says hello and talks and touches me i love that a lot
but it doesn't happen much i am very alone and i love all those things a
lot but it is hard for me to tell the lady doctor that's what they call her
she said to me they love you i wish i could talk like her but i can't i talk

without even opening my mouth if they knew all the things i say without opening my mouth i hear everyone but nobody hears me i talk to the inside talk to me talk to me a lot please i hear them i understand them i understand everything they say they think i don't understand because i don't talk but yes i do understand everything they don't tell me much because they think i don't understand i don't know how to say the things i want and i don't know how to say the things i think and without talking i say what they say i understand them very well you are intelligent the lady doctor says intelligent intelligent i understand them very well but they don't know that and that's why they don't talk to me they just talk about me but they don't talk to me they should know that i understand everything even if it's hard for me to talk the doctor should realize that i understand because if i didn't how could i laugh so much when once a week on the day called sunday sunday sunday they put us all together and show us cartoons of dogs mice cats that make us all laugh at first i didn't know what to do watching the duck get angry and break plates because he was so angry and i started to laugh when i saw all the other kids laugh it was OK to laugh it wasn't bad to laugh everyone laughs watching the duck all angry but i only see the children on sunday sunday sunday they keep me away the rest of the time and the lady doctor whispers to the nurses that's what they are called all of them in white white white you see i do understand white sunday sunday sunday white duck angry the doctor talks in whispers i don't know what she tells them i am all alone except on sundays now i have changed because i am growing up like they say to me i am not a little boy anymore be careful with your hands i don't know what to do with my hands i ask them why don't i see anyone else i am always all alone before they used to pat me on the head and now they don't even do that now all they say is careful with your hands but the lady doctor her eyes get filled with water and she whispers to the other nurses in white white white now nobody ever comes to visit me like when i was little and i used my hands to play ball careful with your hands when you play ball Lencho they call me Lencho or Lenchito now i want to ask them why they look so pale what is wrong what is going to happen i don't know anything outside this place who knows what there is behind the walls why do they get sad when they look at me why do they move their heads like that when water falls they close the windows i don't know what happens there outside where i used to play hide-and-seek now they lock me up in a dark room what did i do what did i do what did i do i don't know i feel my head spin even though i don't move i am alone in a dark room and i say i am nice to the plants and the animals and the trees i love them i smell the plants i stop at the trees i am like them i am them i have nobody else except the garden before now they don't let me out into the garden i am the tree i am the plant i am the animal i have nobody but them i don't see the other children i can still see the squirrel a dog some flowerpots with flowers but the trees no not anymore now they don't let me out all i have is a blue blue blue notebook i heard them say let him scribble in his blue book when i scribble i write things down like these things i write without ink the notebook has letters i only have a finger to write on these white papers i remember the man and the lady that used to come and visit me and now don't ever come i don't ask them anymore if i will ever see them again and sometimes i think i never saw them i only dreamed them i ask the lady doctor who were they why don't they come and see me anymore she says Lencho love is real Lencho love is real Lencho love is real write it in your blue notebook with your finger remember everything you think and dream because you won't see them again they are very important people i knock on the door don't they hear me? won't they come to see me? can't they see me all alone? don't they know a boy can't forget? why do they tie my hands behind my back? how can i play like that? how can i write in my blue notebook?)

CARLOS FUENTES was the author of more than twenty books, including *Destiny and Desire*, *Happy Families*, *The Eagle's Throne*, *This I Believe*, *The Death of Artemio Cruz*, and *The Old Gringo*. The recipient of many awards and honors, including the Miguel de Cervantes Prize, the Belisario Domínguez Medal of Honor, the Rómulo Gallegos Prize, France's Legion of Honor medal and Spain's Prince of Asturias Award, he also served, from 1975 to 1977, as Mexico's ambassador to France. Carlos Fuentes died in May 2012.

ABOUT THE TRANSLATOR

KRISTINA CORDERO is a translator of fiction and nonfiction, including *In Search of Klingsor* by Jorge Volpi, *The Country Under My Skin* by Giaconda Belli, *The Best Thing That Can Happen to a Croissant* by Pablo Tusset, and *This I Believe* by Carlos Fuentes. She is presently at work on an anthology of the writings of Saint Teresa of Avila.

Printed in the United States
by Baker & Taylor Publisher Services